BROTHERHOOD PROTECTORS

BOOKS 1-3

ELLE JAMES

TWISTED PAGE, INC

BROTHERHOOD PROTECTORS

VOLUME 1

New York Times & *USA Today*
Bestselling Author

ELLE JAMES

MONTANA SEAL

BROTHERHOOD PROTECTOR SERIES
BOOK #1

New York Times & *USA Today*
Bestselling Author

ELLE JAMES

New York Times & USA Today Bestselling Author
ELLE JAMES
MONTANA
SEAL
BROTHERHOOD PROTECTORS

This story is dedicated to the men and women who risk their lives daily to protect others. Military, police, firefighters, paramedics, bodyguards, FBI, CIA, fathers, mothers, siblings and good Samaritans. When you put your life on the line to save others, you're a hero. Thank you to all the heroes we have in this world. You don't need superpowers, guns or capes to be a hero.

Elle James

1

"MONTANA, TAKE POINT," Big Bird said. "You'll need to move in fast, once I take out the guard."

Hank Patterson, aka Montana, adjusted his night vision goggles, gripped his M4A1 rifle with the SOP Mod upgrade and rose from his concealed position on the edge of the Iraqi village. U.S. Army intelligence guys had it from a trusted source that an influential leader of the ISIS movement had set up shop in the former home of the now dead Sheik Ghazi Sattar, a paramount chief of the Rishawi tribe. The once palatial estate had taken mortar fire from the Islamic State of Iraq and Syria—or ISIS—rebels. The sheik and his fighters had succumbed to the overpowering forces and died in battle.

In the process, ISIS had gained a stronghold in the village and captured an aid worker the U.S. government wanted returned. When ISIS offered the aid worker in exchange for captured members of their party, the current administration held to its stand that it didn't negotiate with terrorists.

That's where the navy SEALs came in. Under the cover of night, armed with limited intel and specialized sound-suppressed weapons, SEAL Team 10 was to infiltrate the compound, kill the leader, Abu Sayyaf, and liberate the aid worker, who happened to be the Secretary of Defense's niece.

Piece of cake, Montana assured himself. This was what he lived for. Or at least he'd been telling himself that for the past year. He was coming up on the anniversary of his enlistment, and he had to decide whether to get out of the military or re-up. Reenlistment meant more wear and tear on his body and more chances of being shot, blown up or bored out of his mind. When they were called to duty, the missions were intense, yet the downtime gave him too much time to think.

Besides, he wasn't getting any younger. If he didn't leave active duty, he'd end up training SEALs, rather than conducting missions. That would give him even more time to think about what could have been back in his home state.

How many years had it been since he'd visited home? Eight? Ten? Hell, it had been eleven years since he'd been back to Montana. He could remember that defining night like it was yesterday. He'd just broken up with Sadie. He was hurting and wondering if they were insane to give up the best thing that had ever happened to them. Then he and his father had a big blow out. His father called him a lazy, good-for-nothing son and told him to get to work or get out.

Looking back, breaking up with Sadie had been the best thing, all the way around. She'd gone on to become a Hollywood mega-star, and Montana had gotten the hell away from his father, joined the Navy and become a member of an elite force. Life had turned out pretty good for them both.

So why did he still think about home...and Sadie? Hell, he knew why. Every time his reenlistment came up, he started thinking about home. Most of his friends from high school were married and had children. He'd always wanted kids, but SEALs made crummy parents and spouses. They were gone most of the time, sometimes without a way to contact loved ones back home.

"Be ready." Lieutenant Mike lay next to Montana. "Big Bird, hold your fire until I give the cue."

"Roger," Big Bird responded.

New to the team, Lt. Mike wasn't new to being a SEAL. With four years and ten deployments under his belt, he was a seasoned warrior, although his recent marriage seemed to have slowed him down. He wasn't as quick to leap into a bad situation. And if rumor had it right, his wife was expecting their first child.

"Let's do it," Lt. Mike said.

The muted thump of Big Bird's rifle discharging was Montana's signal to take off.

The ISIS guard who had been pacing the top of a roof slumped forward and fell to the ground with a soft whomp.

Montana held his breath, straining his ears for the shout of alarm that didn't come. With the sentry eliminated, Montana had a clear path to the wall. He took off running, hunkered low, his weapon ready, his gaze scanning the top of the wall, searching for the tell-tale green heat signature of a warm body through his night vision goggles.

Swede and Stingray were right behind him.

His skin crawled and his gut clenched. Something didn't feel right. But the mission had to move forward. They had an enemy target to acquire and a woman to rescue before they could go home to Virginia.

Montana knelt at the base of the wall, slung his rifle over his arm, cupped his hands and bent low.

Swede ran up to him, stepped into his cupped hands and launched himself into the air. He hooked his arms over the top, dragged himself over and dropped to the ground below.

Stingray came next, then Nacho, Irish and Lt. Mike.

Big Bird would remain on top of a nearby building and be their eyes and ears for anyone approaching the compound. He'd also provide cover fire for them as they exited with the aid worker.

Lieutenant Mike, the newest member of the team, paused at the top of the wall and reached a hand down to Montana, pulling him up and over.

Swede and Nacho had already moved forward to the main building, one side of which was caved in, like an open wound. The remaining walls bore pockmarks from bullets and shrapnel. The huge wooden door still stood, closed and strangely unguarded.

"It doesn't feel right," Swede whispered into Montana's headset.

"Stay the course," Lt. Mike responded.

"Going in," Swede acknowledged and slipped into the broken corner of the structure, climbing over the half-wall still standing.

Nacho waited a moment until Swede said, "Clear."

Nacho hopped over the wall and through the crumbled bricks, disappearing into the gaping hole.

Lt. Mike went next, then Montana. Irish brought up the rear.

Once inside, what walls still stood seemed to close in on Montana.

Lt. Mike forged ahead, hurrying past the crumbled bricks and mortar.

Swede and Nacho stood at a door leading deeper into the once ornate residence. Swede wedged a knife into the door-jamb, while Nacho aimed his rifle at the door, ready for anything. A quick jab and the lock gave. Swede nodded to Nacho, yanked open the door and stood back. Nothing happened. Nacho dove through the opening and to the side, leaving room for Swede to follow. Lt. Mike entered next.

The team moved through the building, room by room.

"There's nobody here," Montana said.

"Then why the guard on top of the building?" Big Bird asked, still connected via the two-way radios in their helmets.

"Suppose it's a trap?" Irish asked.

"We have to check all rooms." Lt. Mike said.

Montana fought a groan. The place had to be over twelve thousand square feet. And that didn't include any underground bunkers that might be a part of the former Sheik's defense plan. Lt. Mike was right. If they didn't check all the rooms, they couldn't say with one hundred percent certainty their ISIS target and the captured aid worker were not there.

Once they'd completed checking the ground floor and

upper levels, they started down a set of stairs. These steps weren't finished in the opulent granite tiles of the main level. They were plain concrete, leading to a steel door, heavily reinforced.

Montana took the lead again, fixed C-4 explosives near the handle and pushed a detonator into the clay-like substance.

Everyone backed up the stairs to the main level and held their hands over their ears.

Montana pressed the detonation button. A dull thump shook the floor beneath his feet. A cloud of dust puffed up the staircase.

Lt. Mike held up a hand. "Let it clear a little." Finally, he lowered his hand and led the way back down the stairs to the door.

It hung open on its hinges, a dark, ragged hole blown through the metal. The entrance led to a tunnel-like hallway with doors on either side. Yellowed, florescent lights flickered in the ceiling. Another door marked the end of the long hallway.

The team split, each clearing the rooms, one at a time. None were locked, but the locking mechanisms were on the outsides of the doors. A chill slithered down the back of Montana's neck, partly because of the coolness in the basement and partly from knowing the sheik had probably used the rooms to incarcerate people. Nothing in any of the rooms indicated the aid worker had been imprisoned there.

At the end of the corridor, the final door was locked. Once again, Montana set the charge, the team hid behind the doors of the cell-like rooms, waiting for the charge to blow. Montana only used enough explosive to dislodge the lock mechanism, no more. He didn't want to destroy the structure of the underground portion of the building and risk trapping his team or causing them injury with the concussion.

"You have a gift." Nacho grinned as he passed Montana and followed Lt. Mike into a much narrower tunnel.

"We're in a tunnel beneath the compound," Lt. Mike said into the two-way radio.

Montana doubted Big Bird would hear on the outside. Where the tunnel would lead, they'd know soon enough. Unfortunately, they wouldn't have a sniper on the other end providing cover for them when they emerged from whatever building.

His gut twisting, his nerves stretched, Montana clenched his weapon, holding it at the ready as he continued forward. If they had any chance of rescuing the aid worker, it had to be soon. ISIS rebels had a habit of torturing and killing anyone they could use as an example, rather than hanging on to them. Prisoners only slowed the attack and hampered their determination to take everything in their paths.

The tunnel opened into the bowels of what appeared to be a warehouse.

"I feel like we're on a wild goose chase," Swede muttered.

"And the goose is leading us to the slaughter. Not the other way around," Irish concurred.

They climbed a set of stairs to a huge, empty room.

"Damn," Swede said and bent to a dark lump on the ground.

Nacho released a string of profanity in Spanish.

"We've found the aid worker."

What Montana had assumed was a pile of rags, was in fact a woman, her clothes torn, her body ravaged, her face battered. Her eyes were wide open, staring up at the ceiling.

Swede knelt beside her and touched his fingers to the base of her throat.

Montana's stomach roiled at the sight of the woman's damaged body. He could have told Swede she was already dead. What a waste of life. And for what? "We need to get out of here."

The sound of footsteps made Montana glance up. A man stood on a catwalk twenty feet above them. He shouted something in Pashtu, ending in *Allah*, pulled the pin on a grenade and tossed it into the middle of the team.

"Fuck!" Montana yanked his weapon around and shot the man. He fell to the ground, but killing him was a little too late.

The grenade rolled toward Swede, still crouched beside the woman's body.

"Get down!" Lt. Mike shouted, and then threw himself over the grenade.

Montana shouted, "No!" as the grenade exploded beneath their leader.

The force of the concussion reverberated throughout the room, knocking Montana to the ground. His last thoughts were of the home and the girl he'd once loved.

2

—————

Sadie McClain hadn't slept much the night before. She told herself it was because she was in a different bed, different climate and different state than she was used to, but it would only be half of the truth. She was home in Montana, but she didn't receive the homecoming she'd expected. She didn't feel any more relaxed than when she'd been surrounded with the people, traffic and pollution of Los Angeles.

That old saying *you can never go home* was true. Eagle Rock wasn't the same as it had been all those years ago when she'd left to go to UCLA. Perhaps, if she'd maintained close ties with the people with whom she'd grown up, she would have felt differently. Instead, the weeks away had turned into months, the months into years, and all those kids she'd known in school had moved on in their lives, or moved out of the area.

In California, chance audition had led to a screening and an offer to be the star in a movie— an unheard of coup for a fledgling actress. Even more miraculous, the movie had been a hit. Who'd have thought the country girl from the wilds of Montana would ever make it as big as she had? Six feature films grossing billions of dollars had made Sadie McClain one of the highest-paid actresses of all time. Her busy filming schedule and public appearances had kept her away from home. For ten years. Yes, she'd been back for brief visits, long enough to attend her parents' funerals and her brother's wedding. But she didn't stay for long. She couldn't. Memories made being there hurt too much.

The town of Eagle Rock hadn't changed much. The general store had closed. Most people had to drive thirty miles now to do any major grocery shopping. Sure, the one convenience store stocked the basics—pantry staples, eggs, bread, some processed meats and dairy products. For greater choices and lower prices, a person had to drive farther to get it.

After his four-year stint in the Marine Corps, her brother seemed happy enough to return to Montana, go to college and get his degree in architecture. That's when he'd married Carla. When their parents died, Fin had returned to the family ranch, content to raise cattle, train horses and grow a garden for fresh vegetables during the summer.

Sadie wouldn't have come back at all, except she needed a refuge from a highly persistent stalker. Tim Wallis had followed her career from the first time she appeared on screen. Everywhere she turned, the man was in front of her. He tried to pass himself off as part of the paparazzi, but none of his photographs had appeared in any of the magazines or tabloids. He'd even trespassed on her property in LA to get closer to her. She'd had her agent hire an attorney and file a restraining order against him. But she still saw the man everywhere she turned.

The stress of constantly being in the public eye, and the loneliness of being surrounded by people she didn't know or care about, finally drove her to the home she'd abandoned years ago. She had to get away and breathe, re-evaluate her career and life choices.

Sadie stared out the window of her old bedroom on the second floor of the old house. The window was the only thing that hadn't changed. Since her parents' death, her brother Fin and his wife had made their old house their home. His wife, Carla had completely redecorated, changing everything from the curtains to the furnishings. Gone were Sadie's four-poster bed and the quilt her mother had lovingly made for her sixteenth birthday.

In their place were a modern fabric-covered headboard and a sterile, white duvet similar to the ones Sadie found in the hotels she lived in of so often when she was on a shoot. This wasn't home. She didn't feel comfortable in the house in which she'd been raised. Her mother and father were gone and so were all of her things. Nothing was the same. Sadie pushed back a niggle of resentment, squared her shoulders and reminded herself that she was in another woman's home, now.

Though she owned a half-interest in the White Oak Ranch, she'd left it to her brother to manage on a daily basis, infusing cash when he needed new equipment or expensive stud service for his horses and cattle.

As she gazed out of the window, her thoughts drifted back to a time long ago when a certain young cowboy used to climb the trellis to her bedroom window, and stayed until well past midnight. Sadie had fallen in love with that cowboy and dreamed of living in Montana and raising babies.

She'd sacrificed her dream for his.

Sadie sighed and turned away from the incredible view of the Crazy Mountains, thinly capped with the first snow of the season. After holing up in the farm house for the past two days, she was finally ready to venture into town for a few things at the general store and maybe to stop by Al's Diner where she'd held her first job outside ranching.

Fin had assured her Al was still alive despite his propensity for greasy food and cheap whiskey. The crusty old cook had been good to Sadie, always looking out for the sixteen-year-old when the rowdy cowboys got too fresh.

Sadie descended the stairs to the main floor and called out, "Fin? Carla?"

No one answered. Fin hadn't been back to the house since he'd left to take care of the animals before the sun was up. He'd mentioned something about a fence being down on the north forty and not to hold lunch for him.

Carla must have taken him at his word. She wasn't

anywhere around. A quick glance out the window proved the theory. Her car was gone from the driveway. Glad to walk away from the house without an interrogation about where she was going and whom she was going to see in town, Sadie climbed into the Jeep she'd rented and drove out of the yard and down the gravel road toward the highway.

The view hadn't changed much. This was the same land she'd grown up on. She'd played in these fields, climbed the hills, and ridden across the pastures like a wild child. The horses were different, and there was a fresh coat of paint on the house and barn, but what struck her was how much *she'd* changed. And how much she wished she hadn't. Sadie missed the carefree days of summer and the midnight visits from Hank.

If she were honest with herself, she'd call it as it was. She missed Hank Patterson and the young, stupid love they'd shared when they were teenagers. That was the real reason why she hadn't come home much during the past eleven years —Hank wasn't there.

Her heart constricted. After all these years, she'd thought she could handle coming home for an extended stay. She was wrong.

The drive into Eagle Rock didn't take long. She passed the entrance to Bear Creek Ranch and slowed to stare down the winding road disappearing into the evergreens. After a moment, she shook herself. What did she expect? Hank had been eager to shake the shackles of a small town and tight community off his shoulders. He was even more determined to break free of the iron grip of his father. Lloyd Patterson had always been civil to her, but she'd known from Hank's simmering anger and the way he clenched his jaw whenever he spoke about his father, that they weren't close, and never would be.

From the moment she and Hank started riding together, Sadie knew he'd have to get away from Bear Creek Ranch to make a life of his own. Where Sadie would have been content to stay in the area, Hank had to leave to prove to his father and himself he had a mind of his own and could make his own way in the world.

Sadie's heart swelled with the pride she'd felt when she'd gone to Hank's graduation ceremony. She'd read everything she could get her hands on about SEAL training. Hank had made it through where more than seventy percent of those who tried failed and washed out in the first few weeks. He hadn't known she'd been there, and she hadn't walked up to him. The man was still following his dream. If she'd come back into his life then…well, she hadn't wanted to be the force that derailed him. Hell, he probably had forgotten about her, once he'd swept the dust of the ranch from his boots.

Not so for Sadie. She thought of Hank often and worried about him. SEALs lived dangerous lives. They went into some of the most hostile environments, going up against some of the most heinous terrorists imaginable.

As she neared Eagle Rock, she slowed for a stop sign. A truck loaded with bags of feed pulled through the stop sign and one of the fifty-pound bags slid off the back, dropped to the ground and split open, spilling its contents on the road.

Sadie waved at the driver, pulled to the side of the road and got out.

The driver of the other vehicle edged the truck to the side of the road and climbed down, frowning.

Sadie's heart twisted in her chest. She'd recognize the tall, gray-haired man anywhere. His son looked so much like him, it made her chest ache. "Good morning, Mr. Patterson." Hank's father had always had a fierce countenance. Permanently etched on his face, the man's frown had frightened more than one foreman away from the Bear Creek Ranch where Hank grew up.

He grunted in response to her greeting and stared at the feed spilled across the road. "Damned kids. Can't stack a load so as it won't fall off. I'll have words with Bergman about that boy he hired to load feed."

Sadie squatted beside the torn edges of paper and scooped feed into what was left of one half of the bag. "I'm sure he didn't know better. How have you been?" she asked, when she'd really rather ask about his son, Hank.

"Arthritis is giving me fits in my knees and Allie's been nagging me to go to the doctor." He snorted. "Ain't got time to be driving all the way to Bozeman to see a doc who will charge me a fortune to tell me what I already know. I'm gettin' old." He dropped to his haunches beside Sadie and went to work salvaging what he could of the feed.

"I haven't seen Allie since she was fifteen. She must be all grown up by now." Sadie commented.

Lloyd hefted the larger of the two halves of a bag and straightened with a groan. "That she is. And a thinks she runs the place. Need to get her married off before she makes me crazy."

Sadie laughed, scooped the other half up and followed Lloyd to the back of the truck.

The old rancher settled his burden in between the stack of feed and the wheel well and then turned to take the other half from Sadie. He jammed the feed bag in beside the one he'd just settled and turned to face her. When he did, the lines in his forehead deepened. "You're that McClain girl from the neighboring ranch, aren't you?"

Sadie grinned and stuck out her hand. "Sadie McClain. I'm surprised you remembered me."

"I remember you used to ride over on that old nag and hang around my barn every Saturday afternoon. Couldn't get a lick of work out of Hank when you were around."

Sadie's smile slipped, her thoughts filling with memories of a happier time. "I'm sorry I disturbed your work day." But she wasn't sorry for the memories she and Hank had created together. "Speaking of Hank—" The bag Mr. Patterson had just jammed into the back of the truck split open again and fell toward the pavement. Sadie dove to catch what she could.

The crack of a rifle rent the air. The man in front of her staggered backward, clutching his shoulder, a bright red stain spreading across his blue chambray shirt. "What the hell?" he said, his eyes wide as he stared at the blood oozing between his fingers. His face blanched and he shot a look at Sadie, as he dropped to his knees.

"Mr. Patterson?" She abandoned the feedbag and reached for the older man. Another sharp report sounded and something hit one of the bags of feed next to Sadie's head. A trickle of grain spilled out.

Sadie ducked, pulling Lloyd the rest of the way to the ground beside her. She blocked his body with hers and automatically reached for her cell phone in her back pocket. That's when she remembered she'd left it in her bedroom. Not that it mattered. Cell phones rarely worked outside of Eagle Rock. The nearest cell tower wasn't close enough to make a difference. Most people still owned landlines.

"Mr. Patterson, are you okay?" she asked.

"Hell, no, I'm not okay. I've been shot and I can't breathe." His angry retort faded. "Help me up."

Sadie pressed a hand to his uninjured shoulders. "Stay down. We don't know if the shooter will fire again."

"Then get my gun off the rack over my back seat and shoot back," he demanded, a surge of his anger returning. "I can't stay on the ground all day or I'll bleed to death."

He was right about the bleeding part. Already a pool of blood spread across the pavement.

Sadie's pulse hammered inside her veins. None of the parts she'd played in any of her movies had prepared her for dealing with a situation like this. But her upbringing on a ranch made her keep a level head and think.

She had to get Lloyd to a doctor before he passed out. "Stay here."

"I will not."

"I'm going to get my Jeep and bring it around to block anymore bullets that might come this way. I'll only be a moment."

Sadie left Lloyd's side and crawled toward her rented vehicle. Another shot rang out, spitting gravel up in her face. Crawling took too long. She had to move. Sadie pushed to her feet and launched herself toward the open door of her vehicle.

She dove through, landing in a heap in the driver's seat. Keeping her head below the dash, she shoved the shift into drive and angled the vehicle closer to Patterson, placing the bulk of metal between him and the shooter.

Once she had him covered, she climbed over the passenger seat and out onto the ground.

Lloyd's skin was an unhealthy gray and his jaw was clamped tight.

Sadie had to stop the flow of blood before she moved him. Ripping the hem of her shirt, she folded the fabric into a pad and reached for Lloyd's hand covering the wound.

"Let me," she said.

"You a nurse, now?" he said through clenched teeth.

"No, but I played one in a movie."

"Don't need no play actors monkeying around with my arm," he grumbled.

Sadie didn't have time to argue with the curmudgeon. "Well, it's all you get. Now, let me help you." She shoved his hand aside, pressed the wad of fabric to the wound and slapped his hand over his shoulder again. "Hold that while I get you into the vehicle."

"Damned bossy woman. You sound like Ally."

She slipped an arm around him and lifted with all her might.

Lloyd helped, but he wasn't steady on his feet and it was up to Sadie to guide, lift and shove him into the back seat of her Jeep.

"I can drive my own self," Lloyd said, his voice slipping into a moan.

"Like hell you can." She tucked in his leg, shut the door and climbed into the front of the Jeep, crawling over the console, keeping her body below the windows, hoping the exterior of the vehicle would stop anymore flying bullets, should the shooting begin again. "We're taking you to the clinic, and then I'm calling the sheriff."

"Won't do no good. Probably some fool hunter who can't tell a deer from a bus," Lloyd said, through gritted teeth.

"Might be, but it needs to be reported." If the shooter had been a hunter, the big question on Sadie's mind was what was he hunting? He'd hit Lloyd, and then almost hit Sadie, twice. As close as the bullets came, the shooter had to have been aiming at her.

A shot blew out the driver's side window, blasting tiny shards of glass over her hair and arm. Sadie ducked lower, her heart lodging in her throat.

With Lloyd counting on her getting him to medical care quickly, she didn't have time to succumb to fear. Settled low in the driver's seat, she shifted into drive and jammed her foot on the accelerator. Peeking through the steering wheel, she managed to avoid leveling the stop sign and put a hundred yards between her vehicle and the intersection. As she drove toward Eagle Rock, she eventually straightened in her seat, her gaze alternating between the road, Lloyd and her rearview mirror.

Deer hunter my ass. Someone had purposely tried shooting her and Lloyd. Sadie wouldn't feel safe until the shooter was caught. In the meantime she'd be blowing through that intersection without slowing down. The sheriff would just have to write her up. These were the times she really disliked being in a remote town. Houses were few and far between, and if she'd had her cell phone, she'd still have been out of luck due to the lack of towers passing signals. Where was a tall, dark and handsome alpha hero when you needed one to swoop in with a satellite phone or, better yet, a rescue helicopter?

3

"I TOLD them it was only a flesh wound, and what do they do?" Hank shrugged into the leather jacket Tuck had found in his closet and brought to the hospital in Bethesda, where he and Swede were being treated for their injuries.

Swede sat in a sterile, white hospital bed, wearing a faded gown with the ties in the back, while eating the swill from the hospital kitchen. He still had a swath of bandages wrapped around his head where shrapnel had hit, and his hand was wrapped like a mummy's, making it hard for him to hold his fork. As far as the docs knew, they'd dug all the metal shards out of his back and thighs. He'd find out if the surgeon had done his job the next time he went through the metal detector in a commercial airport.

Swede paused with his forkful of rubber chicken halfway to his mouth. "What did they do?"

"They're running me through a medical review board." Hank walked to the window and stared out. Cloudy skies matched his murky mood. "I might be discharged based on this goddamn leg." He kicked his leg out and winced, his hand going to the side of his knee that had taken the bulk of the hit.

"If *you're* discharged, what are they going to do to *me?*"

Swede raised his bandaged hand to his head, fork and all. "Isn't it an automatic career-ender when you get a TBI?"

Traumatic brain injuries were serious business. One minute a guy could be fine, the next, he could be on the floor, unconscious.

"Any headaches?" Hank asked.

"Sometimes," Swede admitted. "Hell, I got hit in the head. I have stitches. They shaved my hair."

Hank laughed. "Was that where all your strength was? In that headful of hair?"

Swede had worn his blond hair long and shaggy, like a Norse god.

"Damn right, it was. I feel as weak as a kitten." He glanced at his bandaged hand. "Can't hold a fork, much less a nine millimeter pistol. Forget an M4. The only good thing about being stuck in this bed is the pretty nurse who comes in on the evening shift."

"Any confusion or dizziness?" Hank's brow furrowed. "You're thinking clearly, aren't you?"

"Just confusion over where to tie the damned strings on this gown—not that I can manage them on my own with this bandage on my hand. No dizziness." Swede nodded. "I'm thinking pretty damned clearly. I want out of this hospital. Yesterday, if it were possible."

"How's the steak?" Hank asked, his lips twitching, his eyelid dropping in a wink.

"It's garbage. Tastes more like chicken." Swede glared. "I only wish it was steak. I can't wait to get back to my own place."

Hank rubbed a hand across his face. "The medical review board doesn't meet for another month. They recommended I go on leave until they come to a decision. The orthopedic surgeon doesn't want me to start running again until I've been through a couple months of physical therapy. How the hell am I going to stay in shape if I can't exercise?"

Swede shook his head, his lips twisting into frown. "Have

you ever considered you're looking at everything all wrong?" his friend asked quietly.

"I'm a SEAL. What good am I if I can't work out?"

"As much as I can't stand hospitals, you and I were the lucky ones." Swede set his fork on the rollaway table and pushed it aside. "Lt. Mike won't be going home. His wife won't be kissing him goodnight. His kids won't know their daddy."

Hank eased into the chair beside Swede's bed and stared at the wall, his heart and stomach twisting into a hard knot. "Why did he do it?"

"The same reason you or I would have done it, had we been closest to the grenade. Lt. Mike just had the shit luck to be standing there. He saved all of us."

"We could have run—"

Swede shook his head. "We wouldn't have made it." The big man sighed. "What's important is that Lt. Mike bought us a second chance at life. We can't go around second-guessing the past. We have to move on and make a difference in our futures. Lt. Mike would have wanted us to."

"We have to do right by him."

"Exactly. We can't waste this opportunity to live our lives to the fullest."

Hank glanced up and nodded. "And do some good, while we're at it."

"What about going back to Montana for a visit? Or better yet, you could go back to ranching. Isn't that what you did before you joined the navy?"

Hank shook his head. "I joined the navy to get away from Montana."

"Or did you join the navy to prove to your father you didn't need him?"

Swede knew Hank better than Hank knew himself. "That's part of it. I can't go back to Montana flat on my ass, jobless and not fit to do anything but blow shit up. Going home isn't an option."

"I know you and your father didn't see eye to eye, but what about your sister? Doesn't she like it when you visit?"

The frown eased on Hank's forehead. "Allie would be beside herself, she'd be so happy. But every time I return home, my father makes it a point to reminds me that I'm wasting my life in the navy. He thinks I should get back to what I do best."

"And that is?"

"To him, it sure the hell isn't blowing shit up. No, he thinks I should be a rancher."

"And if the MRB boots your ass out of the military, is that what you'll do?"

Hank shook his head. "I couldn't go back to work on my father's ranch. He and I butt heads too much."

"What about working on another ranch?"

"I don't know. I like what we do as SEALs—taking out the bad guys and rescuing the good ones."

"Isn't that what you do as a rancher?" Swede asked. "You take down the wolves that would feed off the innocent cattle."

"It's different." Hank scrubbed a hand through his hair.

"If you like protecting the innocent, how about security work?"

"No way. I can't be a mall cop." Hank shoved a hand through his hair. "I'd shoot myself first."

Swede laughed. "No, not that kind of security. I mean, more like personal protective services, like a bodyguard. You could hire out to protect a high-powered CEO or politician."

"Now that you mentioned it, I kind of like the idea of doing something in Montana."

Swede raised his mummy hand. "Hell, isn't Montana filled with rich guys and celebrities? Don't they need bodyguards?"

"I guess." Hank hadn't considered protective services as a potential civilian occupation. All he'd ever done was ranching and the SEALs. But the idea held merit.

"All I'm saying is you should think about it." Swede settled back against the pillow, pinching the bridge of his nose. "If you end up medically discharged, you have to do something. I hear the Crazy Mountains where you're from are pretty spectacular. I hope to go there some day."

"You should. There's no place on earth quite like it." Hank's cell phone vibrated in his pants pocket. He pushed to his feet, trying not to wince as pain shot up his leg. He reached into his back pocket for the device. The caller ID indicated the call was from his sister Allie. He tipped his head toward Swede. "It's my sister. Mind if I take it?"

"Go ahead. Tell her I said hello, and ask her when she's going to marry me." Swede grimaced and closed his eyes.

Hank turned and walked into the hallway, jabbing the key to receive the call. "Hey, Allie Cat."

"Hank, we need you at home," she said without the back and forth banter they usually shared as a form of greeting. "Dad's been shot."

$\sim$

THREE DAYS AFTER THE SHOOTING, Sadie made the hour-long drive to Bozeman to check on Lloyd Patterson. She found his twenty-six-year old daughter, Allie, pacing the hallway outside his room.

"How's your father today, Allie?" Sadie asked.

Allie wrinkled her nose. "He's cranky and ready to be out of the hospital. But he's alive, thanks to you." She hugged Sadie. "I know he's an old grump, but he's *my* old grump of a dad."

Sadie chuckled. "I know what you mean. I'd give anything to have my parents around." Her heart pinched painfully every time she thought of her parents and their untimely deaths due to an auto accident on their way to Helena for their anniversary dinner. Sadie missed them terribly.

"I'd like to think he's cranky because he's getting better." Allie sighed. "But he's cranky all the time. Seems he's been double angry since Hank left eleven years ago."

"Really? You'd think he'd be over it after all this time."

"He never forgave Hank for leaving." Allie puffed out her chest and dipped her chin, lowering her voice. "The ranch is his heritage. He has an obligation to preserve it for his children and his children's children."

Her imitation of her father's gruff voice made Sadie laugh

out loud. "He's got a point. I don't know what I would have done if my brother hadn't wanted to stick around and run the ranch our parents left us. I haven't been around enough to do it myself."

Allie's lips spread into a wide grin. "No, you haven't. But you have been busy making a big name for yourself in the movie industry. Congratulations on the Oscar nomination."

Sadie shrugged. "I didn't win."

"But you were nominated. I'd be turning cartwheels at the honor." Allie hugged her. "And I can say I knew you when you were a country bumpkin in the Crazy Mountains of Montana."

"I'm still a country bumpkin. Don't let the fancy clothes fool you." Not that she'd worn a single designer outfit since she'd left LA. In Eagle Rock, she didn't have to dress up to go to the grocery store. She'd managed to slip out of California on a private jet and land in Montana without the paparazzi getting wind of her movement. That in itself was just short of a miracle.

Sadie tipped her head toward the closed door. "Will he mind if I pop in to say hello?"

Allie waved her by. "Please. I could use the break from his constant complaining about the food and stump water they call coffee around here." Her lips twisted. "His words, not mine. I gotta warn you, though. He's madder than a hornet. The doc thinks he needs surgery on his shoulder. He's waiting for the orthopedic surgeon's opinion before he releases Dad."

"That bad?"

"Yeah, it seems the shot hit the rotator cuff and shattered the bone."

"I'm sorry to hear that."

Allie touched her arm. "I'm glad the bullet didn't kill him. We can deal with a bum arm."

Sadie wished she could have done more to protect Mr. Patterson from the shots fired. But she couldn't have known someone would target that intersection on that day. "Agreed. Rather have him around than not."

"I'm going to the cafeteria for more stump water," Allie

said. "I think I'll need it, if he's this cantankerous the rest of the afternoon. Can I bring you anything?"

"No, thank you." Girding her loins, Sadie pushed through the swinging door, the scent of rubbing alcohol and disinfectant filling her nostrils.

Mr. Patterson sat up in bed, his hospital gown worn on one arm, the other draped over his chest, exposing the swath of bandages covering his right shoulder. He was frowning, fumbling with the controls for the bed, punching the button that raised his feet. "Damned bed has a mind of its own." He hit another button and the other end of the bed lowered. "Goddamn it!"

"Mr. Patterson?" Sadie called out softly.

He glanced up, his frown deepening. "I hope you have news about that son of a bitch who shot me."

"Sorry, but I don't."

"Then why the hell did you come all the way to Bozeman?"

She fought the grin teasing the corners of her lips. The man had the personality of an angry badger even back when Sadie had been a teen, hanging out at the barn, waiting for Hank to finish his chores. Time and age hadn't softened his edges one bit. If anything, they were even sharper.

"I came to see how you were feeling," she said.

"How do you think I'm feeling?" he groused. "Got hay to stack in the barn, the first snow is right around the corner and I can't use my arm. The doc says I might not get full use of it… ever." Lloyd laid has hand over the bandages and winced. "What's he know anyway? He's young enough to be my son. I'll get a second opinion before I accept that quack's sentence."

"I'm sorry about your arm, Mr. Patterson." Though she was quite grown up, Sadie couldn't bring herself to call the man by his given name. As Hank's father, he would always be Mr. Patterson to her. "Is there anything I can get for you?"

The grouch glanced down at the controls again and punched a button. Once again, the foot of the bed rose, tipping him backward. "You can get me the hell out of here before this bed kills me."

"I'm sorry, but that's not up to me. Allie and the doctor will have to spring you." Sadie closed the distance between her and the bed and took the controls from him. "What is it you're trying to do?"

"I want to sit up, not put my feet over my confounded head."

Sadie studied the directions and pressed the button to lower his feet, and another that raised his head. "Better?"

"A little higher," he muttered.

She pressed again and the head of the bed rose a little higher.

"There," he said.

Sadie handed him the control and pointed to one of the buttons. "When you get tired, press that one, and the head of the bed will go down." She fussed with the sheet and blanket, pulling them up around his chest. The air was cool in the room and his skin was puckered with gooseflesh.

"I can do that," he said, brushing her away. "I still have one good arm."

"Yes, sir." She set her purse on a chair and reached for the plastic pitcher of water, filled his cup and set it within his reach on the bedside table.

"What are you still doing here?"

"I thought I might visit with you for a while. I'm sure you must be bored out of your mind, lying in bed when you're used to being out working from dawn to dusk."

"You got that right. But I don't need some Hollywood actress to entertain me."

She nodded. "I'm not here as an entertainer. Just here as a friend." Sadie sat in the chair beside the bed and pulled a magazine about ranching out of her purse. She'd borrowed it from her brother's stack of reading material. The man tried to keep up with the cattle industry and best practices for raising livestock and the crops to feed them. "You don't mind if read out loud, do you?"

"I'd rather you left me alone so I can get some rest. When the doctor comes in, I'm going to demand that he release me."

Sadie didn't mention anything about the possibility of his staying longer or that he might be undergoing surgery. Allie could tackle that with her father. She had more practice. In the meantime, Sadie opened the magazine and read aloud about the latest in organic fungicide to battle such diseases as leaf spot, mildew and black patch in alfalfa. She went on to the next article about symptoms, diagnosis and treatment of corneal ulcers in horses. The next article was a personal account of a North Dakota rancher's encounter with a bear in his barnyard.

Mr. Patterson had stopped complaining and grown quiet.

Sadie glanced up.

Hank's father leaned back in the bed, his eyes closed. When he wasn't frowning, he reminded her of Hank so much hear heart squeezed tightly in her chest. What would it have been like if she'd stayed here, married Hank and lived on the Bear Creek Ranch? They'd have had a kid or two by now. She'd always imagined them growing old together. A sharp pang of regret hit her hard, and she swallowed the lump in her throat. No use crying over choices made. She had her life. Hank had his. They didn't fit in each other's worlds anymore.

Not knowing whether or not he was asleep, Sadie leaned forward, studying the gentle rise and fall of his chest.

Lloyd frowned and propped one eye open. "Don't stop, now. I want to know how he got the bear out of the barnyard." He settled back. "Had a bear in my barnyard once. Left before I could get back to the house for my rifle."

Sadie went back to reading the story about the bear in the barnyard, keeping her voice soft and soothing, hoping to calm Mr. Patterson.

A few paragraphs later, the door swung open.

Expecting the doctor, a nurse or Allie, Sadie glanced up with a smile on her face.

The smile froze as a tall, broad-shouldered figure filled the doorway. The blood rushed from Sadie's head and she swayed, glad she sat in a chair, or she might have melted into a puddle of goo on the floor. "Hank?" she whispered. "Is it really you?"

4

———

Hank stood transfixed, his hand on the door as he stared into the room. Sadie McClain sat in a chair beside the hospital bed, her blond hair hanging down around her shoulders, her sky-blue eyes wide, soft pink lips forming an O of surprise. She pushed to her feet and swayed, her face turning pale and then flushing a pretty pink.

His heart stopped for a long, moment, as if time had frozen. Then his pulse kicked in, hammering against his veins, reminding him he was still alive and he was there for his father, not for Sadie.

Hank nodded his head toward her. "Sadie," he said, and then dragged his gaze away from her to the bed.

His father blinked his eyes open and focused on Hank. "What the hell are you doing here?" He held up his hand. "No. Let me guess. Allie!"

The door opened again and Allie entered backward. "Dad, stop your bellerin'. They can hear you all the way down the corridor. I thought you might like some real coffee. It's much better than what they served for breakf—" She turned, balancing two cups of coffee. "Hank!"

Hank snatched the coffee cups from her before she dropped them. "Hey, Allie Cat." He set the cups on the nightstand and pulled his little sister into his arms. "It's good to see you, squirt."

She wrapped her arms around his waist and squeezed hard. "I missed you, you big jerk."

"Hey, watch your mouth." He rubbed his knuckles across her head like he had when she was ten years old. "Tell me what's going on."

"Nothing's going on," his father assured him. "You don't need to be here. You might as well go back to your unit. You're not needed here."

That hurt. Fortunately, Hank had heard worse from his father. For some reason, his father never had a kind word to say to him. Ever since his mother died.

"Dad, I'm here for a month." Hank crossed his arms over his chest and stared down his father, not out of disrespect, but out of the very same stubbornness he'd inherited from his father. "So, you might as well get used to it."

"I'm not getting used to anything. I don't need you here."

"Fine. Then I'll stay in Eagle Rock at Ruby's Bed and Breakfast."

"Ha! Ruby sold it," his father said and winced. "Damn it. I could do without the aggravation." He shot a glance at Allie. "Why did you go and call him?"

Allie's lips thinned. "Dad, be reasonable. You were shot."

"I know that. I was there." Hank's father slapped the bed and doubled over, his face turning white. "Damn it. What does my being shot have to do with your brother?"

"I don't know." Allie stared up at her brother. "What does this have to do with you?"

Hank was tired of the arguments and exhausted from the flight. His knee hurt, and he didn't have it in him to argue. "You want me to leave? Fine." He spun on his heels and would have headed out the door, except he caught the disturbed expression on Sadie's face. All his anger melted away in that one look from Sadie. He couldn't leave. Not yet. Not without clearing the air between him and his first love.

Allie hooked her arm through Hank and Sadie's and herded

them through the door. "Sadie, tell Hank what happened while I try to talk sense into Daddy." She pushed them into the corridor, and let the door swing closed behind them.

Relatively alone with Sadie in the corridor, Hank stared down at her. She'd broken his heart when she'd told him she didn't want to get married, and that she wanted to pursue her dream of going to California to become a big movie star.

"Hi, again."

She chuckled softly. "Your father is still the same."

"If by the same, you mean cantankerous, ornery and pig-headed, you're right." Out of habit, his hand rose to touch her, to bring her into his arms and kiss her, but he stopped himself before his fingers made the connection. They weren't teenagers in love anymore. She was a celebrity. He was a SEAL. By the nature of their chosen occupations, their worlds would never collide.

Except in Eagle Rock where they'd both been raised. In Hank's case, he'd never wanted to come back. Had he known Sadie would be there..."How long have you been in town?" he asked.

"Five days."

"I thought you lived in LA."

"I do—did." She stared down at her cowboy boots. "It's complicated."

Hank nodded. Complicated probably meant it was personal, and she didn't want to share her reasons for coming home with him. There was nothing between them but a few old memories. Even if those memories were carved into his mind and had been what kept him going during his darkest days, whether in battle or in recovery from injuries.

"You look good," Sadie said, a strained smile turning her lips upward on the corners.

"You look too thin," he said, his tone flat, a frown pinching his forehead.

She'd lost the rounded corners of baby fat, her cheekbones and arms were more angular, toned and beautiful in a more mature, upscale fashion. This woman was now Hollywood royalty. She'd walked the red carpet with people way out of Hank's league, gone to private parties with some of the most elegant and famous people of their time. She'd even had dinner with the president of the United States.

Hell, Hank worked for the president, yet he'd never actually met the man in person.

Sadie's lips formed a crooked smile that had the added effect of turning his insides to mush. "I can always trust you to give it to me straight. No sugarcoated platitudes. Just the ugly truth."

Hank shook his head and made the mistake of gripping her arm. Now there was no going back. Ever since he'd seen her in his father's hospital room, he'd wanted to yank her up against him and kiss away all the years they'd wasted apart. As his fingers curled around her arms, he slowly, inexorably drew her toward him. "What I meant to say is you look incredible." He brushed a strand of hair behind her ear like he used to do after horseback riding across the prairie grasses.

Her eyes widened and she tipped back her head. "It's so very good to see you again, Hank," she said, her voice breathy. Her tongue darted out to moisten her lips. "You look pretty good yourself."

God, he wanted to kiss her.

A nurse pushed a cart down the hallway toward them. The front wheel wobbled, making a grating sound, reminding Hank they were in a hospital corridor, not alone. He leaned his forehead against hers and slid his hand down her arm to capture hers. "You want to tell me what happened?" As soon as he uttered the words, he realized there was deeper meaning in the words. He held his breath wishing Sadie would catch it.

She drew in a deep breath and let it out. Then she met his gaze. "You know the intersection with the stop sign right before you get to town?"

His lips curled in a smile. "We used to meet there when we wanted to get away from our respective homes."

Her expression hardened. "Your dad seems to think someone might have been out hunting and mistook us for a deer. I might have gone along with that theory if that someone hadn't fired two more rounds, narrowly missing me as I crawled across the ground to my car."

Hank's grip tightened on her hand. "You think whoever was shooting was *trying* to hit you and my father?"

She nodded.

Anger boiled up inside Hank. "Why?"

Sadie shrugged. "Could be someone with mental problems, for all I know. I've heard of nutcases nailing passersby for no reason other than they were practicing their shooting skills."

"Do you suppose my father's flawed personal skills pissed off someone? Hell, he's probably pissed off everyone in the county at one time or another."

"Why now? Everyone knows him and what he's like. He's cranky, but he's hard working, and he'd help a neighbor in a heartbeat. Why would someone decide to hurt him, now?"

"And that doesn't account for the shots fired in your direction." Hank pulled her into his arms. "I'm sorry you had to go through that. But I'm glad you weren't hit."

"Thanks." For a long moment, she leaned against him, her hand resting on his chest. Then Sadie glanced up at him. "I don't know if this has anything to do with the shooting, but had several incidents with a stalker, back in LA."

"Stalker?" Hank pushed her to arm's length. "What stalker?"

She shrugged. "I have the usual paparazzi ganging up on me, but one guy in particular has been following me, anticipating my every move. The obsessive, freaky way he shadowed me forced me to pull up stakes and head home."

"I suppose overzealous fans are part of the life of a celebrity, but couldn't you have him served with a restraining order?"

"He'd been pretty good about disappearing before I could get a name and address to have him served. But I got one just before I left LA. The guy's name is Tim Wallis, if he happens to show up in Eagle Rock." She squeezed Hank's hand and let go. "Anyway, that's what happened, and one possibility of who could have done it. Your father took a bullet, and I got away with nothing more than a skinned elbow."

"In a town as small as Eagle Rock, it shouldn't be hard to find the culprit."

"I don't know about that. There have been a lot of tourists in the area, coming to get in the last hike of the season back in the mountains. When they cleared out, the hunters moved in. And there've been geologists and oil speculators sniffing around, looking for the next big oil reserve. The Crazy Mountain Bed and Breakfast, which used to be Ruby's, has been booked solid for the past couple of weeks, and the campground south of town has been full."

Hank frowned. "Hunting season started last week?"

Sadie nodded. "I checked with the sheriff. He said he'd keep an eye peeled for anything out of the ordinary. He checked the area where we were and all around, but he didn't find any leads."

"No bullet casings?"

She shook her head. "Nothing."

"It doesn't make sense," Hank said. "Who would want to kill my father or you?" Hank tilted his head. "I can see my father making someone mad, buy why you?"

"Getting rid of the witness?" she offered.

"Well, you both lived, and no one has been brought in for attempted murder. Seems whoever did this is off the hook."

"Your father and I go through that intersection every time we come to town. Many others do, too. What if the shooter decides he wants to conduct target practice again?"

Hank shook his head. "He has to be caught."

"Agreed. The sheriff said he'd check the usual suspects. The rowdy teenagers, the county rabble-rousers and anyone else he can think of. They did manage to pull a bullet out of your father's truck. He sent it to the state crime lab for analysis."

"Good. In the meantime, we have to be aware at all times."

"Tell your father that. He's already madder than hell at being confined in this hospital."

Hank glanced at the door and braced himself for facing his belligerent father.

Sadie touched his arm. "For what it's worth, I'm glad you're here. Despite what he says, your father needs you."

The warmth of her hand on his arm filled Hank with the fortitude he needed to deal with the situation. She'd always calmed him, made him step back from the blowups with his father and think logically. Patterson men were stubborn to a fault. That's what made him and his father butt heads all the time. Now was no different. Only this time, Hank really did need to be there to figure out who the hell shot his father and tried to kill Sadie.

SADIE FOLLOWED Hank back into the room, her heart still hammering, her hand tingling from where she'd touched Hank's arm. Eleven years had done nothing to quell the hunger that flared each time she was near him. She was still the same girl inside, but she had to consider who she'd become on the outside. Even if she wanted him to be a part of her life, she couldn't drag him into her world. The red carpets, paparazzi and living in LA would kill him. At the very least, it would kill any kind of relationship they could hope to have. If he was even interested. The best thing she could do for him was to not encourage a resurgence of old desires. They lived vastly different lives now. She had contracts to fulfill, press conferences, media events and more that went along with being a star.

Sometimes she wished she could go back to being that girl who knew that boy and wanted nothing more than to be his wife and have his babies. But if she'd said yes to his proposal when they were teenagers, they'd have stayed in Montana, barely made a living, and Hank would have been as grumpy and bitter as his father. He never would have pursued his dream of joining the Navy and becoming a SEAL.

Walking into the hospital room behind Hank, Sadie couldn't help noticing how broad his shoulders had become.

And he must have grown another two or three inches. He was all lean muscle and dangerously handsome.

She frowned.

Was Hank limping? If so, he was hiding it well.

Neither his father nor his sister had noticed.

But Sadie had, and her heart contracted. Had he been injured in battle? All the years away from him, Sadie had forced aside images of Hank fighting for his life against terrorists. Every time she heard a news report about military personnel dying in battle or a helicopter crash, she stopped everything and waited for the names, nearly fainting in relief when not one of the names listed was Henry Patterson.

"I changed my mind," Lloyd said before the door closed completely behind Hank and Sadie.

"About what?" Hank asked.

"About needing your help." Hank's father waved his hand. "Of course, I don't need your help, other than helping Eddy get the hay into the barn. But besides that, I don't need you."

"Dad, you're not making sense."

"It's the damned drugs. They're making my head fuzzy."

Allie touched her father's good arm. "Tell him what you told me."

He patted her hand. "I'm getting to it." Lloyd cleared his throat. "I want you to find out who shot me and tried to shoot Miss Sadie. There." He glared at Allie. "Are you happy, now?"

Allie smiled at her father. "Yes, Daddy. I'd feel better having Hank around."

"I'm not concerned about having him around. In fact, if anything, he needs to stay close to the girl. I won't be straying far from Bear Creek Ranch for the near future. But Miss Sadie wasn't injured. If whoever was shooting at us decides to shoot again, she needs someone to protect her."

Sadie raised her hand, alarmed at the direction in which the conversation was going. She couldn't be around Hank on a regular basis. Keeping her distance was predicated on just that —keeping her distance from the man who had the ability to flip her belly and make her knees turn to goo. "I can take care of myself, Mr. Patterson. No need for your son to follow me around."

"Nonsense," Hank's father said. "I might have been in pain, but I'm not blind. Whoever was shooting only took one shot at me and two at you. In fact, if you hadn't moved when you did, that first bullet would have hit you instead of me."

Hank turned to her, his brows furrowed. "Is that the way you saw it?"

Sadie thought back to where she'd been, and her movements prior to Mr. Patterson being struck by a bullet. She'd been standing in front of him and bent to catch the broken bag of feed when the shot was fired. Her breath left her lungs, and her vision blurred. Damned if the man wasn't right. She looked up at Hank and nodded. "I was standing in front of him. If I hadn't moved, the bullet would have hit me. Then, when I tried to get to my vehicle, two more shots were fired close to where I was on the ground. Both bullets missed, but were close enough to spit gravel up on me."

Hank slipped an around her waist and pulled her against him.

Sadie was glad for the support. Not only had she had a near miss, Mr. Patterson had taken the hit meant for her. "If someone is after me, I'm not safe to be around." She pushed away from Hank. "Thank you for thinking of me, Mr. Patterson, but I can't put Hank at risk."

Hank reached for her hand. "Sadie. Don't be ridiculous. As a Navy SEAL, I'm used to being shot at. If you were the target all along, whoever was responsible might come after you again."

She shook her head. "Then I'll hire a bodyguard. I don't want you to be hurt because of me."

"If you're hiring a bodyguard, I'll apply," Hank said. "I don't have to report back to my unit for four more weeks. I could use the work to keep me busy."

Allie stepped toward Sadie. "Let Hank help. He's got combat experience. If you hire someone to be your bodyguard, you don't know what you'll be getting. Hank's a Navy SEAL, he can probably do the job with his hands tied behind his back."

Sadie backed away from Allie and Hank. One Patterson was hard enough to stand up to—three was impossible. "Okay. But only until I can interview and hire a bodyguard from a reputable agency."

Lloyd Patterson lay back in his bed and closed his eyes. "Now that we have that settled, you can all leave my room. Seems the pain medication they gave me is kicking in." He yawned. "Allie, tell the nurse to wake me when the doc gets here. I want my discharge papers as soon as possible." His words faded off, and he was snoring a moment later.

Sadie turned to leave, the urge to turn and run almost too strong to resist. As she pushed through the swinging door, Hank's hand descended on her shoulder.

"We need to talk," he said.

"I know." Sadie dreaded having that talk. As soon as they got someplace they could be alone, she'd tell him never mind. She would risk being on her own.

Hank took her hand in his and led her to a nearby waiting room. A family of five adults turned toward them when they entered, probably hoping for a doctor with news of their loved one.

"Not here." Hank pulled Sadie to a stop and swung her out of the room.

They walked back toward the nurses' station. Along the way, Sadie spied an empty room. "In here." She grabbed Hank's hand and pulled him through the door.

Hank disengaged the doorstop, and the door swung closed. Light shined through the window onto a bed made up with fresh sheets.

Sadie crossed to the window and looked out onto the parking lot. The usual big, blue Montana sky had clouded over while she'd been visiting Mr. Patterson. "Hank…" she started, struggling to find the words to inform Hank that she didn't want to hire him as a bodyguard, without telling him why. How could she tell him she didn't want him to work for her because it meant they would be together? That she couldn't risk her heart, when she knew it would be broken again as she returned to California and he returned to active duty? "I don't think…"

Hank gripped her shoulders, turned her and drew her into his arms. "That's your problem," he said, staring into her eyes, making it difficult for her to remember what she was about to say.

Oh, yeah. "You're fired," she blurted out.

He chuckled. "You haven't hired me yet."

"What do you mean?"

"You haven't actually made me an offer, and I haven't accepted."

She frowned. "You mean you don't want to work for me?" She hadn't thought in those terms. Sadie had assumed Hank might still have feelings for her, and that she would be hurting him by sending him away.

"I didn't say that." He smoothed a strand of hair behind her ear. "What I want to make clear is that, if I do agree to be your bodyguard, the condition will be that we go into this as a business deal. You're the client. I'm the paid labor."

Sadie's eyes narrowed, and disappointment stirred a flash of anger in her belly. "And?"

He brushed his knuckles along her cheek.

It was all Sadie could do to refrain from leaning into his palm.

"Look," he said, his gaze locking with hers. "What we had when we were kids was puppy love. We're both grown. Our lives and careers have taken us in different directions. I don't expect anything more from you than a bodyguard would expect from his boss, and vice versa."

Another spike of anger bolted through her, and she propped a hand on her hip. "What exactly are you trying to say?"

"If I'm to be your bodyguard, our relationship will be strictly business." His gaze captured hers and held it as he moved closer. "There can be none of this." Hank leaned forward and pressed his lips to her forehead.

Sadie's breath caught and held in her throat as his firm, soft lips met her skin.

Every last ounce of resistance evaporated and she braced her hands on his chest.

"And at all costs," he whispered, "we can't do this." He leaned his head to the side, caught her earlobe between his teeth and nibbled gently. "Or this," he said, his voice pure smoke and gravel as his mouth skimmed across the line of her jaw, stopping when his lips came in contact with hers.

Too soon, he lifted his head.

"You're right," she whispered. "We can't do this. It would be wrong." Sadie leaned up, touching her lips to his. She couldn't tell whether he was claiming her, or she was claiming him. It didn't matter. What did was that everything about the kiss felt so right, she couldn't back away. Instead she moved closer, leaning her breasts against his chest, her hips melding to his. The hardened evidence of his desire nudged her belly, reminding her of how very long it had been since she'd made love.

None of that mattered when Hank kissed her, his mouth moving over hers, his tongue tracing the seam of her lips. She opened to him, allowing him through to stroke her tongue, caressing it in a long, sensuous glide. He tasted of coffee and mint, a familiar blend that brought back so many memories of kisses long ago.

What had started as her desire to fire him, had turned into fiery desire. How could she hope to keep him at arm's length, when all she wanted was to be in his arms?

When they finally broke apart, Sadie was breathless, and her body trembled from head to toe. This was Hank. The man she'd given her heart to as a teen. Her first love. Since they'd parted, no other man had ever measured up to him.

She'd dated other Hollywood stars and had been the target of many tabloid rumors, but she hadn't committed to anyone.

In the back of her mind, she couldn't help comparing them to Hank.

She stepped away and pushed her hair back from her face, squaring her shoulders as she got a grip on herself. "Look, if we're going to make the arrangement work, we have to treat it as a business-only deal. I'll hire you as my bodyguard. But we can't do…" she waved her hand between them, "this."

He reached for her. "Why?"

She edged backward, out of range. "We're different people now."

"You're still Sadie McClain. I'm Hank. You know me."

Sadie shook her head. "We have different lives. Vastly different lives. And when I leave Montana, I'm going back to my life in LA, and you'll go back to your unit." She couldn't risk breaking her heart again. The first time, she'd pushed him away for his own good. This time was no different. Hank didn't belong in her world. He'd be miserable.

Hank's eyes narrowed. "What if I don't return to my unit?"

Sadie's heart fluttered against her ribs. A glimmer of hope rushed in, only to be squelched by common sense. She shook her head. "You love being a SEAL. I wouldn't want you to give that up. Besides, LA can be ruthless, heartless and a completely foreign environment compared to Eagle Rock, Montana."

"And I wouldn't fit in. Not even as your bodyguard? Surely they have bodyguards in LA." When she opened her mouth to explain, he raised his hand. "Don't worry. I'm not pressuring you into taking me back to your world. I got the memo. I'm just the hired hand, here to protect you while you're in the wild backcountry of Montana. That's it. No kissing the boss. And we won't talk about what just happened in this room. As far as I'm concerned, nothing happened." He strode to the door and held it open.

Sadie stepped through. She couldn't deny the tightness in her chest, or the way her eyes stung. Yes, this was the way it had to be. But she didn't have to like it.

5

———

As Hank followed Sadie's vehicle back to Eagle Rock, he could still feel the heat of their kiss on his lips. After all those years, she still made him hot all over and want so much more than a simple kiss. Not that their kiss had been simple. It still radiated throughout his body, making him count the seconds until he could hold her again.

But after the kiss ended, Sadie had made it perfectly clear—their association would be purely platonic. She didn't want to rekindle a childhood infatuation. No. She was a big star now. She'd made it abundantly clear that he would not, and could not, fit into her world of glitz and glamour. Not that he wanted to.

Unless it meant being near her, holding her in his arms and making love to her through the nights.

Hank groaned. His best bet was to tell her to hire that bodyguard she desperately needed. Someone with whom she didn't share a past. Someone who didn't burn to kiss her again and hold her close. Damn. But hiring a bodyguard wasn't as easy as making a phone call. She had to get someone she could trust. In the meantime, Hank couldn't let her go gallivanting around Montana with a shooter on the loose, gunning for her.

Instead of driving straight through to her family ranch,

Sadie pulled to a stop at Al's Diner on Main Street in Eagle Rock.

Hank parked his rental beside hers and got out.

Before Hank could round Sadie's vehicle, a decrepit pickup zoomed up to the driver's side of her SUV. A heavyset man leaped out, wearing a fedora, sunglasses and carrying a camera. "Miss McClain, could I have a moment of your time?"

Sadie had opened her door and was about to step out when the intruder converged on her, snapping pictures with a bright flash right in her face.

Anger surged through Hank. He vaulted over the hood of her car and dropped to the ground in front of the cameraman. "Back off," Hank said, his voice a low growl, his instincts that of a male wolf guarding his territory ready to rip the man in two if he didn't leave Sadie alone.

"I'm a dedicated fan of Miss McClain's. I only want a few pictures." He leaned around Hank, still snapping pictures, as Sadie stepped out of her car.

Hank positioned himself directly between the man and Sadie, hoping to block any attempt to harm her.

"Please, Miss McClain, I only want a picture of you," the man begged. "I'd go to the ends of the earth to get one picture of the beautiful Sadie McClain."

"Please, not now." She raised a hand in front of her face to deflect the bright flash.

If this was what Sadie had to put up with on a daily basis, Hank was surprised she hadn't hired a bodyguard already. When the cameraman refused to back away, Hank planted a hand against his chest and pressed firmly, angling the man away from Sadie, giving her enough room to make a dash for the diner.

Once her path was clear, she ran into the building.

Giving the man his meanest, junk-yard-dog look and puffing out his chest, Hank glared at him. "Leave. Sadie. Alone."

The man lifted his chin. "I have just as much right to go into the diner as anyone else."

With a snarl curling his lips, Hank said, "If you go in while she's there, I'll be forced to break something."

His eyes rounding, the man backed away. "Is that a threat?" he said, his voice shaking.

"No," Hank said. "Count it as a promise."

From a couple feet out of Hank's immediate reach, the cameraman stood with his feet braced. "You can't go around slinging threats. I could have you up on charges."

"And I could break…things…before anyone from the sheriff's department had a chance to get to you." Hank glanced around deliberately. "Seems it's just you and me out here. My word against yours. You still think anyone will give a rat's ass what you say?"

The man's lip curled. "I only wanted her picture."

Hank took a step toward the jerk who couldn't take a hint. "Then write to her publicist. I'm sure she has a collection of headshots she'd be wiling to autograph for you. In the meantime…" Hank lowered his voice. "Leave her alone." He crossed his arms and flexed his muscles, making his chest and shoulders appear even bigger.

The man glanced at Hank, his gaze shifting from Hank's shoulders to his hands, bunched into fists. Then, without a word, he dove into his truck and spun up gravel as he floored the accelerator and raced out of town.

Thankful his intimidation efforts had ended without him having to get physical, Hank watched until the banged-up truck disappeared. If it had come down to it, Hank would have pounded some sense into the guy.

Once he was convinced the man wasn't coming back anytime soon, Hank entered the diner, his gaze scanning the interior, searching for Sadie.

She stood with a man dressed in a business suit, who was gripping her arm, his frowning countenance and the proprietary way he held her, sending Hank's pulse skyrocketing. "Sir, I'll have to ask you to unhand Miss McClain."

"I'm talking to her." The man didn't even glance in Hank's

direction, his attention on Sadie. "Sadie, be reasonable. You can't ignore your fans."

"I can, and I will." Sadie shook off his hand.

If Sadie hadn't knocked the man's hand away at that moment, Hank would have shoved the man aside. "Look, Ray. The studio can wait for my answer until I'm good and ready to give it to them. In the meantime, I'm here to get some rest, and arguing with you is far from restful."

"If you don't sign the contract in the next twenty-four hours, they might withdraw their offer."

"Then let them. I could do with a longer break between films. My schedule has been brutal."

He grabbed her arm again. "You can't slow down now. Your fans will forget your and move on."

Sadie frowned at his hand on her arm. "Let go of me, Ray. Right now, I could use a little less adoration from my fans."

Hank reached out and laid a heavy hand on Ray's shoulder. "Back away from Miss McClain."

Ray glared at Hank. "I'm Raymond Holt."

Cocking his brows, Hank stared down at the shorter man. "And that's supposed to mean anything?"

Ray snorted. "I'm with the Holt Agency. I'm Sadie's agent. Who the hell are you?"

Hank pushed Ray back and stepped between him and Sadie. "I'm her bodyguard, hired to protect her. And the way I see things, you're bothering her."

Sadie touched his arm. "Hank, I can handle Ray. You don't have to."

Hank stood for a moment longer, giving Ray a narrow-eyed glare. "Hurt her, and you'll answer to me."

Ray raised his hands. "I wouldn't hurt her. She's my bread and butter."

"Then let her have the space she needs."

"But I need...she needs to sign this contract before the studio decides to go with another actress. She's not the only one they had lined up."

"Then it wasn't meant to be." Sadie stepped up beside Hank. "Ray, I'll think about it."

"But—"

"You heard the lady," Hank crossed his arms over his chest. "She'll think about it."

Ray's lips pressed into a thin line. "I'll be here for a couple of days."

"And I'll be thinking about it for a couple of days. You might as well go back to LA. I won't be pressured into making a decision during the time I'm here in Montana."

"And how long do you plan on being in Montana?" Ray persisted.

"I don't know." Sadie waved her hand. "A week, maybe two."

"Hi, I'm Daisy. Would you three care to sit down?" The pretty, young waitress smiled at them and leaned closer to Hank, a conspiratorial gleam in her eyes. "You're scaring the customers."

Hank shot a glance around the nearly empty diner and frowned at Daisy.

She winked. "Okay, so you're not scaring the customers, you're scaring the cook."

Sadie gave Daisy a thankful smile. "Yes, please. Hank and I would like a table for two." She gave her agent a pointed stare. "Ray was just leaving."

"If that's the case, you'll want your check." Daisy pulled a slip of paper from her apron and handed it to Ray. "If you'll step up to the register, I'll happily take your money." Her smile was infectious, but Ray wasn't any happier about being separated from Sadie and herded out the door.

"Sit anywhere you like," Daisy called over her shoulder as she led Ray to the cash register. "I'll be with you in a minute."

Sadie chose a booth in the far corner and sat with her back to the door. Hank sat opposite her.

Sadie pulled a menu from behind the napkin holder and stared down at it. "So you see, my life can be complicated, and not really my own."

"It doesn't have to be that way."

"As long as I'm a celebrity, it will be this way." She laughed, the sound not at all cheerful, more tired and resigned.

"Isn't this what you wanted?" Hank's jaw tightened. "The dream you left Montana to pursue?" Weren't those the words she'd used when she'd turned down his proposal? She wanted to follow her dreams, and he should follow his.

Sadie nodded. "Yes. Acting was something I always wanted to do. Playing great roles, making people laugh, cry, feel the pain of the characters in the story, was a dream come true."

"But the other stuff that comes with being famous?" he prompted.

She shrugged. "Normally, I can deal with it. But every once in a while, I need a break."

"Like now."

Again, she nodded. "Like now. Making two movies in one year may not sound like much, but it's emotionally and physically draining. I need a chance to recuperate. To be away from the crush of people, away from LA."

Daisy walked Ray to the door, and then joined Sadie and Hank at their table, pulling out her order pad and pencil. "Now that you're settled, let me say welcome home." She grinned at them both. "I remember you two from high school."

Sadie's brows wrinkled, and Hank stared at the pretty brunette. "I'm sorry, but I don't remember you."

She laughed. "You probably wouldn't. I was a kid back then. You were a senior when I was a freshman, and the only girl Hank could ever see was Sadie." Daisy sighed. "Not that I blame you. Sadie, you're our Hollywood legend. And Hank, you're our hometown hero."

"I'm not a hero," he muttered, his gaze shifting to the window. An image of Lt. Mike throwing himself onto that grenade flashed through his mind and his hands tightened on the plastic-coated menu. "There are others more deserving of that label."

"You're a hero to us," Daisy said with a nod. "Eagle Rock's never produced a Navy SEAL." Her expression turned serious.

"Thank you for your service." She raised the pad and pencil. "Now, what can I get for you two?"

They placed their orders and waited until Daisy walked away.

Sadie's lips twitched on the corners. "How does it feel to be a celebrity?"

"I'm not. You're the celebrity."

"You're a Navy SEAL. In my book, that trumps Hollywood, any day."

Her words were meant to cheer him, but Hank couldn't help the stabbing pain in his chest. If the medical review board decided his injury was sufficient to medically discharge him, he'd be out of the Navy. He'd be just Hank from Montana. "Being a SEAL doesn't make me special."

Sadie reached across the table, laying her hand over his. "Who you are makes you special, Hank. You became a SEAL because you already were special—loyal, dedicated and strong. I could see that before I witnessed your graduation from BUD/S training."

Hank's gut tightened and he shot a glance across the table, his hand curling around hers. "You came to my graduation?"

She nodded, a smile spreading across her face. "I was working in LA as a waitress. I saved all of my tips so that I could afford to drive down for your graduation."

His chest filled with a combination of pride and pain. He'd been so happy to make it through the grueling training, and sad no one cared enough to come to his graduation. "Why didn't you tell me you were there?"

She shrugged. "You were busy celebrating with the men who made it through with you. That's where you needed to be."

"I would rather have celebrated with you." Once again, she'd proven she didn't want him in her life. "Why did you bother to come, then?"

"I was so proud of you. I couldn't stay away."

"How did you know? I thought when you turned down my proposal, you didn't want anything more to do with me."

"I turned down your proposal because we were too young. Hell, we were just kids. We still had a world to explore, to make our own way and figure out who we wanted to be."

"And now?"

Sadie opened her mouth, but didn't get the chance to respond.

"Here we are. A loaded club sandwich and the house special, chicken salad." Daisy set the plates in front of them and stood back. "Is there anything else I can get you?"

"No, thank you." Sadie said, her gaze dropping away from his.

Hank shook his head, his gaze on the woman sitting across from him as he waited for Daisy to leave so that Sadie could answer his question.

When Daisy tuned away, Hank fixed Sadie with a look. "You were saying?"

Sadie stared down at her salad. "It doesn't matter. We live different lives. You have your SEAL team. I have my work."

Hank didn't correct her. In thirty days, when the board had their say, he might not have his SEAL team. He'd have to start over, find out where he fit in the civilian world.

Rather than pressure her for a real response, he lifted his sandwich and asked, "How long do you plan on being in the movie industry?"

"I like what I do, but I'm becoming more selective about the projects I accept."

"I guess that comes with being one of the most sought-after actresses in the world." He nodded. "If I haven't told you before, congratulations on realizing your dreams. I've seen every one of your movies. You have a gift."

Her cheeks heated, and she smiled. "Thank you. That means a lot, coming from you."

"Why me?"

"I could always count on you to tell me the truth. If you didn't like the movie, you'd tell me."

"Sometimes, I could be painfully honest."

"Like the time you told me you didn't like me wearing braids—that it made me look like a little girl."

He grinned. "I didn't feel right kissing you. It made me feel like a pervert. Besides, you are so much sexier with your hair down around your shoulders. Like it is now." He reached across the table and lifted a strand of her hair. It felt natural to touch Sadie's. He'd always been casual with his hands and quick to give a caress. Time hadn't changed that. And she didn't seem to mind. "If anything, you're even more beautiful than you were in high school, though you were pretty damned gorgeous then."

Her cheeks flushed a soft pink. "Thank you."

They spent the rest of their meal eating in silence. When they left the diner, Hank exited first. He checked both directions, looking for the cameraman, Sadie's agent or anyone else who might cause problems. When he was convinced the coast was clear, he held the door for her.

Sadie shook her head. "You take your job seriously."

"Your life is serious business." He rested a hand at the small of her back, telling himself it was to keep her close. So wrapped up in the warmth of her body against his hand, he forgot about the curb and nearly fell. Though he caught himself before tumbling, the jolt sliced pain through his injured leg and he winced.

Sadie reached for his elbow. "Are you okay?"

Hank straightened, pushed back the pain and the urge to curse. "I'm fine," he said through clenched teeth. As fine as he could be two weeks after having surgery to remove shrapnel from his knee and thigh. The stitches had been removed the day he'd gotten word his father had been shot. The scars were tender, but he would heal.

"If you need to take it slowly—"

"I said, I'm fine," he snapped and stepped out like he had no injury, biting down on his tongue to keep from letting go of a sting of profanity. "Where to?"

Her glance searched his face. "I'd like run by the general

store for a few items, then I'll be ready to go back to the ranch."

"We can ride together," he said.

"No need. It's just around the corner." She climbed into her Jeep.

Hank eased into his own, rubbing his sore leg, willing the pain to subside. "Some bodyguard you are," he muttered. The woman he was guarding had asked if he was okay, not the other way around. If he planned to establish a new career in the personal security business, he wasn't starting out with a bang. Hank supposed it wasn't unreasonable to have a learning curve. He hoped the curve and his injury didn't put Sadie at risk.

SADIE GLANCED in her rearview mirror, a frown settling between her brows. She'd noticed Hank's limp, but until he'd stepped off the curb and nearly fallen in front of her, she'd assumed his limp was a twisted ankle or a blister from wearing his combat boots. She hadn't wanted to consider he might have been injured in a battle. All these years, she'd tried not to think of the danger he faced on a daily basis.

It made her little incident seem minor in comparison. Except, Hank's father had taken a bullet for her. Nothing had happened since the first attempt, making Sadie rethink the scenario. Maybe it really had been a kid getting stupid with a gun. With the sheriff looking for him, he might be running scared. In which case, hiring a bodyguard might be overkill.

Sadie shot a glance in the mirror at the SUV following closely behind her. She pulled into a parking space in front of the general store and shut off her engine, admitting she was happy Hank had been there to add additional support in getting rid of the overzealous photographer. If Sadie wasn't mistaken, the intruder was Tim Wallis, the man who'd stalked her for the past few months, showing up at every public event, and even finding his way into her backyard to snap pictures of her. He'd cut his hair and shaved his beard, or she'd have recognized him immediately.

Sadie needed to notify the sheriff that she had a restraining order against the man. In a small town like Eagle Rock, it wouldn't take the sheriff's deputies long to find Mr. Wallis and remind him to keep his distance. After shopping, she'd pay a visit to the local law enforcement.

Inside the store, she grabbed a small cart and rolled up and down the few aisles. When she reached the pantry staples aisle, she ran into her brother's wife, Carla. Sadie gave the woman a friendly smile. "There you are. You're an early riser."

Carla frowned. "If you needed anything, all you had to do was ask. I would have bought it for you while I was in town."

"Thank you, Carla. I figured since I was coming into Eagle Rock anyway, I'd stop by and get a few things."

"The pantry's pretty full. We might not have room to store more items. I've been after Fin to remodel the kitchen. It's too small. I want to gut it and start over. It's way too dated."

Sadie's heart clenched. Their mother had remodeled the kitchen a couple of years before she'd died. She'd loved every-thing retro. From the black and white tiles on the floor to the bright red chairs around the small table nestled in the alcove with the view of the Crazy Mountains out the window. Jeanie McClain had loved her house in Montana, and never tired of the view.

Sadie swallowed her natural inclination to tell Carla she couldn't touch a thing. But then she tried to think of how Carla must have felt to be a young bride brought to live in a house decorated by her dead mother-in-law. If she couldn't change the decorations, how would she make the house her home?

Carla's gaze shifted to glance over Sadie's shoulder. "Hank? Hank Patterson?" Her eyes widened. "I didn't know you were back in town."

A warm rush of awareness washed over Sadie. Hank hadn't taken long to catch up with her. She hated to admit to the certain sense of satisfaction filling her. He'd always been able to find her when he went looking, as if she was his homing beacon.

"Got in today," he said.

Carla stared at him, her cheeks flushing pink. "You look amazing." She blinked and glanced down at her near-empty shopping cart. "I mean, I'm sorry to hear about your father. I hope he's doing better."

"He appears to be on the mend."

Carla pouted. "Does that mean you'll be going back to your unit soon?"

Hank shook his head. "No. I'm on leave for four weeks. I plan on spending it here."

"I'm surprised." Carla tucked a strand of hair behind her ear.

If Sadie wasn't mistaken, her sister-in-law was flirting with Hank.

"Oh?" Hank's lips twitched. "Why?"

"You haven't been back for any length of time since you left."

Hank glanced at Sadie. "Haven't had a reason to come back. Until now."

Carla's gaze followed Hank's.

Sadie's cheeks heated. Hank had made it sound like she was the reason he'd come home. But she knew she wasn't. However, she might be the reason he stayed, rather than returning to active duty. Lloyd Patterson hadn't been all that happy to see him, or that interested in him helping out at the Bear Creek Ranch. If Sadie hadn't hired him to be her body-guard, he might already be on his way back to Virginia.

Her pulse quickened. And she hadn't had to twist his arm all that much for him to agree to watch out for her.

Carla's eyes narrowed. "You two were a thing back in high school. I remember. No other girl could get the great Hank Patterson's attention when Sadie was around. Whatever happened? One minute you were a thing, the next you were going opposite directions."

Sadie didn't respond. The memory of Hank's proposal and her response made her stomach hurt like it had back then.

Hank slid an arm around Sadie's waist. "We made a conscious decision to go our separate ways. Didn't we, Sadie?"

Sadie swallowed hard and nodded, afraid her voice would crack if she answered. She'd hurt him back then. He'd been devastated, and so had she. More than anything, she'd wanted to be with him. But his relationship with his father had always been edgy. He'd needed to get out of Eagle Rock, and realize his dreams of joining the Navy and becoming a SEAL. That would never have happened if she'd accepted his offer. She'd wanted to, so very badly.

"And yet, here you are." Carla smiled. "Hometown hero and Hollywood legend together again. It's like a fairytale come true."

"Oh, we're not—" Sadie started.

"We're not," Hank interrupted, "ready to let the world in on our relationship." He hugged Sadie closer and kissed the top of her head. "Although I don't know how we'll keep it from everyone, when I move in with her."

"Move in?" Sadie shot a startled glance at him.

He skimmed his knuckles along her cheek. "Like we talked about. We want to make sure we're still compatible. You know, like learning each other all over again." Hank grinned at Carla. "You and Fin won't mind, will you? The house is big enough, isn't it?"

Carla's brows dipped lower. "I suppose it'll be all right. You're only going to be here a short time, anyway, right?" Her gaze went to Sadie.

Sadie nodded. "That's right. Two weeks. Max." Two weeks with Hank living with her. Panic rose in her belly. But along with the panic was something else. Desire. Hot. Burning. Desire. If Hank stayed with them for the next two weeks, how would she keep him at arm's length?

He stared down at her, his eyes warm—and was that laughter crinkling the edges? The arm around her waist tightened. "It's been so long since we've seen each other. But there's no denying the chemistry. It's still there."

Oh, how right he was. Sadie felt herself slipping under his spell, even though she figured his actions were all for show. On his part. The rush of emotion and lust was all too real on her part.

Holy hell, what had she done?

6

───────

Hank almost laughed out loud over the expressions playing across Sadie's face. From sheer panic to the rosy flush of desire. She might be a good actress but, with him, Sadie had never been able to lie or hide how she really felt.

Carla's lips tightened for a moment, and then she smiled. "I guess I'd better buy more groceries if Hank's coming to stay."

Holding up a hand, Hank shook his head. "No. No need. That's why we stopped by the store. We figured you might not have sufficient provisions for another person in the house. We'll take care of it."

"If you're sure." She glanced down at her empty cart. "I was going to get fresh vegetables, fruit, milk and bread."

"If you leave your list with us, we can get them," Sadie said.

Carla shook her head. "That's it. Just the vegetables, milk, fruit and bread."

"We'll take care of it." Sadie gave her sister-in-law a weak smile. "Thank you for being so patient with me. I know it must be an inconvenience, going from just the two of you to the four of us."

"No. I'm sure Fin will be delighted." She nodded to the two of them. "Well, then I'll see you two back at the house in a little while." Carla breezed past them and disappeared around the corner of an aisle.

When she'd gone, Hank followed to make sure Carla left the store completely before he returned to Sadie.

"Why did you tell Carla we were back together?" Sadie asked in an urgent whisper.

"I'd rather not let everyone in the community know that I'm your hired bodyguard. I think we have a better chance of finding whoever shot at you if we play this…arrangement… close to our chests. When Carla jumped to the conclusion we were back together, it was natural to say we were. Everyone else will follow our lead. If I remember correctly, Carla was one of the biggest gossips back in high school. I bet by the time we get back to the White Oak Ranch, everyone in Eagle Rock will know you and I are back together."

Sadie chewed on her lip. "But we're not. That was the agreement."

"You and I know that, but the rest of Montana won't."

She stared at her hands on the handle of the cart. "I don't know…"

"Just go along with it. The sooner we discover the culprit behind the shooting, the sooner we can reveal the truth to everyone." He touched her arm. "Besides, if I moved in as your bodyguard, the rest of Eagle Rock would either come to the same conclusion, or tip off the shooter that you know it wasn't just an inexperienced hunter with more bullets than brains."

Sadie looked around, as if not happy about the turn of events and searching for a way to escape.

Guilt rose in Hank's chest, but, at the same time, he knew he had to be with her, in order to protect her. "I can't protect you from Bear Creek Ranch, unless you come with me or I go with you. I have to be with you, twenty-four-seven. This is the best way to do that, and to keep it under wraps. Our past will make it easy and believable." He held up his hands. "Unless you've changed your mind, and want to hire someone else."

"No. I haven't changed my mind." Sadie chewed on her fingernail, something she used to do when she was nervous.

Out of a long-forgotten habit, Hank grabbed her hand, pulling it away from her mouth and pressed a kiss to the tip of her finger. "It's going to be all right," he said, his tone low, the way he used to talk to her when she was down or upset.

"You're right. Everything will be okay." She snorted softly. "And to think, I came here for rest and relaxation." She shook her head, a smile playing at the corners of her lips. "I'm beginning to think it's safer for me in LA with its gang violence and insane traffic."

"Or you need a full time bodyguard no matter where you go."

She looked up at him. "If you ever stop being a SEAL, you have a career for yourself in personal security." Sadie glanced around the small store. "Especially here in Montana. Do you know how many rich people purchase huge ranches in this state, just to get away from it all?"

Now she was babbling, her nervous energy going from biting her fingernail to talking. Hank nearly smiled. If being near him made her nervous, he hoped it was because she felt the electric currents he was feeling. Standing in the store, between the canned goods and the breakfast cereal, made the spark no less potent.

"Come on. We have shopping to do. And then we need to make a quick stop at the sheriff's office for a status on your shooter and to warn him about your paparazzi-stalker dude." He took over the cart from her and pushed it toward the processed meat section. Loading up on the only lunchmeat the small store carried, Hank moved on to find the fresh vegetables and fruit.

Sadie followed. When he purposely reached for overripe bananas, she stepped in—as he guessed she would.

After they checked out, he helped her load the groceries into his rental and followed her to the sheriff's office.

When they entered, the sheriff straightened from behind a desk. "Miss McClain. I'm glad you stopped by."

Hank stared at the sheriff a moment before he recognized

the man in uniform. "Joe? Joe Barron?" He stuck out a hand. "Remember me? Hank Patterson."

"Remember you?" Joe's face stretched into a huge grin. "How could I forget the best running back in the history of Eagle Rock?"

Hank shook the man's hand.

Joe wasn't satisfied with just a handshake. He pulled Hank into a bear hug. "About time you came back to Eagle Rock. Are you staying, or just passing through?"

"I'll be around for a couple weeks. Maybe more," he said.

Joe nodded. "I'm sorry about what happened to your dad. We're working on identifying the one responsible." Joe turned to Sadie and shot a look back at Hank. "You two back together?"

Hank answered for Sadie. "We're testing the water. But it's looking good." He grabbed Sadie's hand and pulled her close. She settled against his side, a little stiff, but she didn't refute his comment.

"I'm glad to hear it. I always thought you two should be together." Joe's smile faded. "We canvassed the nearby campground and hunting outfitters, asking if anyone had been out hunting near the intersection where Mr. Patterson and Miss McClain were fire upon. So far no one has seen, heard or owned up to firing those shots. I sent the bullet slugs we found embedded in Mr. Patterson's truck to the state crime lab, but haven't heard anything back from them. I'm sorry I don't have any more news than that."

"We actually stopped by to let you know that Sadie was accosted outside Al's Diner by an overzealous fan. You might want to check him out." Hank gave Joe the description of the man, his old truck and the California license plate he'd managed to pick up as the guy sped off.

Sadie added, "I think he's the same stalker I had in LA. Tim Wallis. I had to file a restraining order against him."

"I'll check the local bed and breakfasts, lodges and campgrounds and see if he turns up. I can't get inside his room or vehicle to look for a weapon without a search warrant. Just because he wanted a picture of Sadie doesn't make him an attempted murderer. If he's your Tim Wallis, I can arrest him on charges of violating his restraining order. You don't happen to have a copy of it, do you?"

Sadie reached into her purse. "Normally I wouldn't be carrying it around, but I got the official document the day before I left LA, and stuck it into my purse."

The sheriff took the document, made a photocopy and handed the original back to Sadie. "I'll put out a be-on-the-lookout."

Hank nodded. "Understood. But you'll let us know if you find him?"

"Will do." Joe reached out for Hank's hand. "It really is good to see you. I hope you decide to stay. Montana needs more men like you in the state. If you ever give up the glamour of being a SEAL, I have a *real* job waiting for you here as a deputy sheriff."

"Thanks," Hank said, and meant it. With the possibility of being medically discharged from the navy, Hank was happy to know there were jobs in the civilian world. He could hire on as a deputy sheriff, or like Sadie had suggested, and he'd been considering, start his own protective service. The idea had merit. What did most SEALs do once they left active duty? It wasn't like they quit being a SEAL. Once a SEAL, always a SEAL. But how did the sharply honed combat skills translate to employment on the outside? Well now, he had two possibilities. And with him and Swede facing the potential of being booted out, he had to start thinking past active duty.

He'd run the ideas by Swede and see if he was serious about starting a protective service made up of former SEALs and other combat veterans. And if they could base out of Montana, he would at least get to see Sadie whenever she came home to visit. Hank had no desire to live in LA, unless he lived with Sadie. Then, anywhere in the world would be fine with him.

Who was he kidding? Sadie was a huge celebrity, with every man in the country wanting to be with her. She could have her pick. Why would she pick a washed-up SEAL?

Hank led the way out of the sheriff's office and checked both ways before holding the door for her. "Why don't you ride with me? We can leave your vehicle in town."

She crinkled her brow. "I might want to have it handy."

"You'll have to get used to having me around. I'm not letting you go anywhere I don't go. That's kind of how it works, you know." He winked. "Being a bodyguard, means guarding the body. I can't do that if we're too far apart."

She climbed into the passenger seat of his vehicle, albeit reluctantly. "Are you certain this is all necessary? No one has taken a shot at me since the first incident."

"Do you want to put yourself up as a target and see what happens?" He forced a shrug when his insides clenched. "It's up to you. You're the boss."

She glanced out the windows, as if debating his words, then finally leaned back against the seat. "No. I actually feel safer with you around."

Hank let out a long breath, drove out of the parking lot and onto the road leading out of town. "For the record, I don't want to put you up as a target. But I also don't want you to feel smothered."

She gave a shaky laugh. "Thanks. It's just all so new to me. It's not like I'm anything special."

"Darlin', that's where you're wrong. You're a beautiful, amazing actress; capable of making your fans laugh, cry and *feel* something. And if that's not enough, you're Sadie McClain from Eagle Rock, Montana, one of the smartest, brightest young women I have the pleasure of calling my friend."

She reached across the console. "We were always that, weren't we?"

"Friends?" He nodded. "And if that's all you want us to be now, I guess I can be okay with that." Although he would really have to work on squelching his desire to kiss her whenever she smiled. Or laughed. Or chewed on her fingernail. Hell, he had his work cut out for him.

SADIE DIDN'T LET GO of Hank's hand until they left town. Then he'd needed both on the wheel to handle the curving, winding road into the hills that led to the White Oak Ranch, the place she had called home. She didn't have to give Hank directions. He'd been there often enough her parents had more or less adopted him. Hank and Sadie's brother had played football together with Joe. In a town as small as Eagle Rock, every able-bodied young man played on the football team. Some pulled double duty, playing in the band as well, marching in their football jerseys during halftime. Sadie had been content to watch from the sidelines. Neither in band, nor a cheerleader.

Sadie had been a quiet child, satisfied to let others shine. She read voraciously and felt deeply. Nobody quite understood why Hank, one of the best-looking guys in high school would find her at all interesting. What they hadn't known was that Hank and Sadie had been friends long before they were boyfriend and girlfriend.

Their ranches bordered on each other's. Hank and Fin had grown up throwing a football back and forth, riding horses and going out to the hunting cabin whenever Hank could get away from his father's demands. Only a year younger, Sadie had tagged along, preferring the company of her brother and his best friend over the company of the silly girls in high school. Though she'd enjoyed reading, she'd also liked riding, and the beauty of the Crazy Mountains had never ceased to fill her with wonder.

"Have you been riding since you left Montana?" she asked.

Hank shot a glance her way. "No. Have you?"

She shook her head. "Not much chance of riding in LA. I only ride when I'm home."

"For a land-locked farm boy, becoming a Navy SEAL was a stretch." He laughed. "All those years of swimming in the freezing lakes with you and Fin helped prepare me."

"I've seen the videos of SEAL BUD/S training. What you did to make it through was amazing."

"BUD/S helped me to grow and learn what it takes to trust my teammates to get us through the hard times."

"And I imagine there were some hard times." Sadie glanced at him, noticing how his jaw hardened, and his hand drifted from the steering wheel to his leg. "Were you injured recently?"

He frowned. "Why do you ask?"

"I've seen you rub your leg several times, and you walk with a slight limp."

His brows dipped. "I can still do the job of bodyguard."

"I'm not doubting your ability. I just wanted to know."

For a long moment, he didn't respond. Finally, he said, "Yes. I was just being discharged from the hospital when I got the call about my father."

Sadie's chest tightened. "Were you hurt badly?"

He raised his hand back to the steering wheel, his fingers wrapping around it so tightly his knuckles turned white. "Not as badly as others."

Sadie wanted to know more, but didn't want to push. Apparently his team had taken a pretty bad hit. Maybe losing one of their own. "I'm sorry."

"For what?"

"For whatever you and your team went through."

"Danger is part of the job."

"Yeah, but I know what it's like when someone you love is lost or hurt badly. You feel helpless. Or you second-guess yourself, asking if you could have done something differently to keep it from happening." Sadie stared out the window, remembering when she'd gotten word her parents had died in a car wreck, coming to visit her in LA.

"You miss them, don't you?" Hank glanced her way, his gaze softening.

Sadie nodded. "My folks were what kept me grounded. For the first year after they passed, I felt completely lost. My career had taken off, but I couldn't find the joy I thought I'd feel in it. I didn't have anyone I cared to share my success with."

"What about your brother?"

She smiled. "Fin was too busy picking up the slack on the ranch. He held down the fort, working through his grief. At least, he had Carla." Sadie sighed. "I worked through the toughest time, throwing myself into making movies. I'd make myself so tired, I'd fall into bed, too numb to feel."

The road continued up into the hills, the light of day fading as the sun dipped below the peaks of the Crazy Mountains.

"What about you? I take it your father never forgave you for leaving Bear Creek Ranch."

"No. He was highly disappointed when I didn't choose to stay in Montana and work for him."

Sadie laughed without humor. "He never understood how difficult a man he was to work with."

"No."

"How does Allie do it?"

"Thankfully, he isn't as hard on her as he was on me. I think it's because she looks so much like my mother."

Sadie nodded. "I remember the photos your father kept on the mantel. Allie does look a lot like her."

"She tells me she's getting serious about someone she's been dating from Bozeman. A lawyer she met when she went skiing with the church group up in Big Sky."

"I'm glad she's found someone." Sadie sensed Hank wasn't as happy. "Are you concerned?"

"I haven't met the man. I don't know if I should be worried."

"You'll be here a while. Perhaps you'll have a chance to meet the guy who's stolen your sister's heart."

"We'll see." The road grew steeper and curved around a bluff. Hank slowed the SUV before he entered the curve, and then slammed on the brakes. "Damn!"

The seatbelt kept Sadie from sliding forward and crashing face-first into the dash or windshield. She yelped and clutched the armrest. "What the hell—"

Two rocks, each the size of concrete blocks, lay in the middle of the road.

Hank swerved to miss them, careening off the road and down the steep embankment.

Bounced, jolted and thrown against the door, Sadie held

on, her heart banging against her ribs, as the SUV raced toward a stand of trees in the ravine at the bottom of the incline.

"Brace yourself!" Hank yelled. He pulled hard to the left. The SUV tilted on two wheels and teetered a moment before coming to a halt on all four tires.

Sadie sat for a moment, trying to remember how to breathe, her body bruised and her breath coming in ragged gasps. Then she turned toward Hank.

He sat with his fingers gripping the steering wheel, his face white beneath the tan. When he met her gaze, he asked, "Are you all right?"

She nodded. "I'm fine. Are you?"

His hand went to his leg and he rubbed it, wincing. "I am." He glanced up the hill. "Guess we'll find out if this vehicle has what it takes to climb a hill." He pressed the button to engage the four-wheel drive. "Do you want to climb out on your own two feet or risk the ride up?"

Sadie wrapped her fingers around the oh-shit handle above the door. "Go for it."

Hank eased his foot onto the accelerator. At first, the tires spun on the loose rocks and gravel, then they gripped the terrain and propelled the SUV up the hill.

Sadie closed her eyes, the angle of the slope on the way up feeling even steeper than it had on the way down. She practically lay on her back as the vehicle climbed. Any minute, she fully expected the SUV to perform a backflip and tumble back down to the line of trees waiting at the bottom.

Only when they crested the top and leveled out did Sadie open her eyes and let go of the breath she'd been holding.

Hank pulled the vehicle forward on the very narrow shoulder and shifted into park. He pointed at Sadie. "Stay here and stay low, while I move those rocks."

She swiveled in her seat to peer out the back window, watching Hank as he studied the two big rocks before lifting and tossing them over the embankment he and Sadie had been down moments before.

When he climbed back into the SUV, he shifted into drive and headed toward the ranch, his jaw tight, his hands gripping the wheel. He drove much slower than before, creeping around every curve.

Sadie touched his arm. "You couldn't have done anything different than what you did, if that's what has you worried. If I'd been driving, I'd have swerved off the road, too."

His lips pressed into a tight line before Hank responded. "If I had followed you home, you would have either hit those rocks and crashed, or you would have driven off the side of the hill in your Jeep. Although I'm sure you can handle a vehicle in rough terrain, keeping us from crashing into those trees took all of my strength."

Sadie frowned. "It's one of the hazards of living in the foothills of the Crazy Mountains. Rocks fall on the road all the time."

"Those rocks didn't fall from that bluff. They were placed there, deliberately."

Sadie's stomach clenched. "Do you think it was another attempt to hurt me?"

"No. I don't *think* it was." Hank stared across at her. "I *know* it was."

7

THE WHITE OAK Ranch nestled in the foothills of the Crazy Mountains, bordered on one side by the Bear Creek Ranch and on the other by protected national forests, with an abundance of wildlife. The ranch house was a two-story, mountain cabin in stone and cedar with a wide, wraparound veranda and windows overlooking the mountains on one side and the valley on the other.

Sadie had always loved her home. It was the root of every great memory of growing up with her brother Fin and her parents. Memories, she wouldn't have traded for all the fame and fortune in the world. This place had been her sanctuary. Until her parents died. Fin had given up his career as an architect to return home and take over the running of the ranch.

He'd brought his bride from Bozeman and settled her in the house. Carla had made so many changes, it made Sadie wince, like someone was poking at an open wound. She realized it made sense for a bride to make her house her home, but nothing felt the same without her parents.

Carla had moved the four-poster bed from the master bedroom into Fin's old room and decorated the master suite in a modern style of stark white and tan. The pale, tan fabric-covered headboard had been screwed to the wall. A king-sized bed had replaced her parents' queen mattress, and a sterile white comforter and pillows gave more of the appearance of a hotel suite than a cozy bedroom at home.

The redecorating hadn't stopped at the bedrooms. The living room had been converted to a modern style as well, which clashed with the exterior of the mountain cabin. The sofas were stiff and white, hardly conducive to relaxation after a long day in the saddle.

Fin had insisted she leave his leather recliner alone, so that he didn't have to shower and change clothes before he could take a load off his feet and rest. Sadie almost felt sorry for him, but he'd allowed the changes.

Hank parked on the gravel drive at the side of the cabin and stepped out.

Before he could round the front of the SUV, Sadie had already climbed down to avoid any physical contact with the man. The less they touched, the less chance she had of falling completely under his spell. When she left Montana, she couldn't take Hank with her. He had his life with his team. She had her life as a celebrity. Her chest tightened. After all the years of struggling to make it in the movie industry, now that she was there, she found it to be as lonely, if not more so, than when she was a nobody living in Montana. In fact, she'd felt more like somebody when she'd been with Hank than she'd felt with anyone else.

He waited for her to join him before climbing the steps to the porch.

The sound of voices arguing came to them through the screen door.

Sadie paused and glanced at Hank.

"Should we give them some privacy?" Hank asked.

"Maybe we can help." Sadie squared her shoulders and entered the house. "Fin? Carla? Is everything okay?"

Carla stalked toward her, carrying a suitcase, her face set in an angry scowl. "Just peachy." She pushed past them and slammed through the front door.

Fin appeared in the entryway, carrying a suitcase, his lips

twisted. "Sadie, Hank. Carla said you'd be here soon. It's great to see the two of you together, again."

Sadie wanted to correct him, but Hank slipped an arm around her waist at that moment. Sadie swallowed the words she'd been about to say, opting for something else. "Are you going somewhere?"

Fin glanced down at the suitcase. "Carla's mother called and wants her to come stay with her for a couple weeks in Reno. I can't leave the ranch right now. There are a couple of cows still up in the high country that need to be brought down before the snows start."

"Carla didn't seem happy about it," Sadie commented. "Did she want you to go with her?"

"No. It's just that her mother drives her nuts. Even so, she takes her shopping, and they have fun at the casinos." Fin glanced away. "She's upset because she didn't want to miss being here when you were here."

"Could her trip wait until I leave?" Sadie asked.

"No. Trust me. When her mother calls, Carla needs to go. It gets her out of the country life and back into more of an urban setting for a while. I think she'd be happier if we lived in the city. She's never much cared for the ranch life."

Sadie frowned. "I thought you two were happy living here?"

"I'm happy. Carla, not so much." Fin ruffled Sadie's hair like he had so many times when they were kids. "She'll get over it. The main thing is that you take time to unwind and relax. Your schedule has been insane." When Carla's car horn blared, Fin grimaced. "I'll be right back." He carried the big suitcase down the steps and loaded it into the back of the vehicle. He'd barely closed the hatch and backed away when Carla shifted into reverse and swung around. Without a kiss or a wave goodbye, she spun up gravel as she headed down the driveway.

Fin stood for a while watching his wife, a frown denting his brow. Then he turned to Sadie. "I'm going to take care of the animals before I call it a day."

"We'll help," he offered.

"No need." He waved, and started around the side of the

house. "Just enjoy your time off. You do enough by funding this place to keep it running."

Alone again with Hank, Sadie felt panic rise up inside. Her natural inclination was to lean into his arms and kiss him in the light of the fading sunlight. The scent of pine and pinion and the cool, crisp air reminded her too much of when they would sit on the porch, wrapped in a warm blanket, watching the sun set over the top of the mountains.

Life had been so much simpler then.

Hank's arm dropped from around her. "I'll get the groceries."

Sadie turned. "I'll help." She followed him to the back of the SUV. They bumped into each other several times collecting the bags. Each nudge sent a shower of electrical sparks through her, and she nearly dropped a carton of eggs.

Hank dove to catch them, his lips quirking at the corners. "You seem nervous. Is something bothering you?"

She glared up at him. "You."

He raised his brows, all innocence, making her want to crunch the eggs against his chest. "I'm just playing the part. Nothing else. Unless, of course, you prefer to take it a step further." His gaze challenged her.

"No." She jerked the carton of eggs out of his hand. "I meant it. We live in different worlds. You would not be happy in my world. I won't drag you into it."

"Spoken like a true snob." He winked. "Don't worry. I'm just the bodyguard. I know my place."

Sadie's heart skidded to a halt. "Is that what you think? That you're not good enough for LA?" She set the eggs down in the back of the SUV and cupped her hands around his face. "Oh, Hank. You have it all wrong. Hollywood isn't good enough for *you*. It's a terrible place with all the backstabbing, money-grubbing catfights, everyday of the week. The press never leaves you alone, and they make up stories if their ratings fall. They can be so vicious and insensitive. One minute, you're a rising star, the next, they're tearing you down or printing disparaging lies about you."

"Then why do you do it?"

Sadie laughed. "I ask myself that question often." She looked out at the pastures with the mountains rising up behind them. "I love acting. The idea of taking a script and bringing the character alive is like a form of art to me. That drive came from my love of adventure and fantasy when I read books during the long winters. I could feel everything the characters felt. The physical as well as emotional obstacles were just as much mine as the fictional characters in the stories. When I acted in school plays, I found I enjoyed bringing those characters to life, helping the audience see and feel the struggles through the way I portrayed them. I felt that if the audience laughed or cried, it was like giving them a gift, inviting them into another world, if only for the length of the show."

When she turned back to Hank, heat rose in her cheeks. "It sounds silly. I know."

Hank set his grocery bags aside and took her hand in his, drawing her closer. "Far from it. You have a passion for acting. It shines from your face and in your work. It doesn't come from wanting to be rich and famous. You give your characters the voices they deserve. They're rich in emotion and feeling. Just like you." He raised her hand to his lips and pressed a kiss into her palm. "You're amazing. And that's why everyone loves you."

Sadie's breath caught and held, waiting for him to say that he loved her, too. When he didn't, she hid her disappointment. What did she expect? She'd told him his services would no longer be needed once she left Montana and returned to LA. Their limited time together would be strictly platonic.

What kind of stupid was she? Platonic with Hank was like throwing a shark into a tank with a seal and expecting the shark not to eat the seal. Not loving Hank went against every grain of her nature. Separated by years and distance, she'd never stopped loving the cowboy she'd grown up with. Never stopped measuring other men by the standard he'd set. Now that he was a grown man, with years of military service behind him, hardened by battle, he was even more desirable. She was doomed to fall in love with him all over again.

"Sadie—"

She dropped his hand. He had his life. She had hers. "Let's get these groceries in. I'm cooking dinner, since Carla won't be here."

He stared at her a moment longer. "I'll help."

Together, they unloaded the SUV and stowed the items in the refrigerator and pantry. Hank carried his duffle bag into the house and set it on the floor in the entryway.

Her heart fluttered, and a deep ache pressed hard, low in Sadie's belly. If they were just two people who lived in Montana, and didn't have other outside commitments, she'd tell him to park his things in her room, where they'd make love until the sun came up. Oh, sweet Jesus, how she wished she could go back to being that simple girl from Eagle Rock, Montana. She could feel the words on her lips and imagine Hank's reaction.

With a sigh of resignation, she headed for the kitchen, calling over her shoulder. "You can put your things in Fin's old room. First door on the right at the top of the stairs." They'd both come too far to go back to the simple life.

HANK DITCHED his bag in Fin's old room, which didn't look anything like the room he remembered. Gone were the football trophies, rodeo buckles and posters of his favorite bull riders. In their places were abstracts with splashes of red, tan and black. The walls had been painted a flat tan, and the solid wood four-poster bed sat at an angle in the corner of the room. Hank had the urge to center it on the wall where the bed used to be when Fin had been in high school. Instead, he turned and left the room as it was.

He found Sadie in the kitchen, settling steaks and chicken breasts on a tray. "Grill?"

She nodded, handing him the tray. "You know where to find it."

Hank cranked up the gas grill and placed the steaks and chicken on the grate. When he returned to the kitchen, he stood at Sadie's side, chopping lettuce, tomatoes and sweet onions for a salad, while she cleaned the ears of corn on the cob and wrapped them in foil to go on the grill.

"When did you learn to cook?" Hank asked as he tossed the salad in the bowl.

She smiled. "When I was a starving waitress in LA, trying to break into the movie industry. I couldn't afford to eat out, and I needed all my tip money to pay my rent. I even learned how to make Ramen Noodles taste good."

"Hey." He twisted a damp dishtowel and popped her bottom. "Don't be talking bad about Ramen Noodles. I've eaten them more times than I can count, out of pure self-preservation."

They talked and moved in and out of the kitchen checking the food as it cooked. By the time the chicken breasts and steaks were ready to come off the grill, Fin showed up.

He stopped beside the grill and sniffed the air. "Something smells good."

"Go get cleaned up while we put this on the table," Sadie said.

The pure domesticity of working in the kitchen with Sadie made Hank long for more experiences just like it. It was what it would be like if they were married. Living under one roof, cooking in the same kitchen, sleeping in the same bed...

"Why the big sigh?" Sadie asked.

Hank hadn't realized he'd even done it. "Just that it's a beautiful evening, and I can't think of a place I'd rather be."

She nodded. "I was thinking the same thing." She took one of the plates full of steak and chicken up the steps of the back porch.

Hank followed. As they entered the house, the telephone rang. Fin's voice sounded in the hallway, "Hello...Oh, hey,

Joe… Tonight? Sure, I'd love to meet you there… I'll check with them. Either way, I'll be there after supper. See ya."

Sadie set the bowl of salad on the table and glanced up as Fin entered the kitchen, shaking the water out of his hair. "I jumped in the shower since I smelled more like a horse than a man." He padded to the table barefooted, buttoning his shirt. "That was Joe on the phone. He's off duty and headed to Blue Moose Tavern for a beer after dinner. He wanted us to join him. He said something about the state crime lab identifying the bullet slug they pulled from Patterson's truck."

"We'll go," Sadie answered, then looked to Hank. "If that's all right by you."

"I'll go wherever you go," he said, without adding, *After all, I'm just your bodyguard.*

She gave him a grateful smile and waved at the table. "Gentlemen, don't let the food get cold."

Hank held her chair while she seated herself. Then he and Fin took their seats and dug into the food. The steak was so tender it melted in his mouth. "Is this from one of your own?"

Fin nodded. "It is."

"Best I've ever had." Hank went into a long discussion with Fin over the merits of different breeds of cattle. Sadie joined in, laughing and smiling as they shared memories of growing up on ranches. By the time they finished the meal and cleaned the kitchen, darkness had settled around the ranch house while the stars made their grand appearance.

Fin patted his belly and stretched. "I just have to pull on a pair of boots and a jacket, and I'll be ready."

"I want to change into something fresh." Sadie hurried after Fin, leaving Hank in the kitchen, drying the last plate.

He wandered into the hallway where the photographs of the family had hung ever since he could remember. When he'd visited Fin and Sadie, he'd waited in the hallway, staring at pictures of the McClain family, working the cattle, playing football, on vacation or gathered around the Christmas tree, smiling and laughing.

Hank had vague memories of a time when his family had

been happy. When his mother was still living. She'd been the life force that held the family together. After she died, his father had gotten meaner and crankier, never finding anything nice to say about anyone. Especially Hank. No matter how hard he'd tried, he couldn't please his father. For many years, he'd busted his ass for his father's acceptance. Now that he was grown and had gone through all he had to become a SEAL, he had to give the credit to his upbringing. If his father hadn't been so hard on him, he might not have made it past the first week of BUD/S training.

Pausing in front of Sadie's senior picture, his pulse quickened and a rush of longing filled his chest to the point he felt it might explode. This was the photograph he'd carried in his vest for years until it disintegrated. Sadie was the woman who'd held his heart and gave him a reason to live through the worst firefights. Even knowing he couldn't compete with her costars, he dreamed of being with her some day. Never had he thought it would be so soon. Now that he was with her, he didn't want their time to end.

Fin appeared beside him. "She was such a brat back then. I don't know how you put up with her."

"Hey." Sadie joined them in the hallway and slapped her brother's arm. "That's no way to talk about your sister."

"I didn't do it until I knew you were eavesdropping." Fin rubbed his arm. "You didn't have to hit me so hard."

"Baby."

"Brat." Fin pulled his sister into his arms and hugged her tight. "It's so good to have you home."

Sadie smiled up at her brother. "It's good to be here." Her smile faded. "I'm just sorry Carla couldn't stick around."

Fin's face darkened, and he set Sadie at arm's length. "It worked out for the best. She gets a little too flustered when company comes to stay with us, and her mother is always happy when she goes to visit."

"Are you two all right?" Sadie whispered.

Hank heard the worry in her voice.

"We're fine," Fin said. "Now, let's get going. Joe will be one beer ahead of us if we don't get there soon."

"I'll drive," Hank said. "Might as well put the miles on the rental, since I have unlimited miles."

"You won't get an argument out of me." Fin held the door for Sadie. "I call shotgun."

"I swear we could all be back in high school," Sadie said.

Hank disagreed. Though their words were spoken like they had been ten years ago, each of them had gone through a lot. From taking on more responsibility, learning new skills and suffering the loss of loved ones, they'd weathered storms and come out stronger.

Hank drove the curvy roads a lot slower heading back into town than when he'd drive out earlier.

Fin joked, "You're driving like an old man. What happened to the kid with the lead foot on the accelerator?"

"Let's just say I've encountered my share of obstacles. Driving like my hair's on fire doesn't hold the same appeal."

"Realizing your own mortality?" Fin nodded. "I don't ride the orneriest horses anymore. I've learned to tame them, rather than break them. Actually, I guess I learned there was a difference."

Talking with Fin and Sadie felt like old times. Before Hank knew it, they were pulling up in front of the Blue Moose Tavern.

Hank hopped out and held the rear door of the SUV for Sadie, and then held her hand all the way into the bar.

Joe met them with back-thumping hugs. A cheer went up from the occupants of the room for the hometown hero and the local celebrity. After a few minutes of handshaking and hellos, they finally settled at a table in the corner.

About the time Hank sank into his chair, he spied Sadie's agent, entering the tavern.

Sadie must have seen him as well. "Damn," she muttered.

"Say the word and I'll throw him out," Hank said.

"No. I can handle him. He's really one of the best agents in the business."

"Yeah, but he doesn't know when to back off."

"True."

When Raymond spotted Sadie, he made a beeline for their table.

Sadie straightened in her seat. "Here we go."

"Sadie, I'm so glad you're here, tonight," Ray said as he came to a halt in front of her. "I hope you've had time to consider the contract."

Her lips thinned. "Ray, I told you, leave it until I get back to LA."

Hank leaned forward and gave the man a glare that made most SEALs new to the unit cringe. "Listen to her, Ray," he said in a deep, threatening tone.

Ray frowned at Hank, and turned back to Sadie. "I have the document in my car. All I need is a signature."

"Ray," Sadie said, her voice smooth, controlled, "you're fired."

"It will only take a second for me to get the papers," Ray went on. "You can sign, and I'll be on my way back to LA in the morning."

Hank stood and placed himself between Sadie and Ray. "Maybe you didn't hear Miss McClain. She said you're fired."

Raymond blanched and stepped backward. "You can't fire me."

Sadie rose to stand by Hank. "I can, and I did. Now leave me alone."

Ray looked from Sadie to Hank. He opened his mouth and snapped it shut. "We'll talk when you get back to LA."

Sadie crossed her arms over her chest. "I won't change my mind."

Ray dragged in a breath and let it out on a huff. "Fine. I'm leaving. But this isn't over." He performed an about face and left the tavern.

Hank slipped an arm around Sadie. "You handled that well."

"Yeah, but now I need a new agent." She shook back her hair and smiled. "But that can wait until I get back to LA. I'm here to visit with my friends."

Someone fed money into the jukebox, and a cry-in-your-beer love song filled the room.

Hank leaned close. "They're playing our song."

"We had a song?" she asked.

He winked. "We do now. Dance with me." When she hesitated, he added. "It'll reinforce our cover."

Still she hesitated. When a cowboy got up from a barstool and headed straight for her, Sadie grabbed Hank's hand and pulled him toward the dance floor. "Show me what the navy taught you about dancing."

"Go easy on me. I'm not fully recovered." Though his injury gave him a recurring twinge of pain, and he couldn't do a decent squat without tearing open the newly formed scar tissue, he could sway to a slow song and hold his girl in his arms.

His girl.

Profound yearning filled him as he pulled her into his arms.

Sadie slipped her arms around his neck and nuzzled her cheek against his shoulder. Her warmth pressed against him, made Hank long to be away from the crowd, in a room by themselves where they could peel away their layers of clothing and make love like they used to beneath a summer's moon shining down from the big Montana sky.

No words were necessary—just touching, feeling, and breathing in the essence of Sadie. When the song came to a close, she lifted her face.

He took her offering, his lips closing over hers in a long, deep kiss that heated him from his toes to the tips of his ears, filling his heart until he was sure it would burst.

A lively song replaced the slow one, and several younger couples hurried onto the dance floor.

"What was the name of that song?" Sadie asked.

"I don't know." He took her hand and led her back to their table. "Why?"

"I want to remember it." Rather than take her seat, she glanced around the barroom. "I'm going to find the restroom." She stepped away from him.

"I'll go with you," he said.

Sadie raised her hand. "Don't worry. I won't go outside without you."

Hank stood while Sadie weaved through the tables. When she disappeared down the hallway leading to the restrooms, a panicky feeling filled his chest.

"Sit." Fin patted the chair beside him. "I ordered a beer for you. The waitress is coming."

Reluctant to let Sadie out of his sight for even a moment, he lowered himself into the chair.

A waitress arrived with three longneck beers.

As she set the bottles in front of them, Hank leaned around her to keep an eye on the darkened hallway. He knew it took women longer to make use of the facilities than men, but the longer Sadie took, the more anxious Hank became. Finally, he pushed back from the table and stood. "I think I'll hit the head."

Fin ducked and grinned. "As long is it's not mine you're aiming at."

Hank shook his head. "Navy-speak for latrine."

"Oh. Gotcha." Fin tipped his head in the direction Sadie had gone. "I'll be on my second beer by the time you two get back."

Hank hurried through the crowded tables and chairs and was blocked once by a waitress carrying a huge tray of drinks. The longer it took to get across the room, the faster his pulse beat. Where was Sadie?

8

———————

Sadie wet a paper towel and blotted her face with the cool dampness, her insides still on fire from the dance with Hank. Desire raged through her, making her want to take him home to her bed and make love to him until night turned to day. And then they'd start all over again.

She'd never intended for her trip home to be a reconnection with her first love. It was about grounding herself and giving herself time to think about the next steps in her career. She was at the top of her game, but reaching the top wasn't nearly as satisfying as she'd expected it to be. What was success without love?

Every night, she went home to the gorgeous, spacious mansion she'd purchased in the Hollywood Hills. She could buy anything she wanted, but she found she didn't want for anything. For the past couple of grueling years, working on the sets of her latest movies, she'd dreamed of going home to Montana. Now that she was there, she didn't want to leave.

And it all had to do with Hank.

She stared at herself in the mirror. "How the hell can I live without him?" she whispered to the anguished woman in the glass. Maybe, if she let herself succumb to her desires, she might find that having what she thought she couldn't have would diminish the heart-wrenching longing she'd lived with for over ten years.

Butterflies fluttered in her belly. She glanced once more into the mirror, a smile lifting the corners of her mouth. *Yes.* She'd make love with Hank—assuming he still wanted to—and get him out of her system.

In the back of her mind, she knew it was like lying to herself, but her heart pushed her forward and out of the bathroom. She turned toward the bar, but was stopped when a dark cloth was flung over her head, a gloved hand twisted her arm up behind her, and cold hard metal pressed into her back.

"Scream and I'll plug a hole through your back," a gravelly voice said behind her.

Unable to see her assailant or where she was being taken, she danced on her toes to lessen the pain in her arm. A door opened, and she was shoved out into the cold night air. Fear and desperation spiked through her. If she didn't put up a fight, her captor could take her anywhere, do anything, and perhaps even kill her.

Sadie refused to go down without a fight. As the door swung closed behind her, she planted her heels in loose gravel, backed up and twisted around, hoping that if the gun went off, it wouldn't hit her square on.

The person holding her arm grunted and stumbled backward.

Sadie jerked free, swept her arm wide, connecting with the weapon. Metal clattered against pavement. Her heart hammering against her ribs, she swept the cloth off her head and spun to face her attacker.

Dressed in dark, baggy clothing and wearing a black ski mask, her attacker dove for the gun. With the man between her and the doorway, and not wanting to stick around to take a bullet, Sadie did the only thing she could. She ran.

Racing to the end of the building, she ran around the side and turned toward the street. Footsteps pounded behind her, making her run even faster. If she could make it to the front of the tavern, surely someone would be there to help, or she might make it back inside before being shot dead.

As she rounded the corner, she plowed into a soft, pudgy man. He staggered backward and fell to the ground with a grunt, still holding her, his hands gripping her arms.

Afraid the gun-toting attacker would round the corner at any moment, Sadie yelled, "Let go of me." She struggled to get free, but couldn't untangle herself.

~

By the time Hank made it to the hallway where the restrooms were located, his gut told him something wasn't right. The door to the ladies room opened and a woman exited, frowning at him.

"Was there another woman in there with you?" he asked.

Her frown deepened. "No." She scurried past him and ducked back into the barroom.

Hank shoved the door open to the ladies room. "Sadie?" The room was empty, and every alarm bell inside Hank rang loud and clear. Back in the hallway, he noticed an exit sign over the door at the end. Without hesitating, he rushed toward it and burst out into the night. The alley was empty, but a woman's voice sounded from around the front of the building.

"Let go of me!"

Dear God, it was Sadie.

Hank sprinted for the front of the building and found Sadie struggling to her feet, the cameraman from earlier that day on his knees, trying to stand.

Closing the distance between them, Hank pulled Sadie into his arms and hugged her briefly and then shoved her behind him. Rage fueling him, he grabbed the collar of the photographer and jerked him to his feet. "Go inside, Sadie, and call 911."

"But I didn't—" the man stammered. "I was minding my own—"

Hank's fists tightened and he half-lifted the guy off his feet.

A hand grabbed his arm, and Sadie said, "Not here." She pulled him through the entrance to the tavern.

Hank held onto the photographer, dragging him along.

Once inside, Sadie said, "Let go of him, Hank. He didn't do anything."

"What do you mean?" Hank snarled at the man. "He tried to hurt you."

"No, I ran into him, and knocked him over." Sadie tugged at his arm. "Please, put him down."

For a moment, Hank glared at the guy then slowly lowered him to his feet. "You better have a good story. What happened?"

"I was about to go into the tavern to find something to eat when I heard someone running around the side of the building. When I turned around, Miss McClain plowed into me, and knocked me on my ass."

Hank glanced from the man to Sadie.

Sadie nodded. "It's like he said. Let him go. He did me no harm."

With a narrow-eyed glare at the man, Hank released the fist he had bunched in the front of the man's shirt. "Leave, before I change my mind."

The rotund photographer dove for the exit, the door slamming shut behind him.

Hank turned his attention back to Sadie.

Her face was pale and she trembled.

"Why were you outside?" Hank asked. "I thought you were in the restroom."

"I was. When I came out, someone threw a scarf or bag over my head, stuck a gun in my back and shoved me out the back door."

Hank's gut clenched, and he slid an arm around her waist, cinching her to his side. "I knew I should have gone with you."

She leaned into him, her arms circling around his neck. "I would never have thought someone would attack me in the tavern."

"I see I can't let you out of my sight for even a moment." He kissed the top of her head. "Let's report this to the sheriff. They're going to want a full description of the assailant."

Sadie shook her head. "It was all a blur. The man wore baggy black clothing, black gloves and a black ski mask. I couldn't even tell what color his eyes were." She snorted. "I was too busy running to stop and ask."

"We have to find out who's targeting you and put an end to it."

"You're telling *me*? I thought all I had to worry about was paparazzi showing up shooting photos of me. I'd take the photos any day. Bullets can be a little more difficult to overcome." She leaned her forehead against his chest. "I can't live like this."

"Me either." He tipped her chin up and dropped a kiss onto her lips. "Come on. Let's talk to Joe and then go home." Hank led her back to the bar. Joe and Fin surrounded Sadie at the bar. The bartender offered a free round, but no one felt like drinking. Especially, Hank. He'd failed her by not escorting her across the room. In such a short amount of time, she'd been accosted, and nearly kidnapped or shot. What if she hadn't been able to knock the gun out of the man's hand? Hank's heart dropped to the pit of his belly, and he felt ill.

Thirty minutes and a slew of questions later, Hank was in the front seat of the SUV with Sadie sitting behind him. They had just pulled away from the tavern and were on their way back to the ranch.

"Damn, Sadie," Fin said, turning to look at her in the backseat of the SUV. "Who the hell would want you hurt? You're a national treasure. Everyone loves you."

"Obviously, not everyone," she said.

Hank glanced at her in the rearview mirror. "Are you okay?"

She nodded, her lips quirking on the corners. "I'm alive."

"And that's what matters," Hank concurred.

Sadie stared out the window. "I can't remember making anyone angry enough to want to hurt me."

"Could it be a jealous rival? Someone who didn't get the

part that rocketed you to fame?" Fin asked. "How could anyone be mad at you? As kids, even *I* couldn't stay angry with you for long."

She smiled at her brother. "We had our fights."

Fin's jaw hardened. "Yeah, but this is worse."

Hank glanced in the mirror at Sadie's pale face, illuminated by the streetlights.

"Well, we have to let Joe do his job," Sadie said, her voice even. "I'm just ready to be home. Out of harm's way."

When Hank pulled up to the McClain house, he shifted the truck into park. "Stay here until I check the house."

Sadie touched his shoulder over the back of the seat. "You don't think whoever is doing this will show up here, do you?"

"I don't want to risk it. Wait until I give the all clear." Hank climbed down from the SUV and closed the door. He half-hoped the perpetrator was there. He'd choke the life out of the man for putting the look of fear into Sadie's eyes. The bastard would die for that.

Hank circled the house, checking the bushes, behind the trees and finally climbed the steps of the porch. With the key Sadie had given him earlier, he unlocked the back door and entered. Moving silently, he cleared each room, much as he would have done as a SEAL, only he didn't carry a weapon. That would change. Fin had to have a pistol he could use while he was there.

He continued checking. Nothing moved and no one lay hidden in the closets or under the beds.

He walked out the front door and down the steps to open the SUV door for Sadie. "It's safe." Normally, Sadie wouldn't have waited as long a she had for him to check every room in the house. She'd have declared it nonsense. That she had remained in the vehicle the entire time, spoke to the level of fear she must be harboring.

Hank held the door until she was out of the vehicle and standing beside him. Using his body as a shield, he hurried her into the house. Fin brought up the rear, closed the door and twisted the deadbolt.

Sadie stood in the hallway, a shiver rippling across her body. Even in the relative safety of the house, she didn't move out of the curve of Hank's arm.

"I'll leave you two alone." Fin hung his coat in the closet. "I have to get up early and check on a fence in the high pasture before the snows come." As he turned to head of the stairs, he paused. "I'm glad you're all right, sis."

Which left Hank holding Sadie in the foyer where they hadn't moved since they'd walked through the door.

"Want me to build a fire?" Hank asked.

Sadie shook her head. "No." She walked away from him, rubbing her arms. "I'm cold, but a fire isn't going to warm me."

"Do you want me to stay up with you until you're ready to go to bed?"

She turned to face him. "No." Sadie closed the distance she'd put between them and rested her hands on his chest. "I want to go to bed, now."

His hands rose automatically to rest on her hips, like they used to when they were teens. "I'll walk you to your door and check your room again."

"That would be nice," she said, staring up into his eyes.

Hank swallowed hard, pushing back the rush of lust threatening to overwhelm him. He took her hand in his and lifted it to his lips. Then he led her up the stairs to her room. The one beside his. "Wait here." He entered, checked the closet and under the bed. "All clear." When Hank straightened, Sadie no longer stood at the door. He turned and almost bumped into her.

"Stay with me, Hank." Her fingers fumbled with the buttons on her blouse, pushing them through, one at a time, until she reached the hem.

His pulse pounding and his cock swelling, Hank dragged in a deep breath and let it out. "Are you sure that's what you want?"

"Never more certain." She shrugged out of the blouse, letting it fall to the floor. Her hands moved to the button on her jeans.

Hank grabbed her hands and stopped her from flicking the rivet open. "I thought you wanted to keep this all business."

She nodded. "I was wrong. That one dance proved it to me." Sadie wrapped her arms around his neck. "I have a life in LA. You have a life with the navy. But while we're in Montana, we can be together." She leaned up on her toes, her lips a breath away from his. "Take it or leave it." With a brush of her lips across his, she whispered. "Please. Take it."

Hank hesitated. What Sadie offered was a temporary arrangement. A fling with an old lover. On the one hand, it made Hank feel cheap, like he wasn't good enough to be with her forever. On the other, he couldn't resist the heaven of her naked flesh pressed against him. "What about tomorrow? Or the end of the few weeks we'll both be here?"

She brushed her lips across his again. "I don't want to think about the future. I want to live now. With you. Inside me. Tomorrow is another day. We'll worry about it then."

"I have a feeling I'll regret this," Hank muttered, even as his hands gripped her hips and pulled her against his burgeoning desire. "But right now, all I can think about is holding you in my arms." He claimed her lips, his tongue plunging inside her mouth to caress hers, slipping along the length. She tasted of salted peanuts, beer and her own sweet essence, and Hank wanted to drink his fill.

In a frenzy of movements, she unbuttoned his shirt, and he shoved her jeans over her hips and down her legs.

"Oh, my." Sadie ran her fingers over the tattoos covering his shoulders and back. "I love the tats."

He brushed his fingers down the length of her neck, over her collarbone and down to her breast. "I love everything about your body."

Soon they were naked, breathing hard and laughing. He lifted her in his arms and laid her across the bed. Then he straightened and forced himself to say, "This is your last chance to back out of this. As it is, I'm almost too far gone to stop, now." His cock stood rigid, jutting forward as if reaching for her sex.

"Heaven forbid, Hank. Don't stop now." Her frown eased and a look of challenge rose, as did the tilt of her chin. Sadie trailed one of her hands over a breast, pausing to tweak a peaked nipple between her thumb and forefinger. Then she lowered her hand, skimming across her belly to the triangle of hair at the juncture of her thighs.

Hank couldn't take it a moment longer. "You're a tease, Sadie McClain."

She frowned. "Apparently, I'm not doing it right, or you'd be on this bed with me."

"I'm enjoying the view. It's foreplay just watching you."

"Oh, yeah?" Her frown lifted, and her eyelids sank to half-mast. "Then maybe you'll like this, even better." She parted her folds and stroked the nubbin of flesh between.

Hank could remember when he'd tasted her there, flicking his tongue across that very spot. She'd cried out and begged him for more.

His cock twitched, eager to take her, to move in and out of her tight, slick channel. But Hank held back, savoring the moment, anticipating the pleasure. "Show me how much you want me to lie down with you." With his fists clenched to keep from reaching out to her, he watched as she trailed her finger lower to dip into her glistening pussy, slathering her fingers with her juices before dragging them back up to toy with her clit.

Hank almost came. His swelled even bigger, the tip oozing a drop of come.

Sadie's gaze swept over him, stopping at his dick. She slid her tongue across her bottom lip, and then raised her gaze to his. "Do you have protection?"

His mind on her center, he couldn't think straight. Inhaling deeply to slow his pulse, he had to pull back and focus before he realized what she was asking. "Protection. Yes!" Hank dove for his jeans, found his wallet and pulled out the stash of condoms he always kept on hand, hoping they hadn't expired. How long had it been? Oh, who cared?

Sadie leaned forward and plucked one from his hand. "Not yet. I want you to be as ready for me as I am for you."

"Oh, sweetheart, if you can't tell I'm ready, Hollywood must have blinded you." Hank's last word came out on a gasp as Sadie wrapped her fingers around his staff.

"I can see quite clearly, but I want to *feel.*" She slid her hand up to the tip of him and back down to cup his balls. "Um, I do believe you're almost there."

Hank sucked in a ragged breath and let it out, willing himself not to come too soon. "Please tell me this isn't one of the scenes you played in your latest movie."

"I have a body double for something like this." She rolled his scrotum between her fingers and leaned forward to touch her tongue to the hooded rim. "I don't need a body double tonight. I want to play this scene myself."

"Damn, Sadie, when did you learn to be so fuckin' hot?" Hank dug his hands into her hair. "If you don't stop talking all sexy like that, I'll be done before we start."

Sadie laughed, sucked his cock into her mouth and then let go, smiling up at him. "You always liked it when I talked sexy before. Why not now?"

"Because I'm a little limited on my self-control where you're concerned. Let's shut up and fuck."

"I'm not finished." She sucked his dick into her mouth again, cupped his ass and pulled him closer, taking him all the way to the hilt.

Hank's hold on his control took a hit. "I'm telling you, I can't last much longer..."

She leaned back, letting his cock slide out of her mouth until only her lips touched the tip. "In a minute."

With her hands clenching his buttocks, she maneuvered him in and out, increasing the speed until Hank's fingers dug into her scalp and forced her to stop. "That's it. I'm there, already."

"Well then, let's get his show on the road." She grabbed the condom, ripped it open and rolled it down over his straining shaft. Then she scooted back on the bed and let her knees fall open. Her pussy shone with the wash of liquid slicking her channel.

Hank climbed her body like a conquering hero and settled between her legs. "I can't take it slow like I wanted."

"I don't want it slow," she said. "I want you to fuck me hard and fast. Make it hot and wicked. I want to feel every bit of you inside me."

Hank sent a silent hallelujah to the heavens and slid into her. If he couldn't have a tomorrow with Sadie, he'd capture the memory of tonight. He'd make sure it was branded into his mind where he would never forget. Like he could forget her. She'd haunted him since he left Montana. Sadie would be on his mind until the day he died.

9

Sadie lay back against the pillows, her core on fire, her body moving to the rhythm Hank set.

When he finally entered her, she drew her knees up, planting her heels into the mattress, pushing up to meet him thrust for thrust.

As her channel adjusted to his length and girth, he increased his speed until he pounded into her, his balls slapping her ass, the sound making her even hotter. This was where she wanted to be, and with the man who'd filled her dreams. No one else could ever equal Hank Patterson. He was the one she would never forget. As she lifted her hips to bring them even closer, she reveled in the way he filled her, making her complete—the half she'd been missing all those years.

His body grew rigid against her, and he drove into her one last time, all the way in, until he could go no further. Hank flung back his head and cried out, "Sadieee." His cock throbbed inside her, pulsing, spilling his seed into the prophylactic.

For a moment, Sadie wished they didn't have a condom between them. In her mind, she could picture a miniature Hank running around the yard, yelling and laughing at the top of his lungs, loving life and filling hearts. What would it be like to carry Hank's baby inside her? To feel it grow, kick and squirm until it finally arrived?

As the tension eased from Hank's body, he lay down beside her and draped his hand over her belly.

When she started to turn toward him, he pressed his palm flat on her tummy. "Not yet. I want you to come, too."

"You don't have to—"

He parted her folds and slipped his finger between to stroke the nubbin of flesh swollen from need and desire.

Sadie's breath lodged in her throat, and her pulse hammered through her veins.

"You were saying?" He leaned over and flicked the tip of her nipple with his tongue. "If you don't like this, I can stop." Hank tongued her nipple again, and rolled it between his teeth. "Although you taste exceptionally sweet." While his tongue teased her breast, his finger dipped into her center and came out wet and dripping. He applied the moisture to her clit, and swirled around and around until Sadie gasped and raised her hips, urging him to continue.

His strokes quickened as he flicked and teased her clit until she couldn't think past that magic finger doing what it did to make her insanely crazy for more.

Tingling began at her center and shot outward, the sensation so intense it made her cry out. She caught and held her breath, riding the wave of her orgasm to the very end. All the while, Hank swirled and stroked, the pace slowing as she drifted back to earth. When at last she drew in a breath, she released it on a joyful laugh. She rolled over to face him, warm, replete and so relaxed she didn't think she could move from where she was. Nor did she want to. Hank was amazing. Even as a teen, he'd known exactly how to coax her body into a full, unadulterated orgasm.

Hank kissed the tip of her nose. "You're amazing."

Sadie chuckled. "I was thinking the same thing about you. I'd forgotten how good you were at taking me there."

"Sweetheart, your body is like a fine instrument. You just needed the right artist to bring the music out."

She cupped his cheek. "Did the navy teach you to be a poet?"

"You bring out the romantic in me."

"I think it's kind of sexy for a big, tattooed SEAL to say things like that." She leaned closer, rubbing her breasts to his chest. "It makes me all wet and needy inside."

"Oh, baby, you make me want to go for round two." He sucked in a breath and let it out. "Give me a few minutes, and I'll be up for it." He rubbed his leg, wincing.

Sadie frowned. "I'm sorry." She leaned back. "I got so caught up in what we were doing, I completely forgot about your injury."

He grimaced. "It's not something you want to mention in the middle of making love. And I really didn't notice. I was kind of caught up in the moment."

"You should have let me be on top."

"I wouldn't have changed a thing."

Sadie shook her head and kissed his lips again. "Well, for round two, I get to take charge and be on top." She pressed a finger against his lips. "No argument."

He cupped her hand and moved her finger away. "Darlin', I wasn't going to argue. I was going to say you're sexy when you get all forceful about your sexual positions." He winked and pulled her into his arms.

Sadie rested her head on his bicep, and nuzzled her nose against his chest. He smelled of the outdoors and male musk, the combination heady and so very intoxicating. If she could have frozen the moment, she would have. Instead, she committed it to memory, the sight, scent and feel of Hank holding her so very close, skin against skin. Two hearts coming together as one.

Hank's breathing grew deeper and steady, and soon he slept.

Not Sadie. She didn't want to sleep through this consummation of her love for this man. She didn't want to sleep because having made love to Hank didn't change anything. In fact, it made everything worse. She couldn't ask him to give up his life with the SEALs to follow her to every movie set. He'd be miserable without his team, and she'd be miserable watching him become disillusioned by life as the famous movie star's man. They'd call him "Mr. McClain", instead of Mr. Patterson, and reduce him to just some schmuck who won the lottery by marrying Sadie McClain. She didn't want him to be viewed as any less than a hero, because that was what he was. A hero who'd fought for his country. Sadie was a household name because she could act. Not because she'd defended people or a way of life.

Too bad they couldn't be together like this forever. Tomorrow would be there all too soon.

Hank rolled onto his back.

Sadie lay there until the dull gray light of the predawn hours edged through the window.

The sound of movement in the hallway alerted her to her brother rising, dressing and heading down the stairs. A rancher's life started early in Montana. She'd offered to hire a foreman to relieve Fin of some of the work. He'd refused, claiming he preferred to run the ranch. He let her help pay for ranch hands. A single man could only spread himself so far. As he'd increased the size of the herd of cattle, the workload had become more than he could handle on his own.

Sometimes, Sadie felt guilty about leaving the running of the White Oak Ranch all on Fin's shoulders. But when she came to visit, she could see how much the ranch meant to her brother. He loved being there and doing all the tasks that were part of ranching in Montana. With the snows coming soon, he had to make sure all the animals were brought down from higher pastures and accounted for. Had Sadie not made it in Hollywood, she'd have returned to work the ranch alongside her brother. As it was, she'd hired the help to make up for her absence.

She'd never understood Carla's aversion to ranching. The work was hard, but it made you feel good about what you'd accomplished, about yourself and the land you called home. The ranch had been part of their family for over a century. It was a proud legacy to pass down to future generations of McClains.

Sadie slipped from the bed, pulled on a robe, gathered clean clothing and headed for the bathroom across the hall. Fin would have had breakfast and left for the barn before she finished, so she took her time, enjoying the feeling of the hot spray pelting her skin. With the bar of soap, she worked up a lather and spread it over her closed eyes and raised her soapy face to the showerhead, imagining Hank joining her, running his hands over her body.

The shower curtain shifted with a waft of cool air. Big, warm hands slid around her middle and tugged her hips, pulling her back against a solid wall of muscles. "Ready for round two?"

She shivered at his deep, teasing tone. "I thought you'd never wake." Sadie melted into him, guiding his hand downward to the tuft of hair covering her sex.

He nudged her with his hardened cock. "I wasn't awake, but another part of my body was missing you. Bad. Really bad." Hank nibbled at her neck and tucked the hair behind her ear so that he could access her earlobe, sucking it into his mouth. His hand cupped her pussy, one finger diving between her folds to stroke that sensitive strip of flesh.

Sadie moaned and reached behind her to curl a palm around his taught ass, pulling him closer, forcing his cock between her butt cheeks.

He adjusted himself, fitting his staff between her legs, the velvety thickness rubbing her entrance, making her flame with desire. His finger flicked and teased her clit until her knees grew weak and her belly clenched, and she came in a rush, the tight, achy tingles spreading deliciously throughout her body to the tips of her fingers and toes. She rocked her hips with her release, until she burned again to have him inside her, sharing her incredibly cosmic orgasm with one of his own.

She turned in his arms and pressed her hands to his chest. "It's my turn to please you."

"Oh, Darlin', in case you haven't noticed, you're already pleasing me."

She laughed. "You woke up with that. I'm talking about being on top."

He winked. "I know what you're talking about. I woke from just such a dream."

She turned, twisted the handle, shutting off the shower and whipped the shower curtain aside. "I can't do this in the shower. It's physically impossible." Sadie grabbed his hand and led him out of the tub and across the bathroom floor.

"Aren't we going to dry off first?"

"I can't wait." She opened the door and called out. "Fin, are you in the house?"

When she received no response, she flung the door open, crossed the hallway, naked, dripping wet and hotter than she'd ever been in her entire life. Tugging Hank behind her, she was on a mission to ride this man like he was a wild stallion—hard, fast and fierce.

Once in the bedroom, she pointed to the bed. "Assume the position, frog man." She frowned. "That's what they call SEALs, right?"

He laughed and stepped in front of her, tipping her chin upward. "Yes. That's what we're called." Hank didn't move to get into the bed immediately; instead, he trailed a line of kisses along her jaw and back to her lips. "Um, you taste good."

Sadie brushed his lips with hers. "If I'm going to fuck you this time, you need to be flat on your back." Tipping her head, she motioned toward the mattress.

He stepped back, his gaze running the length of her, from her dripping hair downward, raking across her breasts and lingering at the juncture of her thighs. "You're even more perfect than you were at eighteen."

Her glance met his, and she performed the same perusal, taking her time to admire the bulging biceps, his incredibly broad chest, angling downward to a narrow waist. His cock jutted forward, hard, proud and thicker than she recalled. She didn't stop there, forcing herself to view the angry red scars on his leg. She bent to run her finger over the lines in a feather-soft caress. "I'm sorry you were hurt."

"I'm okay." He gripped her arm, bringing her back up to him. "And I'm about to explode with my need for you." He sat on the bed and then stretched out, his dick standing at attention. Then he turned on his side, propped his head on his hand and grinned. "Now, Darlin', you have me where you want me. Whatcha gonna do?"

She laughed, her heart lifting, her desire building once again. Soon she would have him inside her again. She crawled up on the bed beside him. "I'm going to fuck you like the wild stallion you are."

"I love it when you talk dirty to me." He reached for one of her breasts. "But I'd like to participate a little more than just being a horse to ride."

About to lift her leg to straddle him, Sadie paused. "What do you mean?"

"Come here."

She leaned over him, her lips quirking. "Tell me what you want. I'll do it."

He hooked her leg with his arm. "Turn around." Hank had her straddle him, but not over his cock. Instead, he had her facing his strident staff, her pussy hovering over his head. Then he gripped her hips and drew her down to where he could touch her with his tongue. "Getting the idea, now?" With his thumbs, he parted her folds and tongued her clit.

"Oh, dear heaven, yes." She lowered herself even more and licked the tip of his cock, running her tongue along the ridge.

As he tongued and sucked on her, she wrapped her lips around his dick and drew it into her mouth.

Hank thrust upward.

Sadie took him all the way until he bumped into the back of her throat. Never, had she been in this position before. Never had she had someone take her with his mouth while she went down on him. It was the most erotic experience she'd ever had, and it rocketed her to the heavens and back. Within seconds, she felt the rush of fire burning a path from her center outward, firing synapses, and scorching her nerve endings in every part of her body.

Hank thrust into her mouth, pumping in and out, faster and faster. Just when Sadie thought she might come apart with the force of her orgasm, Hank lifted her off him, turned her around and positioned her over him.

Lost in the moment, she was halfway down on him when she remembered. With every ounce of control she could muster, she rose up and squeaked, "Protection?"

His face strained, his body rigid beneath her, Hank grabbed a foil packet from the nightstand beside him and slapped it into her open palm.

Sadie released a tense laugh. "A man after my heart—always prepared." She took the packet from his hand, tore it open and rolled it over his engorged staff, all the way to the base, taking a moment to fondle his balls. Then she lowered herself until she was fully seated. Leaning over him, she cupped her hand around the back of his head and kissed him, pushing her tongue past his teeth to claim his in a long, sensuous stroke. When at last she allowed him air, she said, "Now, it's my turn."

Rising up, she tightened her channel as she went, squeezing him from inside until he almost slipped out. Then she lowered herself, easing down, slowly, savoring the intensity of the feelings it elicited.

Hank groaned. "Sweetheart, you're killing me."

"Oh, but it feels sooo good," she said, practically purring. How had she ever thought making love with Hank would get him out of her system? If anything, it only made her want him more.

HANK LET Sadie take the lead, riding him like he was a slow-motion mechanical bull. At first it was good, then it was painfully erotic and finally, he thought he would explode. "Darlin', seriously, you're killing me." He grabbed her hips and slammed her down on him, impaling her with his cock. Then he lifted her and slammed her down again.

"Is that the way you like it?" She winked. "I can do that." She got with the program and rocked up and down. Bracing her hands against his chest, she moved with a ferocity and fierceness that rivaled the burning desire inside Hank.

Her breasts bobbed in front of him, and her bottom smacked his thighs. The minor amount of pain in his sore leg was worth it to see the determination in Sadie's face as she made love to him like she was riding a bucking stallion. When he thought it couldn't get better, he was catapulted into the stratosphere. He rammed into her and held her hips to keep her from rising. He remained that way until his cock stopped throbbing, and he fell back to earth and consciousness.

Then he gathered her in his arms and held her close, his heart thundering against his ribs, her breasts smashed to his chest. God, he loved this woman more than life.

They lay entwined, connected and warm, until the light of day filtered through the window and reminded them there was a whole world outside the bedroom.

"I could lay like this forever, but I think you might like to breathe." Sadie lifted herself off him and rolled to the side.

Hank's stomach rumbled, and he laughed. "I think I might have worked up an appetite."

Sadie's tummy gave an answering growl, and she laid a hand across it. "I can cook a mean omelet."

"I'll take you up on that omelet." Hank rolled out of bed and pulled her into his arms. "Ready to face the day?"

She leaned against him and chuckled. "As soon as my legs quit wobbling. Guess I'm out of shape."

He slid his hands from her waist downward to cup her ass. "From where I'm standing, you're in perfect shape." Then he kissed her neck and sniffed. "Something smells funny."

"Hey!" She leaned back and swatted his arm. "That wasn't nice."

Hank set her aside, instinct telling him something wasn't right. "No, really. I smell gas. As in propane or natural gas."

"We use propane to heat the house." She sniffed the air and frowned. "Now that you mention it, I smell it too." She walked toward the door. "Maybe Fin didn't turn the burner off on the stove." As she reached for the doorknob, Hank made a grab for her hand.

"Don't."

"I need to turn off the stove, before the house catches on fire."

"We need to get out of the house." He pulled her toward the window. "Now."

"But—" She struggled to free her wrist.

Hank wouldn't let go. "If there's enough of a gas smell to reach this bedroom through the door, we're in trouble."

"How much trouble." Sadie grabbed her clothes from the night before, slipped her arms into her shirt and dragged her jeans up over her hips.

"Deep trouble." Hank unlatched the window and shoved it upward. "Step out on the roof and scoot on your bottom to the trellis. If it's as sturdy as it was when I climbed it as a teen, it'll hold you. Get down quickly and run as far from the house as possible."

She held onto his hand, her brows puckering. "But you're coming, too."

"I'll be right behind you," he said, shoving his feet into his jeans, and pulled on his cowboy boots.

Sadie turned back toward the bedroom door. "But what about our photo albums and the family bible?"

Hank caught her arms and stared down at her, capturing her gaze. "If you don't get out now, you won't be alive to care."

"I need shoes!" she cried.

"I'll throw them down. Please, for the love of Mike. Go!"

Sadie sat on the windowsill, ducked her head under and swung her legs out onto the sloping roof. A moment later she'd scooted to the edge, lay on her stomach and found her footing on the trellis. With a thumbs-up, she started down.

Hank darted for Sadie's boots. A moment later, he shouted, "Watch out!" He sent the boots sailing toward the ground. Then he exited through the window and scooted across the roof. He turned and placed his foot on the first slat of the trellis, when Sadie appeared below him, staring upward. "Get away from the house!" he yelled, waving an arm. "Run!"

She shook her head. "Not without you."

"Go!"

Sadie turned and ran toward the barn. She tripped, fell, scrambled to her feet and kept running. The farther away she went, the better Hank could breathe.

He'd just placed his foot in the next slat, when the world exploded around him, thrusting him into the air. He flew through the sky and landed on the ground, the air knocked from his lungs, his head bouncing on the hard earth, hard enough he saw stars, then nothing.

10

———————

SADIE HAD ALMOST REACHED the barn when the house exploded behind her. The force of the blast knocked her off her feet. She slammed onto her belly and slid across the dirt. As debris fell to the ground, she covered the back of her head to protect herself. When the air grew still, she pushed to her feet, and turned back toward the house.

Where was Hank? Oh, God, he wasn't behind her like he'd said he'd be. She started toward the burning house and stopped when a figure stepped in front of her.

He wore dark, baggy clothes and a black ski mask, and he held a handgun in his gloved hand. "Damn you."

Sadie recognized the gravelly voice from the night before. This was the same person who'd attacked her outside of the bar, and probably the same person who'd shot at her and hit Lloyd instead.

"You did this." Rage roiled in Sadie's belly and erupted upward in her chest. "You shot Lloyd, destroyed my home and…and…Hank." Sadie took another step forward, desperate to find the man she loved more than her career, her house in LA and more than breathing. He could be injured, possibly dying. She had to get to him.

"He's dead, and soon you will be, too." The person in black pointed the gun at Sadie and pulled the trigger.

Sadie's breath caught. She didn't have time to move, nor could she dodge fast enough to avoid a bullet. Thankfully, the gun jerked in the attacker's hand and the bullet went wide, missing Sadie completely.

Sadie dove, rolled and came to her feet, rushing toward the person in black.

"Bitch!" Before the attacker could aim, Sadie hunkered low and plowed into him like a bull into a matador. All her pent-up fury took both of them several feet back, landing in a heap on the ground. The gun bounced out of her assailant's gloved hand and skidded across the dirt, out of reach.

Sadie landed on top of the attacker and pinned him to the ground. "You bastard! If you've killed Hank, I'll choke the living shit out of you and sling your sorry ass into the house so you'll burn in hell where you belong." Furious, she could feel the fire burning inside of her as well in the blaze of her home going up in flames, she was beyond caring if the fiend had another weapon.

The body beneath her struggled, bucked and kicked. It felt too small to be a man and didn't have the strength to throw Sadie off. Grabbing the ski mask, she yanked it off his head and gasped.

Long, bleached-blond hair spilled out onto the ground, and a familiar face glared up at her.

"Carla?" Sadie shook her head. "You?"

She spit at Sadie and bucked again. "Damn you to hell. You should have died, damn it. You were supposed to fucking die!" Carla swung at Sadie, catching her in the side of the head with a balled fist.

Sadie fumbled for her wrists, dodging the blows. When she finally had both of them, she pinned her to the ground. "You're family. Why do you want me dead?"

"You're making money hand over fist, living the good life. While I'm stuck here, buried on a ranch I hate, cleaning up after a man who doesn't know I exist. Then you waltz back into town, snag the man I dated first in high school, and rub my nose in all your fucking glory. I hate you. I hate this ranch. I hate my husband, and I want you all to die."

"You're making no sense. If we die, you're on your own. No better off than if we lived."

"Bullshit. If you and Fin die, the ranch comes to me. Me!" She fought again to free her hands. "I'd sell this shit hole. Some Californian with more money than brains would pay top dollar for this little corner of hell, and I'd have enough money to move as far away from Eagle Rock and Montana as I could get."

"Well, you're going to get part of your wish," a deep voice said behind Sadie.

She turned, and her heart squeezed hard in her chest.

Fin's jaw was tight, his gaze dark and his face ashen. A horse stood behind him, dancing backward, nickering, the flames reflecting in its frightened eyes.

"You knew what you were getting into when you married me." He took another step forward. "I made no bones about staying in Montana."

Sadie rolled off Carla and stood.

Carla staggered to her feet, her hair wild about her shoulders and her lip curled in a snarl. "I was a fool to think your four years in the marines would show you there was a whole other world out there. I married you because you'd been somewhere beyond Eagle Rock. I was sure I could change your mind. Make you move. Ha!" Carla spit on the ground at Fin's feet. "You're never going to leave this place."

"Damn right. When I was taking live fire in the hills of Afghanistan, all I could think about was home. Montana. This ranch. I have no desire to go anywhere else in the world." He flung his arm out. "Why should I? This place is paradise compared to where I've been."

Sadie could feel the pain in Fin's voice. He'd come back from his four years in the Marine Corps a changed man. Gone was the carefree teenager who'd run wild through the Crazy Mountains. For the first year after he'd returned, Sadie's parents said he'd jumped at every loud noise and had night-mares where he'd yell so loud, he woke himself and everyone else in the house.

"You can have this place." Carla stepped away from Sadie. "I'm done. I'm going to move to Reno with my mother."

"Are you forgetting something?" Sadie crossed her arms over her chest. "You've committed a couple of crimes: arson and multiple counts of attempted murder."

Carla's eyes narrowed. "You won't turn me over to the sheriff. It will be too much negative publicity for your career."

"Sweetheart, as a celebrity, any publicity is good for my career." Sadie jerked her head toward the burning house. "And I'm not the one who started the fire."

"Sadie won't have to turn you over to the authorities," Fin said. "I'll do it." He reached for her.

Carla dodged his grasp and dove to the ground.

Before either of them knew what she was going for, she'd grabbed the handgun, rolled to her back and fired.

The bullet hit Fin in the leg and he went down, clutching his thigh. "Damn you."

"Fin!" Trying not to think about the crazy woman waving the gun, Sadie dropped to her knees beside him. Her hand covered the wound, applying pressure to staunch the flow of blood. Blood leaked through Sadie's fingers. "I need to stop the bleeding," she said through chattering teeth.

"My shirt." Fin sat up shrugged off his coat, then quickly removed his shirt, and handed it to her.

She pressed it against the wound, praying Carla didn't take the opportunity to shoot her in the back. Sadie needed to get help for Fin and find Hank. The last she's seen him, he was still on the roof of the house. Had he made it down before the building exploded? The force of the blast could have thrown him.

Sadie had to assume Hank lay somewhere unconscious, or he'd have been there when Carla pulled the gun on her. She refused to think for a moment he'd fallen into the burning inferno that used to be her family home.

From the corner of her eye, she saw Carla push off the ground, rising to her feet and holding the gun in front of her. "I'm not going to let you condemn me to some stinking Montana jail, while you two go on about your charmed lives. I put up with years of living in this hell. I've done my time. Now, it's time to make you pay."

"Then do it," Sadie said. "Shoot us and get it over with." She glared at the woman, heat from the fire warming her face, anger searing through her soul. "But you won't get away with murder."

"Sure I will. You two had a quarrel—a falling out." She sneered. "I'll leave the smoking gun in your hand, *sis*, and a note written in your handwriting."

"Only one flaw in that plan," Sadie said. "You're not going to do it. You can't shoot straight, and you're too much of a coward."

"Is that what you think?" Carla held the gun out in front of her. "Just watch me."

"Hey!" A deep voice called out over the roar of the fire.

Sadie's heart leaped with joy and then crashed with fear. "Hank! Watch out! She has a gun!"

Carla spun to face Hank, the pistol pointed at his chest. She backed toward the position where Sadie knelt beside Fin. "Stay back or I'll shoot Sadie." Carla stood between Sadie and Hank, the hand holding the weapon shifting between them, pointing at Sadie.

Hank ground to a halt and held up his hands. "Give it up, Carla. It's over."

"The hell it is. As long as I have this…" Carla waved the gun at Sadie, "I'm still in the game." Her eyes narrowed.

A cool wind blasted between the barn and the burning house, lifting the flames higher. The first flakes of snow mixed with falling ash. Sadie shivered, wearing nothing but a shirt and jeans, she was exposed to the chilled air.

Carla reached out and grabbed a handful of Sadie's hair, pulling her to her feet, while pointing the gun at her head. "Come one step closer to me, and I'll shoot a hole in her head so big, there won't be anything left to put back together."

"Carla," Fin said. "Put down the gun. You can't shoot us all. One of us will get to you before you finish the job. You'll go to jail for murder."

"I'm not going to jail for anything. I'm leaving, and Sadie's my ticket out of here." Holding onto Sadie's hair, she shoved her toward the front of the house where the cars stood in the light of the fire. Carla leaned close to Sadie. "And if you're thinking of tripping me or make a break for it...know this: I'll shoot Hank first, and then I'll finish off Fin. You can run, but you won't have anyone left to come home to. Got it?"

"Sadie," Hank said. "Do what you have to do. Don't worry about us."

"Shut up!" Carla jerked the gun toward Hank, and fired off a round.

Taking a chance, Sadie twisted, and slammed into Carla, hoping to knock her over. But, Sadie couldn't get enough leverage, and Carla still had a hand in her hair.

"Bitch!" Carla screamed.

She pulled so hard, Sadie's head snapped backward and her eyes filled with tears of pain, temporarily blinding her. She couldn't see if Hank or Fin had been hit. The snow was now coming down in earnest, and the house fire raged on. Carla shoved and pushed her forward, kicking her shins and kneeing her in the sides. "Move!"

When they were close to Carla's car, the woman let go of Sadie's hair.

Sadie twisted around, flinging out an arm hoping to catch Carla's hand holding the gun.

Carla was ready for her to fight back and got in the first hit, knocking Sadie in the temple with the butt of the pistol.

Sadie staggered backward, pain knifing through her eye. Out of the corner of her uninjured eye, Sadie saw Carla's trunk pop open. Before she realized what Carla had in mind, she was shoved. She lost her balance, and fell backward, the trunk catching her beneath her bottom. Sadie threw her arms in the air, flailing for purchase, finding none.

Another shove sent her falling into the trunk, her legs shoved in after.

"No!" Sadie grabbed the edges and tried to pull herself out, but the trunk lid was slammed downward. She had less than a second to pull her hand back before the lid crashed down and crushed them.

Complete darkness enveloped her.

The muffled sound of Carla yelling came to Sadie through the metal surrounding her, "Come near me, and I'll fire into the trunk. I swear I'll kill her now."

The engine revved. Shots were fired, and the vehicle jerked backward, spinning around. Then they were moving forward.

Shivering, her eye aching, the tissue around it swelling, and her sockless feet so cold she could barely feel them, Sadie refused to give up. Her only saving grace was Carla was a lousy shot with a pistol. Hopefully, she'd missed Hank and Fin. She prayed Hank would stay with Fin and make sure he was all right before attempting to do anything about finding her.

Carla's vehicle lurched along the gravel drive leading out of the ranch, driving faster than was advisable on the sloping road. She slowed slightly, bumped over the metal cattle guard at the entrance and veered sharply, the tires sliding across pavement as she turned onto the highway, heading away from Eagle Rock.

Sadie felt along the darkened interior of the trunk, searching for release catches on the rear seats. Didn't most new vehicles allow the seats to fold down to get long items into the trunk, stretching into the back seat? She worked her fingers around what she assumed was the back seat, searching for a hard plastic button, and prayed she'd find one. Finally, she located a plastic button and pushed it. Nothing happened. She mashed the button again and shoved as hard as she could. Half of the rear seat flopped forward at the same time as the car made a sharp turn off the road and bounced down another gravel road, going so fast, it skidded sideways, throwing Sadie across the trunk. Doing her best to brace herself against the trunk lid, she grabbed the side of the seat still standing and pulled herself through the opening.

She glanced toward the windows. The snow had thickened into near whiteout conditions.

Carla leaned forward in the driver's seat, peering through the windshield, the wipers working overtime to keep up with the developing storm. She was concentrating so hard on the road in front of her, she didn't hear Sadie, or see her in the rearview mirror until Sadie reached around the back of her seat and wrapped her arms around her neck. "Park it, Carla," she said.

Carla screamed and slammed on the brakes.

Sadie lurched forward, but held onto the seat and kept one arm tight against Carla's throat.

Carla clawed at her arm with one hand. "Let go of me," she gasped, "or I'll crash the car and we'll both die."

"Don't do it, Carla. You don't want to die anymore than I do. Just park it and let's talk this over."

Instead, Carla jammed her foot onto the accelerator, and the car leaped forward. The road ahead was little more than a trail, climbing up into the Crazy Mountains, twisting and turning. "I'd rather die than go to jail," she said, pushing the car faster and faster up the mountain.

Soon the road grew narrower, and the sides fell away, plunging down jagged slopes.

Sadie loosened her hold and rested her hands on the other woman's shoulders. "Carla, please stop the car. We can talk this over."

"No. We can't. If I have to die, you're going down with me." She reached over to grab the gun off the passenger seat. When she did, she took her attention away from the road. A curve loomed ahead.

Sadie saw it but Carla didn't, until it was too late.

The car flew over the edge of the road, and raced down a steep slope. Carla flung her hands into the air and covered her face.

Sadie was thrown into the backseat floorboard and couldn't pull herself out.

As if in slow motion, the vehicle bounced, slid, and careened down the hill.

Sadie closed her eyes and braced herself for what would surely come.

The vehicle slammed into something hard and unforgiving. The front and back seats squashed together like an accordion. Trapped between them on the floor, Sadie lay, bruised and dazed.

Metal creaked and cold wind whistled through broken windows.

A low moan filled her ears, and it took a moment to realize it came from her own throat. Sadie wiggled her toes, moved her arms and legs, and made a tally of all her muscles and bones. She was alive. For a moment, she rejoiced.

Then the pungent scent of gasoline wafted in the air, stinging her nostrils and spiking her fear.

<h1 style="text-align:center">11</h1>

Hank started after Carla's disappearing vehicle, but stopped and went back to Fin.

"Don't worry about me." Fin waved at Hank. "Go! Save Sadie. Carla is completely insane. There's no telling what she'll do to her."

"I can't leave you to bleed to death. Sadie would never forgive me."

Fin shoved the shirt Sadie had used to staunch the blood at Hank. "Then use this."

Hank made quick work applying a pressure bandage, using the shirt. Then he helped the other man back into his coat, and half-lifted and carried Fin to his rented SUV, where he deposited him in the passenger seat.

Less than two minutes behind Carla, he peeled out of the drive, leaving the burning house behind.

Fortunately, the falling snow made it easy to follow Fin's crazy wife. As long as the snow didn't thicken and cover her tracks too quickly, they should be able to catch up.

"I'm sorry about all this," Fin said. "I knew she was losing it, but I thought she'd be all right if she went to visit her mother in Reno."

Trying not to think about what might be happening to Sadie at that moment, Hank asked, "Do you still love her?"

Fin held his hand over the wound on his leg, his gaze ahead on the road in front of them. "I'm not sure I *ever* loved her. I'm not sure I know what love is. But out here in Montana, the pickin's are slim. I liked her in high school. We got along okay. I thought we'd make a good team." He shook his head. "I was wrong."

"Wrong or right, we have to find her before she hurts Sadie."

The snow fell in big, fat flakes, blowing sideways and blanketing the ranch road. Hank slowed as they neared the cattle guard. For a moment, he lost the tracks. Which way had Carla turned? Toward Eagle Rock, or away?

Fin leaned forward, staring hard out the window. "There! She turned right!"

Hank bumped over the metal cattle guard and turned onto the highway, headed away from town. The tracks in the snow were getting harder to see. He floored the accelerator, pushing the rented SUV faster than was safe on the slick roads. If he didn't find Sadie soon…

Well, he couldn't think that way. He *would* find her and she'd be all right. Then he'd beg her to let him be with her forever, even if she wouldn't marry him. He'd take her crumbs, follow her to the ends of the earth, and even to LA where she thought he wouldn't fit in. He could be her bodyguard, though he'd done a crummy job so far. Carla blew up her house, and Sadie would have been inside had they not smelled the gas in time. Making love with the client had shaken his focus.

"I'm losing the tracks, and my vision is starting to blur." Fin wiped a hand down his face. "I won't be much help if I pass out."

"Hang in there, Fin. I'll get you to the hospital as soon as I find Sadie."

"Don't worry about me," Fin said, his voice slurring. "Find my sister."

"Do you think Carla would be desperate enough to turn off any of the side roads?"

"Maybe. One of these leads to a hunting cabin." Fin shook his head and blinked, then stared out the windshield again. "It's up ahead in a curve, if I'm not mistaken."

Hank slowed, wishing the snow would slack up enough he could see farther ahead than ten feet in front of the SUV.

"Damn!" Fin turned his head. "We just passed the turn-off. I think I saw tire tracks."

Hank jammed his foot on the brake pedal and sent the SUV skidding sideways and almost off the side of the road. Letting up the pressure, he straightened the vehicle and brought it to a halt. Then he swiveled in his seat and shifted into reverse, backing up several yards.

"There," Fin said, pointing. "Do those look like tire tracks to you?"

With a nod, Hank's jaw tightened as he shifted into drive and pulled off the highway and onto a dirt road that was barely wide enough to call a path. Flanked on both sides by evergreens, the road itself wasn't as thick with snow as the highway was quickly becoming. The tracks in the dirt were evident and fresh.

Hope filled his chest, but soon faded as the road wound upward into the hills. Soon, they came to a curve barren of trees, with a rocky drop off falling away into the darkness. Thankfully, the tire tracks led past it, up the road, into another stand of trees.

As they neared a sharp curve, Hank jammed his foot on the brakes and came to a complete halt.

"What?" Fin's head jerked up, his face pale, his mouth set in a thin line, pain clouding his eyes. "Do you see them?"

Hope dropped like a lead weight into his belly. "Stay here." The tracks led off the road and down the side of a very steep hill.

Fin started to unbuckle his seatbelt. "I'm coming with you."

"Look, you're hurt. This terrain is rough. With my bum leg and yours, I wouldn't be able to get both of us back up the hill.

If I don't come back soon, get in the driver's seat, go back to Eagle Rock, and get the sheriff out here. And while you're at it, call for an ambulance." Hank stepped out into the snow.

"Hank!" Fin called out.

Hank paused.

Fin leaned forward, shucking his jacket. "At least take this. You'll freeze to death if you're gone long."

Hank accepted Fin's offering and turned toward the edge of the road, shrugging into the coat.

Before he'd taken one step over the side, an explosion ripped through the air, knocking him backward. He fell hard on his ass, the landing jolting the hell out of his leg. Pain radiated from the injury through the rest of his leg and stole his breath away.

Flames rose into the sky, the glow enhanced by the low-hanging clouds.

Hank scrambled to his feet, his heart banging against his chest, panic making his breath catch in his throat. *Sadie.*

Holy hell, what had happened? He went over the edge, limping as fast as he could. Skidding on loose rocks, he slid toward the bottom of the hill where a ball of flames reached for the sky, puffing black, acrid smoke like a steam engine.

"Sadie! Dear God, Sadie!" he cried and ran toward the vehicle. The trunk remained closed. The doors on the side closest to him were closed. Nobody had gotten out of the vehicle that way, and the fire was too hot for him to get close.

Hank had a flashback of when his team had taken that hit with the grenade. His heart raced and he couldn't breathe. Dropping to his knees, he ignored the pain in his leg as tears ran down his face. He'd lost Lt. Mike. He'd almost lost Swede in that last battle. Now, in the beauty of his home, in the Crazy Mountains of Montana, he'd failed the one woman he'd ever loved. Hank buried his face in his hands. "Oh, Sadie."

A hand settled on his shoulder. "Hank." Her voice came to him as if in a dream. "I'm okay. I'm here."

He looked up, blinked the tears from his eyes and stared into Sadie's beautiful, dirt-streaked face. Then he was on his feet, pulling her into his arms, his aching leg forgotten in the joy of holding his Sadie, his heart, his love.

She nestled against him, her body trembling.

"You're cold." He yanked the jacket off his back and wrapped her in it.

Sadie laughed, her teeth chattering. "Thanks, but now you'll be cold."

"I may never be cold again in my life." He kissed her forehead, the tip of her nose, and finally claimed her lips in a deep, soul-defining melding of their mouths.

When she pushed her hands against his chest, he didn't want to loosen his hold, afraid if he did, she'd disappear, and he'd realize this had all been a dream.

"Hank. I'm okay, but Carla isn't. I barely got her out of the car before it caught fire. She's unconscious and needs medical help."

Hank frowned. At first, he couldn't comprehend helping the woman who'd tried to kill Sadie and Fin. When his heart stopped racing, he knew he couldn't leave the woman to die in the falling snow. "Show me where she is."

Sadie took his hand, and led him toward the burning vehicle, and around to the other side where the doors stood open. Carla lay on the ground, somewhat sheltered from the snow beneath a tree.

Hank bent, his leg screaming with the pain of the effort, the scar tissue stretching, threatening to pull apart. Scooping his hands beneath the woman, he lifted her into his arms, when he'd rather be lifting Sadie and carrying her out of the woods.

Step by painful step, he climbed the hill, slipping twice. If not for Sadie, walking up the hill beside him, steadying him when he would have fallen, he wouldn't have made it.

Fin stood at the edge of the road. "Carla?" His gaze met Sadie's.

"She's alive, but pretty banged up," Sadie said.

Fin hobbled to the back door of the SUV and flung it open. "I was just about to climb into the driver's seat, and go to town for that ambulance." He stood back so that Hank could settle Carla in the back seat. Then Fin climbed in with his wife.

Hank closed the back door and held open the front door for Sadie.

She paused and leaned up on her toes to kiss him. "We have a lot to talk about."

"Yes. We do." Hank wrapped his arm around her waist and hugged her to him, his mouth finding hers, kissing her hard. "But first, we have to get to the hospital."

Sadie smiled, her eyes filling with tears. Then she slid into the seat and buckled her belt.

The arctic wind found Hank, blowing through the thin shirt he wore, sinking all the way through his skin to his bones. He and Sadie needed to talk, but what did *she* want to talk about? Was she going to push him away again?

He limped around to the driver's side, the pain returning to his leg in full force. He gritted his teeth and climbed into the SUV.

All the way to Eagle Rock, he held it together, refusing to start the conversation with Sadie until everyone was taken care of. The best Eagle Rock had to offer was the volunteer fire department's first responders. The town was too small to afford a trauma center or hospital, and, as they discovered when they pulled into the station's parking lot, the town's only doctor was on vacation.

Carla and Fin were stabilized and loaded for transport to the hospital in Bozeman. Hank learned that Allie had noticed the light in the sky from the White Oak Ranch. When she'd called the ranch's number, and didn't get an answer, she'd dialed 911 to have the fire department take a look. They'd sent the full contingent in response and were handling the blaze. Thankfully, they were able to save the barn, but the house, and everything in it, was a complete loss.

Sadie leaned into Hank, tears falling silently down her face as she listened to the emergency medical technician's account of what had happened since they'd left the ranch. "All the pictures of my parents. Their wedding rings. My grandmother's rocking chair…"

"Things can be replaced. People can't." He brushed the stray strands of hair away from her damp cheeks. "And nothing can take away your memories."

She smiled. "I know all that. But it still hurts."

Hank's heart squeezed. He wished he could take away the pain of her loss.

He and Sadie followed behind the ambulance, both quiet on the trip into Bozeman.

While the emergency room doctors worked on Fin and Carla, Hank insisted on someone checking Sadie over.

Allie arrived while Hank waited for Sadie.

"Thank goodness you're all right." She hugged him and stood back, checking him from head to foot. "What the hell happened?"

He filled her in on everything, his gaze shifting to the ER doors every time they opened.

"And Sadie? Will this make her cut her visit short and go back to LA?"

"I hope not." Hank wouldn't let himself believe that after all they'd been through together, she'd leave him behind. But he didn't know for certain, and it was eating away at his insides.

Finally, Sadie appeared, smiling. "Other than a few bumps, bruises and a shiner, I'm fine," she said. "While we're waiting for the doctor to finish with Fin, I'd like to see how your father is doing."

"I'll stay here and wait for Fin," Allie said. "Tell Dad I'll be by to see him next. Hopefully, he'll be getting out of the hospital soon."

A few minutes later, Hank and Sadie entered Lloyd Patterson's room.

Hank's father was sitting on the side of his bed, buttoning his shirt over his hospital gown.

Sadie hurried forward. "Mr. Patterson, what are you doing?"

"Getting out of this dadgum morgue. Half the county is on fire back home, and I'm stuck here."

"The fire department is taking care of things," Hank said. "Besides, how did you hear about it?"

"I have my sources." Hank's father caught Sadie's hand. "What happened to your face, girl?"

Sadie touched the corner of her eye. "Would you believe I ran into a door?" She winked and winced.

"Hell, no." Hank's father's brow drew into one of his deepest frowns. "Did my son do that to you?"

Sadie laughed out loud. "No, sir."

Hank drew Sadie away from his father and into his arms. "I'd never hurt her."

"Then why did you leave her to join the Navy?" his father demanded. "I never saw a sorrier face than Sadie McClain's after you ran out on her."

"I asked her to marry me. She said no."

"Ladies don't like to appear too eager. Don't you know nothin' 'bout womenfolk?" Hank's father shook his head. "When you find one as special as your mother, you hold onto her, woo her, convince her you love her more than life itself. She's worth it." Mr. Patterson's frown softened as he stared at Sadie, his eyes clouding. "I loved my Maggie more than I loved to breathe. I'd give anything to have her back." His shoulders slumped, and he seemed to get smaller.

"Mr. Patterson, you need to lie down," Sadie said softly. "You're not yet well enough to be out of bed."

He let her help him back into the bed. "Maggie hung the moon, in my books."

"I remember her. She was always so happy." Sadie tucked the sheet around him and kissed his cheek.

"She never had a harsh word to say. Not even to me. And I was no saint."

Hank snorted. His father had been angry for so long, he couldn't remember when he hadn't worn a frown.

His father lifted a hand to Sadie's cheek and then stared

across at Hank. "Make it right with Miss Sadie. She loves you and, you love her. I can't believe you let her get away."

Hank remembered the raw hurt he'd experienced the day Sadie had said no all those years ago. That pain had never let him.

"He didn't let me get away. I pushed him away." She stared down at Hank's father. "Hank needed to follow his dreams. He'd always wanted to join the Navy and become a SEAL. If he'd married me straight out of high school, he never would have gone."

"He'd have stayed where he belonged. Here in Montana, ranching like his ancestors."

Hank started to say something, but Sadie beat him to it.

"He needed to go away, to do those things he'd dreamed of, so that when he came back, he'd know whether he belonged in Montana or somewhere else. Now that he's been all over the world, he can make an informed decision." She turned to Hank. "By now, he should have an idea of where he really wants to be, and who he wants to be with."

"This is not the place to have this discussion." Hank circled Sadie's waist with his arm. "Dad, I love this woman and would do anything for her. But I need to talk with her."

His father raised his hands. "I'm not keeping you." He pointed his finger at his son. "But don't screw it up this time. She's a keeper."

For the first time he could remember, he fully agreed with his father. "I'll do my best." Then he led Sadie out of the hospital room and down the hall until he found an empty room. He pulled her inside and closed the door.

The corners of Sadie's lips quirked upward. "We have to stop meeting this way."

Hank cupped her cheek. "If it's the only place I can get you alone, without the house exploding, I'll take it." He brushed his thumb across the bruise near her eye and shook his head. "Does it hurt much?"

"Only here," she said, and touched her hand to her chest.

"Tonight, in the back of Carla's trunk, I thought I might never see you again."

Hank laid his hand over hers. "Sadie, Darlin', I might not have a place in your life in LA, but I'd follow you to the ends of the earth just to be with you."

Sadie's eyes filled and tears slipped down her cheeks. "You belong with your SEAL team. I can't take you away from the life you love."

"My heart is with you." He pulled her into his arms, molding her body to his. "If all you want from me is a body-guard, I'll do it."

"I don't want you to give up your life as a SEAL for mine."

Hank pressed a finger to her lips. "I'm leaving the navy."

Sadie's eyes widened. "But, Hank. You love what you do."

He gave her a kiss and then pulled away. "I love you."

More tears slipped from Sadie's eyes. "I never stopped loving you."

"Then what's stopping you from being with me?"

She raised her hands. "I don't know."

He kissed the tip of her nose. "I'll prove to you I can handle your life in LA."

"I don't want to live in LA. I want to live here." She sniffed and smiled. "I can cut back to one movie a year, or quit altogether. I don't need the money. I have more than I know what to do with." She laid her cheek against his chest. "I want to be with you."

Hank smoothed a hand over her hair, loving the silky feel of it. "I won't be your kept man."

Sadie laughed. "Like you could ever do that." She looked up at him. "Will you go back to being a rancher and work with your father?"

He shook his head. "Maybe part time. But I thought I might start a business of my own."

"Doing what?" She laid a hand on his chest.

"I want to create an agency providing protective services for individuals who need it. I'll hire prior military who need jobs. It combines the best of both worlds. People who need help will get it, and good men who have fought in wars, and are highly skilled at what they do, will have honorable work following their military service."

"I love it." She wrapped her arms around his neck and leaned up on her toes to kiss him. "What will you call this agency?"

"Brotherhood Protectors."

"Hmm. Seems you have it all figured out." She pulled his head down to hers. "What about us?"

"I only have one thing left to do." Hank set her away from him.

Sadie tilted her head. "And what's that?"

He knelt on his good knee, his bad knee aching at being bent, but he didn't care. The woman he loved was standing in front of him, confessing her love for him. There was only one thing he could do to make this day better. "Sadie McClain, love of my life, for the second time in our lives, I'm asking you... will you marry me?"

Sadie dropped to her knees and lifted his hand to her face. "Hank Patterson, I love you. I've never stopped..." She pressed a kiss into his palm.

"You might love me, but you didn't answer my question." Hank drew her to her feet and pulled her into his arms. "Will you marry me?"

"Yes! Yes! Yes!"

Hank kissed her, holding her tight. If he could, he'd never let her go again. This was where he belonged. In Montana, his home. In this woman's arms.

BRIDE PROTECTOR SEAL

BROTHERHOOD PROTECTOR SERIES
BOOK #2

New York Times & *USA Today*
Bestselling Author

ELLE JAMES

New York Times & USA Today Bestselling Author
ELLE JAMES
BRIDE PROTECTOR
SEAL
BROTHERHOOD PROTECTORS

This story is dedicated to military men and women who separate from active duty and find it hard to fit in with the so-called real world. You are loved and appreciated for all you have done to protect this great nation!

Elle James

1

AXEL SVENSON, or Swede, as he preferred to be called, flexed his hand before he stuck it out. He found the scars were less disconcerting than proffering his left hand to shake. "Nice to meet you, ma'am."

"You can call me Allie. Ma'am makes me sound old." Alyssa Patterson took the hand without flinching. "No offense, but I can't say that I'm as thrilled to meet you. I really don't need a bodyguard, despite what my brother says."

"Yes, you do," her brother, Hank 'Montana' Patterson, said.

His first day on the job with the Brotherhood Protectors and Swede's first client didn't want his services. It wasn't exactly the way he'd pictured his initial assignment. From the way Montana had described the work, he'd expected to be allocated to a helpless rich person who needed someone to chauffeur, him or her, around. All he'd have to do was look big and tough. With the scar on the side of his face, he had no doubt he could intimidate the hell out of most people.

Instead of a rich socialite, Montana had tasked Swede with protecting his kid sister. And she wasn't thrilled with the idea.

"If your sister doesn't want a bodyguard, why force one on her?" Swede asked.

Allie's eyes narrowed. "Wait, you're taking my side?"

127

Swede shrugged. "You're a grown-ass woman. If you don't think you need a bodyguard, you shouldn't have to accept one."

Allie turned to her brother and flashed a smile. "I might like this guy after all."

Sadie, Montana's wife, laughed.

Montana shot a brief frown at Allie and Sadie, and turned to Swede. "After several suspicious events, Allie's fiancé is concerned about her. And frankly, so am I."

"I have too much to do between now and the wedding to have someone on my heels slowing me down," Allie argued.

Montana gave her an "I'm the big brother" look. "You already agreed to Swede tagging along. Just shut up and let him."

Allie crossed her arms over her chest. "I'm going to a fitting, having my nails done and shopping for lingerie for the wedding night. That's when I'm not hauling hay, cleaning stalls and checking fences not only on the Bear Creek Ranch, but on the Double Diamond." She gave Swede a look that sized him up and found him lacking. "What do you know about any of those activities?"

He shrugged. "Nothing."

Allie rolled her eyes and turned back to Montana. "Let me guess, he's never been on a ranch, and doesn't know one end of a horse from another?"

Rather than allow himself to feel inadequate, Swede stiffened his back and straightened to his full six-feet-four inches. "I might not know my way around a ranch, but I'm good with a gun, I learn fast, I'm quick on my feet and highly observant."

She opened her mouth.

Swede pressed a finger to her lips. "Let me demonstrate." He gave her the same assessing stare she'd given him. "You came straight from the horse stalls you spoke of because you smell like manure, and you're tracking it into the house. You didn't take time to brush your hair this morning, likely because you had to clean the stalls and take care of the animals. Your hands are shaky, probably because you drink too much coffee. You haven't slept well in days, if the circles under your eyes are any indication. The lack of sleep has everything to do with all of the things you mentioned, plus you're worried your brother might be right and you might be in danger." He crossed his arms over his chest, much like she had. "Did I miss anything?"

"Great. And he's a smartass." Allie glared at her brother.

Montana raised his hands. "Hey, don't look at me. Take it up with your fiancé. He was the one who thought you needed protection. Maybe if you'd decided to marry one of the locals instead of a rich man who just bought a ranch in Montana because he could, you wouldn't be in any more danger than getting thrown by a horse."

"Do you hear yourself?" Allie asked. "You sound like our father."

Montana scowled and his jaw tightened.

His wife, Sadie, touched his arm. "Sweetheart, Allie has the right to choose her partner. Let her take up the bodyguard issue with Damien. He's the one who thinks she might need one. He can better explain his concerns."

Montana slipped an arm around Sadie's waist. "You're right." He turned to his sister. "I'm sorry. You can marry any rich jerk you want. I don't have to like it, and I'll tell you so, but if this is what you want, I won't stand in your way."

"Damn right, you won't." She lifted her head.

"At least let Swede tag along. If Damien is set on hiring a bodyguard, perhaps he can convince you." Montana held open his arms. "You know I love you, kid. I only want what's best for you."

Allie sucked in a deep breath, let it out and stepped into her brother's hug. "I guess that's your job."

"Yup. I wouldn't be a big brother unless I told you how I see it." Montana sniffed. "And Swede is right. You do smell like manure."

Allie punched him in the belly. "Thanks. Love you, too." She hugged her sister-in-law and patted her stomach. "Take care of my niece."

Sadie laid a hand over her flat abdomen. "I will." She

hugged Allie. "Let Swede take care of you. I want our baby to know her Auntie Allie."

"I'll be around. I might be marrying a rich man who travels all over the world, but my life is here in Montana."

"Don't forget…" Sadie touched her arm. "We have the final fitting for your dress the day after tomorrow."

Allie sighed. "I don't know why I had to have it altered. It fit just fine."

"The dress was too loose around your waist and too short," Sadie reminded her. "And no, you can't wear your favorite cowboy boots under it."

"Why?" Allie protested. "Nobody will see my feet."

"Because they'd smell like you do now. Like the inside of a horse stall." Montana turned her around. "Go on. Talk to Damien before you go back to the ranch."

Swede's chest tightened over the back-and-forth arguing between the siblings. Montana was lucky. He had a wife, a baby on the way, his sister and his father. For Swede, one of the hardest things about being processed out of the military was losing the only family he had. His SEAL team. The soldiers he'd met during his recovery had family members come visit them. Not Swede.

The whole recovery process would have been a lot harder but for two things: the Australian shepherd he'd rescued from the animal shelter, and the Delta-Force soldier he'd met during his physical therapy sessions. Bear Parker had been in the same boat as he was. No home to go to, no family to greet him when he got there. They'd gone out for a beer several times after therapy sessions. Which reminded Swede…

He hesitated before following Allie. "You know, Montana, when you start getting more business, I know another man you might want to hire."

"Yeah?" Montana's brows rose. "Tell me."

"He's not a SEAL, but he's former Delta Force."

"I might have work for him. Is he available now? Or do we have to wait until his enlistment is up?"

"Available now. I met him in Bethesda during my recovery. I'm sure he'd be interested."

"Pass on his details, and I'll contact him."

"And Montana, thanks for the opportunity." Swede held out his hand.

Montana took it and pulled the big man into a bear hug. "We're in this together."

Swede hugged him back. "Once a SEAL, always a SEAL."

"Right. We just have to find out where we fit now that we're not fighting wars in foreign countries."

"If you're going to follow Allie, you'd better get going," Sadie said. "She's pulling down the drive now."

Swede sprinted from the room, feeling only a slight twinge in his thigh from the shrapnel wounds. He hurried to his truck, parked in front of the house. Ruger barked a greeting and moved out of the driver's seat.

"Good boy." Swede started the engine and spun the truck around, spitting gravel in his wake.

ALLIE WAS furious Damien hadn't asked her first before contacting her brother about a bodyguard. She'd made it perfectly clear to her fiancé that she was a very independent woman who liked doing things her way. If he wasn't okay with that, he shouldn't have dated her or asked her to marry him. She wasn't changing for any man.

A glance in her rearview mirror made her smile. She'd left without waiting for Swede. If he was to be her bodyguard, he'd have to do a whole lot better at keeping up.

He didn't catch up to Allie until she slowed to turn onto the highway.

Yes, she was driving like a bat out of hell, racing along the highway like she was actually trying to lose him. Maybe she was. Having someone follow her around like she needed a babysitter wasn't her idea. Why make it easy on the man?

Apparently, Swede wasn't so easily deterred. He caught up

and rode her tail, even though she was breaking the speed limit.

The gate to her current home with her father at Bear Creek Ranch came and went. She didn't slow down until she reached the grandiose stone and wood monstrosity with the words Double Diamond Ranch seared into the cedar archway. Unlike most gravel ranch roads, the Double Diamond road was paved all the way up to a huge mansion of a house, spreading across the top of a knoll.

Damien had purchased it from a movie star who'd gotten tired of the cold winters and moved back to sunny California to retire. The drive was lined with trim white wood fencing and trees spaced perfectly along the way. Horses grazed in the pastures if they weren't being cared for in the massive stable. The stable was magnificent with twelve stalls, a spotless tack room and an office for the foreman.

Allie had a love-hate relationship with the ranch. She loved what wealth could buy, but, at the same time, hated the waste of so many dollars on things that weren't necessary to have a working ranch in Montana. But, this wasn't a working ranch. It was a gentleman's retreat where riding was done for exercise and fun, not out of the necessity of managing cattle.

When she married Damien, she hoped to change that. She wasn't the kind of woman who sat around the house eating bon bons with servants who tended to her every need. *Bleck!* She got the sour taste in her mouth, and felt the need to spit to clear it.

Allie pulled to a stop in front of the mansion and slid out of the driver's seat. Without waiting for Swede, she marched up to the front entrance and pounded on the door, her anger fueling her fist.

Footsteps sounded on the steps behind her. The bodyguard was getting faster. Darn it all.

A man in a uniform opened the door. "Ah, Miss Patterson. Mr. Reynolds is out at the stable. Perhaps you'd like to come inside and wait for him?"

"No, thank you, Miles. I'll find him." Allie turned and ran

into Swede. Beside him was a blue merle Australian shepherd with ice blue eyes much like his master's. "Why are you standing so close?"

He stepped aside with what could only be regarded as a sarcastic flourish. "Maybe if you looked before you rushed headlong into things, you wouldn't have a problem with where I stand."

She snorted. "This your sidekick?"

"You could say that. His name is Ruger."

Her expression softened, and she reached down to scratch the dog's ears. She had a soft spot for dogs, especially working dogs, which she was almost sure this one was not.

Ruger leaned against her leg, his tail thumping against the stoop.

Allie could get lost in eyes so blue. Her jaw hardened, she straightened and gave Swede a narrow-eyed glare. "Just stay out of my way, will ya?" She ducked around him and marched across the manicured lawn toward the stable. "Damien!" she called out. "I need to talk to you."

Her fiancé, dressed in freshly pressed khaki slacks, a dark polo shirt, and black leather jacket emerged from around the far side of the stable, his brows pulled into a deep frown. "Alyssa, what are you doing here?"

Not *'Alyssa, darling, I'm so happy you came to see me'*. Was the honeymoon over before it had even begun? And without the requisite sex? That was another thing she would take up with Damien when she had a moment alone with him. Why hadn't they gone all the way yet? This waiting for the wedding bullshit was positively archaic. What if he was lousy in bed? Worse yet, what if she was lousy in bed with him? She wasn't a virgin, but it had been a while since she'd slept with someone.

Frustrated by all she had to do before the wedding and adding the aggravation of having to put up with a shadow following her around, she launched her attack. "What's this about you going behind my back to hire a bodyguard for me?"

He glanced back in the direction from where he'd come. "Darling, I think it's best. It appears that I've made a few enemies along the road to success. Some would like to steal away my good fortune."

"What kind of enemies?" Swede asked, stepping up beside Allie. He held out his hand. "I'm the bodyguard you hired. Axel Svenson. Most people call me Swede."

Allie crossed her arms over her chest as the men shook hands.

"Damien Reynolds. I'm glad to meet you. Let me show you the latest in what has me concerned." He hooked Allie's elbow, turned and walked around the side of the stable. He stopped and waved his hand at the wall. Splashed across the side of the well-maintained structure were bold letters spray-painted in red.

TAKE WHAT'S MINE
I'LL TAKE WHAT'S YOURS

A chill slithered down Allie's spine at how the red paint resembled blood, with long trails dripping from the letters down the side of the stable. She shuddered and straightened. "Damien, it's just paint."

His mouth pressed into a thin line. "It's a threat. A promise to take what I've accumulated here. Whoever did this might also target the people I care about."

Swede turned to Allie. "Didn't your brother say something about cut brake lines on your truck?"

Damien's brows dipped. "Have you had anything else happen since then?"

Allie shot a narrow-eyed glare at Swede. "No. And that could have been a fluke."

"I'd rather be safe than sorry. Less than a week remains until our wedding. Then we'll get away on our honeymoon, and leave all of this behind."

"If there really is a problem," Allie pointed to the stable wall, "which it seems there is, we'd only delay dealing with the issue."

Damien shoved a hand through his immaculate hair. The gesture barely ruffled the dark locks.

Sometimes that irritated Allie, considering she looked like she needed to brush her hair the minute she stepped outside.

"How about us tackling one challenge at a time?" He lifted her hand and pressed a kiss to her callused fingers. "Let Mr. Svenson get you to the wedding on time and intact. When we get back from the honeymoon, we can deal with whoever is causing the problems."

"I can take care of myself," Allie insisted. "I have a gun, and I know how to use it."

"I know you do, darling. But you can't always be watching over your shoulder. I know you have last-minute preparations for the wedding. You don't need to worry yourself about some lunatic stirring up trouble. Leave it to your bodyguard."

Allie bristled, biting hard on her tongue. One of the things she liked about Damien was also one of the attributes that really pissed her off. He treated her like a lady. As a hardcore rancher, it was a nice change to be seen as a woman, not just another ranch hand. But then, Damien sometimes took it a little too far, treating her like a woman who didn't know one end of the gun barrel from the other. Rather than call him on his patronizing attitude, and show any discord between them to the hired bodyguard, Allie swallowed the words she wanted to say. "Okay, I'll let him tag along."

"Good, because I have to go out of town for the next few days."

Allie frowned. "Our wedding is in less than a week. You promised you'd be here to help with last-minute details."

"Now, Alyssa, I still have a business to run. I can't just let it go." He glanced at the stable wall. "Some emergencies have come up and I need to handle them."

"Fine," she said. "Just be sure to make it to the church on time for the rehearsal and the actual ceremony." She'd be damned if she got stood up at the altar like some pathetic female in a romance novel. In this case, she'd have to get in line behind her father and brother to shoot him. "When are you leaving?"

"This evening. I'm catching a flight out of Bozeman." He cupped the back of her head and bent to kiss her.

As soon as his lips touched hers, an explosion rocked the earth beneath Allie's feet. Damien dropped where he stood.

Swede grabbed Allie and threw her on the ground, covering her body with his as a second explosion blasted through the side of the stable, shooting splintered boards over their heads.

Fire shot up from the far end of the stable, and smoke filled the air. Horses screamed inside the remaining walls. Ruger barked in response.

Allie bucked beneath Swede. "Let me up!"

Swede rolled to the side, and pushed to his feet.

As soon as his heavy weight was off her, Allie jumped up and ran into the burning building.

2

———

SWEDE RACED AFTER ALLIE, his body shaking, the explosion having thrown him back to his combat days. Only this wasn't Afghanistan or Iraq. His primary job was to protect a woman hell-bent on running headfirst into danger.

Seeing Allie run into the burning stable, Swede had no other choice but to chase after her into the smoke-filled structure. Ruger tried to follow, but Swede pointed his finger at the dog's nose. "Stay." He could only pray the dog would remember the one command long enough for Swede to get Allie out.

Inside, the smoke hit him immediately, burning his eyes and lungs. He pulled his T-shirt up over his mouth and blinked to clear his eyes. Hunkering below the bulk of the smoke, he hurried toward the pair of legs encased in blue jeans, standing in front of a stall, struggling to throw open the latch.

A horse on the other side pawed at the gate, its eyes rolled back, nostrils flaring.

Swede brushed aside Allie, slammed the lever to the side and jerked the door open.

With a shrill scream, the horse pushed through and raced toward the exit.

Allie had gone deeper into the smoke-filled stable and threw open another stall.

The horse inside reared, thrashing its legs.

Swede grabbed Allie and dragged her out of the way of the deadly hooves.

"Let go of me!" she cried, struggling to be free.

"Get out, now." Swede coughed and ducked low. "I'll take care of the rest of them."

"No way." Allie's eyes streamed with tears, making tracks in the soot clinging to her face. "One person can't get them all." She pushed away, and ran to the next stall.

Rather than fight her, Swede pitched in and helped her free the remaining horses from the stable. When the stalls were empty, he waved to Allie. "Get out. Now!" The heat from the fire bore down on him, but he wouldn't leave until she was out.

Allie ran for the door and Swede fell in behind her. At the last minute, just before he passed through the open door, a movement caught his eye. He reached between two feed barrels and snagged a cat by the scruff of its neck. With the feline clawing at his arm, Swede dove for the door. Once outside, he didn't let go of the cat until he was far enough away from the stable the cat wouldn't run back inside. When he set the creature on the ground, it ran back toward the stable. Ruger blocked its way, growling fiercely. The cat changed directions and ran toward the house.

ALLIE'S LUNGS burned with every breath. She knelt on the ground fifteen feet from the barn, coughing so hard her entire body shook with the force.

Swede dropped down beside her, his lungs burning, and coughing equally as hard. "We need to get you to a hospital," he said, between fits of hacking. "Smoke inhalation can be fatal."

She raised her hand, swallowed hard and shook her head. "I don't need a hospital. I just need fresh air." Her gaze went to the stable. "What kind of monster targets a stable full of horses? What did the horses ever do to him?"

"Some people have no respect for life," Swede said. "Animal or human."

"People like that need to die a really terrible death." Her chest still tight, Allie lay down on the ground and closed her eyes. A moment later, she sat up straight when a thought came to her. "Where's Damien?"

Swede shook his head. "He wasn't in the stable. I made a final sweep before we got out."

Allie glanced around. "Thankfully, all of the animals survived. When the fire burns down and the horses can be gathered, we can assess injuries."

"Alyssa!" Damien came running from the direction of the house. "Thank God, you're okay. The fire department is on its way."

Allie wanted to ask him where the hell he was when the horses were trapped inside their stalls. The call to the fire department could have waited until all the animals were safe. She stood, brushing the grass and dust off her jeans.

Damien opened his arms for her, but she didn't step into them.

"I'm covered in soot. I wouldn't want to mess up your jacket with the smell."

He glanced down at the garment. "I don't care about the jacket." And he pulled her into his arms. "I'm just glad you're all right." He tipped her face up to him, pulled a cloth handker-chief out of his pocket and dabbed at her lips. Then he kissed her. "You shouldn't have gone into the stable."

"I wasn't about to let those horses burn in the fire."

"But you could have died." He kissed her again and then set her to arm's length. "Now, do you see why I wanted to hire a bodyguard?"

Witnessing the tender moment, Swede turned away from the couple. He'd have to get used to disappearing if he wanted this bodyguard gig to work out. He imagined the first rule of being a bodyguard was to keep one's mouth shut. A good bodyguard was there all the time, but not to be seen or heard, except when necessary. Or at least, that's how he figured it should be. He wondered if Hank had drafted a set of standard operating procedures for the company. He made a mental note to ask the next time he saw his friend.

Ruger leaned against his leg, a low whining sound rising up his throat. Swede bent to pat the dog's head and scratch behind his ears. "It's okay, boy. You did good."

"So, it's all settled then?" Reynolds was saying.

Swede turned back to Allie and her fiancé.

"Mr. Svenson, you're in charge of my bride's safety," Reynolds said. "I expect you to guard her with your life, and make sure she gets to the church for the wedding." He glanced down at Allie. "From what your brother said, this man is one of our nation's finest. A navy SEAL, a combat veteran skilled in almost every weapon imaginable. Who better to guard my precious Alyssa?"

Swede fought to keep from rolling his eyes or snorting. In the brief amount of time he'd known Allie, he could imagine she was fighting not to gag. The woman had spunk and valued her independence. *Precious* wasn't one of the words Swede would use to describe her. It was too frilly.

Allie stepped back. "You be careful, too. You're in more danger than I am. Whoever is mad at you blew up *your* stable, not mine."

Damien nodded, his jaw tightening. "I hope to find out who it is while I'm away, but it pays to be overly cautious, especially after we've seen what he might do. Now, if you'll excuse me, I have to pack a bag and get to the airport. I trust you can answer any questions the fire department might have." Without waiting for a response, the man turned and left Allie and Swede standing in front of the burning stable.

Less than five minutes later, Reynolds drove away in a white Land Rover, before the fire trucks could arrive.

Swede shook his head. The man had narrowly missed being blown up in an explosion, his fiancée had almost died in the ensuing fire, and he'd been willing to let his expensive horses die. Swede violated his first rule of being a bodyguard and opened his mouth. "You're engaged to him?"

"Don't judge." Allie turned and walked away.

"Right. I'm just the bodyguard," Swede muttered under his breath and followed her. "Where are you going?"

"The horses need to be caught and put out to pasture before the fire truck spooks them and they run out onto the highway." She walked up to a horse standing in the corner of a fence, its eyes wild, its feet dancing in the dirt, stirring up a small cloud of dust.

Allie spoke in a calm voice. "It's okay. That big bad fire won't get you." She slowly reached for the animal's halter.

The gelding reared, pawing at the air, nearly knocking over Allie.

Swede grabbed her around the middle and pulled her out of reach. Only thing was that, once he had her out of harm's way, he didn't want to let go. The woman tried his patience and had a mouth on her, but she cared about the horses and risked her own life to save theirs. He admired that in the infuriating woman.

"What are you doing?" Allie demanded, struggling to free herself from his hold.

When he realized he'd held on too long, he abruptly let go.

Allie broke free and backed away in a hurry. Her movement startled the gelding. Again, the animal rose on its hind legs.

And, once again, Swede grabbed her and pulled her away from the flailing hooves. This time, she was facing him and her hands rested on his chest.

For a moment, she froze, her fingers curling into his shirt. Her gaze rose from his chest to his mouth.

For a brief, unexplainable moment, Swede had the undeniable urge to kiss the woman.

Her eyes widened, and she pushed against his chest. "Let go of me."

"The horse is understandably afraid. Let me try to catch him." Swede held her a moment longer. "I'm going to release you. Please don't make any sudden moves."

"I know what I'm doing," she insisted with a glare. "I grew up around horses."

"Just let me do this."

"How many horses have you been around?" she asked.

"Counting the ones we got out of the stable?" His lips twisted. "Five." The total number of horses they'd rescued from the fire.

"My point, exactly." Allie pushed her sleeves up her arms. "You'll get hurt."

"Give me the benefit of the doubt," Swede said. "Stay here with Ruger. He's never been around farm animals, that I know of. Keep him from coming after me."

Allie waved an arm. "Fine. Go ahead. Get yourself killed. Then I won't have you following me around." She dropped to her haunches next to Ruger. "Poor dog. What did you do to deserve him?"

"I'll have you know he was on death row at a dog pound when I rescued him." But, if Swede was telling the whole truth, Ruger had been the one doing the rescuing.

Standing in front of the frantic beast with the heat of the still-burning fire behind him, Swede studied the animal. Having grown up in the city, he'd never really thought much about horses. Like most kids, he'd always dreamed of living on a ranch and riding horses, but the opportunity had never presented itself. Now that he was in Montana, he would make a point of learning how to ride and care for a horse.

Starting now.

He eased toward the horse, maintaining eye contact with the beast. When he'd brought Ruger home, he'd treated him with kindness and respect, he noticed how the dog responded to the tone of his voice even when he talked nonsense. If that worked with a dog, perhaps it would work with a horse. He spoke in a low, steady, monotone, advancing slowly, holding out his hand, praying the horse didn't take a bite out of it or trample him in his crazed state of mind. This horse was like most creatures when they were scared, it needed reassurance and comfort.

Swede inched toward the horse, and it whinnied and pawed at the dirt, but it didn't rear. Hoping the smell of smoke wasn't still clinging to his skin, Swede let the horse smell his hand and touch his fingers with its big lips. The sensation was new and exhilarating to Swede. The horse was like a big dog. When he thought of it that way, he relaxed and smoothed his hand over the nose and up to scratch behind his ears, wrapping his other hand around the halter.

ALLIE HATED THAT SWEDE, a greenhorn who'd never been near a horse, had walked up to one who was so clearly spooked and calmed him.

She snorted. "Beginner's luck. We have four more to catch. You better get cracking." She walked with Ruger over to a gate and held it open.

Swede led the animal through and released it on the other side.

The horse galloped across the pasture, moving as far away from the smoke and flames as it could get.

The other four horses were easier to round up, and they soon had all of them in the fenced pasture. Just in time, too. The wailing of sirens grew louder, and soon the driveway filled with a pumper truck, a paramedic's vehicle, and a sheriff's deputy. Several ranchers' trucks arrived, all part of the volunteer firefighters who served the county.

Swede and Allie moved back as the fire-fighters made use of the nearby pond and pumped water onto the flames. Unfortunately, the stable was a complete loss, but the firefighters kept the blaze from spreading to the house and grassy fields.

After the paramedics checked out both Swede and Allie for smoke inhalation, they gave them a blast of oxygen. The pair was released, with the recommendation that they go to the clinic in Eagle Rock.

But, that would have to be later. The sheriff and fire chief had questions. Allie answered them as best she could. Someone had left a threatening message on the side of the building, and then the building exploded. She had no idea who the perpetrator might be. The only person who might have the answer to that question had left to catch a flight out that afternoon. Yes, he should be back within the week. He had a wedding to attend, after all.

What else could she say? Less than a week out from her wedding, and this incident hit her full in the face. How well did she know her fiancé? She knew so little about his business and why someone would want to hurt him. She swore she'd grill Damien thoroughly before the wedding. How had she been so caught up in her own life she hadn't bothered to get to know her future husband's? Had she thought the man was independently wealthy just because his parents were rich?

For the first time since she'd agreed to marry Damien, Allie started to get cold feet. Up until now, the relationship had seemed like a fairytale. She'd met her prince charming at a local fundraiser for charity. He'd taken her out on several dates, and then flown her in his private jet to have dinner in Seattle. Yeah, he'd swept her off her feet, and shown her a life so foreign she couldn't help but be dazzled. Best of all, he treated her like a woman, instead of another one of the guys.

When he'd popped the question less than a month ago, he'd been so romantic. He'd gotten down on one knee and asked her to marry him. Just like in the movies. It was every girl's dream. Allie had been no different. She couldn't say no to the man, or the life he promised. And his ranch was something she had only fantasized of. She couldn't wait to dig in and make it all it could be, not just a show place.

Hell, was she more in love with the ranch than the man? She shook her head. No. Damien might not know how to be a rancher, but that wasn't why she was marrying him. She cared for him. When she'd had disagreements with her cantankerous father, she'd turned to Damien, who'd been there to just hold her and let her vent. He hadn't offered advice, presumably because he trusted her judgment on how to handle her family.

He was an excellent horseman, having ridden in competitive dressage since he was a teenager. His parents had spared no expense in his education, sending him to private schools and then Yale. As a child, he'd traveled all over the world, and then again for the business he'd built for himself in contracting.

The tension slowly released from her shoulders. Maybe she knew more about him than she thought. So, she didn't know the particulars about his contracting business, only that he made a lot of money doing it. He had building projects all over the world, with a concentration in the rebuilding efforts going on in Afghanistan. He'd been there twice already that year, and maybe he was headed there now. When he called to check in, she'd ask.

A pickup pulled in behind the fire truck and emergency vehicles. Will Franklin got out, his eyes rounding. He walked up to where Allie and Swede stood near the sheriff and the fire chief. "What happened?" he asked.

Allie filled him in on the explosion.

Will started toward the stables. "The horses?"

Placing a hand on the man's arm, Allie answered, "Swede and I got them out." She turned to her bodyguard. "This is Will Franklin, Damien's foreman. Will, this is Swede Svenson. A… friend of mine."

Will shook hands with Swede and then glanced around. "Where's Mr. Reynolds?"

"He left shortly after the explosion," Allie said. "Apparently, he had to take care of business before the wedding."

"I'd better check the horses."

"I'll help." Allie followed Will through the gate to the pasture.

Swede followed with Ruger trotting alongside.

The horse he'd sweet-talked came trotting up to him.

Grinning, Swede held out his hand, and the horse nuzzled his open palm.

"Has he been around horses much?" Will asked Allie.

"No." Allie shook her head.

Will's lips twisted and he shook his head. "That horse doesn't usually come up to anyone."

Swede held the gelding's halter while Will and Allie looked over the animal. Other than smelling like soot, he seemed to be okay.

They performed the same inspection on the other four horses. When Will and Allie were satisfied they hadn't suffered any lasting ill effects, Allie checked in with the fire chief and sheriff once more.

"If you need us for further questions, we'll be at the Bear Creek Ranch."

Without waiting for her escort, she crossed to her truck, climbed in and left the Double Diamond.

Swede, with Ruger, stayed right behind her all the way to the ranch house.

As Allie drove up to her family home, she wondered what sleeping arrangements she'd have to make for her new bodyguard. She snorted. Her father would be thrilled to know she was bringing a man into his house. As her bodyguard, he couldn't sleep in the barn. Nor could he sleep in the foreman's quarters, as that was already taken. Unlike larger ranches, they didn't have a bunkhouse for ranch hands. It was up to her, her father, and Eddy, their foreman, to manage the herd. During cattle roundup days, they hired extra hands who slept in the barn, and Mrs. Edwards cooked for them.

No, Swede would have to stay in her brother's old bedroom. A tingle rippled down her spine at the thought of the big SEAL sleeping in the room next to her. But then, he was a bodyguard. What good was a bodyguard if he wasn't close to the body he was guarding?

She parked the truck beside the old house with its wide porches. Yeah, the paint was peeling and the steps needed repair, but the place was her home. At least, for the next week. Allie's heart squeezed in her chest. It wasn't as big and fancy as the mansion at the Double Diamond, but it had a helluva view of the Crazy Mountains, and it had been the house where she'd lived for the past twenty-seven years.

Allie supposed she'd get used to living on the Double Diamond. She'd be with Damien, when he was home from his trips. She'd have Miles, the butler, and Barbara, the cook, to talk to in the big house. She'd spend most of her time outside, tending horses and the cattle she hoped to bring onto the three-thousand-acre ranch.

She opened the door to her truck, pushing aside thoughts of her future home. First things first. Her father couldn't know Swede was her bodyguard. He'd flip if he knew Damien was having trouble. Her father would find out soon enough when word got around about the explosion and fire that consumed the stable at the Double Diamond.

Swede parked beside her, got out and rounded the front of his truck with Ruger.

"I think I can get a room in the house for you, but my father isn't keen on dogs inside."

He glanced at the porch. "Which room is yours? I can toss a sleeping bag outside your window."

"Seriously?" Allie shook her head. "I can't ask you to do that. I'll see what I can do to bend my father's rule."

"I'm not here to cause you more problems. I'm here to keep you safe. And I've slept in worse places than on a porch."

As a SEAL, he probably had. Still… "You can have Hank's old room. Grab your stuff, you can stow it inside." Allie started up the steps. When she realized Swede wasn't following, she turned back to him. "You and Ruger can have Hank's old room. There. Are you satisfied?"

Swede walked around to the side of his truck, grabbed a duffle bag and an old blanket and followed her into the house.

"Georgia?" Allie called out.

A gray-haired woman wearing jeans and a short-sleeved plaid shirt stepped into the hallway. "Allie, I'm glad you're here. I heard there was a fire out at the Double Diamond, and I was worried you might be there." She studied Allie before hurrying forward and hugging her. "Oh, dear. You were, weren't you? You're all covered in soot and smell like smoke. I'm glad you're okay. What a terrible thing."

Allie almost laughed. News traveled fast in small communities. She should have known it had already made it home. "Do Dad and Eddy know?"

"Not yet. They've been out repairing fences all day. I haven't seen them since breakfast."

Good. She'd get Swede installed before they got back. "Georgia, this is Swede Svenson, a friend of mine from college, who came early for the wedding. He was going to stay in Eagle Rock, but I told him we had room here for him and his dog."

Georgia smiled at Swede and held out her hand. "Nice to meet you. There are fresh sheets on the bed in Hank's old room." Her smile wrinkled into a bit of a frown. "As for the dog, well, you'll have to take it up with Mr. Patterson. He doesn't like animals in the house."

Allie nodded. "I'll take care of it. Could you show him to the room so he can toss his bag? I need to ride out and check on that sick heifer."

"I'm coming with you," Swede insisted.

Allie sighed. "Fine. I'll wait." Again, she didn't want everyone to know Damien had hired a bodyguard. In order to keep that little bit of information on the down-low, she had to play the hostess to her "friend."

This bodyguard business was going to be a big pain in the ass. And having a hunky SEAL following her around might be more difficult than she ever imagined.

3

Swede followed Georgia up the stairs and across a landing to the first door on the right.

"You can use this room. The one next to it is Allie's, and at the end of the hall is Mr. Patterson's." She opened the door and stepped aside. "The bathroom is across the hall. If you need anything, let me know. Dinner is at 6:30. Mr. Patterson doesn't like folks being late." She smiled. "Where was it you met Allie, again?"

"In college," he said.

"At Montana State University?" she queried.

He swallowed hard. "Yes, ma'am."

"How did you like Missoula? I have a sister who lives there."

He shrugged. "It's okay," he said, hating that he was lying to a very nice woman. But, Allie had started the lie and he wouldn't be the one to spill the beans.

"Uh-huh." Georgia's eyes narrowed. "And what was your degree?"

"Engineering," he replied. At least this was the truth. Working on his degree online and in a classroom the semesters he was Stateside, he'd earned a degree in engineering. He dropped his bag on the floor and turned to leave the room, only to find Georgia standing in the doorway with her arms folded over her chest.

"How long have you known Allie?" An eyebrow cocked high.

"Five, maybe six...If you don't mind, she's waiting for me." He started toward the woman.

She didn't budge for a moment and then snorted. "Uh-huh." Georgia stepped out of the way. "Remember, supper's on the table at 6:30."

He hurried past her and down the stairs. Ruger fell in step beside him as he pushed through the door onto the porch where he found Allie.

"Is there a reason you lied to Georgia about who I am?" he asked, his voice terse, anger simmering low in his belly.

Allie glanced at the house where Georgia stood in the window of the kitchen, watching them. "I didn't want them to worry about me."

"Well, you need to tell me more about yourself before you commit me to being an old school chum. In what city is Montana State University?"

"Bozeman."

Damn. "Not Missoula?"

"No. That's University of Montana."

He winced. "You'll have to do some damage control with Georgia. She's on to me." He left it at that and walked down the steps.

"I'll square up with her before dinner."

"Which is at 6:30 sharp. She told me twice. I take it that you don't want to be late."

Allie caught up with him and fell in step. "Welcome to the Bear Creek Ranch. My father likes things the way he likes things."

"And he likes the man you've chosen to marry?"

Allie's steps faltered for a moment. "That's none of your business."

"While I'm your bodyguard, everything about you is my business."

"The hell it is." Allie walked faster. She reached the barn first, and turned to face him. "Remember, it wasn't my idea to hire you. If I had my way, I'd have you sent back to the White Oak with Hank, looking for some rich celebrity to follow around like a lap dog." She shot a glance at the animal beside him. "No offense, Ruger."

She spun toward the door and reached for the handle.

Swede slammed his palm onto the wood, keeping the door from budging. "Look, princess, as long as I'm being paid to protect you, I'm following you around like a lap dog. Only, this lap dog bites. So don't push me."

She turned in the small amount of space between the barn door and his chest and stared up into his eyes. "I'm not a princess, and if you call me that again, I'll show you just how not a princess I can be. Now, move your arm." Her green eyes flashed and color rose in her cheeks.

God, she was beautiful and fearless. Swede had scared newbie SEALs with his full-on glare. Not this ranch woman with fire in her eyes and bright auburn hair. He held his ground for another second, his pulse pounding and his breath mingling with hers, fighting that sudden desire to kiss her.

Her eyes widened and she licked her lips.

As though she could read his mind.

As soon as the thought struck, he dropped his arm and moved away.

Allie lifted her chin, turned and ducked into the barn.

Swede followed at a slower pace, wondering what the hell was wrong with him? Bodyguards weren't supposed to kiss their clients. Especially one who'd told him multiple times she didn't want him around. He found her in the tack room, a blanket and bridle over one shoulder as she hefted a saddle from a wooden stand.

"Here, let me," Swede said, because his mother had raised a gentleman, and gentlemen lifted heavy objects for ladies.

He reached for the saddle.

But, she jerked away. "You'll need to get your own."

He glanced around the room at the seven saddles resting on stands. "Which would you suggest?"

Her lips twitched, and she tilted her head to get a look at his backside. "One big enough for your butt."

His groin tightened at her playful look. Immediately, he turned away before he started thinking about her as anything other than the person he was assigned to protect, who happened to be engaged to the man who'd hired him. At first glance, the saddles all looked pretty much the same. Upon closer inspection, he selected a dark brown one he hoped would fit, grabbed a blanket from a stack and hurried out of the tack room.

Allie had her horse tethered outside a stall. She'd already placed the blanket and saddle on the horse and was reaching beneath the horse's belly for the girth.

Swede knew what these were because, as a kid, he'd dreamed of learning to ride and studied what he could find in his grade school library. He watched carefully as she looped a long leather strap through the metal ring on the girth, pulled it tight, and then looped it again. When she'd used most of the strap, she tied the remainder in a single knot. Then she let the stirrup down.

"Is there a particular horse you want me to ride?" he asked.

She gave him an assessing glance. "Little Joe. Last stall on the left. You get the horse and I'll get his bridle."

Swede walked to the last stall on the left and opened the gate. The horse nudged his way through and would have taken off, but Swede slipped his hand through the animal's halter before he'd gone two steps and brought him under control. He spoke to the horse like he'd done with the spooked one at the Double Diamond. Within seconds, he was able to walk him to the spot next to Allie's horse where a lead rope was tied to a metal loop. He snapped the lead on the halter and quickly laid the blanket and saddle in place. Then he reached beneath the horse and pulled the girth up, looping the leather through the ring, like he'd seen her do.

"Make sure you get it tight. Little Joe likes to blow out his belly while you're saddling him. And you'll need to adjust the stirrups to fit your longer legs."

Following her advice, he tightened the girth and adjusted the stirrups, while Allie slipped the bridle into the horse's mouth.

Once they were out of the barn, Allie led her horse to a gate, opened it and waited for Swede to walk his horse through. She followed and closed the gate behind them.

Then she swung up into the saddle from the left side of the horse. As he'd told her, he was very observant. He mimicked every one of her moves until he found himself up in the saddle. Then the horse danced sideways, whinnied and took off running as fast as the goddamn wind. Where were the damned brakes?

Swede held onto the reins and the saddle horn and sent a desperate prayer to the heavens. He'd almost rather be shot at by a dozen Taliban than be at the mercy of a crazed horse. Over the thunder of his horse's hooves and blood pounding in his ears, he heard a shout.

"Whoa!" Allie, atop her mare, raced up beside him, leaned dangerously toward Swede, grabbed the rein closest to her and pulled back. "Whoa!"

Both horses slowed until they came to a halt. Allie handed back the rein and shook her head. "You really haven't ridden a horse before, have you?"

His heart still pounding, he shook his head. "Never." He wiped the sweat off his brow and breathed. "But I learn quickly."

"Tap the flanks with your heels, gently, to make him go. Pull back on the reins to make him stop." She demonstrated as she spoke. "If pulling back on the reins doesn't do the trick, the horse might have the bit between his teeth. Then you pull back on one side only and make him turn in a circle until he stops."

Swede nodded. "Got it."

"Now, I really need to check on that heifer." She tapped her heels against her horse's flanks, and the animal lurched forward.

Swede did the same.

Little Joe leaped after the other horse.

Swede slipped backward in the saddle, but he righted himself and rode after Allie. Several times, he slowed the horse by pulling back on the reins. The animal didn't like being left behind, but he slowed. Feeling a little more confident, he settled into the rhythm of the horse's gallop. Thankfully, Little Joe was perfectly happy following Allie, giving Swede the opportunity to relax and look around.

The Crazy Mountains were undeniably beautiful, with towering trees and jagged peaks capped with remnants of winter snow clinging to the higher elevations.

Allie led him through a narrow valley, across a stream, up and over a ridge, and then stopped near a copse of trees overlooking a grassy valley.

Swede rode up next to her, pulling back on the reins.

She nodded toward several cows grazing in the field beyond. "She seems to be doing better today. At least she's up and eating."

They all looked pretty healthy to Swede. "Which one is she?"

"The brown and white Hereford at the edge of the others." Allie pointed to one that was a bit smaller and not as filled out. "She's okay, for now. I'll check on her tomorrow."

Allie glanced across at Swede. "How are you?"

"Fine." He shifted in the saddle, knowing he'd be sore later. But he'd never admit it to her.

"Trotting is the hardest gait on the butt. If you stand up in your stirrups every other bump, you won't be beaten to death. It's called posting. Like this." She tapped her horse's flanks and the animal took off at a trot. Allie rose and fell in rhythm with the horse's steps.

Swede nudged his mount and the horse broke into a trot. He tried what Allie demonstrated, but ended up standing in the stirrups the entire time, not quite getting the rhythm.

"When you get it right, it stops hurting," she said. "Then the movement becomes natural."

"How long have you been riding?" he asked.

"Since I was big enough to sit up on my own, so my father says. I think I was about four years old when my father put me on a horse by myself." Squinting in the sun, Allie turned back in the direction from which they'd come. "It's getting close to dinner time. We'd better get back."

They crossed the ridge and eased down the other side into the narrow valley with a stream winding through. Everything seemed so peaceful and different than the hills of Afghanistan, filled with Taliban fighters waiting to blow off his head.

Just when Swede thought it couldn't get more placid, the roar of a small engine echoed off the hillsides.

Swede looked around for the source, but the echoes made it hard to determine. Then a four-wheeled all-terrain vehicle erupted out of the tree line and raced straight for Allie.

Swede urged his horse forward, creating a barrier between the oncoming vehicle and the woman he was supposed to protect. He reached beneath his jacket and pulled out the nine millimeter Glock he'd purchased before he'd left the military and aimed for the man on the ATV. He'd give him five more seconds to turn away.

Five. Four. Three. Two. One.

Just as Swede pulled the trigger, he saw Allie's horse rear, throwing her from the saddle. Spooked by Allie's horse and the oncoming ATV, Little Joe bucked.

Swede's shot went wide of its target.

The sound was enough to make the rider swerve to the right and cross the stream, heading up into the hills.

Swede yanked the reins, turned the horse and trotted back to where Allie lay on the ground, her own horse long gone.

The woman lay perfectly still, her eyes wide open.

Swede started to dismount when Allie said, "Don't move."

"Why? Are you okay?"

"I will be, as long as you don't move a muscle and keep Little Joe from coming any closer."

Then he heard the telltale buzz of a rattlesnake's tail.

Wound into a tight coil, lying in the dirt near a rock, lay the biggest rattlesnake Swede had ever seen.

The slightest move on Allie's part could make the snake strike her in the face.

"Be very still," he advised.

"Duh. You think I don't know that?" she said, barely moving her lips and whispering softly so as not to disturb the creature.

"I'll slide down off the horse."

"Any movement could make him strike. I'd rather you didn't."

"What do you want me to do?"

"I don't know. Feed him a mouse. Wait until he leaves. Shoot him. Something." Her voice was soft and calm for having a huge snake in her face.

Little Joe appeared unfazed by the snake lying nearby. He stood still, waiting for Swede's next command.

Still holding the nine-millimeter in his hand, he raised it and aimed down the barrel at the snake.

"What are you doing?" Allie said, through gritted teeth.

"Close your eyes," he said.

"Oh, no, you are not…" She squeezed her eyes shut and tensed.

Swede pulled the trigger. The bullet hit the snake in the head, flipping it over in the dust.

Little Joe danced to the side, but didn't bolt.

Allie rolled away and jumped to her feet. "Are you crazy?"

Swede holstered his weapon and dropped down out of the saddle. Holding onto the reins, he approached Allie and gripped her arm. "Are you okay?"

"I'm fine, despite the fact you could have killed me."

"But, I didn't." He looked into her eyes, checking her pupils. "Did you bang your head against the ground?"

Allie rubbed her bottom. "No, I hurt my pride more than anything else. I haven't been thrown from a horse in years." She glanced at the snake lying still on the ground. "I guess Major had a good reason to spook." Brushing the dust off her jeans, she looked out across the stream and up the hill on the other side. "Who the hell was on the ATV?"

"I was hoping you could tell me."

"It wasn't one of our vehicles."

"He was aiming for you. And I was aiming for him when your horse reared."

Allie frowned. "I guess I should thank you."

"No need. I was just doing my job."

"Okay, so you aren't a great horseman, but you did shoot the snake without killing me." She drew in a deep breath and let it out. "Thanks."

"You're welcome."

"Now, we'd better get back to the house before we're late for dinner."

Allie balanced her hands on her hips. "Since my horse is halfway back to the barn by now, we'll have to ride double. I'll drive. But you'll need to mount first."

Swede swung up into the saddle, removed his foot from the stirrup and reached for her hand.

Allie placed her toe where his had been, and Swede pulled her up in front of him. For a moment, she was sitting in his lap. Her auburn hair drifted into his face.

Inhaling a hint of strawberry and the fresh, outdoor scent clinging to her, he closed his eyes and tried not to think of her sitting where she was, or that his groin was reacting naturally and hardening.

His eyes snapped open and he pushed backward, over the lip of the saddle and sat on Little Joe's rump.

He tried holding onto the saddle, but as soon as Allie nudged Little Joe's flanks, the animal leaped forward.

Swede slipped backward and almost fell off the horse. He wrapped his arms around Allie's waist and held tight all the way back to the barn.

When they arrived in the barnyard, Swede slipped off the back of the horse and landed on his feet.

Allie swung her leg over Little Joe's back, and dropped to the ground. "You didn't do badly for your first ride on a horse."

The insides of his thighs ached, but it was a good ache. After months in a hospital and physical therapy, getting out into the open, clean air of Montana felt good.

Now, if he could keep Allie safe from whoever just tried to run her over, he'd feel even better.

ALLIE HURRIED into the house to get cleaned up and dressed for dinner. Her father believed in punctuality. As children, if they weren't at the table on time, they didn't eat. Of course, when their mother was alive, she'd sneak a snack into their rooms, later. After she'd passed away, Georgia continued the tradition.

When Allie got married and had her own house, she wouldn't be as strict. She might even have dinner at different hours other than 6:30pm every single day. She ran up the stairs, calling out, "I have the shower first."

A low chuckle sounded at the bottom of the stairs, warming her from the inside.

When she made it to the top, she glanced over the banister.

Swede stood at the base of the staircase, his hand resting on the banister, staring up at her, his mouth tipped upward in a smile.

Allie stumbled, recovered and ran for her bedroom, her cheeks burning.

The man had no right to be so very handsome when he smiled. And how different from Damien. Not that Damien wasn't handsome. He was. Like a prince. Not like a rugged navy SEAL with boundless muscles and a wicked grin.

Grabbing fresh jeans and a soft green pullover blouse, she entered the bathroom, locked the door and ducked under the shower's cool spray. By the time she'd rinsed off the dirt, smoke and sweat from her body and shampooed her hair, she had her head on straight. Without wasting any time, she was out of the shower, dried and had combed the tangles out of her long hair, thinking for the hundredth time she needed to cut it short. But she couldn't bring herself to do more than trim it. Every time she looked into the mirror, she saw her mother, the parent who'd given her the auburn hair and green eyes her father had fallen in love with.

Dressed and brushed, she ducked back into her room, pulled on socks and a pair of clean boots and ran down the stairs to see if Georgia needed help getting the food on the table. She didn't run into Swede, figuring he was in his room unpacking.

Georgia stood at the stove, stirring gravy in a pot. "You can take the roast out to the table."

Allie did, and returned to the kitchen. "Mmm. That smells good."

Having been the housekeeper since before Allie's mother passed, Georgia was like a surrogate mother. She lifted the pot off the stove and poured the gravy into a bowl. "Before your father comes down, you want to tell me why you lied to me, your father and Eddy?"

With a spoonful of gravy halfway to her mouth, Allie grimaced. "I'm sorry I lied."

"I wasn't born yesterday." Georgia planted a fist on her hip. "Swede didn't go to school with you, did he?"

Allie had hated lying to Georgia. It gnawed at her belly, making her feel nauseated. "No. I met him this morning, at Hank's."

"So, why did you invite a complete stranger to stay in the house?"

"He's a buddy of Hank's from his navy SEAL team. Damien hired him to be my bodyguard until the wedding."

"Bodyguard?" Georgia's brows furrowed. "Does this have anything to do with the fire at his place?"

Allie nodded. "And my cut brake lines. Someone is mad at Damien and is taking it out on him. Damien thinks he might be targeting me, as well."

"And what do you think?"

She hated to admit it, but… "I think he's right. When I went out to check on the sick heifer, I was almost run over by someone on an ATV. Swede kept that from happening." Allie didn't add that Swede had shot a snake next to her head as well. No use worrying Georgia any more than she already was, based on her deepening frown.

The older woman took her hands. "What has that fiancé gotten you into?"

"I don't know, but he's working on it." Or so she assumed. Why else would he take off before the sheriff and firefighters arrived at his place to put out a fire?

Georgia held her at arm's length. "You know you can back out of the wedding any time between now and the actual ceremony."

Allie smiled at her. "I'm okay. The wedding is going on as planned. Just a few more days, and I'll be a married woman with a house of my own to run."

"You hate household chores."

"Yeah, but I'll have people to do them for me. The way I like them done." Allie pulled Georgia into a quick hug. "Not that you haven't done a terrific job taking care of us all these years. Have I ever said thank you?"

"Yes, dear. You have." Georgia hugged her tight. "We're going to miss you around here."

"I'll only be a couple of miles away."

"Maybe so, but it will seem like a long way to me. I'll be outnumbered by the men."

Allie laughed. "I'm sure you'll keep them in line."

"Are you two going to stand around gabbing or come eat?" Eddy, the ranch foreman and Georgia's husband, entered the kitchen, sniffed and rubbed his belly. "Something smells good."

Georgia stepped back, dabbing her eyes with the hem of her apron. "Did you wash up?" she said, her voice brisk as she turned toward the stove and retrieved a pan full of corn.

"Yes, I did." Eddy sneaked up behind her, pulled her back against his front and nuzzled her neck. "You smell good enough to eat."

Georgia smacked his hands playfully and giggled. "Oh, go on with yourself."

"Not until I get me some sugar."

She set the pan of corn on the stove, turned in his arm and kissed him. "Now, go set the table."

Eddy grinned and smacked her bottom.

"Dang it, Eddy!" Georgia waved a wooden spoon at him. "I'm not above spanking you with this."

"Promises, promises." He fished silverware from a drawer and laid them on the table, whistling as he did.

Allie was used to their playful antics. The childless couple had always been loving and unabashed at showing it in front of others.

"It's 6:30, are we eating or not?" Allie's father entered the big country kitchen, pulled back the chair at the head of the table and sat.

Allie carried the bowl of corn while Georgia brought a basket full of fresh-baked rolls.

"It's 6:25, not 6:30. Remember, Daddy? You always set your watch five minutes ahead." Allie shot a glance toward the doorway, wondering what was keeping Swede.

Just as she looked that way, he entered the room.

"Pardon me if I kept you waiting."

Allie's father frowned at Swede. "Who the hell are you? And what are you doing in my house?"

For the next hour, Eddy and Mr. Patterson grilled Swede about everything from letting Ruger in the house, to what he knew about horses and cattle, to the types of weapons his team used on special operations.

With admirable patience, Swede answered every question. Eddy and Allie's father seemed satisfied with the man's answers, even when he owned up to knowing nothing about livestock. When the meal was over, he got up like the inquisition hadn't fazed him a bit.

Allie, on the other hand, felt like she'd been run through the wringer. And the worst part was, she'd seen another side of Swede she hadn't wanted to see. A proud military man who'd served his country and now had to figure out how to fit into a life without the SEALs.

He even helped clean the table and wash dishes.

Damn it, if she wasn't careful, she might end up liking the exasperating man.

Tired from a long day, full of stress and trauma, she trudged up the stairs and brushed her teeth. When she exited the bathroom, she ran into Swede. He'd shed his shirt and boots and wore only jeans.

The moisture in Allie's mouth dried as she stared at his broad, muscular chest.

"Are you okay?" Swede asked.

Dragging her eyes upward, she couldn't make her gaze quite reach his eyes, stopping on his full, sexy lips. "I'm fine," she managed to squeak out. Then she dove into her room and slammed the door behind her.

This just would not do. The man was far too attractive to be a bodyguard.

Allie stripped, pulled on an old MSU T-shirt from her college days and crawled into bed, reminding herself that her wedding was only a few days away. Closing her eyes, she tried to picture Damien in a tuxedo, standing at the altar. But the face she saw wasn't Damien's, it was Swede's.

Double damn.

4

SWEDE WOKE EARLY the next morning after a crappy night's sleep. Thankfully, he hadn't had any of the dreams that had plagued him since he'd left the service. He dressed in sweats, a T-shirt, and tennis shoes and took Ruger outside. Staying within sight of the house, he performed his morning calisthenics—pushups, sit-ups, leg-lifts and more. It paid to stay in shape. Even while he'd been recovering from his wounds in the hospital, he'd done everything he could.

Today, his hand and thighs ached from riding the day before. He stretched his legs and ran to the end of the driveway and back several times before he finally reentered the house.

The smell of bacon lured him to the kitchen where Georgia cooked breakfast. "This will be ready by the time you're out of the shower," she promised.

"Thanks," Swede said. "It smells good." He took the stairs two at a time, grabbed a pair of clean jeans, and hit the shower.

When he was done, he stepped out of the tub, toweled dry, and tossed the towel to the floor. He was reaching for his jeans when the door swung open. Swede straightened as Allie started in.

When she saw him standing there naked, she widened her

eyes and her mouth dropped open. For a long moment she stared. Then her cheeks turned a brilliant red, and she backed out of the doorway. "Pardon me." She pulled the door shut. Through the panel, she said, "Oh, my God."

Swede laughed out loud, and then tried to pull on his jeans over a rock-hard erection. He waited a minute, thinking of everything that could douse his desire, from babies to grand-mothers. Nothing seemed to work when the image of Allie's face kept coming to mind. Carefully tucking himself in, he pulled his T-shirt over his head and let it hang down over the ridge of his fly.

He found Allie downstairs in the kitchen with Georgia. Allie didn't look him in the eye, her cheeks still a pretty shade of pink. "My father and Eddy are out cutting hay, so I'm working the barn today. Have you ever mucked a stall?" Finally, she glanced his way.

Swede shook his head, feeling a little inadequate for the job of ranch hand. "No, but I'm game." *As long as I'm near you.*

"I know the task is not part of your job description, so don't feel like you have to."

Swede shot a glance toward Georgia.

The older woman nodded. "I know. I'm just glad someone is looking out for our girl." She held up a coffee pot. "Coffee?"

"Please," Swede said.

"I still think you should tell Eddy and your father what's going on." Georgia gave Allie a stern look as she poured the steaming brew into two mugs and carried them to the table. "They could be looking out for you, too."

"Absolutely not," Allie said. "My father would do his best to call off the wedding. I've spent too much money on every-thing, and the event is only a few days away. I pick up my dress tomorrow, and everything is downhill from there."

Georgia raised her brows. "Downhill?"

Allie rolled her eyes and took one of the plates of food from the kitchen counter. "You know what I mean."

"All the preparations are nothing but money and time," Georgia said.

Swede stood quietly, watching the interaction between the two women.

Apparently, Georgia didn't want Allie to marry Damien. Swede wondered why.

Allie ignored Georgia's comment and focused on Swede, her color back to normal, her jaw set in a tight line. "The sooner we get done cleaning the stalls, the sooner we can exercise the horses. After that, we can call it a day. I have to tell you, though, it'll be a long, hard day."

"I'm up for it."

Allie handed him a plate full of eggs, bacon and biscuits. "Eat up."

After breakfast, Swede followed Allie out to the barn. She handed him a pitchfork and pointed to a wheelbarrow. "Tie the horse up outside the stall and start shoveling."

Swede worked through the morning, glad for the physical labor that flexed his muscles and the rich, earthy smell of manure. It beat the scent of diesel smoke and gun powder any day.

Ruger stood guard outside the barn, lying in a patch of sun, watching as Swede and Allie wheeled barrels full of soiled straw out to a pile behind the barn. By noon, they had all the stalls cleaned, the horses brushed, and the chickens and pigs fed.

Georgia had sandwiches waiting when they came inside. Then they were right back out in the sunshine to exercise the horses.

Allie lunged a couple of mares in the corral and then had Swede take over. She watched him, giving tips on how to handle the animal and the lunging rope.

Swede was glad the horse knew what to do. The work wasn't hard. In fact, it had a certain rhythm that bred a sense of calm.

Georgia shouted from the house that Allie had a call from the caterer.

"This horse is about done. You can turn her out into the pasture and then bring out another horse. Just stay clear of

Diablo, the black gelding in the last stall. He's a work in progress, and he hasn't quite got the hang of anything."

"Who rides him?"

"No one, yet. Like I said, he's a work in progress. In other words, he's too wild to handle easily." Allie waved at Georgia. "I have to go. No need to follow me. You can keep an eye on the house from the corral, and I really doubt anyone will attack me there."

Swede nodded. She was right. He had a good view of the house and the road leading to it from the corral.

As Allie hurried inside, Swede couldn't help but follow her progress. He told himself it was part of his job, but the truth was the way her hips swayed in her jeans was completely mesmerizing.

The horse he held on a lead tossed her head, pulling Swede back to the task at hand. He walked her through the gate into the pasture and unhooked the lead.

She pranced away and joined the other horses already grazing.

Glancing back at the house and drive, Swede returned to the barn and walked along the stalls, most of which were empty now. One mare stood placidly, watching him as he passed her and walked down the line of stalls to the end.

When they'd been cleaning, Allie had led Diablo in and out. She'd also taken charge of brushing him.

As Swede neared, the animal stuck his head over the top of the gate and nickered.

"So, you're a real ball-buster, are you?" Swede spoke softly and reached out a hand to rub the gelding's nose.

Diablo nuzzled his hand.

"Do you want out?"

The horse pawed at the dirt and tossed his head as if saying *yes*.

"How hard can it be to walk you around a corral?" Swede snapped the lead onto Diablo's halter and opened the stall.

As soon as the latch was free, Diablo hit the door, knocking Swede backward. He staggered and held on tightly to the lunging rope, while being dragged out of the barn by the bolting horse.

When Swede got his feet under himself, he dug his heels into the dirt and slowed the horse.

Diablo reared and jerked the lead, but Swede held steady and started talking. Soon, the horse stopped fighting and settled on all fours.

Ruger stepped up beside Swede as if to show his support.

Diablo lowered his nose to the dog, and the four-legged creatures sniffed each other.

"You're not so bad, just a little spirited." He raised his hand slowly to stroke the horse's nose. "See? I'm not here to hurt you." The gelding tossed his head as if to disagree. "Ruger wouldn't be beside me now if I hurt him. He trusts me because he gave me a chance. I gave him one, too." Swede continued to talk to the horse as he led him into the corral and closed the gate behind him. Still holding the lead close to Diablo's halter, Swede walked the horse around the outer circle. He kept a running monologue going, to calm the animal.

Ruger stood outside the pen. Every time they passed the dog, the horse looked his way.

After walking around the pen for five minutes, getting the gelding used to the environment, Swede picked up the pace and settled into a slow and steady jog.

Diablo matched his pace and trotted alongside Swede. Slowly, Swede lengthened the lead, still running with the horse, but putting more distance between them. Whenever Diablo slowed, Swede clicked his tongue and jogged faster, encouraging the horse to keep moving. When the lead was long enough and Swede was standing in the middle of the corral, the horse slowed. Swede clicked his tongue, and Diablo broke into a trot.

After several more circles around the corral, Swede let Diablo come to a stop. He pulled in the lead until he could rub the horse's nose. "You're a good boy," Swede soothed, running his hand across the horse's nose and up to scratch his ears. Then he swept his hand along the gelding's neck to his back.

Diablo pawed the earth and whinnied, swaying on his hooves.

Swede scratched the animal's back, side and around to his belly. He moved his hands up to the horse's back again and laid his arms over the top, scratching the other side, while leaning his weight on the animal.

Diablo tossed his head, but didn't move away.

Holding onto the lead rope, Swede grabbed hold of a handful of Diablo's mane and swung his leg over the top of the horse. He leaned forward and wrapped his arms around Diablo's neck, speaking to him the entire time, fully expecting to be thrown, but hoping it wouldn't happen.

Diablo backed up and then moved forward, whinnying.

Ruger whined behind the rails of the corral, capturing the gelding's attention.

Diablo trotted to where the dog stood and lowered his head to sniff.

Swede molded his body to the horse, still rubbing his neck and speaking softly.

Seeing Diablo and Ruger greeting each other with their noses, Swede slipped off the horse's back and patted his neck. "See? It's not as bad as you think."

When Swede straightened, he noticed he had an audience.

"Damnedest thing I've ever seen." Eddy leaned against a corral panel, his arms resting on the top rail.

"That horse doesn't like anyone," Lloyd Patterson said, scratching his head.

"And to beat it all, Swede never rode a horse until yester-day." Allie joined the two men at the fence, a smile tilting the corners of her lips. "You're lucky he didn't take you for a ride."

Swede rubbed Diablo's neck. "I think he just needed a friend." He tipped his head toward Ruger. Diablo and Ruger sniffed at each other. Ruger's tail thumped the ground.

"The man we bought him from said he had another gelding raised with Diablo," Mr. Patterson said.

"You might want to check and see if he still has him," Allie said. "Seems Diablo needs a friend."

"Why? Swede's dog seems to be doing the job," Eddy said.

"And why feed another horse?" her father added. "It's cheaper to feed a dog."

Allie's smile slipped. "Swede and Ruger are only here until after the wedding." She opened the gate. "I think we have one more horse to exercise. Dad, is there anything else you want done before we call it a day?"

"Not a thing. We could use a little help hauling the first cutting of hay the day after tomorrow. It should be dry enough, and we need to get it in before the rain."

As he walked Diablo though the gate, Swede glanced at the bright blue Montana sky. "Is a rainstorm expected?"

Lloyd flexed his shoulder. "I can feel it in my bursitis. If not tomorrow, then the next day. By the end of the week for certain."

"Great. It'll probably rain on my wedding day," Allie muttered

"You can always put it off," her father said. "No need to rush into marriage."

"I'm getting married on Saturday," Allie said, her tone flat but firm.

Mr. Patterson faced his daughter. "If you're going to get married, why Reynolds?"

"Because he asked me, and I said yes."

Lloyd nodded toward Swede. "Why not marry a real man— like a war hero?"

"Dad!" Allie's face burned a bright red. "You don't even know Swede. Besides, who said he wanted to get married in the first place?" She threw her hands in the air. "What did Mom see in you? All I'm getting is a grumpy old man who is stubborn and insensitive."

Her father's face grew rigid, his eyes a stormy gray. "I loved your mother and would have done anything for her. And she loved me, too." He lifted his chin. "Can you say that about Reynolds?"

Swede could feel the tension between father and daughter, as palpable as electricity singeing the air.

"I'm getting married on Saturday. You can come to the wedding and wish me well–or not. But I don't want to hear another negative word about Damien." She stomped into the barn, leaving the men outside, scratching their heads.

"Women," Lloyd grumbled. "Can't live with them…and can't live without them."

"Guess you'll find out in a few days." Eddy pounded Lloyd's back and turned to Swede. "Good job with Diablo. You might have a knack for ranching after all, city boy."

Swede nodded. "Thanks."

Inside the barn, Allie had grabbed a lunging rope, snapped it onto the last mare needing exercise, and led her past Swede and Diablo. "Don't say a word."

Swede grinned. "I wasn't going to."

"My father raised me, but he doesn't know anything about me, or how I feel."

"Maybe he just wants you to be happy."

Allie raised her hand. "I said, don't say a word." She walked out, leading the mare, her lips pressed into a thin line.

Swede chuckled.

"No laughing, either," Allie's voice sounded from just outside the barn door.

Swede fed Diablo and brushed his coat. Ruger lay nearby. It seemed the dog's mere presence had the same calming effect on the horse as it did on Swede. *Go figure.* All Swede knew was that if not for Ruger, he'd still be suffering the effects of his nightmares and breaking out in cold sweats over loud noises. Yeah, he'd pulled Ruger off death row at the pound, but Ruger had pulled Swede out of a life of misery, suffering from PTSD.

Now, if only the dog could perform miracles and dampen the increasing urge Swede felt to kiss the feisty Miss Patterson.

AFTER THE LAST horse had been exercised and all the animals fed, Allie trudged back to the house and sat on the steps to remove her boots. "Thanks for the help."

Swede dropped down beside her and pulled off his boots,

as well. He smelled of sweat, hay and manure. Not the kind of smell Allie associated with Damien. Her fiancé never seemed to sweat. Even when they rode horses together, he came back smelling like his aftershave, not the leather and dusty scent of being in the great outdoors.

Allie should prefer the clean scent of aftershave, but leather and dust, to her, was more manly and satisfying.

She drew in a deep breath, trying not to be too obvious. Yeah, Swede smelled like how Allie considered a man should. But then, she wasn't marrying Damien because of his scent.

Then why was she marrying him?

Because he'd asked, and she didn't want to marry any of the local men she'd grown up with. They were too much like brothers, who didn't even consider going anywhere else but Montana or the nearest stock show or rodeo. Some didn't even want to cross the border into Canada, preferring to remain on their ranches where they'd been born, lived all their lives and where they'd die.

"Do you like to travel?" Allie blurted out without thinking.

Swede shrugged. "I do. But some day I hope to have a place to call home. Traveling is all well and good, but roots help you appreciate where you're going. You're lucky you have a place to call home."

"You don't?" Allie wanted to travel, but like Swede said, she liked to have a home base to come back to.

"Not since my folks died. The closest I came were the apartments I rented near the bases where I was stationed. I rarely saw the insides of those places, having deployed often."

"I'm sorry." She pulled off the second boot and set it beside the first. "Where did your parents live?"

"In Minneapolis, Minnesota."

She smiled softly. "So you have a vague idea of what cold winters are like."

"I do. Not as cold as it gets in Montana, but I know my way around snow."

She gave him an assessing glance. "Ever play hockey?"

Swede nodded. "That's how I got this scar." He pointed to the one on his chin."

"And I thought you'd gotten that working as a SEAL."

He shook his head, his glance shifting to his hand, which he lifted to the scar that ran along the side of his face, from his hairline to his cheekbone. "I got this one in Kandahar Province, on my last mission in Afghanistan."

Allie took his hand in hers and studied the jagged scars between his thumb and forefinger. "And these?"

"Syria."

"Does it still hurt?" she traced the jagged scars with the tip of her finger.

He clenched his hand, only closing it halfway. "A little. I haven't gotten full range of motion yet, but don't worry. I can fire a weapon accurately with either hand."

Her eyes widened and she stared into his. "Holy hell. It didn't even dawn on me that you shot that snake with your left hand. Are you even left-handed?"

Swede shook his head. "Not naturally, but I've learned to be since I joined the navy and became a SEAL. It was a challenge to learn to shoot with both hands. Now, I'm glad I did."

Allie felt warmth filter from his hand into hers and up her arm. She let go of him, grabbed her boots and stood. "You can have the shower first."

"You're not going back out?" he asked.

"No. I thought I'd feed Ruger for you, if you like." She bent to scratch the dog's ears. "He's proving to be useful around here."

Swede's lip quirked up in a half-smile. "He's smart and learns quickly."

Allie chuckled. "Like you?"

"I like to think I can do anything I set my mind to."

"I'll give you that. From what I've seen or read about SEAL training, anyone who can make it through to graduation has to have a lot of stamina and fortitude." She glanced toward the house. "You better get going. I'd like to wash the stink off me, too."

Swede grinned. "I never thought I'd say this, but horse manure smells pretty good on you." He winked and held the door open.

She twisted her lips into a crooked smile. "Thanks. I think."

"Ruger's food is in the mud room," Swede said. Then he turned to the dog. "Stay."

Ruger sat on the porch and whined softly.

"I'll be right back with food and water for you," Allie said, and followed Swede inside.

Swede set his dirty boots inside the mudroom door and headed for the stairs.

Allie set her boots on the floor and straightened, her gaze following the man up the stairs. He had a great butt that looked exceptional in jeans. And he didn't wear fancy, expensive jeans like Damien. Swede wore the kind most of the cowboys around Eagle Rock wore. Plain, serviceable and tough. Like the man. Well, he wasn't exactly plain.

His face wasn't classicly handsome like Damien's, with all his features completely symmetrical. Swede's nose must have been broken more than once and didn't sit exactly straight on his face. He had the scar on his chin, and the one on the side of his face, marring his otherwise rugged good looks. It was the breadth of his shoulders, the trimness of his waist, and the thickness of his thighs that made Allie's heartbeat flutter.

Damn! There she went again. Thinking about the SEAL, rather than dreaming about her future husband.

She picked up Ruger's water bowl, strode into the kitchen and filled it. When she came back out on the deck, the dog sat exactly where Swede had told him to stay. His tail thumped against the porch boards.

Allie set the water in front of Ruger and went back inside for his food. When she came out, she saw he'd lapped up every drop of the water. Then he wolfed down the food she put in front of him, and looked up at her expectantly.

"More?" Allie laughed and gave him more.

When he was finished, she let him into the house.

The telephone rang on the stand in the hallway. Allie answered. "Bear Creek Ranch."

"Allie, Hank here."

"Hey," she said, always glad to hear from her brother since he'd returned from the war in Afghanistan. "What's up?"

"Sadie and I are going out to the Blue Moose Tavern tonight for some drinks and dancing. We thought you and Swede might want to join us."

Allie frowned. Not *you and Damien*. But then, Damien was out of town, and Hank knew it from the fire. She sighed. "Sounds good." She arranged for the time and place to meet and then ended the call.

She'd almost said no. After a hard day's work, she wasn't sure she had the energy to drink and dance. But, it did break the monotony of ranch life. Allie sniffed. First, a shower.

Allie headed upstairs.

Ruger followed and plopped down in front of the bathroom door to wait for Swede. "Traitor. I fed you, he didn't."

The dog stared up at her through soulful blue eyes.

"Fine. Stay here. See if I care."

The door opened, and Swede stood there with a towel looped around his bare shoulders, his wet hair slicked back and wearing nothing but blue jeans, half buttoned up.

The air caught in Allie's lungs, and she fought to push some past her vocal cords. When she finally did, she said, "Fed your dog."

"Thank you. I'm sure Ruger appreciated that." Swede smiled with that melt-me-to-the-core twist of his lips. "Your turn."

Allie had to really focus to make sense of what he was saying. When she did, she nodded. "Great." Then she spun on her socks and ran for her bedroom, where she pressed her palms to her burning cheeks. "What is wrong with me?" she whispered. Then she remembered.

"Oh, Swede?"

The man leaned into the doorway. "Yes, darlin'?"

Don't do that!

She gulped to swallow past the constriction in her throat. "I'm going to meet Hank and Sadie at the Blue Moose Tavern for drinks after dinner."

"Sounds good. What's the dress code?"

"Dress code?" Allie laughed. "We're in Montana, not the military." She laughed, shut her door and leaned against it. She never laughed like that with Damien.

Why was she suddenly comparing everyone to Damien?

Not everyone. Just Swede.

Damn.

5

———————

Swede dressed in clean jeans, a white, button-down shirt, and his best cowboy boots he'd purchased before moving west to work in Montana. He didn't know why he hadn't owned a pair before. They were comfortable and easy to get into.

He stood at the bottom of the stairs waiting for Allie to come down. They'd had dinner with Lloyd and the Edwards. After dinner, Allie excused herself to get dressed for their night out with her brother.

Swede didn't see anything wrong with the jeans and T-shirt she'd worn. And her hair, though wet from her shower, was neatly combed and smelled like strawberries. Nope. He didn't see anything wrong with that.

Ruger would remain out on the porch until they returned from the bar. No use keeping him up with loud music. Besides, they might not allow dogs inside.

Georgia stepped into the hallway, wiping her hands on her apron. "My, don't you look nice?"

"Thank you, ma'am," Swede said.

She untied the apron in the back and lifted the strap up over her head. "I was about to leave and go to our house. Is there anything you need before I call it a night?"

"No, ma'am," he answered.

176

Georgia glanced up the staircase. "There you are. You've kept this man waiting long enough." The older woman smiled. "I'm sure he'll agree it was worth it."

Swede followed Georgia's gaze, his eyes widening, a low whistle escaping from his lips. "Wow."

Allie wore a short white dress that caressed her body perfectly, the skirt brushing against the middle of her thighs with every step she took. She'd dried her hair and it lay in big, soft curls around her shoulders, framing her face. The makeup she'd applied naturally enhanced her cheeks and made her green eyes stand out.

"Wow," he repeated.

Her lips quirked. "You said that." She came down the steps in strappy sandals that drew attention to her toned and tanned calves.

Swede struggled to pull his jaw off the floor and act like a bodyguard, not a teenager on his first date. He couldn't help but look at her several times as if she weren't real, but a figment of his imagination. She was stunningly beautiful in a fresh, girl-next-door way.

"Well, I must say that dress is you." Georgia took her hands and smiled, her eyes misting. "Isn't it one you bought for your honeymoon to the Cayman Islands?"

Allie shrugged. "I felt like wearing it. After all, I'll be out in public with Sadie McClain. Not that I can compete with her. She's amazing."

"Sweetie, you don't have to compete," Georgia said. "You're beautiful in your own way."

"Thanks." Allie hugged Georgia and then turned toward Swede, her shoulders thrown back, making her breasts rise. "Ready?"

Swede was almost certain he wasn't ready to take Allie for a night on the town. Thankfully, it was only to Eagle Rock, a village with a population of maybe a thousand, counting all of the outlying ranch owners, ranch hands and hound dogs. Surely they'd roll up the sidewalks by 9:00.

"I'll drive." Swede hooked her elbow and guided her to his truck, opened the door and handed her up.

He couldn't get over the transformation from the sweaty, dirt-covered ranch girl to the sexy redheaded temptress. His gaze swung her direction several times on the drive into Eagle Rock.

At least two dozen trucks lined the parking lot and the street around the Blue Moose Tavern. The thumps of drums and a bass guitar could be heard all the way out into the street even before Swede opened his door.

"I see Hank's truck," Allie said. "He and Sadie must already be inside." She waited for Swede to get out and come around to open her door. He reached in to capture her around the waist and helped her to the ground. He held on a moment or two longer than he should have, but he couldn't get his fingers to loosen their hold on her body.

"Ready to go?" she asked.

Oh, hell no. "Yes."

From the outside, the bar didn't look like much. Inside, it was a lot bigger than the exterior storefront indicated.

A three-man band played country-western music, and several couples were two-stepping their way around the dance floor.

"I see them." Allie grabbed his hand and led him, weaving between the tables, saying hello to almost everyone in the room. Several cowboys whistled when she walked by. One reached out to touch her leg, but a hard stare from Swede made him back off and turn his reach into a wave.

Hank and Sadie sat at a table facing the front entrance, with a broad-shouldered man seated in front of them with his back to the room.

Swede and Allie arrived at the table and the stranger turned and jumped to his feet, with a smile and a wince. "Swede. You son of a bitch. Good to see you." Bear, the Delta Force friend he'd made during rehab, pounded his back and hugged him so hard it hurt his ribs. The guy didn't know his own strength. The leg wound had done nothing to diminish his arm strength.

"And this must be your assignment." Bear winked. "Hi, Tate Parker. But call me Bear."

"Alyssa Patterson, but you can call me Allie." She shook his hand, but was pulled into a hug similar to the one Swede had endured.

Bear set her to arm's length and raked his gaze over her. "Allie, wearing a dress like that, you need to be on the dance floor. Care to dance with me?" He held out his arm. "I can't promise I won't step on your toes. The docs said I'd never dance again. But I fooled them. I never could dance, but what I lack in skill, I make up for in enthusiasm."

Allie laughed and followed Bear to the dance floor.

Swede stepped aside, wanting to punch his friend for taking off with his girl. Then he had to remind himself Allie wasn't his girl. In fact, she was Reynolds's girl, soon to be wife.

"What's wrong, Swede? You look like you swallowed a lemon." Hank nodded toward Bear. "I thought you would be happy to see your friend. He got in an hour ago and insisted on coming with us, even though he's been up since four this morning."

"Bear's a force to be reckoned with. I swear, he knows no limits to his physical abilities." Another glance Allie's way and Swede turned back to Hank. "I take it Bear will fit in with the team you're building?"

"Perfectly. I talked with him on the phone yesterday evening and had him on a plane first thing this morning."

"Great." Swede really was glad for the friend who'd been at his side through his own physical therapy and re-introduction into the civilian world. But did he have to hold Allie so close?

"I spoke with the fire chief. They found evidence of C-4 explosives and a detonator similar to the ones used by the military."

"Great. That tells me that whoever set that charge probably knew what he was doing."

Hank's lips firmed. "Afraid so."

Sadie leaned forward. "What I don't understand is how Damien could walk away from it all and leave his fiancée to answer to the sheriff and fire fighters." The pretty actress frowned. "If I were Allie, I'd dump his ass and call off the wedding."

"Before the explosions, he said he had a business emergency he had to deal with and the plane was waiting," Swede said. "But no business emergency is enough to leave the woman you love behind with the lingering threat of someone trying to blow you and her away."

Sadie smacked her palm on the table. "Damn right. I've got half a mind to tell her that."

Hank slipped his arm around Sadie. "That's what I like about you. Your passion." He kissed his wife. "Our baby is going to be hell on wheels when he's born."

Sadie lifted her chin. "She."

Swede smiled at the happy couple, glad his teammate had found the woman of his dreams. But they still had a big problem on their hands. One involving Hank's sister and her fiancé. "What do you know about Damien Reynolds, and any of the people who work for him?"

Hank retained his hold on his wife's hand, but he turned his attention back to the case. "I searched the web, looking for anything linked to Damien and found an article about him and his corporation being awarded a big government construction contract. I have a call in to a friend of mine who works in procurement in D.C. I'll let you know what I find."

Swede nodded toward Bear. "What have you got for Bear to work on?"

"I take it you haven't heard about the national guardsman who was attacked in Bozeman last night?"

Swede swung his gaze back to Hank. "No, I didn't. What happened?"

"I don't have all of the details. What I do know is that he was cut up pretty badly. Fortunately, someone found him shortly after the attack, and he was rushed to the hospital. Whoever did it sliced him open, basically eviscerating him."

Sadie gasped and covered her belly. "That's terrible!"

Swede's own gut clenched. "And he survived?"

"The guy who found him performed basic first aid, applying pressure to the wound. The first responders were able to get to him before he bled out, and the surgeon put his intestines back together. He's in ICU. He's not good, but they're hoping he makes it."

"Why would someone do that?" Sadie sat back in her chair, her face pale, her hand resting over her flat tummy.

"I don't know, but I'm putting Bear on it. The investigation doesn't pay, but the victim is a fellow serviceman. I feel we owe it to him to do something. He's a twenty-year-old kid, just back from deployment and only been home a day."

Swede's fists clenched. He wanted to kill the bastard who'd hurt the kid. He'd seen his share of stomach-turning atrocities, but that was in the Middle East where the Taliban and ISIS rebels had no regard for life. But this…Hell, they were on American soil with baseball and mom's apple pie. "Things like that shouldn't happen here," he said.

"Agreed."

"What do the Bozeman Police Department have to say about it?" Swede asked.

"They don't know what to think. As far as they could tell, they have no suspects, and they couldn't find a motivation for the attack. The guy's wallet was still on him, and he had five hundred dollars inside. For now, they're calling it a random act of violence."

"Bullshit." Swede's fists bunched. "It's just another way of saying they don't have a suspect or a clue as to who might have done it."

"Exactly. I want Bear to talk to the kid's family and his CO. I'm sure the police will be doing the same, but I won't feel right unless we do something to help find the bastard. In the meantime, you need to stick to Allie like glue. I don't think the two incidents are related, but I'd rather not take any chances. I love my little sister and don't want anything bad to happen."

"I'm on it." Swede pushed to his feet as the song ended. He crossed to the dance floor and tapped Bear's shoulder. "Mind if I cut in?"

Bear backed away, grinning. "Yes, I do mind, but I guess since it's you, I won't protest too much." He turned to Allie and raised her hand to press a kiss to the backs of her knuckles. "Thank you for the two-step lesson."

She nodded. "You're a quick study. Thank you for the dance."

Swede took her hand as the music transitioned into a slow, heart-breaking, belly-rubbing song.

Allie glanced up at him. "We can wait for a faster song, if you were hoping to two-step."

"No, this one is perfect." Perfect if she wasn't engaged to another man. Perfect to hold her close and sniff the strawberry scent of her hair. Perfect if she wasn't the body he was supposed to guard, and wasn't a woman getting married on Saturday.

ALLIE MELTED into Swede's arms, her body pressing close to his. She fit against him like they were made for each other. God, she had to stop thinking that way. On Saturday, she was supposed to marry the man of her dreams. What she was feeling was only pre-wedding jitters. Damien was the man for her, not Swede.

Then why was she leaning into his body, resting her cheek against his chest and wishing the song would never end?

With their hips touching, Allie knew immediately that she wasn't the only one feeling whatever it was building between them. The hard ridge of his fly pressed into her belly, the slow song lending itself to false dreams and dangerous passion.

As if of their own volition, her hands slipped up his chest and wrapped around the back of his neck.

Swede cupped her face, turning it up to his. "Do you know what you do to me?" he whispered.

"I have an idea," she said, her voice breathy. Allie couldn't seem to breathe normally. Not with Swede so close and the heat building between them.

His head dipped lower, and his lips hovered over hers. If

she leaned up on her toes, they'd kiss. It would be wrong. So very wrong. But…

As she bunched her muscles, she heard the music end, and the band announce a fifteen-minute break.

Swede straightened. "We should go back to the table."

"Yes, we should." Allie couldn't make her feet move.

"Look." Swede gripped her hands and squeezed hard. "Whatever this is, whatever we're feeling right now, isn't real."

Allie's chest tightened, and her eyes stung. "Of course, it isn't," she agreed, though her body felt otherwise.

"You're getting married on Saturday, and I'll move on to my next assignment. Let's not make this any harder than it has to be."

She nodded, knowing what he said couldn't be truer, even though she still wanted to feel his lips against hers. "You're right."

Swede stepped back, his arms falling to his sides.

Allie pasted a smile on her lips and forced air past her vocal cords. "Thank you for the dance. If you'll excuse me…" She made a beeline for the ladies' room. Once inside, she stood in front of the mirror, staring at the face of a woman who was engaged to one man and lusting after another. Her mother and father had raised her better than that. She ran cold water from the tap, stuck her hands beneath the spray and then splashed her cheeks with her wet hands.

"Hey." Sadie entered behind her and slipped an arm over Allie's shoulder. "Are you okay?"

Too disturbed to come up with a lie, she shook her head. "I don't know."

"You look a little flushed." Sadie ripped a paper towel from the roll, wet it and squeezed out the excess before patting Allie's face with it. "For a moment out there, I thought you and Swede were going to kiss."

Allie met Sadie's gaze in the mirror. "The bad part about it is that I wanted to," she admitted.

Sadie sighed. "Baby, are you sure Damien's the right man for you?"

Throwing her hands in the air, Allie spun and paced all three steps across the room and back. "I'm getting married on Saturday. No man I just met is going to derail my plans."

Sadie held up her hands. "Okay. You're getting married on Saturday." She tossed the wet paper towel in the trash and tore off a dry one. "If it's Damien you're determined to marry, then you have to stop drooling over your bodyguard."

Again, Allie's gaze met Sadie's in the mirror. Her shoulders slumped, and she nodded. "You're right. It's not right. I need to go home, get a good night's sleep and wake up with the right frame of mind."

"Don't forget, tomorrow we pick up your wedding dress," Sadie reminded her.

Allie's chest pinched. Instead of being giddy with excitement, like a bride should be, she dreaded going. She needed to call Damien. Maybe hearing his voice would help get her back on track. He was the man she was going to marry on Saturday. This was only a case of cold feet. Straightening her shoulders, she stepped out of the bathroom and ran into a wall of muscles.

Sadie squeezed by them and darted back into the bar room. Some friend she was.

Swede's arms came up around her and crushed her against his chest. "Are you all right?"

"Yes." She nodded, and then shook her head. "No. I need to go home."

"We've only been here twenty minutes. Are you sure you don't want to stay and visit with your brother?"

"No. I'm tired and have a big day ahead of me." She stepped back. "If you want to stay, I can see if Bear will take me back to the ranch."

Swede's jaw hardened. "I'll take you." He hooked her elbow in a tight grip and led her back to the table where they said their goodbyes and then left the tavern.

Once outside, Allie sucked in deep breaths, hoping the fresh Montana air would clear her head.

Swede opened the truck door for her and handed her up

into the passenger seat. The touch of his fingers against her elbow shot electric currents throughout her body and left her tingling. This couldn't be. Maybe she'd had too much to drink. Then she remembered, she hadn't had a chance to order a drink.

As she watched Swede walk around to the driver's side, Allie moaned softly. She needed to talk to Damien. What she was feeling was lonely and neglected. That was all.

Swede climbed into the driver's seat and shifted the truck in gear.

Allie stared out the side window, refusing to look his in direction. How he must be laughing at her, thinking she was a two-timing woman, eager to cheat on her fiancé while he was out of town. Allie wanted to tell him that wasn't the case. That she wasn't that kind of woman. But she'd had those feelings. And feeling it was almost as bad as actually doing it.

They'd driven past all the houses and continued onto the highway leading to the Bear Creek Ranch when headlights flashed brightly in the rearview mirror.

Swede squinted and tipped the windshield mirror upward. He decreased his speed a little, but the vehicle wasn't interested in passing.

Allie watched through the side mirror and finally turned in her seat to glance through the rear window. "What the hell is he trying to prove?"

Swede lowered his window and waved the guy on.

The headlights seemed to get larger as the vehicle sped up. Instead of swerving to go around, the SUV rammed into the back of the truck.

Allie jerked forward. The seatbelt snapped tight, keeping her from slamming into the dash.

"Hang on!" Swede yelled. "He's going to hit us again."

Allie braced her hand on the dash, her body already bruised from the first attack.

The trailing vehicle rammed them again, hitting at a bit of an angle.

Swede's truck fishtailed. He fought to straighten it before it ran off the road into a ditch. Just when he had it under control, the attacker raced up beside them and slammed into the driver's side.

The truck ran off the pavement onto the gravel shoulder.

Allie held onto the oh-shit handle above the door as Swede fought with the steering wheel to bring the truck back onto the blacktop.

It was hard to do with the attacking vehicle pushing him further off the road.

Swede changed tactics and slammed on his brakes. The truck skidded in the gravel but slowed faster than the attacking full-sized SUV. His maneuver bought them a few seconds, allowing Swede to drive back up onto the highway.

No sooner had he righted the truck, something hit the front windshield dead-center between the driver and passenger sides.

Allie's heart plunged into the pit of her belly. The hole in the windshield was perfectly round. "They're shooting at us!"

"Get down!" Swede shouted. He spun the steering wheel and hit the accelerator at the same time. The truck did a complete one-hundred-eighty-degree turn.

Another bullet blasted through the back windshield, through the headrest of the passenger seat and exited through the front windshield. If Allie hadn't ducked when Swede told her to, she would have been hit in the back of the head. Her stomach flipped, and she remained low in her seat.

"Switch places!" Swede yelled.

"What? Are you insane?"

"They're coming around. Hurry. Switch places." Swede shifted the seat back and slammed his foot on the accelerator.

Allie slid across the console and into Swede's lap. Once she had control of the steering wheel, he crawled out from under her and lifted his foot off the accelerator.

He fell across the other seat, righted himself, lowered the window and poked out his handgun.

The other vehicle had performed a slower version of the

turnaround Swede had executed moments before and was now quickly catching up.

Her heart pounding against her ribs, Allie slammed her foot all the way down on the accelerator, while Swede leaned halfway out the window and fired.

The trailing SUV swerved, but kept coming.

Swede fired again, hitting one of the headlights.

Another bullet hit the back windshield, spraying glass fragments throughout the truck's interior.

Allie kept her head low and her gaze on the curving road ahead. Reaching town meant the guy behind them might veer off and leave them alone.

Swede fired again, but the SUV kept coming.

Allie rounded a curve, reaching out to grab Swede's belt to keep him from flying out.

He stayed with the truck and fired again on the SUV.

After flying around another curve and over a rise, Allie nearly cried out in relief when the lights of Eagle Rock twinkled from below. She drove faster, refusing to slow for the curves leading into town. The lights behind her disappeared as she made the last turn, drove onto Main Street and straight toward the local sheriff's office.

Swede dropped back into the passenger seat, still holding his handgun in one hand, while his other covered his right shoulder.

Allie pulled into the parking lot of the county jail and sheriff's office, honking the truck's horn. She shoved the shift into park, dropped down out of the driver's seat and ran toward the door.

Sheriff Joe Barron stepped outside, his hand resting on the handle of his service weapon. "What the hell's going on?"

Allie stopped in front of him, breathing hard and shaking from head to toe. "Someone tried to kill us." She turned back to look at the road leading into town, happy to see it empty of traffic. Especially the kind of traffic that fires bullets.

Swede dropped down out of the truck, having holstered his handgun beneath his jacket. He held his hand over his right arm. "You don't happen to have a first aid kit in your office, do you?"

"I do."

"Good." Swede pulled his hand away from his arm. His palm and fingers were drenched, and the sleeve of his black leather jacket shone with wet, sticky blood.

Allie swayed, and her heart leaped into her throat. "Damn, Swede, you've been shot."

6

———

Within minutes, the volunteer firefighter paramedic, local doctor, Hank, Bear and Sadie converged on the sheriff's office. Between all of them, they insisted on moving Swede two buildings down to the only medical clinic in town.

Swede shook his head, insisting the injury was nothing but a flesh wound. Upon closer inspection, the doctor and paramedic agreed, but it had nicked him deep enough to cause a significant amount of bleeding.

"Did you get a look at the license plate?" Sheriff Barron asked.

Swede shook his head. "I didn't.'

"Me neither," Allie confirmed. "It all happened so fast, and bullets were flying. We didn't have time to breathe, much less jot down a license plate." She hovered near Swede, offering to hold the adhesive tape or hand them a bottle of rubbing alcohol when needed.

Swede let the doctor treat the wound. He'd seen what happened when soldiers didn't take care of themselves. Infections could be lethal, or cause the loss of a limb. But he drew the line at stitches. "Just slap on a butterfly bandage. It'll heal."

The doctor flushed the wound with water and alcohol and then pressed a couple of bandages across it. "Change the bandage daily, or if it gets really dirty. Other than a nice scar, you'll probably live."

"Thought so."

"But not if that guy is still running loose." Allie held out Swede's jacket. Sadie had rinsed the blood out of it as best she could and dried it with towels and a blow dryer while the doc worked on him.

Sheriff Barron shook his head. "I don't know what's going on around here, but we have to get to the bottom of it. We can't have the good citizens of the county afraid to come outside."

"So far, Reynolds and Allie seem to be the targets," Hank said.

"Yeah. We're trying to track down the source of the C-4 and the paint used to deface the stable before it burned to the ground. The state forensics lab is working on it, and a hundred other hot cases." The sheriff drew in a deep breath and let it out. "In the meantime, to make sure you get home safe, I'll escort you to the Bear Creek Ranch, personally."

Allie smiled at her friend. "Thank you, Joe."

He draped an arm over her shoulders, and hugged her. "I'm sorry this is happening to you, but I'm glad you had someone like Mr. Svenson with you. Your own personal SEAL to keep you safe when the crap hits the fan."

Allie nodded, her gaze seeking and connecting with Swede's.

Swede felt a warmth flooding through him that had nothing to do with the jacket he'd shrugged into. The arm felt fine, but he'd like to get back to Bear Creek Ranch where Allie was surrounded by people who loved and looked out for her. After the attack that evening, Swede wasn't sure his skills were enough to keep Allie safe.

"You know, Allie," Sheriff Barron was saying. "You really might consider postponing your wedding. With the way things have been going, it would make too big a target for these yahoos to pass up."

Allie's eyes narrowed and her lips thinned. "I'm getting

married on Saturday. Scare tactics aren't keeping me from my wedding."

The sheriff raised his hands. "Just saying, it might not be safe for you or your guests."

Her brows furrowing, Allie seemed to chew on Joe Barron's words. "I don't want anyone else to get hurt because of me." She looked up at her friend. "I'll think about it. But as far as anyone knows, the wedding is still on."

Swede's stomach bunched at the determination in Allie's voice. What did he expect? She was engaged to a wealthy man and had been, well before Swede showed up in Eagle Rock. Besides, he wasn't in the market for a long-term relationship. Not with his hang-ups. Hell, he was barely satisfactory at his new job. A man who was at one hundred percent would have taken out the attackers. But he'd missed, allowing the bastards to live.

Sheriff Barron waved toward the door. "Allie, if you're ready to go, I'll escort you two to the ranch gate."

Allie glanced at Swede.

Swede nodded. "We're ready."

"Call me when you get home." Hank pressed a kiss to Allie's forehead. "I like to know you're okay."

Sadie hugged her. "I'll see you tomorrow."

"Do you want us to swing by and pick you up for the trip into Bozeman?" Swede asked.

Hank shook his head. "No. We will all drive in at the same time. Sadie and I will meet you at the gate to the Bear Creek Ranch."

"And I'll bring up the rear," Bear said. "I want to swing by the hospital and check on the soldier, and then I'll go by his unit to talk to his commander."

Swede had wondered how it would be as a civilian, without the support and camaraderie of his SEAL team. Not much had changed. With Hank and Bear nearby, Swede knew they had his back. He hoped, between the three of them, they could keep Allie safe.

Allie insisted on driving Swede's truck back to the ranch.

With the sheriff's SUV behind them, they had no repeat performances from the earlier attacker. The sheriff parked at the entrance to Bear Creek Ranch and waited until Allie was halfway to the house before he turned to go back to town.

"You have some good people here in Montana," Swede noted.

Allie snorted. "Except the ones trying to kill me?"

"With that exception. I think the good people outnumber the bad."

She nodded. "You're right. I love living here. I love the people I grew up with and the sense of community. Although, sometimes they can get into your business when you don't want them to. But for the most part, everyone looks out for everyone else."

"You're lucky to have them." Swede's hand rested on his pistol. Even though they were on the Bear Creek Ranch, he couldn't let down his guard for a moment. He had done so earlier, and it had almost gotten them killed. All because he'd wanted to kiss Allie.

And still did.

He sat in silence as Allie drove up to the house and parked.

"What will you tell my father about your truck?" Allie asked, staring at the holes in the windshield.

"I'll tell him I got behind a gravel truck."

"What about the dent in the door?"

"It could have been a rude driver in the Blue Moose parking lot, backing into me and driving off."

She nodded. "He might buy it."

"You need to talk to Damien," Swede said.

She stared at the house in front of her. "I know."

"He has to know more than he's telling us about this threat. If we could talk to him about it, we might have a better starting point in our search to locate the attacker."

"I'll try to get in touch with him tonight. If he's on the other side of the world, it might be difficult to contact him." Allie unbuckled her seatbelt and reached for the keys in the ignition.

"Why are you marrying Reynolds?" Swede asked before he could stop himself. It wasn't the kind of question a bodyguard asked his client. But there it was.

Her hand froze on the keys. "Why do you ask?" she countered. She didn't glance his way. Instead, she stared at the keyring.

Swede studied her face, looking for a reaction, a clue to her feelings about the man she had promised to marry. "I don't know him well, but you two just don't seem right for each other. Like you don't fit." Again, as soon as the words left his mouth, he wished he could have taken them back.

Allie's fingers curled around the keys, and her mouth pulled into a tight line. "You're right. You don't know Damien. And, for that matter, you don't know me." She pushed open the door, stepped down on the running board and dropped to the ground.

Swede rounded the front of the truck and took the keys she held out to him. "You didn't answer the question. Why are you marrying Damien?"

Allie pushed back her shoulders and met his gaze. "That's none of your business. You're just the bodyguard my fiancé hired to protect me. After the wedding, I'll be on my way to the Cayman Islands, and you'll be on to your next assignment. What does it matter?"

Swede gripped her arms, wanting to wring the truth out of the woman. But, he knew she was right. It wasn't his business. Still, he didn't understand the relationship between Allie and Damien, and one thing was bugging the hell out of him. "You never said you loved him."

Allie stared up into his eyes, her hands pressed to his chest, neither pushing him away nor bringing him closer. "I don't have to say the words to you."

Swede pulled her closer until their bodies touched, hip to hip, breasts to chest. "Do you want to kiss him when you're dancing?"

"Why are you doing this?" she whispered. "You said you aren't into relationships. Why are you interested in mine?"

"Answer my question." He leaned closer, his mouth moving nearer to hers.

Allie licked her lips, sending a burst of flame through Swede's system. He couldn't go back now that he'd started down this path.

Swede's voice dropped lower, his groin tightening as the ridge beneath his fly rubbed against Allie's belly. "Does he make you want to fall into bed and make love to him with only a glance?"

"You don't know what you're doing," she said, her gaze slipping to his mouth, her tongue sweeping across her lips again.

"*Me?* I think *you* don't know what you're doing. Or what you really want."

"And you know me well enough to know what I want and need?" she challenged.

"No, but I know what *I* want." His hands slipped down her arms and around to rest on her lower back. "I want that kiss." Then Swede broke all the rules he associated with being a bodyguard and kissed the woman he was sworn to protect. Not only did he kiss her, he branded her with his mouth, taking everything she would give and sweeping past her teeth to take even more.

Their tongues danced a sensual tango, thrusting and parrying.

Allie's hands slid beneath Swede's jacket, curled over his chest and locked behind his neck, pulling him closer.

Swede knew what he was doing was wrong, but something drew him to Allie. Something he found irresistible. Unfortunately, one kiss would never be enough. With her imminent marriage to a man who didn't care enough about his fiancée to be with her when someone was out to kill her, looming, Swede's stomach knotted and his heart hurt. He tore his lips away from hers.

"No." Swede lifted his head and stared down into her face. "No."

Allie looked up into his eyes, her green ones glazed, her breathing coming in labored breaths. Her body still pressed to his, her hands flattened against his chest. She blinked and the glaze cleared. Her eyes widened, and she gasped. "Damn you." Allie stepped back and swung her arm, her palm connecting with his face in a resounding slap.

Swede's cheek stung with the force of the blow. He stood there, unmoving, knowing he deserved every bit of it. "I'm sorry. I shouldn't have done that."

Through gritted teeth, she said, "Don't. Ever. Touch. Me. Again." She spun on her heels and ran in the house.

If he wasn't mistaken, Swede could swear he heard a sob before the door closed behind Allie.

She didn't stop running until she reached the sanctuary of her bedroom. After she shut the door, Allie leaned her back against it and slid to the floor. Tears rolled down her cheeks. Allie touched her fingers to the tears. What was wrong with her? She was never this emotional. The last time she cried was the day her mother died. Since then, her father insisted crying was only for babies. She wasn't a baby; she was a grown woman with a wedding ahead of her.

For a minute more, she allowed herself to sink into the depths of despair, sobbing quietly so that her bodyguard couldn't hear her break down. Then she got up, stripped out of the pretty dress, wadded it into a ball and stuffed it in the very back of her closet. If she never wore the dress again, that was just fine with her.

Pulling a T-shirt over her head, Allie peeked out into the hallway. Nothing moved. A light shined beneath the door of Hank's old bedroom, her father's room was dark and the bathroom door across the hall was open with the light on. She crossed to the bathroom, closed and locked the door, then brushed her teeth and scrubbed off the little bit of makeup that hadn't washed away with her tears.

Allie brushed her hair and secured it in a ponytail on top of her head. Looking in the mirror, she appeared much like the little girl who'd lost her mother. Right now she missed her mom more than ever. When she opened the door, she half-feared, half-wished she'd run into Swede in the hallway. Again, it was empty.

After trudging across the corridor to her room, she closed the door and collapsed on the bed. She lifted the phone, dialed Damien's number and waited. She heard one ring and his phone rolled over to voicemail.

Damn.

Tomorrow she really needed to talk to Damien. That kiss had only made matters worse. Now, not only had she cheated in thought, she'd cheated in deed. How could she go into a marriage with the guilt of that kiss weighing on her mind? Then again, how could she tell Damien without hurting him?

Allie curled up on the bed, hugging a pillow to her chest. For a long time, she lay still, willing herself to sleep, hoping everything would appear brighter with the morning sunshine.

After tossing and turning until the wee hours of the morning, Allie finally drifted to sleep.

It was her wedding day. She wore the dress she had picked out, and had her hair piled high on her head with ringlets falling down her back. Her father walked her down the aisle very slowly, his face grim. As they passed the rows of guests, people whispered and pointed. They knew. Her face heated and her belly churned.

When Allie finally reached the altar, she turned to face the man who would become her husband until death should they part. But Damien wasn't the one waiting for her. The man in the tuxedo stood taller and straighter. A man of military bearing and discipline. Waiting to marry her was the man who'd been hired by her fiancé to protect her.

Swede.

Pounding on her door woke her at 8:00 the next morning. Her father's voice boomed through the paneling. "If you want to eat, you need to come down, now. Georgia is cleaning the kitchen, and she's waiting on you."

"I'm coming," Allie responded. One glance at the clock made her throw back the comforter and leap out of the bed. "Why didn't anyone wake me earlier?"

"Swede said you didn't get to bed until late. We decided you needed your beauty sleep."

Allie crossed the room to her dresser and selected a pullover blouse. "Are you saying I'm looking more like a hag lately?" She ripped her sleep shirt over her head, put on a bra and dragged on the clean shirt she'd wear to town.

"I wouldn't say that," her father said. "But you have had dark circles beneath your eyes. I think you work too hard."

Allie stuck her feet into her jeans and pulled them up, securing the zipper. "Well, that plays right into my plans for today. I'm going to Bozeman to pick up my wedding dress. That means I won't be around to help out in the hay field until late this evening." She grabbed a pair of walking shoes and the high heels she'd wear under her wedding dress and opened her bedroom door.

"The hay won't be dry enough to bale until tomorrow. Take your time."

"Thanks, Dad." She glanced at her father, sensing he wanted to say more, but couldn't come up with the words to express the emotions playing across his face. Well, as much emotion as Lloyd Patterson ever expressed. The man was taciturn and rough around the edges, but Allie knew deep down he loved her and Hank, and only wanted the best for them.

Her father stared at her for a moment longer. "I heard what happened last night."

Allie's fists clenched. She shouldn't have slapped Swede for kissing her, and she sure as hell shouldn't have kissed him in the first place. Today, after she picked up her wedding dress, she'd call Damien and confess that she was confused and scared and…well…she'd come up with a good reason for kissing her bodyguard. Although, she couldn't at the moment, other than she'd wanted to more than she wanted to breathe. "Look, Dad, what happened last night won't happen again."

His brows furrowed. "How do you know it won't happen again?"

She squared her shoulders. "Because I'm not going to let it."

Her father shook his head, his gaze narrowing to a slit. "I

don't see how you can keep it from happening again until they catch the guy who did it. From what Sheriff Barron said, you didn't even get a look at the license plate. How will they find the shooter if you didn't even get that?"

Allie almost laughed out loud at her father's words. Holy hell, she'd thought he was talking about the kiss. Thank goodness the people who knew about that would remain the only two. Until she confessed to her fiancé. *If* she confessed. "You're right, Dad. It could happen again. We just have to hope it doesn't."

"I'm just glad your friend Swede was with you. I can't imagine what would have happened had you been alone." He took her hands. "With the wedding so close, and this shooter still on the loose, don't you think you should consider postponing?"

What was with everyone trying to convince her to postpone or call off her wedding? "It was probably a random act. I'm getting married on Saturday. I've spent too much money on everything, and it's non-refundable."

"That's no reason to get married. Here you are in trouble, and your fiancé isn't anywhere around to keep you safe." Her father dropped her hands, a scowl making deep grooves in his forehead. "What kind of man doesn't take care of his woman?"

"He'll be back before the wedding. You can ask him then." Allie stepped past her father. "In the meantime, I have a wedding dress to pick up at the bridal shop."

"I really wish you'd stay here at the ranch. I don't want to see you hurt."

"I'll have Sadie, Hank and Swede with me. If I need help, they have offered to provide it." She didn't wait around to argue further. Allie hurried down to the kitchen.

"You'll have to hustle if you want breakfast before you leave for your appointment at the dressmakers." Georgia held out a plate of fluffy scrambled eggs. "Hank called. He and Sadie will be at the gate in ten minutes."

"I'm not hungry. But thanks." Allie aimed straight for the coffee pot, poured half a cup and downed it, burning her tongue. With her father's words and the images of her dream still rattling around in her head, Allie braced herself and stepped out on the porch.

Swede sat on the porch steps, scratching Ruger behind the ears. When he heard the door open, he stood and faced her. "I've been thinking."

Allie marched down the steps and out to her truck, her keys in hand. "That's nice."

"What happened last night—"

"It didn't." Allie turned to face him. "Nothing happened last night. Get it?"

Swede pressed his hand to the cheek Allie had slapped the night before. "Sure felt like it happened."

"Don't ever let it happen again."

"I wasn't the only one kissing." He grabbed her arm and forced her to stop and look at him. "You weren't fighting me."

Allie glared and looked back at the house. "Shh. Whatever happened cannot happen again. On either side."

"Trust me. I won't kiss you again." He let go of her arm, walked to her truck and stopped next to the passenger side. "Not unless you ask me." His lips twitched on the corners.

Allie contemplated hurling her keys at him. How dare he laugh at such a huge mistake? She refused to rise to his bait. Instead, she climbed into the driver's seat, fit the key into the ignition and started the engine.

Swede tried the handle on the passenger side. "Hey, unlock the door."

For a moment, Allie considered driving off without the infuriating man. One glance at the bullet holes in his truck changed her mind. She popped the locks and waited for him to climb in.

"I thought you were going to leave without me."

"Believe me, I almost did." She slammed the gear into reverse, backed up and turned around, heading for the gate.

As agreed upon, Sadie and Hank were waiting in Hank's pickup. Bear, in one of Hank's White Oak Ranch trucks, waited behind them.

Allie waved as she passed the two trucks and drove all the way into Bozeman without saying another word to Swede.

"Stop at the hospital. Hank, Bear and I want to talk to the kid who got cut up."

With a nod, no words, Allie turned and headed for the hospital, pulling into a visitors' slot.

Allie turned off the engine but made no move to get out. "I'll wait out here."

Swede was halfway out of the truck. "Like hell, you will." He rounded to the other side and grabbed her door handle.

Moving quickly, she hit the door lock. Her gaze went from the lock to his eyes.

Swede frowned and tried the door handle. "Allie, don't be ridiculous. You can't stay out here by yourself. Please, unlock the door."

She stared at him for a long moment and then sighed. Who was she kidding? She might as well paint a big red bulls-eye on her and the truck.

She tapped the button releasing the locks and slid out of the truck.

Swede let out a long breath and touched her arm. "I'm sorry for anything I've said or done that makes you not want me to protect you. I promise not to touch you or make you uncomfortable. But please, don't lock me out."

Allie shook her head. "No, that was childish of me. I won't do it again." She held up her hand. "I promise."

The other two trucks pulled in and parked nearby. Sadie joined Allie and took her hand. The men surrounded the women as they entered the hospital.

At the information desk, Bear asked for Thomas Baker, the soldier brought in with knife wounds.

The volunteer keyed something into the computer and waited a moment. Then she looked up and smiled. "He's in ICU."

"How is he?" Bear asked.

The gray-haired lady shrugged. "You'll have to speak with the nurses in ICU. They'll be able to tell you more."

They rode the elevator up to ICU.

Nurses hurried from room to room, tending to seriously ill patients, taking vital signs, administering medication and trying to make their patients more comfortable in an uncomfortable situation.

Hank approached the nurses' station and asked to see Thomas Baker.

"Are you a relative of Mr. Baker?" the head nurse asked.

"No," Hank responded. "I'm a war veteran, come to pay my respects to the young soldier. He deserves a whole lot more than what he got from the low-life who did this."

The nurse nodded. "Agreed. But rules are rules. Only relatives are allowed into the room. Unless Mr. Baker requests to see you."

"We'd like to talk to him about the attack, in case there is anything we can do to help, or keep this from happening to others."

"Isn't that what the police are doing?" asked the head nurse. "They were in an hour ago, after Mr. Baker woke."

"I imagine they are doing a fine job of finding the attacker," Hank said. "But we'd still like to help."

The woman behind the counter stared at Hank for a long moment and finally said, "Get the family's permission to visit with Mr. Baker, and I'll bend the rules for you this once." Her eyes narrowed. "But, if you do anything to upset my patient, you'll be thrown out of here so fast you won't know what hit you."

Hank held up both hands. "We're here to help, not hurt."

"His mother and father are in the ICU waiting room. You can catch up with them there. They must agree or you're not getting in to see the young man."

"We understand," Bear assured her.

As they walked away from the nurses' station, Allie asked, "What if you can't get in to see Baker?"

"Bear will be making an appointment to visit with the soldier's commander," Hank said. "Maybe he can shed light on what happened."

In the ICU waiting room, the only other people present were a man and a woman appearing tense and exhausted.

Hank stopped just inside the door. "The rest of you should find a seat. I'd like to talk to Baker's parents with just me and Bear, so as not to overwhelm them."

"Right." Swede followed Allie to a seat on the far side of the waiting room. He sat on one side, and Sadie sat on the other.

A few minutes later, Hank, Bear and Baker's parents left the waiting room.

Swede wished he could be a fly on the wall in Thomas Baker's room, but he was content to be next to Allie. With all of the attacks on her and then this one on Baker, he wasn't comfortable leaving her alone here in the hospital. Forget about leaving her out in the parking lot.

Allie turned to Sadie. "Have you had any morning sickness, yet?"

Sadie shrugged. "A little, but nothing unmanageable. I still can't believe we're having a baby in seven months."

Allie grinned. "I can't wait. Hank's going to make a great father. And I'm over-the-moon about being an aunt."

Swede listened to the ladies talking, a little envious of Hank. The man had a family and a baby on the way. Wow. Nothing could be more grounding than having a child and a wife. A glance at Allie made him wonder what it would be like to be married to a woman like her, and to have children. He could picture an auburn-haired little girl running through the yard, her curls bouncing on her shoulders. She'd laugh and play with her mother, beautiful and carefree.

Too bad that child wouldn't be his. That thought caught him by surprise. He'd never considered himself good husband material, especially after all the operations he'd been on. Shooting other people and being shot at did something to a man. As if the nightmares, ducking at every loud noise, always easing around corners and looking behind you for the enemy weren't enough, trying to fit into a society at once familiar and yet foreign was a challenge in itself. Most people Stateside were only worried about what they were cooking for dinner, not whether they would live to see their next meal.

Like so many other combat veterans, Swede found the transition hard and didn't wish his problems on anyone. Especially an attractive, independent woman like Allie.

Sitting with Allie and Sadie, hearing talk of renovating a

room for the baby reminded Swede that his buddy Hank was getting on with his life. He'd been through everything Swede had, and more. If he could move on and give himself a chance at a real life with a family and children, why couldn't Swede?

He glanced at Allie.

Reynolds didn't know how good he had it. His fiancée was amazing. She'd make a great aunt, and an even better mother.

Hank and Bear entered the waiting room five minutes later, their faces grim.

Swede stood. "What did you learn?"

"Baker is lucky to be alive," Bear said.

Hank pushed a hand through his hair. "From what his parents and the nurse said, his attacker gutted him and left him to die."

"Was he able to give a description of the attacker, or any kind of motivation?" Swede asked.

"No," Hank said.

"He wasn't involved with a girl, so no ex-boyfriend issues." Bear's jaw tightened. "The kid was jumped walking home from getting a lousy hamburger yesterday evening. He didn't provoke anyone or start a fight. Hell, he'd barely said two words to the server at the hamburger joint."

"Bear is headed to Baker's unit," Hank said. "Since it wasn't a robbery, and he just returned from a deployment, maybe his commander can tell us whether or not he'd had any troubles with other unit members."

"I'll be with the ladies all afternoon." Swede nodded toward Hank and Bear. "Let us know what you find out."

"Will do." Hank glanced at Allie and Sadie. "You two stay close to Swede. If there's a nutcase walking around stabbing people, we don't want him taking a crack at you."

Sadie and Allie stood and edged a little closer to Swede.

"We'll stay with him," Sadie said, giving Swede a sad look. "Poor guy. He'll have to put up with sitting in a bridal shop while we try on our dresses."

"I can handle it," Swede said. Better to suffer through a

female shopping trip than to worry whether or not they'd make it home alive.

Bear smirked. "Better you than me, buddy." He winked at the women. "Not that spending an afternoon with two beautiful women sounds bad at all, it's just all that talk about fabric and lace makes me itch."

"Same here," Hank agreed.

Sadie pointed toward the exit. "We could do without your negativity. The final fitting of the bride's gown is supposed to be a happy, optimistic time. We're better off without the two of you."

She hooked Swede's arm. "Come on, Swede, we'll have a nice afternoon, despite those two."

Hank snagged Sadie around the waist and hugged her to him. "Kiss me, you ornery woman, before I turn you over my knee and spank you."

She laughed up at him. "Not in front of the others." And she kissed him, long and hard, melting into his body.

Swede shifted uncomfortably, bumping into Allie.

"Disgustingly mushy, if you ask me," Allie whispered.

"I heard that," Sadie said, breaking off the kiss.

They walked to the elevator together, returned to the ground floor and exited the hospital.

Hank left in Bear's truck. "I'll have him drop me off at the bridal store when we're done poking around."

Sadie drove Hank's truck while Allie and Swede rode together the few blocks to the bridal shop.

Inside the building, the attendant hustled Sadie and Allie to the dressing rooms. Another attendant showed Swede to a cushioned seat to wait. Around him were full-length mirrors and more seats. He chuckled quietly. If his SEAL teammates could see him now, they'd howl with laughter. Badass SEAL surrounded by tulle and taffeta, or whatever it was they made wedding dresses out of.

Sadie was first to emerge from the dressing room in a pretty sky-blue dress. She lifted her skirt and walked toward Swede. "What do you think?"

He shrugged. "It's nice."

"Allie wanted sky-blue to remind her of the Montana skies. I like the sentiment." She turned away and stared at herself in the mirror. "Although, it's a good thing she's getting married Saturday. I don't know how much longer I'll fit in this dress." She ran her hands over her belly. "It won't be long before I start showing." She smiled, her eyes glazing with tears. "I'm going to be a mommy. And Hank's going to be a father." Sadie glanced at Swede in the mirror. "It's a big change from fighting the Taliban and ISIS, huh?"

Swede nodded.

"Ta, da!" The attendant who'd disappeared with Allie opened the dressing room door and stepped aside with a flourish. "And we have the bride. Isn't she beautiful?"

Allie stepped out of the dressing room, her cheeks a rosy red, her gaze locked on Sadie.

"Oh, Allie." Sadie clapped her hands together. "You look amazing."

Swede swallowed hard past the constriction in his throat.

Allie, the cowgirl who could ride like she was born in a saddle, who loved ranch life and getting her hands dirty, had transformed from girl next door to...Oh, hell, a radiant and beautiful princess in a lacy white dress that hugged her body from the strapless neckline all the way down past her hips where it flared out, ending in a long train. The attendant had swept up her hair on her head and fixed it with a pearl comb.

Allie's gaze shifted from Sadie to Swede. She didn't say anything.

Swede could only stare. This woman was preparing to marry another man. How could he comment when all he wanted to do was say *No! Don't marry Reynolds! He doesn't deserve you.*

To keep from uttering those words, Swede had to get outside. Fast. He pushed to his feet and walked out of the viewing room, out of the building and into the fresh Montana air. There he sucked in a long, steadying breath. Then another.

No matter how many breaths he took, he couldn't seem to get enough air into his lungs to ease the pressure.

One thing became very clear to him. He didn't want the bride he was sworn to protect and get to the church on time to marry Damien Reynolds.

"WHAT THE HELL JUST HAPPENED?" Allie stood with her hands on her lace-covered hips, staring at the empty doorframe Swede had just passed through.

"He's a man. They can't handle all this girl stuff." Sadie tilted her head to the side and tapped her chin. "Or, is it that he didn't like seeing you in a dress you'd be wearing to marry another man?"

"Don't be ridiculous." Allie turned her back to Sadie. "Unzip me. The dress is fine. We can leave as soon as you're ready." She couldn't wait to get out of the dress shop. Really, she couldn't wait to ask Swede why he'd run out like a cat with his tail on fire.

"What's up between you and Swede?" Sadie asked.

"Nothing," Allie replied, a little too quickly. She took a deep breath and answered more slowly. "Nothing. I'm marrying Damien on Saturday." *Come hell or high water.*

"Look, Allie, you don't have to go through with this wedding."

"I accepted his proposal. I'm marrying Damien on Saturday." She refused to be a wishy-washy bride. Having made her decision, she should stick to it.

Sadie finished unzipping the back of the dress and turned Allie to face her. "You don't have to marry him."

"I keep my word."

"This is a case where you can break your promise, if it doesn't feel right." Sadie squeezed her hands. "From the look on your face, it doesn't feel right, does it?"

"I don't know." Holding the front of the dress up, Allie turned to the mirror, trying to see what Sadie saw in her face. But all she saw was a cheater who'd kissed her bodyguard. "I need to see Damien. Everything will be okay once he's back in town."

"Will it?" Sadie rested her hands on Allie's shoulders.

"This is all pre-wedding jitters. I'll be fine as soon as Damien is back in town."

Sadie planted her hands on her hips and stared at Allie in the mirror. "Okay, assuming you really love Damien, and you still want to marry him, tell me why. What's so great about him that you can't see yourself with any other man?"

That was the problem, Allie *could* see herself with another man. *Swede.* Hell, he'd been the groom in her wedding dream. What was the matter with her? Damien was everything a woman could want in a husband. "He's handsome," Allie started. In a preppy, businessman way. Not in that rugged, outdoorsy way, like Swede.

Not helping.

"So? Handsome isn't everything. I work around extremely handsome men in Hollywood." Sadie snorted. "Trust me, handsome isn't everything."

"He's a very successful businessman," Allie stated.

"So, he knows how to make money. How important is that to you? You and your father haven't wanted for anything. What can money buy that you don't already have?"

"I can travel more. See the world." *Damn was she that materialistic?*

"With a man you're not sure you're in love with?" Sadie crossed her arms over her chest. "I'd rather stay home. I've been on sets in different countries. Without someone you love to share the excitement of exploring a foreign country, the trip is just sad and lonely."

"Damien's a fine horseman. Swede never rode a horse until he came to Bear Creek Ranch."

Sadie's eyes widened, and she pointed a finger at Allie. "Ah ha! You're comparing Damien to Swede. You *do* feel something there, or you wouldn't."

"I don't feel anything where Swede is concerned." Allie hiked up her skirt with one hand and marched into the dressing room, slamming the door. "You're reading way too much into my relationship with my bodyguard. He's just the hired help. Nothing more. He said so himself."

"But you wish it was more, don't you?" Sadie's voice was soft, barely audible through the door.

Allie let the dress fall to the floor like her heart sinking into her gut. *No.* She didn't wish Swede could be more than the hired help. It would mess up everything. "I'm marrying Damien."

"Allie, the big question is, do you love him?" Sadie said through the door.

Her chest tightened, and her throat constricted. Did she love Damien? Or had she been in love with the idea of getting married? "I'm not getting any younger," she whispered.

"You're only twenty-seven. You have years of dating and meeting more men in front of you."

"I know all the men in Eagle Rock and the surrounding ranches. I don't want any of them."

"Do you want Damien because he's not from Eagle Rock, or because you love him?"

God, why was Sadie pushing her into saying something she didn't want to say? Allie leaned against the door, tears filling her eyes. "Please, Sadie, stop."

For a long moment, silence reigned.

"I'm sorry, Allie. I won't say anything else other than I love you like the sister I never had. I don't want to see you marry someone you don't love. Marriage is hard, even when you *do* love your spouse. It's harder when you have nothing in common, and you don't love one another." She paused. "I'm going to be a mother. I can't imagine letting a child of mine enter a loveless marriage. That would be so unfair to him or her. Think about it, Allie."

Allie stepped out of the dress as several warm tears slipped from the corners of her eyes and rolled down her cold cheeks. She dressed quickly, left the room and handed the wedding gown to the attendant who'd stood patiently and discreetly out of the way during the whole conversation.

"Will you be taking the dress, today?" she asked.

"Yes." Allie didn't want to make another trip to town for it.

Sadie hugged her. "Ready to go home? I'm sorry if I upset you."

Allie shrugged. "I'm okay. I need to get a good night's sleep. We're hauling hay tomorrow."

"Seriously?" Sadie shook her head. "Your wedding, should you choose to go through with it, is in a couple of days."

"Wedding or not, the hay has to be baled and loaded into the barn." The hard work and long day would keep her occupied so much that she wouldn't have time to think. If she was going through with the wedding, the chores had to be done before the big day.

If.

Damn. Now she was thinking *if*, not *when*.

8

SWEDE HELD the door for Allie as she hung the wedding dress in the back seat of the truck and then climbed into the passenger seat. The ride home from the bridal shop was uneventful, and completely and painfully silent.

Hank and Bear had returned from their visit to Baker's unit, arriving as Swede and the ladies left the bridal shop. The commander wasn't in, having gone to Wyoming earlier that morning. They expected him to be back the next day.

Bear had stayed in Bozeman to run by the police station and see if he could get any information from them about the stabbing. Hank and Sadie followed Swede and Allie to the gate of Bear Creek Ranch. As they pulled off the road at the entrance, Hank waved at Allie. "I can be by in the morning to help with the hay."

"Thanks. I'm sure Dad and Eddy can use all the help they can get," Allie said.

When they left, Swede turned to Allie. "I take it we're hauling hay tomorrow?" He didn't like that he'd been left out of the conversation until now.

"You don't have to. It's not part of the job description."

"If you're out hauling hay, I'm out hauling hay."

Allie opened her mouth for a moment and then snapped it shut.

Dinner was much the same. Mr. Patterson and Eddy talked about baling and loading the hay the next day.

Swede wasn't clear on all the terms they used. He nodded when he thought he should.

"Allie, are you driving the truck for us? Or should I get Georgia to drive?" Eddy asked.

"Since Swede will be here, why not let him drive? I can help load the hay," Allie suggested.

Georgia's brows furrowed. "Don't be silly. Your wedding is in a couple days, you can't go out and get scratched and bruised. You want to have perfect skin and no sunburn for the big day. I'll drive the truck, and you'll stay at the house and cook dinner."

"No, ma'am." Allie said. "I want to help with the hay, and you know I can't boil eggs without burning the water."

"Then you'll drive, and Swede can help load," her father said. "Since that's settled, why don't you get some sleep? We have to be up by dawn to get this cutting done in a day."

"But—"

"No buts. Go to bed." Her father left the table and climbed the stairs.

"You'd think I was a little girl," Allie mumbled. "I'm a grown woman, with a mind of my own," she said louder. "I don't need my daddy telling me when to go to bed."

"I heard that," her father said.

Swede's lips twitched, but he fought the smile.

Allie stared at him through narrowed eyes. "Don't laugh. It only encourages him."

Unable to hold back, Swede laughed out loud.

Eddy clapped a hand on his back. "She's as stubborn as her father."

Allie glared at Eddy. "I'm in the room."

Georgia patted her back. "Yes, dear, you are. Now, go to bed. Maybe a good night's sleep will improve your disposition."

"My disposition is just fine, thank you very much." But she rose from her chair, carried her plate to the sink and climbed the stairs to her room.

Swede waited thirty minutes before going to bed, giving Allie enough time to get through the shower and back to her room. He didn't want to bump into her in the hallway. He was afraid he'd try to kiss her again. And that wouldn't do.

Sleep was a long time coming, and dawn arrived too soon.

The sound of boots on the stairs woke him. He hurried to dress and get downstairs before the others left without him.

Lloyd and Eddy were just finishing breakfast when Swede walked into the kitchen.

"You two can join us at the barn when you're done here," Mr. Patterson said. "We have to connect the trailer and fuel the tractor."

"I won't be long," Swede promised.

Georgia set a heaping plate of food in front of him.

He stared down at it. "Looks good, ma'am, but I can't eat all of that."

She laughed. "You'll burn it off before noon. Eat."

Allie entered, dressed in jeans, a long-sleeved shirt, boots and a cowboy hat. She tossed another cowboy hat on the table next to Swede. "That's one of Hank's old hats. You'll need it today. Try it."

Swede settled the hat on his head. It fit perfectly.

Allie sat across from him, but never lifted her head to look him in the eye.

Georgia kept up a running commentary about some of the local gossip, seemingly unaware of the tension between Swede and Allie.

By the time Swede choked down half of the food Georgia insisted he eat, he'd had enough. He pushed back from the table, lifted his plate and carried it to the counter. "Please cover that, and I'll eat the rest for dinner tonight."

"Are you sure?" she asked.

"Positive." He kissed the older woman's cheek. "Thank you for all you do."

Georgia blushed and waved a hand at him. "Get out of here. You'll have Eddy jealous if he catches you kissing me."

Allie stood as well and carried her plate to the sink. "Thank you, Georgia."

"I'll bring sandwiches for lunch," Georgia promised.

Swede walked out of the house first and scanned the vicinity, not expecting trouble, but keeping aware was an essential part of his job. They hadn't expected trouble at Reynolds's stable, and it had exploded in their faces.

Hank arrived as Swede and Allie joined Eddy and Mr. Patterson at the barn. Eddy would bale the hay while the other men loaded the bales on the trailer.

Allie drove the truck through the hayfield, inching along at a snail's pace. Ruger walked along beside the truck, occasionally chasing a rabbit or digging for a prairie dog.

Swede considered himself in pretty good shape since rehab, but the work was hard, the hay was itchy, and the sun beat down on them throughout the day. By noon, Swede and Hank had shed their shirts, their bodies covered in sweat and hay dust.

"It's been a while since I've hauled hay," Hank said. "Now I remember why I disliked it." He ran his hand through his hair, loosening the stray straws. "But, you always feel good about what you accomplish when all the bales are neatly stacked in the barn."

Swede tossed another bale on top of the ever-increasing stack. Hank's father manned the top of the pile, stacking the bales in an overlapping pattern to keep them from falling off. "It's good, hard work." And it helped him keep his mind off Allie. Except she was driving the truck. Every time he glanced up, he could see her face in the side mirror.

As her bodyguard, it was hard not to focus on her. Even out in the hayfield, he had to be on his toes. Whoever shot at them from the vehicle the other night, could be hiding at the edge of the pasture with a high-powered sniper rifle.

Swede glanced around again, his gaze coming back to Allie in the mirror.

"Did Bear hear anything new from the police?" Swede asked. Anything to take his thoughts off Allie.

"Nothing we didn't already know from talking to Baker and his parents." Hank tossed a bale up onto the back of the trailer. "Bear would have come to help here, but he's headed to Baker's unit to wait for the commander to return from Wyoming."

"I'd like to get my hands around the throat of the guy who attacked the kid."

"You and me both." Hank wiped the sweat from his brow and walked to the next bale in the field. "It's bugging the crap out of me that I can't come up with a single motivation for the attack."

"It's some crazy son-of-a-bitch who happened by at the same time Baker felt like having a hamburger."

Hank shook his head. "My gut tells me the attack is more than that."

"I'd like to help with the investigation," Swede said.

"You are, by keeping an eye on my little sister. She's got enough problems." Hank shot a glance toward Allie. "I tried to call Reynolds last night. He didn't pick up. I left a message, but he didn't get back to me."

"Allie doesn't even know where he went on his business trip," Swede said. "What kind of guy leaves his fiancée a few days before his wedding and doesn't share where he's going?"

"Maybe he's having an illicit affair with one of his clients." Hank's jaw tightened. "In which case, I'll have to kill him for hurting my sister."

"Get in line." Swede's fists clenched. He flexed his injured hand, the ache building with each bale. But he didn't stop to cry about it. The ache reminded him to keep focused on what had to be done.

Protect Allie.

"Has Allie said anything about what she'll do if her fiancé doesn't show up for the wedding?"

"Not at all. She keeps repeating that she's getting married Saturday." Swede chuckled. "I believe if Reynolds doesn't show up for his wedding, she'll kill him."

Hank laughed out loud. "Sounds like Allie. She's a very determined and stubborn woman. She gets it from our father."

"What does she see in Reynolds?"

"I haven't a clue, and I really don't know him well enough to judge him. Except that he's not here when shit's hitting the fan with my sister. That's a really big strike in my book." Hank glanced up at his father on top of the stack of hay. "Does my father know why you're here?" he said in a lowered voice.

Swede shook his head. "Allie insisted on calling me a friend from college, here for her wedding. Mrs. Edwards knows."

"It's probably just as well. My father might go off half-cocked with both barrels loaded, looking for the crackpot taking shots at his little girl. And I don't think he approves of this marriage."

"Does anyone, except Allie?" Swede chose that moment to glance at the mirror.

Allie was staring back at him, her eyes narrowed. Had she heard him mention her name?

Swede switched sides of the truck. Seeing Allie in the mirror only made him want to shake her. Why was she insisting on marrying a man who clearly didn't care enough about her to be there when she was in trouble? Trouble that could have been brought on by his own business dealings, and her association with him.

When Reynolds returned from his business trip, Swede wanted to have a few words with the man.

THE DAY CRAWLED by at the pace Allie drove the pickup pulling the hay trailer. She counted the minutes until all of the hay was loaded into the barn. Then, and only then, could she get away from the sight of a shirtless Swede, muscles bulging with the weight of the bales as he tossed them like toys into the air. Every time she glanced into the side-view mirror, he was there, looking back at her. How was she supposed to quit thinking about him when he was larger than life and freakin' gorgeous in all his sweaty glory?

Her call to Damien the night before had gone unanswered. Same with the voicemail she'd left, asking him to return her call. He was probably in some far corner of the world where cell phone reception was as crappy or non-existent as it was in the rural areas of Montana.

Still, the man was getting married in two days. The least he could do was call his fiancée each night to whisper sweet nothings in her ear and tell her how much he loved her.

Allie frowned into the mirror at the same time Swede glanced up.

Come to think of it, Damien hadn't said he loved her since the day he'd proposed. Sure, the occasion had been romantic. He'd taken her to one of the most expensive restaurants in Bozeman and then they'd walked along the city streets afterward, arm-in-arm. When they'd come to the city park, the almost-full moon overhead gave just the right amount of light so they didn't need flashlights to see their way.

Damien had stopped, pulled her into his arms and stared into her eyes.

No man had ever held her like that. Most men she knew treated her like one of the guys, until Damien came along and reminded her that she was a woman, with all the needs and emotions most women had.

Then he'd dropped to one knee and asked her to marry him, and she'd been thrilled that a man thought she would make a good wife. But, was that enough to commit her life to a man she still barely knew?

The more she thought about it, the more she realized she might have made a huge mistake by saying yes.

If only she could talk to Damien. Maybe she'd get back that spark of excitement and be happy about the upcoming nuptials instead of feeling like Saturday would be one big disaster.

She was glad she'd insisted on a small wedding with family and a few friends.

The sooner she spoke to Damien, the better. Waiting until the actual wedding would be too late.

In the meantime, Allie drove a few feet forward at a time, gnashing her teeth, counting the bales until they were done. And they wouldn't be done until all of the hay was neatly stored in the barn.

Could this day get any longer?

By late afternoon, the last bale had been stacked in the barn. Though it was late, the sun wouldn't set for another hour or two. The men shook hands and parted, Hank heading home, Eddy heading for the foreman's house for a shower, her father and Swede for the main house.

Allie entered behind the two men and stopped in the kitchen.

Swede stopped, too, turning back toward her.

"Go ahead," she said. "You can have the first shower. I didn't sweat as much as you did." She wandered into the living room, and waited until she heard the water running.

Georgia had run over to the foreman's house for a few minutes, and Allie's father was in his own room showering.

With no one watching her, and her need to talk to Damien so important to her future, Allie decided to make a break for it. Perhaps Damien was back at his ranch and she could corner him for answers to all the burning questions she'd stored up since he left. Number one being, *why the hell did you ask me to marry you?*

She left the house and hurried to the barn. Catching and saddling a horse would take too long, so she pushed the four-wheeler out behind the barn and pressed the start button. The Bear Creek Ranch and the Double Diamond were both large spreads, but they adjoined on the southern border.

Allie had made the ride on horseback several times, and once on the four-wheeler. The terrain wasn't too challenging, and she could get there and back in less than an hour. Surely Damien would be home by now.

She sped away, hoping no one saw her leave. Since her decision wasn't planned, hopefully that attacker wasn't watching. If he had observed her all day, maybe he'd think she was done for the night when she'd gone inside the house. Either way, she was pretty good on the four-wheeler and confident enough in her skills to elude the bad guys. She hoped.

The trip across the ranch took twenty minutes and wouldn't have taken that long if she hadn't had to dismount, open three gates, drive through and close them behind her. Soon she was driving up to the mansion that could be her home in just two days. The broad columns and huge windows were stunning. But, would she fit in that house? Would the place feel like home? Could she be the kind of wife a businessman like Damien needed?

Did she want to be that kind of wife?

The sight of the burned-out hull of the stable and the scent of charred lumber made her want to gag. Nothing had been done to clean up the mess or start building a new stable to house the fine horses Damien kept. Perhaps that would be her first goal as the new wife of the owner. Allie dismounted, climbed the stairs to the front entrance and rang the doorbell.

Miles opened the door. "Miss Patterson, so nice of you to stop by. But I'm afraid Mr. Reynolds hasn't returned from his business trip. Would you care to come in for a cool beverage?"

Not really. Allie needed to talk to Damien.

Miles opened the door wider and Allie entered, wanting to see again what she was getting into by marrying the most eligible bachelor in the county. Hell, maybe in the whole state of Montana. How had she landed a catch like that?

The entryway floors of marble tiles stretched all the way into the main living area at the back of the house with twenty-foot ceilings and windows stretching the full height and length of the room. She could see from the front to the back of the house and through the windows to the snow-capped peaks of the Crazy Mountains.

"Miss Patterson, if you'd like to have a seat, I can get you that drink. What would you like?"

Allie stared around the room, feeling like an interloper, a stranger, a square peg in a round hole. This place didn't fit her personality. She'd be afraid to put her feet on the coffee table or wear her boots inside.

"Nothing, Miles. I'm sorry, but I can't stay." Though it never had in the past, the pure ostentatiousness of the decor threatened to overwhelm her now that she stood in the middle of the living room without Damien at her side. She'd mistaken the way he belonged for her belonging there, as well. Now she couldn't get out of there fast enough.

Allie turned and started for the door.

"Miss Patterson, Mr. Reynolds asked me to give you a piece of luggage from the set you two will be taking with you to the Cayman Islands on your honeymoon. Would you like to take it with you now, or would you like me to deliver it to your house tomorrow?"

She didn't want it at all. But she couldn't tell Miles she was getting cold feet. And she didn't want him to make the trip to the ranch, wasting his time if she decided to chicken out at the last minute. "No need to deliver it, Miles," she said.

"Then I'll collect it and bring it out to you in just a moment."

Before Allie could correct Miles and tell him she really didn't want the case, she watched him disappear into the cavernous house.

Great. Now she'd have one more thing to lug back to the ranch, and it would get dusty on the cross-country trip. Feeling like a fool, Allie left the house and walked out to the ATV. From where she'd parked, she stared at the shell of the stable, wondering who would have been heartless enough to destroy such a lovely building, nearly killing the animals inside.

Miles hurried out of the house, carrying a medium-sized, brown leather suitcase. When he noticed she was on the ATV, he stopped and frowned. "I thought you had arrived in your truck. Perhaps I'll deliver this tomorrow, after all."

"No worries, Miles. I can strap it to the back of the four-wheeler. It won't get any more roughed up than it would by the baggage handlers at the airport."

"If you're sure." Miles held the case clutched to his chest.

Allie reached for the bag, and Miles handed it over. She strapped it to the rack on the back of the four-wheeler and climbed aboard. "If Mr. Reynolds makes it in tonight, tell him it's imperative that he call me immediately."

"I will," Miles promised. "Stay safe, Miss Patterson."

Allie rode out across the pasture, her heart heavy, the suitcase banging against the rack behind her. The closer it came to her wedding day, the more convinced she became that it wouldn't happen. But, she couldn't call it off without first speaking with Damien. Doing so was only fair. She refused to be a bride who jilted the groom at the altar. A day early was better than when all the guests were seated and waiting.

Halfway back to the ranch, she crested a hill and started down into a valley. So wrapped up in her own miserable decision and the consequences she faced, she didn't hear the other engine over her own until an ATV roared up beside her and rammed into her back tire. Her four-wheeler lurched and swerved toward a drop-off.

Heart thumping, she managed to straighten the steering wheel. She thumbed the throttle, sending her vehicle racing ahead. Fortunately, she was back on the Bear Creek Ranch and she knew every inch of the place like the back of her hand.

Speeding across the rocky terrain, she topped a rise so fast her wheels left the ground for a second and then slammed to the earth on the downward slope. She cursed herself for riding out without carrying the requisite shotgun. Too far from the barn to make it back quickly enough, she had to go in defensive mode. If she could put enough distance between them, she knew of a place she could hide until the attacking rider gave up and went away.

Now would be a good time for her bodyguard to discover her missing and come looking for her.

AFTER ONLY FIVE minutes in the shower, Swede walked out, his towel slung over his shoulders, wearing only blue jeans. He stopped in front of Allie's open bedroom door. Nothing moved inside. He stepped in and looked around. "Allie?" No answer.

Not too worried, Swede entered his bedroom, pulled a clean T-shirt out of his duffle bag and dragged it over his head.

Allie had been downstairs when he'd gone for his shower. He'd let her know it was her turn. Pulling on a pair of boots, he hurried down the stairs, his feet moving faster each step he took, a niggling feeling creeping across his skin. "Allie?"

The back door creaked, and footsteps sounded in the kitchen.

Swede headed that direction only to find Georgia checking the contents of the oven. "Have you seen Allie?" he asked.

Georgia straightened. "I thought she'd gone for her shower."

At that point, Swede's belly clenched. "She's not in her room, nor in the shower. I just came from upstairs."

"What's for supper?" Lloyd entered the kitchen and sniffed. "Something smells good."

"Mr. Patterson, have you seen your daughter since we came inside?" Swede asked.

He shrugged. "Not since I went up for a shower. She might be out at the barn. Although, Eddy said he'd feed the animals. Maybe she decided to help."

"Eddy was in the shower when I left our house," Georgia said. "He didn't say anything about Allie."

"I'll check the barn," Swede said.

"I'll check around the house," Georgia said.

"Why the worry?" Lloyd asked, following Swede out the back door. "She's always fiddling around the barn."

"I just want to make sure she's all right," Swede said.

"Why wouldn't she be?" her father asked.

Swede didn't answer. He opened the barn door and entered. All the horses were in their stalls. Which meant she hadn't taken one out to exercise or ride, she wasn't anywhere around the barn and her truck was in the driveway.

Mr. Patterson stood near the rear of the barn, staring into

an empty corner where a four-wheeler had been parked the day Swede and Allie had mucked the stalls. "You don't suppose Allie took the four-wheeler out to check on that sick heifer, do you?"

Damn. Swede walked out the back door of the barn. As he suspected, he found fresh tire tracks in the dust. Allie had gone out alone on the four-wheeler.

"Sir, do you have another four-wheeler?" Swede asked.

"Nope. Just the one."

"Please, go get Mr. Edwards while I saddle up. We need to find Allie."

"Why are you so worried about her? She does this all the time."

Swede wanted to leave and find Allie, but he owed it to her father to let him know what was going on. "Mr. Patterson, I'm sorry, but we didn't want to worry you. I'm not Allie's friend from college. I was hired by Mr. Reynolds to be her body-guard. Several attacks have occurred around your daughter. We need to find her before someone else does."

"You mean to tell me that shooter from the other night wasn't just a random act?"

Swede shook his head. "Not only did someone take a shot at us on our way back from the Blue Moose Tavern, he tried to run us off the road. And the day we went out to check on the heifer, a man on an ATV tried to run your daughter over. We need to hurry."

9

———

ALLIE ROUNDED A ROCKY CORNER, ducked between boulders, and rode down the middle of a stream for a short distance to hide her tracks and then climbed up the bank into a stand of trees surrounded by low brush. Behind the trees rose a bluff with several caves carved out by centuries of water flowing through the rocks. If she could make it to the caves, she had a chance of hiding inside one she and Hank used to play in as teenagers.

She ditched the ATV behind the brush, jumped off and ran, ducking to avoid low-hanging branches, leaping over medium boulders and glancing over her shoulder every four or five steps.

The sound of an engine nearby made her run faster. She had to make it to the cave before he saw her. The biggest challenge was once she started up the rocky path, she could be visible from below. She clung to the bottom of the bluff for as long as she could until she stood almost directly below the cave entrance. To get there, she had to climb over huge rocks. Eventually, she'd rise above the treetops and scoot along a ledge to enter. A thin waterfall ran out of the mouth of the cave, dropping one hundred feet to a stream. One slip on the climb upward and she could make that same fall and, like the water, splatter all over the river rocks below.

As long as her attacker was still on the ATV, he might not be able to see her climbing up the side of the bluff. He'd have to have a clear line of sight from the bottom of the bluff through the branches of the trees.

Allie took a step, slipped and caught herself before tumbling over the side. Her heart pounded so loudly in her ears she could barely hear anything else. She stopped, crouched low in the rocks, and listened. She could hear nothing but the whoosh of the wind through the trees.

Sweet Jesus. She had to move even faster. If the man had found her ATV, he might figure out she'd gone up the bluff to the caves.

Her muscles ached and her lungs burned with the extra effort to pull herself up the side of the bluff. Finally, she arrived at the cave and fell inside, crawling deeper into the shadows.

She lay still for several minutes, filling her lungs with the cool, damp air, straining to listen for the sound of someone climbing up after her. Allie pushed to her feet, her knees wobbling, her body drained.

Why had she ducked out on Swede? All she had to do was ask him to take her to the Double Diamond Ranch. He would have. If she'd found Damien there, Allie could have taken him aside, out of earshot of Swede, and told him how she was feeling. Yes, the discussion would have been awkward. But she wouldn't be in the situation she was in now.

The sound of a pebble bouncing off other rocks made her freeze. Allie shrank into the back of the cave near a tunnel that led even deeper. She didn't want to go much farther without a light, but she would, if she had to.

A shadowy silhouette appeared in the mouth of the cave.

Allie swallowed a gasp and slipped deeper into the tunnel.

Swede tied Little Joe to the hitch, ran to the tack room and grabbed the saddle he'd used the last time he'd ridden. Blanket, saddle, girth… he fumbled, trying to remember how Allie had looped the leather strap through the girth. Once he had it tight enough, he ran back to the tack room for the bridle.

"We have to find her, Little Joe," he said to the horse, slipping the bit between his teeth.

Outside the barn, Ruger waited patiently for Swede to give him permission to go with him.

"Come on, Ruger, we have to find Allie."

The dog tipped his head.

Mr. Patterson and Eddy came running from the house.

"We had a call from Miles, Damien Reynold's butler. He wanted to know if Allie had made it back to the house all right."

"She rode an ATV all the way over to the Double Diamond? It's over five miles."

"By the highway," Mr. Patterson stated. "She probably went cross-country. She knows the way and can get there and back fairly quickly on an ATV."

Then why wasn't she back already? Swede didn't say it, but he could see the same question in Lloyd and Eddy's faces.

"We'll saddle up and be right behind you." Eddy pointed across the pasture. "Head toward the gap between those two hills. You're armed, right?"

Swede patted the handgun beneath his jacket. "I am."

"Good. We'll catch you as soon as we saddle the horses."

Eddy had already disappeared into the barn. Lloyd followed.

Swede nudged the horse's flanks with his heels, and Little Joe sprang forward. God, he wished he'd had the ATV. He wasn't sure he'd be of much use on horseback. Going on foot wasn't an option. He might not reach her in time.

"Come, Ruger!" he called out.

The dog shot ahead of the horse, racing across the pasture like he knew where he was going.

Swede hoped he did. He hadn't trained Ruger to track a person, nor had he given the dog something of Allie's to sniff. But Swede felt more confident with the animal by his side, especially with Little Joe eating up the pasture beneath his feet. Galloping was much easier on the seat than trotting any day, and the gait got him where he needed to go faster. He just hoped when it came time to slow down, the horse would know what to do.

Riding on wings and a prayer, he charged across the pasture, aiming for the gap between the hills. As he topped a rise, the vista changed. On the other side of the hills were more hills, some rocky with steely gray bluffs. This was a different route than Allie had taken him two days before. As he raced through the divide, he hoped Eddy and Lloyd would catch up to him soon before he compounded the problem by getting lost.

Little Joe slowed, the ground beneath his hooves getting rockier and more treacherous. As Swede neared the base of one of the bluffs, he saw movement out of the corner of his eye. At first, he thought it might be a bird flying up the side of the cliff. When he turned and glanced up, he saw a figure in black entering a cave.

Swede pulled back on the reins so hard Little Joe reared and nearly trampled Ruger. Swede held on to the saddle horn and dug his heels into the stirrups, praying the horse didn't tip over backward.

Finally, Little Joe came down on all four hooves.

"Hey!" Swede shouted.

The man in the cave paused and glanced down. He had one hand braced on the wall of the bluff, and he held something in the other hand. Something small and dark…like a handgun.

Swede nudged Little Joe and leaned forward as the horse plowed through brush and trees, crossed a creek and stopped in front of the rocky escarpment.

Even before Little Joe was completely stopped, Swede swung out of the saddle to the ground.

The man at the mouth of the cave turned toward Swede and fired a round.

Swede ducked behind a boulder and waved at Little Joe, afraid the idiot above would hit the horse.

Little Joe spooked and ran, probably headed back to the barn. Ruger crouched next to Swede.

If Swede guessed right, that man up there was after Allie and might have her trapped. He didn't know how deep the cave went. All he knew was the man was armed and had fired on him first. That gave him the right to defend himself, and Allie. However, in order to be effective with a handgun, he had to get closer.

Taking a deep breath, Swede eased out from behind the boulder, spied the next big rock he could use as cover and made a dash toward it, zigzagging as he ran. Ruger ran with him, arriving at the same time as Swede.

Another shot ricocheted off the top of the big rock they ducked behind. Swede performed this maneuver, again and again, moving higher up the side of the bluff, picking his way through the rough terrain as best he could. Within minutes, he was within a reasonable range to fire.

The figure disappeared into the cave.

Damn. Swede took the opportunity to race as fast as he could, stepping over stones, climbing over boulders and pulling himself higher up the trail.

Still, the man didn't appear, making Swede even more anxious, his heart banging against his ribs.

Ruger, on four legs, had much better balance and nimbly climbed the rocky terrain.

"Get 'em, Ruger. Get 'em," Swede said.

The dog raced the remaining yards up the incline and ran into the cave. A shot rang out.

Swede held his breath, praying Allie or Ruger hadn't taken that bullet. Using the remainder of his breath and strength, he heaved himself up over the rocks and ran into the cave.

Though Ruger was only considered a medium-sized dog, he'd tackled and pinned the gunman.

But not for long. The man knocked Ruger to the side, lurched to his feet and dove for his gun.

Swede reached it first, kicking it out the mouth of the cave. The man switched directions and flung himself at Swede.

Barely inside the cave himself, Swede wasn't in a position to take the full force of the man's weight. In a split second, Swede fell to the ground. It was that, or be knocked over the ledge.

The gunman didn't have time to slow his forward momentum. He tripped over Swede's body, stepped in the middle of the waterfall flowing out of the cave's entrance and tumbled over the edge.

He cried out as he plummeted to the base of the falls, landing with a dull thump.

Wasting no time on the dead man, Swede entered the cave, calling out, "Allie? It's me, Swede."

Ruger disappeared into the darkness and whined softly.

"Allie?"

"Swede?" She materialized in front of him, Ruger at her side, his tail wagging a thousand times a minute. For a moment, Allie stared at Swede, her bottom lip trembling.

His heart swelled and he opened his arms.

Allie rushed into them. "I prayed you'd come," she said into his shirt, her voice catching on a sob. "I don't think he would have found me back in the tunnels. But it was really dark, and I've never gone in very deep without a flashlight."

"You're okay, now." Swede smoothed a hand over her hair, speaking to her like he did to the animals in a slow, calming tone, though nothing inside him was calm. He'd almost lost her. She'd been so close to taking a bullet from that man's gun or falling over the ledge to her death on the rocks below.

Swede buried his face in her hair and inhaled the strawberry scent, mixed with the evergreen fragrance of the trees. "You scared the hell out of me."

"I'm sorry." She stared up at him. "I had to go to see Damien."

"I would have taken you."

"I know, but I needed to go by myself."

"And?"

She snorted. "He wasn't there."

Without releasing her, he leaned back enough to cup her cheek. "What was so all-fired important you had to go without me to escort you?"

She stared up at him, her green eyes darkening. "You."

God, he wanted to kiss her. Every beat of his heart urged him to do it. "Me?"

Allie nodded and reached up to touch his face, her fingers tracing the scar along his cheek. "I can't stop thinking about you."

"Funny," he said. "There must be something in the water." He bent his head, no longer capable of resisting those very tempting lips. Before he took them, he asked, "Are you going to slap me again?"

She chuckled, wrapped her hand around the back of his neck and said, "Not a chance." Then she met his lips with hers, kissing him as long and hard as he kissed her.

Swede slid his hands down her back to the base of her spine and lower, pressing her hips to his. Nothing could stop him from claiming this woman's mouth.

Except the shout echoing off the walls of the bluffs.

"Allie! Swede!" Lloyd Patterson's voice boomed through the gathering dusk.

Swede was first to step away. He stared down into Allie's eyes. "Are you okay?"

Allie nodded, pressing the back of her hand to her mouth. She squared her shoulders and nodded again. "We need to call in the sheriff and an ambulance."

"Or a coroner," Swede said. "I'd be surprised if he survived the fall."

Her jaw tightened and her eyes narrowed. "It's wrong of me to say it, but I hope he's dead."

"Not wrong." He slipped his arm around her waist and eased toward the opening of the cave. "In this case, it was us, or him."

Allie tipped her chin. "I choose us."

"His own actions sent him over the edge. The landing did the rest." He gripped her hand. "Come on, your father will be beside himself until he sees his darling daughter."

She shot a glance his way. "He knows?"

Swede nodded. "You turned up missing, so I had to tell him. He was well on his way to figuring it out by then."

Allie sighed. "He'll be mad at me."

"Probably," Swede agreed. "But he'll be happy you're alive and well."

"After we get down from here safely." She peered over the edge. "If I remember correctly, it's easier climbing up than going down."

Swede winked. "We'll help each other."

Picking their way over the rocks, they eased their way down the bluff.

Eddy and Lloyd were at the bottom of the waterfall beside the body of Allie's attacker.

"We heard the gunshots and followed the sound," Eddy said.

Lloyd stared hard at Allie.

"I'm sorry, Dad. I didn't want to worry you."

"My ass," he bit out. "Being a target of someone bent on killing you is a no-brainer. You tell me and everyone else around you. That way we're all looking out for you."

Allie pushed her shoulders back. "You're right."

"And don't go running off alone." Her father nodded toward the body on the ground. "He might not be the only one gunning for you. I'm gonna have words with Mr. Reynolds."

"I went over to his place to have a talk with him, myself," Allie said. "He's not in town."

"After what's happened, I want to take a bullwhip to the boy."

Allie touched her father's arm. "Then you'd end up in jail."

Patterson scowled. "It would be worth it. Any man who skips out of town when his fiancée is in trouble deserves to be whipped. Hell, he doesn't deserve the fiancée, and she'd be smart to tell him so."

"Daddy…" Allie glanced around. She nodded toward the body, lying face down on the rocks. "Who is it?"

Eddy stepped across the rocks, checked for a pulse and shook his head. "Didn't think he'd survive that fall." He grabbed the man's arm and turned him over.

Allie gasped. "That's Will Franklin, Damien's foreman." Her brows drew together. "I'll bet he was also the one who blew up the barn."

"The bastard was conveniently in town when it happened," Swede agreed.

"If he wasn't already dead, I'd shoot him myself." Allie glared at the corpse. "That explosion and fire almost killed five horses."

Swede was so relieved Will hadn't succeeded in killing Allie, he almost laughed at her statement. The image of Will with a gun in his hand, so close he could have fired into the cave and hit Allie, stole all the humor out of the situation.

"How did you guys get here?" Allie asked, looking around.

"Horseback," Swede responded.

Allie's brows rose. "You? Out here?"

Swede nodded. "Little Joe did good. But, he's not above leaving me here to head back to the barn."

Turning to her father and Eddy, Allie asked, "And you two?"

"Our horses are tied to a branch near the creek," Eddy answered.

Allie clapped her hands together. "Then let's get back to the ranch."

"Swede, you can ride double with me," Eddy offered.

"Allie can ride with me," her father said.

She shook her head. "I ditched my four-wheeler in the brush. As long as it starts, I can make it back to the barn on my own four wheels."

"And I'm going with you," Swede said.

"Tell you what," Lloyd said. "You three head on back and

call the sheriff. I'll stay out here until Eddy brings him out. Don't want the wolves destroying evidence."

Eddy nodded.

Swede followed Allie to the stand of brush where she'd hidden her ATV. It was still there, untouched and undamaged, with that damned suitcase strapped to the back.

Allie climbed on and started the engine. Then she turned to Swede. "Hop on."

He slid his leg over the seat and settled behind her, wrapping his arms around her waist.

Being a bodyguard had its perks, but Swede was sure kissing the fiancée of the man he was working for wasn't supposed to be one of them.

Allie revved the engine and took off. Ruger followed, easily keeping up with the pair on the ATV.

Though he was relieved Will Franklin wouldn't be a threat anymore, Swede wasn't sure Allie was out of the woods yet. What beef could Will have had against Allie? Was he afraid she'd usurp his control of the ranch? Or had someone hired him to carry out the threat that had been painted on the side of the stable?

Swede didn't have the answers and, at that moment, he didn't care. What he did care about was the woman in front of him. The one who smelled like strawberries and evergreen forests. She even had a few twigs sticking out of her wild auburn curls.

God, she was beautiful. The more he was with her, the deeper he fell.

It would be tough delivering her to the wedding and letting go. But, he had to. His job wasn't to steal the bride, it was to protect her and give her to another man in two days.

Pressure threatened to squeeze the air out of Swede's lungs. All those bodyguard rules had flown out the window on his first assignment. He wondered if this was really the job for him in the wilds of Montana, or if he should do something less stressful and go be a deckhand on a charter fishing boat.

A strand of auburn hair floated back on him, brushing

across his face, touching him in a way he'd never considered as poignant. It was like a finger stroking him, teasing him urging him to continue to follow this woman, no matter where she led him.

10

Back at the house, Georgia met Allie and Swede in the barnyard.

Eddy had beat them back, riding fast and hard to get to a telephone and call 911.

"Oh, thank God!" Georgia wrapped Allie in a bear hug that nearly crushed her bones. "You had us all so worried. I think I lost a couple of years off my life and gained a few more gray hairs."

"I'm sorry," Allie said, her teeth chattering. Darkness had settled in and the night sky, clear of all clouds, had already begun to release the heat of the day.

The older woman clucked her tongue. "Never mind the scoldin'. The important thing is that you're okay." She stared at Allie. "Oh, baby, you're cold. Let's get you inside."

"Really, I'm okay. Nothing but a few scratches and bruises. I could use a hot shower, though." Things for her could have ended a whole lot worse. At least she wasn't dead, like Will Franklin. A twinge of compassion flickered across her consciousness over the man's death, immediately followed by the strengthening of her will. He had tried to kill her on multiple occasions. Swede might have been collateral damage. "I'll be upstairs if anyone needs me."

Allie marched up to her room, gathered clean underwear and a pair of pajamas, a change from her usual oversized T-shirt. Once in the shower, she turned up the heat and stood under the spray until her insides were as warm as her outsides. When she stepped out of the shower to dry off, she started shaking and couldn't seem to stop.

Never had she been more afraid than when she'd been trapped in the cave with a man wielding a gun. That was the stuff Wild West movies were made of. Thinking a cup of hot cocoa would help, she left the bathroom and padded down the stairs to the kitchen.

Through the kitchen window she could see half a dozen vehicles in the barnyard. An ambulance, a couple of sheriff's deputy's vehicles, and a small first-responder fire truck. Allie glanced down at her pajamas. Maybe she should get dressed to speak to the authorities. She debated going back upstairs, but decided she was fully covered and wanted the hot cocoa more.

Once she took the mug out of the microwave, she pulled on a pair of boots and a jacket, grabbed her cocoa and stepped outside.

Half a dozen people surrounded her, all asking questions at once.

Swede worked his way through the small crowd and slipped an arm around her.

Allie leaned against him, grateful for his solid strength and willingness to stand beside her during the questioning. By the time they'd loaded Will Franklin's body into the ambulance and everyone departed, Allie was mentally and physically exhausted.

"Come on, let's get you inside." Swede touched a hand to her lower back and guided her back to the house.

Instead of going directly inside, Allie stopped on the second step up to the porch. "I'm tired, but too wound up to go right to sleep. I think I need to stay out here for a few minutes. The cool night air helps clear my mind. Go. Get your shower. I won't go anywhere." She held up her hand. "I promise."

"I can't leave you outside alone," Swede said.

"Go," a voice said behind him. "Get your shower. I'll sit with my daughter." Her dad walked out onto the porch, carrying a steaming cup of coffee.

"I'll only be a few minutes," Swede said.

"Take your time." Her father lowered himself to the porch step and patted the space beside him.

Allie sat. She couldn't remember a time since her mother died that her father had sat beside her on the porch steps. Tears welled in her eyes, and she fought to keep them from sliding down her cheeks. What was wrong with her? She wasn't usually this emotional.

Since her mother died and Hank joined the Navy, Allie had tried to be everything her father needed, sometimes forgetting what she needed. Which was probably half the reason she'd accepted Damien's proposal of marriage. He'd seen in her a woman. Not a daughter or a rancher. She'd felt special for a brief moment, the typical female with dreams of a fairytale wedding to a handsome man. But she'd been blinded by the wedding planning. Now she had a big mess to clean up, and she was so tired.

Her father reached out and took her hands in his big, callused fingers. "Allie, I don't say it enough, but I love you to the moon and back."

Tears slipped from her eyes and rolled down her cheeks. Once they'd started, she couldn't hold them back. "Oh, Daddy." She leaned into his shoulder. "I've missed you."

"I'm sorry, I haven't been much of a father since your mother died. I miss her so badly some days I don't know if I can go on."

"Me, too."

"She should have been here for you, to talk with you about all the woman things I can't begin to understand."

"You haven't done so badly. And I've had Georgia to lean on."

"What have I taught you, other than how to be an old grouch? Hell, I ran off your brother."

"He wouldn't have made it through SEAL training if not for

the way you toughened him up. He told me so himself." She squeezed his hand.

"Tonight, I realized just how close I came to losing you." He looked down at their joined hands. "It scared me. Bad. I don't want to lose any more of my family. I'll fight to keep you safe. So, please, if you're in trouble, let me know."

No matter how independent she was, she still needed her father. "I will, Daddy."

He kissed her forehead like he used to when she was a little girl. "If Damien makes you happy, then I'm all for your wedding. But if he hurts you or you want out, I'll have my shotgun ready."

Allie half-chuckled and half-sobbed. "Thanks, Dad. I'll remember that."

A sound behind them made Allie turn.

Swede stood in the doorway, dressed in clean jeans and a blue chambray shirt, his hair wet, his feet bare.

God, he was the most ruggedly gorgeous man Allie had ever seen.

Her father stood. "I need to hit the sack. We have another load of hay to haul in tomorrow."

"I'll help with that," Allie offered.

"Don't you have to get your nails, hair or some such nonsense done for the wedding?" her father asked.

She smiled. "That happens the day of the wedding." If she went through with it. She needed to talk to Damien. Soon.

Again, her father bent and pressed a kiss to her forehead. "Whatever makes you happy, makes me happy." He entered the house, closing the door behind him.

Swede sat in the spot Allie's father had vacated moments before.

Ruger dropped onto the porch directly behind him and laid his head on his paws.

"Are you okay?" Swede asked.

"I am, now." She wiped the moisture from her cheeks and stared out at the moon, shining high above the Crazy Mountains. "I'm sorry about taking off."

"Yeah. About that…" He leaned his elbows on his knees. "Having a bodyguard necessitates a two-way commitment. I can't do my job if you run away."

"I wasn't running away. I needed to see Damien." She shoved her hand through her wet hair, lifting it off her shoulders. "Alone."

Swede nodded. "And he wasn't there."

She shook her head. "No."

"You could have called ahead and saved a whole lot of trouble."

"I know. I called but no one picked up. And, frankly, I wasn't thinking clearly." *I was thinking of you, you big galoot.*

"Would it help if you got a different bodyguard? Bear and I could switch assignments."

"Is that what you want?" she asked, her voice barely above a whisper. "I know I've been less than cooperative, but I'd rather stick with you…if you don't mind." She plucked at the fabric on the leg of her pajamas.

"Better the devil you know, than the one you don't?" Swede asked.

"No." She glanced up at him, though seeing through the moisture pooling again in her eyes was difficult. "I trust you. I know you really do have my best interests in mind." She leaned into his shoulder. "I promise not to take off without you."

"You won't have to put up with me much longer. The wedding is the day after tomorrow. Then you'll be on your honeymoon in the Cayman Islands."

Yeah, that was the plan. If she chose to follow it. She reached for Swede's hand. "Thank you for rescuing me in that cave today."

Swede turned, his knees touching Allie's. "I think the real hero today was Ruger."

Allie swiveled toward the dog at the same time as Swede. She let go of Swede's hand and ran her fingers over Ruger's soft fur. "He was amazing. Did you have him specially trained?"

Swede scratched behind Ruger's ear. "He's a rescue from

the pound. I picked him up because he was on death row. And to tell the truth, he rescued me."

"How could anyone leave their dog behind when they move on?" Allie shook her head. "How did he rescue you?"

"Since the attack that ended my career in the navy, I've had nightmares. Ruger helps get me through them."

Allie looked up from the dog to his master. "How so?"

"Just by being there. When he senses my distress, he nudges me with his nose. It brings me out of the dream world into the real world. Before Ruger…well, I wasn't coping well."

"He is a hero." She patted the dog's head and pushed to her feet. The more she learned about Swede, the more she wanted to know. With another man's engagement ring on her finger, she had no business learning more about Swede. The personal details only made her see him as a man. An interesting man. One with a love for dogs, which put him way up there on her list of great guys.

No, she needed to see Damien, and end her engagement, or go through with the wedding. Until she did that, she had no right to daydream or night dream about another man.

As she stood, she teetered on the edge of the step and would have fallen if Swede hadn't leaped to his feet, grabbed her arms and pulled her against him.

Allie's hands touched his chest, the hard muscles flexing beneath her fingertips. She had the wild urge to run her hands beneath his shirt and feel the skin stretched over those fabulous muscles.

Jerking away her hands, she got her footing and climbed the remaining steps to the porch. "I'd better go to bed. We have another load of hay to haul tomorrow."

"I'd say stay here and let me handle it, but I need you close, so that I can keep an eye on you. We'll do it the same as last time?"

Allie nodded.

"Allie?" Swede reached for her hand and laced his fingers with hers.

She stared at where their hands entwined, her heart racing, her mouth dry.

"Today scared me more than I've ever been scared in my life." He snorted. "And I've been in some pretty hairy situations." He lifted her hand to his lips and pressed a kiss to her knuckles. "I'm glad you're okay."

Electric currents raced up her arm and down her body to pool low in her belly. This couldn't happen. She couldn't be sexually attracted to a man she'd only known a few days. But she was, and it made her feel more alive than she'd felt...ever. An admission which shook her to the core. Using every bit of control she could muster, she pulled her hand from his, anxious to leave him, before she threw herself into his arms and made a fool of herself.

Swede's hand dropped to Ruger's head. "I'll see you in the morning."

SWEDE WAITED on the porch several minutes after Allie went inside, afraid that if he followed her, he'd stay with her all the way to her bedroom. Once there he'd convince her to make love with him.

Wrong, wrong, wrong!

He stood beside Ruger, the dog nudging his hand, sensing his turmoil.

"Sometimes I wish I were you, Ruger," he said. "Life as a dog is so much less complicated."

The dog whined and licked his hand.

"Yeah. Until you find yourself on death row and a broken-down veteran saves you from the gas chamber." He ruffled Ruger's neck, made a pass around the exterior of the house, looking for anyone lurking, unwilling to presume Will Franklin was the only one stalking Allie. When nothing moved and Ruger didn't snarl or growl in warning, Swede made his way inside to his room on the second floor. Knowing Allie was in the room on the other side of the wall reminded him of how close she was, yet how far she was out of his reach.

He stripped out of his shirt and jeans and lay on the sheets, naked. The heat he'd felt burning inside when he'd touched her hand and kissed her fingers clung to him, making it difficult to go to sleep. For a long time, he stared up at the ceiling, willing his lust to subside. Time and fatigue finally won the fight, and he fell to sleep.

What could only have been minutes after he'd closed his eyes, Swede was awakened by the sound of quiet sobbing.

Ruger nudged his hand and trotted to the door. Thinking he might have been imaging the noise, Swede listened.

There it was again. The soft sobs were coming from the room on the other side of the wall. He leaped to his feet, dragged on his jeans and hurried out of his room. When he stood in front of Allie's door, he hesitated. If he went in, he wasn't sure he could walk out without touching her. And touching her wasn't all he wanted to do.

Another sob was the deciding factor. He tapped on the door and, careful not to wake her father, called out softly, "Allie."

Continued sobbing made him grab the door handle and twist. It opened easily, and he stepped inside, closed the door behind him and crossed to stand beside her bed before the next sob shook her body.

"Oh, darlin'," he said, his heart clenching inside his chest.

Tears stained her cheeks and her bottom lip trembled. Her legs thrashed, trapped in the sheets. Whatever she dreamed was either breaking her heart or terrifying her. Maybe both.

Swede couldn't stand by and do nothing. He scooted her over on the mattress and slid onto the bed beside her, pulling her into his arms. "Wake up, Allie. You're having a bad dream."

She rolled onto her side, burying her face into his bare chest, her hand resting against his skin.

The strawberry scent of her hair was almost his undoing. He couldn't stay long, or he'd be tempted to kiss her.

She took a shuddering breath, her fingers flexing and curling against him.

Swede tried again, his power of resistance waning with

every passing second she lay in his arms. "Sweetheart, you need to wake up. You're dreaming."

"If I'm dreaming, please...don't wake me," she said, her voice low and gravely, spreading over him like melted chocolate.

With a groan, Swede clutched her tighter, his groin tightening, the blood rushing from his brain to parts farther south. He was losing it, and he had no way of letting go.

Allie's hand slid down his chest to his abdomen and lower still to where he'd only half-buttoned his fly.

Swede sucked in a breath, afraid to move lest he encourage her to keep going. This wasn't what he'd come to do. But he couldn't deny the magnetic attraction he had for this woman.

Her fingers slipped beneath the waistband of his jeans.

He covered her hand with his. "Allie, you have to know what you're doing. You can't be asleep on this."

"I'm awake," she said, opening her eyes.

From the little bit of moonlight edging its way through a gap in her closed curtains, he could see her staring up at him. "I should go," Swede said.

Her hand flatted against him. "Please, don't. Stay with me."

"I can't stay and not touch you."

She took his hand and slid it up under her pajama top to the rounded swell of her breast. "Then touch me."

His fingers slowly curled around her breast, weighing the fullness of it in his palm. Swede groaned. "God, you feel amazing."

She reached for the hem of her pajama top and pulled it up over her head, tossing it to the side.

"What about your fiancé?"

"It's over," she said. "I can't marry him."

Swede froze, his thumb and forefinger arrested in pinching her nipple. "Why?"

"After all that's happened, I've learned that I don't love him. I was in love with the idea of getting married, not with the man I was going to marry."

Swede leaned over and kissed the corner of her mouth,

then her lips. "But your wedding is in two days," he said against her lips.

"Not anymore. I'm not going through with it," she said. "I'm telling Damien tomorrow."

Knowing he should wait until after she officially called off her engagement, Swede couldn't stop fondling her breast or kissing her lips. What had started as a means to comfort her had become an entirely different scenario he was ill prepared to fight against. This internal battle was one he was all too willing to concede.

The question was, could he live with himself the next day?

11

The moment Allie felt Swede's arms around her, she knew she couldn't let him go. Her dream had shaken her. She'd been hiding in a dark cave, while a man with a gun stood silhouetted in the light, pointing at her. Her feet had felt cemented to the floor, her heart pounding so hard she couldn't catch her breath.

Then Swede's arms wrapped around her, and more than that, his voice penetrated the dream, bringing her to the surface of consciousness.

Wrapped in his embrace, she turned to him, running her hand across his warm skin, inhaling the light, musky scent that belonged only to him. This was where she wanted to be.

Only she wanted to be closer. Skin to skin. Allie wanted him inside her, filling her, making her complete. What started as a rescue from a dream quickly transformed into an aching need to be with him. A need so strong, she couldn't deny it a moment longer. "Please, stay with me," she repeated.

She laid her hand over his as he fondled her breast, the tingling sensations sending shocks of electricity throughout her body. At a touch of his lips, she opened to him, thrusting her tongue between his teeth, meeting him halfway in a long, sensuous caress. Allie pulled her top over her head, desperate to be with him, to feel him against her, their hearts beating together.

Swede's lips brushed across hers, kissing a path down the side of her neck, stopping long enough to tongue the wildly beating pulse at the base of her throat. As he moved downward, he nipped her collarbone, kissed the top of her breast and sucked a nipple into his mouth, pulling gently, tapping the nipple with the tip of his tongue until it hardened into a tight little bead.

Allie arched off the mattress, wanting him to take more.

He obliged, drawing more of her into his mouth, flicking the tip, again and again.

Taking momentary control, Allie guided him to her other breast. "Please," she moaned softly.

And he did please, nibbling the peak, rolling it around on his tongue and laving it until Allie thought she would come apart.

Swede moved his lips across her ribs, past her belly button and onward to the elastic waistband of her pajamas. Inching the fabric down her legs, he paused to kiss the tuft of hair over her sex. Then again to lick the inside of her thighs, and finally to nip her ankle as he tossed the garment to the floor.

Allie parted her legs automatically, making room for him to slide between.

Swede lifted her knees, positioning them beside his head and then slipped his finger through her curls. He parted her folds, touched his tongue to that little strip of flesh packed with what felt like thousands of nerve endings, sizzling with heat, sending messages to her brain and back to her core, making Allie slick with desire.

Just when she thought it couldn't get better, he pressed a finger to her entrance and swirled.

"Oh, God," she said, digging her heels into the sheets, pushing her hips upward. "Oh, God."

He pushed two fingers into her and licked her nubbin in a long, slow stroke, pushing Allie to the very edge of sanity.

She teetered on the brink until he flicked and teased her

there, thrusting his fingers in and out at the same time. The combination rocketed her to the heavens, flinging her past the stars. She held onto his hair, riding the wave all the way, her core pulsing, her breath lodged in her lungs until she finally drifted back to earth and sucked in a lungful of air. Then need drove her to tug on his hair, drawing him up her body.

He leaned over her, pressing his lips to hers for a brief second.

"You're overdressed," she commented.

"I'm working on it." Swede rolled off the bed onto his feet and shucked his jeans, retrieving his wallet from his pocket as he did.

He was beautiful in a purely male way, with shoulders impossibly broad, narrowing to a trim waist. Firm, six-pack abs and…yes…his shaft jutted out straight and proud.

Allie's channel convulsed, liquid sliding through, dripping onto the sheet. "Hurry," she said, her belly tight, her lungs dragging in air in spasms.

"Protection." He pulled a foil packet from his wallet.

Allie leaned up, snatched it from his hand and applied it, rolling her fingers down his length. She fell back against the mattress. "Oh, sweet Jesus. Please. I can't wait another minute."

"Beautiful, and impatient." He spread her legs, running his hand up the insides of her thighs to the apex where heat radiated. Swede pulled her bottom to the edge of the bed, hooked her legs over his arms and pressed his cock to her entrance.

"Now," she urged. "Take me now."

He thrust into her, driving all the way to the hilt before he stopped. Her channel was so slick with juices inspired by all the foreplay, he slid right in, filling and stretching her deliciously.

Allie grabbed his ass and held him there, letting her body adjust to his length and girth. Then she eased him away and back in again.

Swede took over from there, moving in and out, gradually accelerating until he pumped in and out like a piston on an engine.

Raising her hips to match his every thrust, Allie urged him on, the friction causing the heat to build.

Swede's face tensed, his jaw tightened, and he threw back his head. If they'd been alone in the house, Allie was sure he'd have shouted or called out her name.

Instead, he slammed into her one last time and remained buried deep within, his cock pulsing, his muscles tight, his face set. Then he scooted her back on the bed, crawled up beside her and pulled her into his arms.

Allie nuzzled his chest, finding a little brown nipple. She touched it with her tongue, loving the taste of this man. Pressing closer, she basked in the skin-to-skin contact, her heartbeat slowing, her breathing returning to normal. Gone were the residual effects of the nightmare. In its place was the utterly poignant satisfaction of great lovemaking with an amazing man.

As she drifted to sleep, a nagging twinge of guilt made her stomach churn. Tomorrow, she'd break off her engagement. Tomorrow, she'd call off the wedding. Even if nothing came of her relationship with Swede, Allie knew in her heart, she didn't love Damien. A marriage between them would never have worked.

She wished he had been home earlier that evening so she could have made the break then. Tomorrow would have to be soon enough.

SWEDE LAY FOR A LONG TIME, loving the feel of Allie in his arms, her soft body pressed up against his hard one, the smell of strawberries wafting beneath his nose. This must be what heaven felt like. He couldn't imagine anywhere else being as wonderful.

But the longer he lay there holding the woman he found himself falling for, the more that kernel of guilt grew into a sour wad in his gut. He'd made love to his client's fiancée two nights before their wedding. Not only had he broken the first rule of being a bodyguard, he'd betrayed Hank's trust and risked the reputation of the company his friend was trying to build. With Hank's sister.

Allie slept, seemingly dream-free.

After a while, Swede slipped from the bed, disposed of the condom, pulled on his jeans and left her room, closing the door behind him. From now until Allie called off the wedding, Swede vowed to keep his hands to himself. Touching Allie was strictly forbidden.

He returned to his room and lay on top of the covers, his hand reaching for Ruger's head and the calming influence of a dog who didn't judge. For a long time, he stared up at the ceiling, counting the minutes before sleep finally claimed him again.

MORNING CAME TOO SOON, the sound of Mr. Patterson clomping down the hallway in his cowboy boots waking Swede without need for an alarm. Groggy and with a slight headache pressing against his temples, Swede rose from the bed, dressed, brushed his hair and teeth and went downstairs to the kitchen.

"Eddy and Mr. Patterson already had breakfast." Georgia plunked two plates full of food on the table. "They're gearing up, and said for you and Allie to join them when you're ready."

Allie appeared, her hair pulled back in a ponytail, her face scrubbed clean. No makeup masked the simple beauty of her complexion and eye color.

Her cheeks were naturally blushed and her gaze didn't actually meet his.

"Did you sleep all right?" she asked.

"Yes," he answered. "And you?"

She nodded and took her seat across the table.

They spent the rest of the meal eating, not talking, the atmosphere strained. For such an amazingly close connection the night before, he felt like they were miles apart that morning, even though he could reach across the table and touch her face.

Having only pecked at her food, Allie got up, took her plate to Georgia and gave her a wry smile. "Guess I'm not very hungry. Could you save that for my lunch?"

"Sure can." Georgia's brows dipped. "Are you feelin' okay?"

Allie nodded. "Just a little tired."

"Maybe you should stay in and let me do the driving today."

"I think the fresh air will do me good." Allie kissed Georgia's cheek. "But thanks."

Swede carried his half-eaten plate of food to Georgia. "Thanks for breakfast. You're a great cook." He, too, kissed Georgia's cheek and winked. "See you later."

Georgia touched her cheek, her gaze following Allie out the door. "Look out for my girl out there."

"I will." Swede wouldn't let her out of his sight for a minute. He refused to allow anything to happen to her. His heart was riding on it.

The day flew by in a rush to get all the hay from the second pasture baled, loaded onto the trailer and unloaded into the barn.

Allie drove, not saying much to anyone. Not that the men were in the mood to talk. All of their energy was channeled into the work. By the time the sun crept toward the horizon, Eddy tucked the last bale onto the top of the stack in the barn. "Done."

"What say we have a beer to celebrate?" Lloyd draped a sweaty arm over his daughter's shoulders.

"Thanks, Dad, but I'll pass." Allie lifted her father's arm off her shoulders. "And you smell."

"Good, honest sweat."

For the first time since Swede had met Mr. Patterson, he saw the older man grin.

"That's right, you have a wedding to get ready for." His eyes narrowed. "Aren't you supposed to go out on the town for a bachelorette party or something?"

"No, Dad."

"Why not?"

"I don't feel like it." She turned toward the house.

"What about a rehearsal?"

"Damien and I opted not to do a rehearsal." She gave a weak smile. "I'm headed for the shower."

Swede hesitated before following her.

"Go on," Mr. Patterson said. "Eddy and I will take care of the animals."

"Thank you, sir." Swede hurried after her.

She was up the stairs and in the shower before he caught up.

If he expected any acknowledgement for the best night of sex he'd ever had, he wasn't getting any. He wondered if she really was going to break it off with Damien. Swede's gut tightened. If not, he'd been played for a fool.

But the more he thought about it and everything he'd seen of Allie, she wasn't the kind of woman to play games. That woman was a straight shooter. The more likely reason for her silence today was that breaking her engagement was heavy on her mind. Because she was a straight shooter, she was probably feeling a crap load of guilt for having slept with her bodyguard.

At least that's what Swede hoped.

12

———

ALLIE SHOWERED the dust and itchy hay off her skin, telling herself she'd feel better making the call she had to make with a clean body, if not a clean conscience. After she'd toweled dry, she dressed in shorts and a T-shirt and crossed the hallway. Her gaze drifted to Swede's bedroom, part of her hoping he'd open the door and give her an encouraging smile. She'd need all the encouragement she could get to make that call.

With no one stopping her to engage in conversation, Allie entered her room like she was walking to her doom. Taking a deep breath, she squared her shoulders, lifted the phone and dialed Damien's cell phone number, fully expecting to get the voicemail.

He answered on the second ring. "Alyssa, dear. I'm so glad you called."

"I thought you would be back by now," she said, startled into saying the first thing that came out of her mouth.

"I'm sorry, sweetheart. Business delayed me. I'll be back tomorrow morning."

"The wedding is scheduled for tomorrow, or had you forgotten?" she said, with a little snap in her voice.

"I know. I can't wait for the ceremony that will make you

Mrs. Damien Reynolds. Then we leave immediately for our honeymoon."

"About the wedding—" she started, then had to swallow.

"Don't worry, darling. I'll be there on time. Until then, sweet dreams."

"But, Damien—"

The connection ended.

What the hell?

She dialed his number again and the connection went straight to his voicemail. She hung up and redialed, repeating the process four times until she finally gave up. Mad as hell and ready to end their engagement, she was tempted to do it by voicemail. But she couldn't. No matter how aggravating the man was, he deserved to be told to his face that she wouldn't marry him.

She stared at the clock on the nightstand. As late as it was, she wouldn't have time to contact everyone to tell them not to come to the wedding. What she'd tried so hard to avoid would come to pass. She'd jilt her groom at the wedding.

She stretched out on her bed, fully expecting to lie awake all night long, dreading the next day's confrontation with Damien. And she did. For a while, going back and forth on whether she'd marry him just to save face, and then have the marriage annulled a week later. Of course, she wouldn't go on the honeymoon. But Damien could at least enjoy the time on the beach. The Cayman Islands had been his idea of the perfect honeymoon. Not hers.

Allie would rather have gone to a mountain cabin where they could be alone, making love into the wee hours of every morning. Now, she couldn't picture making love to Damien at all. In her heart, it was Swede. And she couldn't go to him that night because, though she'd gone against her own code of honor and slept with him the night before, she couldn't do it again until she'd made a clean break from Damien.

So she lay in bed, irritated that she couldn't talk to Damien, and so sexually frustrated she thought she might explode.

Finally, she fell to sleep and woke the next day with dark

circles under her eyes and a splitting headache. Which fell in line with the expected wedding day from hell.

SWEDE TOSSED and turned all night long, getting up several times with the full intention of marching into Allie's room and kissing her until she was completely convinced Damien Reynolds was not the man she should marry. Each time, he talked himself out of doing it. Swede was afraid she'd change her mind and marry the bastard anyway.

Allie needed to come to a decision on her own. She said she was going to call it off, but she hadn't come to him to let him know the deed was done.

By morning, Swede assumed it wasn't. Which meant his final duty as a bodyguard was to get Allie to the church on time that morning. He scraped the stubble from his chin, combed his hair, and dressed in pressed black trousers and a white button-down shirt. Strapping on his shoulder holster, he tucked his nine millimeter pistol in place and shrugged into his black suit jacket. Like it or not, he was going to a wedding.

In his best boots, he walked down the stairs, hating that he was taking the only girl he'd ever considered worth the trouble of settling down with to marry another man. He'd talk to Hank and hand over the job of protecting his sister to him. He lifted the phone on the table in the hallway and dialed Hank's number.

"Hello," a female voice answered.

"This is Swede; I'd like to speak to Hank."

"Hi, Swede. This is Sadie. How's Allie holding up?"

"Okay. I guess. She's still in bed as far as I know."

Sadie laughed. "She'd better get moving if she's going to make it to the church on time. Oh, wait. Here's Hank."

"Swede, Bear just walked in the door. Sadie and I are heading to the church as soon as he's debriefed me. I'll see you there." Hank hung up before Swede could ask him to take over his bodyguard assignment. Swede would have to deliver her to the church after all. *Great.*

Footsteps on the staircase made him glance up as he set the phone in the cradle.

Allie descended, wearing her usual jeans and a T-shirt, her hair pulled back in a simple ponytail. She carried a long white garment bag and a pair of white satin shoes. Dark circles beneath her eyes stood out against her pale face.

"Hey," Swede said, reaching for the bag. "Let me."

She held it against her chest, refusing to hand it over. "I can carry it." Allie glanced around him. "Have you seen the others?"

As if on cue, Georgia appeared in the kitchen door. "I've made some muffins you can eat on the way to the church."

"I'm not hungry, but thank you," Allie said.

"You can't get married on an empty stomach," Georgia said. She held up a brown lunch sack. "I packed them for you. You better get going, or Sadie and I won't have time to do your hair. Eddy, your father and I are following you in my van. I have decorations loaded in the back. Eddy's going to help put them on the pews. We'll see you in a few minutes." Georgia disappeared back into the kitchen.

Swede glanced down at Allie. "Ready to go?" He'd wanted to say anything but that. But Allie looked like she had a lot on her mind, and he couldn't make himself bring up the subject of the elephant in the room. Was she going through with the wedding, or would she call it off at the last minute? Swede prepared himself for the former, praying for the latter.

ALLIE LED the way out to her truck. "I'll drive," she stated, climbing into the driver's seat.

On the thirty-minute drive into Bozeman, hardly a word was spoken between them. Swede studied the road ahead and behind, looking out for any signs of trouble. His gut told him Will Franklin wasn't the only one involved in the threat against Allie. And until they found out who was behind it all, he wouldn't consider her safe.

Allie parked in the church parking lot and carried her dress inside. Once through the door, she turned to the right and entered an anteroom where Sadie was waiting with a smile and an assortment of brushes and curling irons. "There you are," she exclaimed excitedly. "Let's get you ready for a wedding."

Swede made a sweep of the room, checking all doors and where they led. He made sure they were locked and secure. "I'll be in the vestibule. If you need me, yell." Swede left the room, not waiting for an answer.

Georgia sailed past him, carrying a veil. "See you fellows in a few minutes."

Swede went in search of Hank, his heart heavy. Hank wasn't in the vestibule so Swede entered the sanctuary.

"There you are." Hank approached him, his face tense. "I have news from Bear."

"Shoot."

"Three more soldiers from that same unit have been attacked since they'd gotten home. All of them were more or less gutted. Those three weren't as fortunate as Baker. They died before anyone could get to them."

Swede swallowed the bile rising up his throat. Three men who'd served their country, killed at home. "Anything stand out other than that they were in the same unit?" he asked.

"Bear talked to the commander and found out the four soldiers had been invited to a party on the last night of their deployment. They came back so intoxicated, they couldn't remember anything about the party the next day."

"Intoxicated? In Afghanistan?" Swede shook his head. "I didn't think they were allowed to bring booze into the country."

"They weren't, but the contractor who threw the party must have smuggled in some. My guess is, that because they couldn't remember anything from the night before, they were slipped some kind of date rape drug."

"Why?"

"Why would they all be cut open when they returned to the States?"

A horrible thought came to Swede, making his belly churn.

"They were being used as God damned mules to smuggle something out of the country."

"Bear dropped by the Medical Examiner who processed one of the men. He didn't find any traces of drugs around the incisions or in the intestines."

"Where did Baker say their unit was stationed?"

"He didn't. But Bear found out from the company commander that they were on the edge of the Badakhshan Province."

"Isn't that province known for the lapis lazuli gemstone mining?" Swede asked, glancing around to make sure they weren't overheard.

Hank's eyes widened. "It is. And for the rampant smuggling of gemstones out of the country."

Swede closed his eyes, anger burning in his gut. "Who was the contractor?"

Hank's face grew taut. "RM Enterprises."

"Aren't they the contracting company that won the majority of the bids to rebuild or construct much of the Afghan infrastructure?"

Hank's lips pressed into a thin line. "Guess who one of the partners in that company is?"

Swede's heart slipped into his belly. "Damien Reynolds, the R in RM?"

"You got it," Hank confirmed. "His partner is a Frenchman by the name of Jean-Claude Martine. From what Bear found out, Martine has a wicked temper. Afghanis who crossed him had been rumored to disappear."

Swede headed for the door. "We need to tell Allie. ASAP. Where's Bear now?"

Hank followed. "He's contacting the FBI, the local police and anyone else he can get on short notice. This place will be lit up like the Fourth of July when everyone gets here."

"In the meantime, we need to keep Damien from making a run for it," Swede said.

"Right. Bear will also have them on the lookout for Martine."

Swede exited the sanctuary and entered the anteroom where Georgia and Sadie were helping Allie prepare for the ceremony.

Georgia was tucking a strand of hair into an updo on Sadie's head when the men barged in.

"Where's Allie?" Swede asked.

Sadie smiled. "She excused herself to go to the bathroom one last time before she put on her dress."

"How long ago?" Hank demanded.

"Not more than five minutes." Sadie's brows furrowed. "Why?"

His pulse racing, Swede responded, "She might be in trouble."

ALLIE KNOCKED on the door of the room the groom should be dressing in.

"Yeah," came the answer.

Still dressed in her jeans, her hair hanging down around her shoulders and no makeup on her face, Allie entered, dread churning her belly.

Damien stood in the middle of the room in front of a long mirror.

Miles stood behind him, brushing his hand over the crisp white shirt, smoothing away imaginary wrinkles.

Allie's gaze swept from the top of his neatly combed dark hair to the tips of his shiny black, patent leather shoes. Damien Reynolds turned heads no matter where he went. Why he'd asked Allie to marry him was beyond reason.

Damien glanced her way. "Darling, I'm not supposed to see the bride before the ceremony."

Allie smiled at Miles. "Could we have a moment?"

Miles nodded and left the room.

"What's wrong?" Damien took her hands and stared down at her clothes, his brows dropping into a frown. "You're not even ready."

"Damien, I can't marry you."

"What? Nonsense. Of course you can. You're just getting cold feet. It happens. Once the ceremony is over, you can relax on our way to the islands." His hands tightened on hers. "You did bring the case I had Miles give you?"

"It's on the back seat of my truck, but I'm serious." She pulled her hands out of his and reached for her engagement ring. "This week, I had time to think about us and I…I'm sorry, Damien." Now that the initial declaration was made, she felt only relief. Allie slid off the ring and tried to give it to him. "I don't love you. I don't think I ever did. I was more in love with the idea of getting married than being married to you."

He held up his hands, refusing to take the ring. "You can't back out on me now. We're getting married in a few minutes."

"I am backing out." She set the ring on a nearby table and moved a few steps away. "I tried to tell you last night, but you hung up on me. I tried calling you all week, but you didn't answer. I would rather have told you all of this before our wedding day. I'm sorry it had to be this way. But our marriage wouldn't have worked."

Damien's face changed from shock to anger. "You can't leave. We're getting married. Go get into your dress."

Allie shook her head and turned to leave.

Damien grabbed her arm in a painful grip and yanked her around. "Look, you can't jilt me. We have to get to the Cayman Islands today. Do you hear me? We're getting married, and that's the end of it."

Throwing up her hand like she'd learned in self-defense class, Allie knocked Damien's grip loose. "Don't touch me ever again. You don't need me to go to the Cayman Islands. Go without me. Goodbye, Damien. Oh, and I hope you figure out who destroyed your barn." Allie stepped out of his reach and hurried for the door.

"Damn you, Allie!" he yelled and made another grab for her.

She'd done what she'd come to do. Allie ran out of the room and down the hallway to the exit. Now that she'd called off her engagement to Damien, whoever was threatening him would have no need to torment her. Footsteps pounded on the tile floor behind her. She glanced over her shoulder at Damien chasing after her.

Allie burst through the side door of the church leading to the playground. She ran around to the front where she'd parked her truck. She could have gone back inside and asked her father or Eddy to drive her home, but right now, she couldn't face them. And Damien was going all whacko on her. She dove into the driver's seat and shut the door just in time.

Damien body-slammed into the side of the truck and slid to the pavement.

For a moment, Allie thought he'd hit his head and hurt himself. She opened the door and got out, stepping over his body.

"Damien?" She bent to shake his shoulder. That's when she saw a bright red stain on the back of his shirt, spreading wider with each second.

As her brain registered that it was blood, she heard a sharp popping sound followed by the window behind her shattering. *Damn.* Someone was shooting at her. Allie threw herself to the ground beside Damien's inert body, glancing all around for the source of the gunshots.

A man ran toward her, his gun held out in front of him.

Allie rolled beneath the truck and out the other side. Before she could get her feet beneath her, someone grabbed her by her hair and slammed her head into the side panel of her pickup.

The blue sky of Montana went black.

13

SWEDE RAN toward the room Damien was supposed to be dressing in for the wedding. He was met in the hallway by Miles, Damien's butler.

"They're gone," the older man said, his face paler than usual.

"Who's gone?" Swede demanded.

"Mr. Reynolds and his fiancée." He pointed to the exit at the end of the hallway. "They ran out that door."

Swede pushed past the man and sprinted for the exit. Outside, he found himself near a playground. A scream sent him running toward the front of the building, Hank close on his heels.

A man in black trousers lay face down on the ground next to Allie's truck, blood staining his white shirt.

"Allie!" Swede shouted, drawing his Glock from the holster beneath his jacket.

"Swede! Be careful! He's got a gun!" she shouted from the other side of the vehicle.

A man who looked like the picture Hank had shown him of Jean-Claude Martine stood, dragging Allie by her hair, a gun with a sound suppressor pointed at her head. "Move, and I'll kill her."

"I'm not moving." Swede held up his empty hand. "Just don't hurt the girl."

"Where's the damned suitcase?" the man said, pulling back hard on Allie's hair. "I want that damned suitcase."

Her face was red, her neck extended back. "What suitcase?" she breathed.

"The one Reynolds gave you. I want it now." He pressed the gun into her temple.

Swede glance around, searching for a miracle to get Allie out of the situation."Martine, let her go. You're not going to get very far."

"Shut up!" He fired into the air and then put the gun to Allie's head again.

"The police and the FBI are on their way. They know you and Reynolds are behind the killings of the soldiers."

"They won't take me. Not as long as I have her." He turned Allie so that her body was positioned in front of him. Again, he spoke next to Allie's ear. "Where is it?"

"In the truck," she said, gasping. "Take it. I didn't want it in the first place. I intended to give it back."

"It wasn't Reynolds's to give in the first place. I made all the sacrifices. Reynolds didn't have the stomach for it, once we started."

"Let go of the woman," Swede said. "Take the suitcase and the truck. Just leave the woman."

"No way. She's my ticket out of here. I'm going, but I'm taking her with me. Make any moves toward us, and I'll kill her. Just try me." He opened the passenger side of the vehicle and tried to shove her inside.

"Swede, don't worry. He's nothing but a rattlesnake." Allie started to climb in, stumbling, her head tipped back so far she probably couldn't see. Then she fell, slipping down to the ground, bringing Martine's hand down.

Swede had only one chance. He had to make it count. He raised his weapon and squeezed the trigger before Martine could jerk Allie back in front of him. The bullet left the chamber.

For a long moment, Martine stood there, his eyes widening. The gun he held to Allie's head slipped from his fingers and dropped to the ground, discharging a round. Then he slumped like a rag doll slipping from a child's hands. His body landed on top of Allie.

Swede ran toward them. "Allie!" Fear knifed through him. Had the bullet from Martine's gun hit Allie?

He rounded the hood of the truck, grabbed Martine's arm and dragged him away from Allie.

She lay still for a heart-stopping moment, her eyes closed, a bruise on her forehead rising into a goose-egg-sized lump. Then she blinked her eyes open and stared up at Swede. "Is he dead?" she whispered.

A huge wave of relieve brought Swede to his knees. "Oh, sweet Jesus, Allie. Yes. He's dead."

Hank rounded the truck and stared down at his sister. "Oh, thank God, she's all right. The cops and the fire department are here. I'll bring them over." Hank left them alone, hurrying over to the emergency vehicles gathering in the church parking lot.

Allie smiled and raised a hand to her forehead, touched the bump and then winced. "That's going to leave a mark."

Swede laughed, gathered her into his arms and held her for a long time, his heart so full he thought it might explode. Allie was alive, the bad guys were dead and all was right with the world, again. His eyes stung with tears, and he blinked them away.

She reached up and cupped his face, her finger tracing the scar on his cheek. "Are you okay?"

He choked on a laugh, his throat constricting. "I'm okay."

"Thanks for killing that rattlesnake."

"You're welcome."

"And for the record, I'm glad you're my bodyguard."

He swallowed against the constriction in his throat. "I am too. You've got a pretty darned amazing body to guard."

She held up her ring finger. "I broke off our engagement before…before that man shot Damien. I'm a single woman."

"That's a good thing, because I'm planning to ask you out on a date."

"What's stopping you?"

"Not a damned thing." He bent to press his lips to hers in a tender kiss. "Allie Patterson, would you go out with a washed-up old navy guy?"

She tilted her head, pausing for a long moment.

Swede held his breath, searching her sweet face until she finally responded.

"No."

His heart skipped several beats and he frowned. "No?"

"No." Her brows dipped low. "But I would consider going out with a highly skilled bodyguard who can shoot like nobody's business." Her smile flashed. "I figure I'll never have to worry about rattlesnakes again."

Swede laughed and hugged her to him.

She pushed away enough to look him in the eye. "I have one condition."

"What's that?"

"Ruger comes along with us."

"Deal."

Then he kissed her, believing for the first time he might just have found his place in the civilian world, on a path to that happy ending he never thought could happen to him. If he played his cards right with Allie, he might be heading in that direction, starting with their first date.

Two weeks later

Swede leaned against the stone fireplace at the White Oak Ranch, a long-neck beer in one hand. He studied the group of men gathered in Hank's house.

Besides himself and Bear, a SEAL from their old unit had joined their ranks, along with another soldier from D-Force who'd worked with them on one of their joint operations back on active duty.

Hank stood in the middle of the room, never more in his

element since he'd left the navy. "Brotherhood Protectors is growing fast. Apparently, there's more of a need for personal security services than I'd originally anticipated, and word is spreading fast. I'd like to welcome you aboard and thank you for giving this organization a chance."

Bear shook his head. "No, Hank, thank you. We're just glad to have jobs."

Hank dipped his head. "You all come highly recommended, and have special training and weapons skills."

"Yeah. For what it's worth." Former D-Force soldier, Carson 'Tex' Wainright rocked back on the heels of his cowboy boots.

Ben 'Big Bird' Sjodin, sat in a leather armchair, his long legs stretched out in front of him. "We're highly trained in combat skills, but there aren't too many opportunities as a civilian to use that training."

"Exactly," Hank agreed. "The challenge is to remember our clients aren't all familiar with the military way of thinking. We need to be open to learning about our clients' lives and what it will take to keep them safe."

Swede chuckled, thinking of Allie and how she'd taught him a few things about ranching. He was getting better at horseback riding and caring for livestock. And he'd taught Allie a few things about shooting she didn't already know. That had been their second date.

"The assignments can be more dangerous than we originally expected," Hank said. "So, don't let your guard down." He nodded toward Swede. "Swede's first assignment was protecting my sister Allie from some seemingly unexplainable attacks. We found out her fiancé was involved in smuggling gemstones from Afghanistan to the U.S., using soldiers as mules. Five people died in that operation. Three American soldiers, Allie's fiancé and his partner."

"His point is, don't think this will be a cakewalk," Swede said.

Hank picked up a handful of file folders. "The good news is we have work. Plenty of it." He glanced in the folders and handed them over to each man, one at a time. "Look over your clients' portfolios and requests. If you have questions, ask now."

The men studied their folders and compared notes, asking various questions about locations and protocol.

After the formal part of the meeting was over, Sadie joined Hank, her hand on her belly, which had begun to show a bit of a baby bump.

"Anyone need another beer?" Allie entered the room, carrying five long-necks. She made her way around the room, dropping them with the men, and coming to a stop in front of Swede. "Who'd you get?" she asked, leaning over his shoulder.

"An older woman afraid her neighbor is planning on taking over the country," he said, liking that she was interested.

Allie's eyes narrowed. "Older woman?"

Swede shrugged. "Really old. Thirty-six."

She crossed her arms over her chest. "I'm not so sure I like the idea of you being a bodyguard to another woman. How do I know you won't fall in love with her?"

"Jealous?" Swede pulled her into his arms and brushed his lips across hers.

"Maybe." She lifted her chin. "You're growing on me, and I don't want to lose you to a cougar."

"We've been out together on fourteen dates, one for each day of the week since we started dating. You're not losing me to a cougar, bobcat or any other kind of feline." He nuzzled her neck. "I have my own little Allie cat. Sweetheart, I'm in this for the duration."

She wrapped her arms around his neck and kissed him back. "Good thing, or I'd have to hire you as my permanent, personal bodyguard."

Swede kissed her long and hard, convinced he'd found the woman for him. Two weeks wasn't a long time, but he knew in his heart he wouldn't find another woman like her. "Babe, I'll guard your body any time you want. How about now?"

Allie threaded her hand in his, glanced around at the others in the room, and, with a wink, tipped her head toward the door. "I'll show you where the teenagers go to neck."

"A woman after my own heart." He chuckled and followed her out of the house. She hadn't been after his heart, but she sure as hell had it in her capable hands.

MONTANA D-FORCE

BROTHERHOOD PROTECTOR SERIES
BOOK #3

New York Times & USA Today
Bestselling Author

ELLE JAMES

ELLE JAMES

MONTANA

D-FORCE

This story is dedicated to women who have been brutally attacked and/or raped. I was raped when I was 13 years old. Looking back, now that I'm much older, I realize what a mistake I made. I should have turned in the young man who raped me, if not to protect myself, then to keep others from falling victim to him. Yes, I knew the guy. He was the brother of my best friend. I don't know where he is now, or what he's doing in life, I just hope he isn't victimizing other women. I should have told... If you are a victim of rape, please, don't keep it to yourself. You could be saving others from being raped by telling your story and putting the rapist behind bars.

Elle James

1

MIA CHASTAIN TWISTED the key in the lock and pushed open the door to her past. Eleven years had passed since she'd been back, for more than a night or two, to the house in which she'd been raised. After she'd left for college, she'd sworn she'd never return to Eagle Rock, Montana. Except for very short visits, and her parents' funeral, she'd kept that promise to herself. Yet, here she was. Entering the house her great-grandfather had built, with the intent to stay for at least a month.

"Are you sure you want to stay here tonight?" Sadie McClain, her old friend from high school stood behind her, carrying the smallest of the suitcases Mia had packed for the trip home. "It's been a year since anyone has been inside this house. It probably needs a good cleaning before you can sleep here."

"I'll be all right. I can cover a lot of ground in the cleaning department in the hours before bedtime."

"I can stay and help, if you like," Sadie offered.

Mia paused with her hand on the doorknob. "You have a husband to go home to. I'll be fine. Besides, I came to Montana for a break from the traffic and noise of city life. I need the chance to regroup and refill my creative well before I start writing my script."

"What you're telling me is that you want to be alone, and I need to scram as soon as I set down this suitcase." Sadie raised her hand. "Don't deny it. I understand your motives. After living in L.A., I needed the peace and quiet of the Crazy Mountains, too."

"Yeah, and I need the time to myself to go through the old place."

"It's been quite a year, hasn't it?" Sadie set the case on the wooden porch and hugged her friend. "I miss your folks, too."

After her parents had passed away the summer before, Mia hadn't had the heart to come home and face the ghosts that lingered in the shadows of Eagle Rock.

Sadie's gaze swept the front of the house. "Don't pay any attention to Marly's comment about this place being haunted. She's just a kid. They enjoy making up stories about deserted places." Sadie rubbed the gentle swell of her belly. She'd just begun to show at five months pregnant. "But if you do get scared, don't hesitate to jump in your car and come stay at the house with us. We have loads of room."

Mia's lips quirked upward at what the waitress at the café had said about her old home. The young people around town thought the house was haunted. It had sat for an entire year without anyone in it, but they swore they saw lights shining through the windows at night.

"Ghosts in the house are the least of my worries," Mia muttered. "I have a deadline. That scares me more than any old ghost."

Sadie smiled. "That's the spirit." She covered her mouth with her hand. "Oops. No pun intended."

The old clapboard home had been Mia's one safe haven in the small town she'd lived in all her young life.

Now that her parents were gone, she needed to decide what to do with the house. Should she sell it, tear it down, or rent it out? To sell or rent it, she definitely had to do some major cleaning and possibly remodeling. At the very least, it needed some repairs. But those would all have to wait.

Deciding what to do with her parents' place was only part

of the reason for her being in Eagle Rock. The main focus of her stay was to work through her writer's block on the script due to her editor in less than a month. Under contract to produce, she didn't have time for a gap in creativity. She had to charge forward and get it done. Or buy back her contract and tell the studio that had optioned the work that she had changed her mind about writing the story after all.

The problem was that the story was too close to home for her. Mia could kick herself for proposing it in the first place. Though it would be a work of fiction, it would drag up so many old, disturbing memories she wasn't sure she could handle it.

Every time she sat down to write, her hands shook so much she couldn't keep them rooted on the keyboard of her laptop. Images flooded her mind and filled her with the terror she'd experienced that day thirteen years ago.

The day she'd been raped walking home from the school bus stop.

A chilling sense of being watched brushed down Mia's spine. She spun to look behind her, but no one was there.

"What?" Sadie glanced around. "Spider walk over your grave?"

Mia shrugged and forced a smile to her lips. "No. I'm just tired from the trip." She stepped into the old house, waited for Sadie to cross the threshold, and then closed the door behind them.

Sadie wandered into the living room. "I remember doing homework with you on that rug." Her lips lifted in a sad smile. "It's too bad you don't live here full time. I could imagine our children growing up in Eagle Rock, going to the same school and coming over to each of our houses to do homework. They'd have sleepovers, go horseback riding and generally raise hell." She laughed softly. "Maybe someday?"

With a noncommittal shrug, Mia said, "Maybe." No child of hers would grow up in Eagle Rock. Not as long as the man who'd attacked her remained free and anonymous.

Mia's gaze went to Sadie's belly.

God, she'd never considered that others might be in danger by her not coming forward and reporting her rape to the police.

Sweet Lord, what if Sadie's baby was a girl? What if she was attacked on her way home from school?

Mia bit down hard on her lip. She hadn't told anyone about what had happened to her. Not even her best friend, Sadie, or even her parents. She'd carried the burden alone, feeling dirty and ashamed, as if she'd brought the attack on herself.

As an adult, she knew how foolish those thoughts were. But as a sixteen-year-old, she couldn't have faced her peers if they'd known she'd been used, her body sullied. For weeks she'd lain in bed, afraid she would end up pregnant with her attacker's baby. He hadn't used protection. Hell, he hadn't expected her to live.

Sadie's hand on her arm brought her back to the present. "What's wrong, Mia?"

Shaking herself out of her morose memories, she forced a smile to her face. "Nothing. It's just sad to see the house this way. Mom always tried to make it cheerful and full of light."

"All you need is to open the curtains and windows to let in sunlight and fresh air." She yanked back a curtain, stirring up a cloud of dust. Sadie coughed. "Okay, well maybe you should slide them back slowly." She waved her hand in front of her face. "Mia, come stay with us until this place is livable again."

Mia shook her head. "Thanks, Sadie, but I've needed to do this for a long time. The only way to get it done fast is to live in the disaster zone." She wiped a finger across an end table, leaving a long streak in the thick layer of dust.

Sadie nodded. "Okay, have it your way. But at least let me walk through the house with you once to make sure nothing is glaringly wrong. Then I'll leave you to it."

"Deal."

Mia and Sadie walked through every room on the first floor, and then on to the second floor. No one hid in the closets or under the beds.

By the time they'd been through the house, Mia felt a little better about staying there alone.

She walked Sadie to her SUV and hugged her. "Thank you for welcoming me home."

"I wish you'd let me do more."

"Maybe tomorrow you can come for a cup of tea?"

"I would love that." Sadie hugged her again. "I've missed you."

"I can't imagine you've had much time to miss me with that big, handsome SEAL keeping you busy." Mia grinned. "I always thought you and Hank belonged together. I'm surprised it took you this long to figure it out."

Sadie's face glowed with her love for the man. "We had to be in the same place at the same time for it all to come together."

"Thank goodness he came home when he did, or you might not be here now." Mia squeezed Sadie's hand. "It's great to see you, again."

"I'm so glad you're here," Sadie said. "I get lonely for female companionship."

"You have Hank's sister, Allie."

Sadie nodded. "When she's not ranching. But you speak the language of the movie industry. It's nice to share stories. I'm just happy." She climbed into the SUV. "See you tomorrow. But remember, if you get scared tonight, come on over."

Mia was already scared, but she'd have to get used to it. "Thanks."

Once Sadie left, Mia entered the house, closed the door and locked it behind her.

Then she faced her past.

She'd left everything as her parents had the day they'd gone to Bozeman for doctors' appointments a year ago.

Their appointments had been in the morning. Apparently, on their way back, they'd been caught in a freak blizzard, had run off the road and rolled down a steep embankment. If they hadn't died in the crash, they would have died of exposure. She could only hope their deaths had been instant and painless.

They'd lain at the bottom of the hill upside down in her father's old pickup, the snow covering their tracks, and eventually, the truck. No one had known to look for them until Mia had called the next day.

They hadn't answered. Having heard about the blizzard in Montana, Mia had been worried. She'd called all the people she knew in Eagle Rock and couldn't find her parents. After a couple of hours, she'd notified the sheriff's department.

The sheriff himself had gone to their house to check on them. No one had answered his knock. Concerned for their safety, he'd broken the lock and entered. He'd found a note on the calendar Mia's mother kept on the refrigerator. The note had indicated they'd had doctors' appointments in Bozeman the day before.

After the sheriff had verified with the doctors' office that the couple had been there the day before, he'd sent his deputy out on the highway to Bozeman to look for any signs of the Chastains' truck.

Mia sighed. The dustcovers over the furniture made the living room appear filled with the ghosts the people in town believed haunted her old home. And really, weren't there? The ghosts were the memories the furniture conjured. Fleeting images of her parents sitting in their favorite recliners, staring at the fire or watching television.

They'd been older when they'd had Mia. She was the baby they'd tried for years to have, and when they'd finally given up in their forties, she'd surprised them.

She couldn't have asked for more loving and giving parents. They'd been a bit old-fashioned compared to some of the younger parents, but that had been part of their charm.

Pushing back the memories, Mia continued through to the kitchen. She'd left all the utilities on throughout the year to keep pipes from freezing. Other than a layer of dust, she could move right in and do what she'd come to do.

She ran her finger along the counter, leaving a clean streak amid the dirt that had gathered since her mother's death.

Standing around staring at the dirt wasn't going to get the place cleaned.

If she planned to live there for the next month, she had to get to work cleaning. Once that was done, she hoped to settle, free of distractions from the internet, and write the script she'd contracted to finish before the end of the month.

Rolling up her sleeves, she pulled back her hair and secured it in a ponytail, and then got out a bucket, rags and soap and went to work.

By nightfall, the kitchen sparkled, and she had the kettle on the stove for tea. She'd also cleaned her old bedroom, replacing the musty sheets with a fresh set she'd brought with her from her apartment in Los Angeles.

At the very least, she could have supper and a place to sleep for the night. Tomorrow, she'd work on the rest of the house. When she had it cleaned, she'd start working on her manuscript.

The hard work had kept her from dwelling too much on the past. Exhausted from the trip and all the work, Mia showered, dressed in her favorite, worn T-shirt and soft jersey shorts and then settled at the kitchen table to drink a cup of tea and eat the crackers and cheese she'd brought with her from L.A.

Night had settled around the house. All of the windows had blinds or curtains she could close to block out the darkness, except in the kitchen. The window over the sink stared at her like a dark specter, making her skin crawl the longer she looked at it. She'd have to go to Bozeman to find a set of blinds to cover it.

During the day, the more windows she could open to let in light, the better, but at night, the darkness frightened her. Yeah, she'd learned to get around, even at night, but it didn't stop the irrational fear of being watched from threatening to overwhelm her.

Mia rose from the table, having eaten very little, dumped her tea down the drain and rinsed her cup. All the while, she refused to stare out the darkened window that overlooked the back garden.

When she turned away to go to her bedroom, she could swear she saw a shadowy figure in the window, just out of the corner of her eye.

She grabbed a butcher knife from the drawer and turned to face the window. The view was just as black as it had been when she'd been drinking her tea.

For a long time, she stared at the window, waiting for that ghostly shadow to reappear. Had she imagined the figure? Were her fears getting the better of her?

After a few minutes, she relaxed and started to replace the butcher knife in the kitchen drawer. On second thought, she carried it with her to her bedroom and laid it on her nightstand.

The shadow could have been a result of her memories and her overactive imagination, but she wasn't taking any chances.

She had a gun, but it was packed away in her suitcase that she had yet to unpack. Perhaps that would be the first thing she dug out in the morning. If she continued to feel insecure through the night, she'd unpack it sooner.

Mia slid between the sheets and pulled the blanket up to her chin. Leaving the lamp shining on the nightstand, she closed her eyes and tried to sleep.

Tired beyond endurance, sleep came despite the debilitating fear, only to be filled with nightmares, her memory regurgitated from long ago.

She'd just gotten off the school bus, on her way home from school. Her house was only a half of a mile out of Eagle Rock, surrounded by hills and ranch land. Her great-grandfather had settled in Montana, homesteaded a six-hundred-acre spread and raised cattle and horses. Since then, the successive generations had sold off portions of the old homestead until all that remained was the original house and ten acres.

Mia swung her backpack over her shoulder and started down the driveway leading to her house, set back from the road, past a stand of trees.

Thinking of the homework she had yet to complete, and going over conversations she'd had with her friends during the day, she wasn't aware she was being followed, until a man wearing a black ski mask leaped from the brush and grabbed her from behind.

At five feet two inches, she hadn't been big or strong enough to defend herself. He'd thrown a bag over her head, tied her wrists together behind her, dragged her into his truck and driven her out to a deserted road in the surrounding hills.

Terrified, she'd strained against her bindings, breathing in her own hot, damp air, tears soaking the burlap.

When the truck came to a stop, her attacker had tied her to a tree and pulled off her clothes. She'd fought, kicked and screamed. No one came to save her when he'd penetrated her, tearing through her virginal wall. He'd pinched, bitten and tormented her for what felt like hours, and then left her there to die in the cold air of an early, Montana spring night.

A loud crash yanked her from the nightmare to fully awake. Mia sat up in bed and looked around. At first she didn't recognize where she was, until she spotted the photograph of her and her parents smiling by the lake that summer before her childhood had ended.

She tried to remember why she'd woken. A sound. Something crashing.

Mia reached for the phone on her nightstand, only to remember she didn't have one. Instead, she grabbed the butcher knife she'd left there earlier and swung her feet to the floor. Her heart thumping hard against her ribs, she poked her head out the door of her bedroom. Nothing moved. Darkness enveloped her. Making a mental note to buy nightlights at the hardware store, she inched her way down the hallway to the top of the staircase and shined her flashlight to the floor below.

Another sound captured her attention, this time above her. It sounded like the soft skittering of leaves blowing across concrete. A shiver slid across her skin.

The sounds above had nothing to do with the crash that had jerked her out of her nightmare.

Mia descended the stairs, slowly, wishing she had her gun. Another mental note: dig the gun out of her suitcase.

At the bottom of the stairs, she felt a cool breeze against her bare legs. The air conditioner hadn't kicked in and she hadn't left any windows open.

Another couple of steps placed her near the front entry and the doorway to the kitchen.

The cool breeze was stronger here, coming from the kitchen.

Mia turned abruptly and flashed her light into the kitchen.

A black shadow scurried across the floor and through the open back door.

Mia screamed and backed away, bumped into the wall and dropped the butcher knife. It fell within an inch of her bare, big toe.

Her heart thundered in her chest, and her breath lodged in her throat. Grabbing her purse from the hall table, Mia jammed her feet into her cowboy boots and ran out the front door.

In seconds, she was on the road to Sadie's house, terror fueling her to press the accelerator to the floor.

She had locked the back door before she'd gone to bed, and the black cat that had wandered in sure as hell hadn't broken open the door, damaging the doorframe in the process.

2

———

Tate "Bear" Parker stood on the dark porch of Hank Patterson's ranch house, stretching the charley horse out of his calf. He'd overdone it that day, and he was paying for it.

New to Hank's brainchild, the Brotherhood Protectors, Bear was in between assignments and couldn't just sit around and live off the goodness of the Pattersons' hearts while waiting for work.

When Hank had asked him to help out on the ranch, he'd gladly volunteered. Yeah, he'd ridden horses as a kid on his grandfather's farm, but that had been a long time ago, and well before he'd nearly lost his leg in a battle in the sandbox of Iraq.

His physical therapist back at Bethesda had told him he could do anything…in moderation. That he should build up to more strenuous activities a little at a time to avoid reinjuring his leg.

The trained Delta Force soldier in him couldn't back down from a challenge. Anything Hank had done that day, Bear had done or tried his best to accomplish.

Horseback riding had seemed like a no-brainer, but his muscles weren't used to that kind of exercise, and now his leg ached like crazy.

At two in the morning, he'd given up on sleep and come

out on the porch to walk out the kinks. Refusing to dope up on medication, he had to find other ways to relieve the pain.

He could think of worse things to do than stand on a porch staring at the stars in a sky so clear he swore he could see them shining from the other end of the universe. They didn't call Montana "Big Sky" country for nothing. With little light pollution, the night skies were filled with diamonds, twinkling in a black sea.

Though he'd worked his hardest all day, he was certain Hank had given him the lighter chores. He still didn't know how he would fit into this organization or how he'd add value as a bodyguard when he limped around like a cripple. Hell, he was a cripple. If he were whole, he'd still be on active duty, avenging the deaths of the members of his Special Forces team.

His fists clenched. He still struggled with guilt. He'd lived, while the majority of his team had died when they'd been double-crossed by their Iraqi informant and led into an ambush. If not for the close air support he'd called in, he might have perished as well.

Too many times during his recovery and rehabilitation, he'd wished he'd died. But if he was meant to live, he wanted to be back in the fight. He'd begged the doctors to send him back to the war. His brothers deserved retribution.

The medical review board had met and sealed his fate, kicking him out of the army, calling him medically retired, labeling him a disabled veteran.

The army didn't want him. They might as well have cut off his balls and sat him on a street corner with a cup to beg. Since he'd graduated high school, all he'd done was fight, and train and fight some more.

If not for the SEAL he'd met in physical therapy, he might have given up.

Swede had been as lost and purposeless as Bear. They'd formed a bond in their attempt to laugh off the indignities and pain of relearning how to function with their respective injuries. After therapy, they'd gone to the nearest sports bar, knocked back a couple of beers and watched a game or two.

Having someone who understood what he was going through had helped Bear get through his own reintroduction into the civilian world.

When Swede had gotten a call from his SEAL buddy in Montana, Bear thought that would be the end of their friendship. Swede's departure had left a void in Bear's life when he'd shipped out for the other side of the continent. At that time, Bear had still been waiting to hear about his own appeal of the decision from the medical review board. Not that it had done any good.

Discharged from the army and graduated from physical therapy, he'd been left staring at the world, wondering, *What next?*

He'd polished up a pathetic excuse for a resume and sent it out to every business advertising a need for a leader. He had leadership experience out the ass in a combat environment. He could handle stress and make snap decisions while under attack. But he'd never led anyone in a business environment. Who needed a guy who could shoot an enemy combatant from three hundred yards away with a 98% kill rate? Or a man who would cover you while you raced into heavy enemy fire?

With no one knocking on his door or offering him a job, Bear had begun to slip into a dark place he'd never gone before. The temptation to self-medicate with alcohol had been so real, he'd nearly succumbed.

Then he'd gotten the call. One rainy day in D.C., his phone rang. He hadn't recognized the number, but he'd crossed his fingers and prayed it wasn't a salesman.

The caller had been Hank Patterson, founder of the Brotherhood Protectors personal security agency. Based on Swede's recommendation, he'd offered him a job to come to work in Montana providing personal security to clients.

Bear hadn't hesitated. He'd packed his duffel bag and boarded a plane the next day.

Fortunately, he'd hit the ground running when Swede's first assignment went code red and every member of the

Brotherhood Protector had gone into combat mode to protect Swede's client.

That had been a couple weeks ago. Since then, they hadn't had a client contact them. Hank had warned Bear that they were a new startup company and they wouldn't be advertising. All of their clients would come to them by word of mouth.

Well, word of mouth wasn't bringing in droves of clients. If something didn't come up soon, Bear would have to find alternate work.

Though Hank promised he could stay at White Oak Ranch until work picked up, Bear didn't like living off the good will of others.

The pain in his leg had dissipated enough Bear was considering going back to bed when lights flashed between the trees, indicating a vehicle coming up the long drive to the ranch house.

His pulse quickened, and he debated waking Hank, but didn't have time. At the speed the vehicle flew up the road, it would be at the house before Bear could climb the stairs to the second floor and wake the boss.

The car skidded to a stop in the gravel, but the driver didn't get out right away.

With his heart racing, adrenaline pumping and, curiosity aroused, Bear waited for the driver to make the first move.

Finally, the driver's door opened, and a woman leaped out. Petite, with dark hair hanging down past her shoulders and wearing a baggy T-shirt and cowboy boots, she ran toward the house.

When she jogged up the steps to the porch, Bear stepped in front of her, blocking her path.

The woman screamed, and would have fallen backward, if Bear hadn't wrapped his arms around her waist and crushed her to his chest.

She struggled, kicked and cried out.

Bear held on, afraid she would trip and fall if he let go. "Hey, it's okay. I'm not going to hurt you."

Either she couldn't hear him or was too frightened to listen. She didn't stop fighting until the porch light blinked on.

Hank slammed through the door, his wife, Sadie, on his heels. "What's going on?"

The woman in Bear's arms slowed her fight and glanced up.

"I don't know," Bear said, his arms clamping the wildcat's arms to her sides. "This woman showed up like her world was on fire and ran toward the house. I blocked her path, and she tried to tear me apart."

Sadie stepped out from behind Hank. Her eyes widened. "Mia?"

Bear's captive sagged against him, and her entire body trembled.

"Oh, my God, Mia." Sadie rushed forward.

Bear loosened his hold, but not all the way. As limp as the woman Sadie had called Mia had gone, he wasn't certain she could stand.

Sadie pulled her from his arms and hugged her. "What happened?"

Mia buried her face against her friend's chest, shook her head and continued to tremble.

"Bring her inside, Sadie," Hank said, holding the door open.

Bear stepped away from the two women, feeling as if he'd kicked a puppy. "I'm sorry if I scared you." He reached out to touch her shoulder.

Mia flinched and stepped sideways to avoid his touch.

"It's okay," Sadie soothed. "Let's get you inside, and then you can tell us what happened."

Bear was the last through the door. This Mia woman seemed pretty shaken by something, and he felt like he was part of the cause. The sooner he figured out what was going on, the better.

Sadie led Mia into the living room where she sat with her on the couch.

Bear stood at the entrance, not wanting to cause the lady any more distress. For some reason, she was afraid of him.

Sadie stroked Mia's back and spoke soothingly to her, until Mia finally stopped shaking and straightened.

"I'm sorry," she said, wiping the tears from her cheeks. "I didn't come back to Eagle Rock to fall apart on your doorstep."

"You know you're welcome here, no matter what. And for the record, I wasn't keen on you staying in your old house until you had it where you wanted it." Sadie gave her a gentle smile. "Tell me what happened that scared you so badly."

Mia glanced toward the darkened window and a tremor shook her body. "I was having a bad dream when something woke me." She drew in a shaky breath and let it out. "I got up to check it out and went down the stairs. I found the back door to the kitchen wide open."

Sadie's brows dipped. "Could the wind have blown it open?"

Mia shook her head and looked at Sadie. "I locked all the doors and windows before I went to bed. Not only was the door open, the doorframe was splintered. Someone broke it open. And no, I'm not buying the ghost theory. Ghosts don't break doorframes."

Sadie's frown deepened. "No. They don't." She pulled Mia into her arms. "I'm glad you came here. You can't go back until you have the deadbolt fixed and a decent security system installed."

Mia shook her head, her lips thinning into a straight line. "I have to go back. Whoever did this can't get away with it. I refuse to let anyone scare me away from my family home. I'm tired of being the victim."

Bear's fists clenched into fists. The bullish frown on Mia's face made him want to go after her demons as much as she wanted to.

Sadie gripped her friend's arms. "What are you talking about?"

Mia's chin lifted, even as tears filled her eyes again. She swiped at them with the back of her knuckles. "Did I tell you about the script I came to write?"

Sadie shook her head. "No."

Drawing in a deep breath, Mia glanced around at the men in the room, as if in challenge. Then she turned to Sadie. "It's about a woman who returns to her hometown thirteen years after she was brutally raped to find the man who did it to her."

Sadie tilted her head to the side. A frown dug a line between her brows. "That's a tough one to write."

"Even tougher when it's based on a true story."

Sadie gasped. "Mia?"

The smaller woman nodded. "On my way home from school, thirteen years ago."

Bear's chest tightened. Mia couldn't have been more than fifteen or sixteen at the time. What kind of animal would have done such a thing?

Sadie's hand dropped to the swell of her belly. "Who?"

Mia shook her head. "I don't know. He wore a ski mask. I never knew who did it."

"Oh, my God." Sadie's eyes filled, and she pressed her hand to her mouth. "Was that at the end of the school year between your junior and senior year?"

Mia nodded.

"I wondered why you didn't participate in anything that summer or during our senior year. Oh, sweet Jesus, Mia." Sadie pulled her friend into her arms again and held her there. "You should have told someone."

"I couldn't," Mia whispered. "I was so ashamed and scared."

"Why didn't your parents go to the police?"

Mia shrugged. "I told them I fell down a hill to explain the cuts and bruises. They even let me stay out of school the rest of that week."

As Mia quietly told her story, Bear's heart hurt for the girl she'd been. "That's why you freaked out when I grabbed you."

Mia glanced his way. "I'm sorry."

"No. *I'm* sorry. I shouldn't have held onto you. I thought you were an intruder. And then I was afraid you'd fall off the steps."

Mia gave him a hint of a smile. "No intruder would have a

chance against you. You've got one helluva grip." She rubbed her arms.

Sadie glanced from Mia to Bear, and then up to her husband.

Bear's eyes narrowed.

The couple exchanged a knowing look, and then Sadie said, "Are you thinking what I'm thinking?"

Hank nodded. "Mia, I have a proposition for you."

Mia's brows puckered. "What kind of proposition? If it's to stay here with you two, my answer is no. You've got enough on your plate with a new business and a baby on the way."

Hank held up a hand. "Though we'd love to have you live here, we know how determined you are to renovate your family home and get some writing done there." He shot a glance toward Bear. "No, my proposition is that you hire a bodyguard to protect you while you're doing that renovation." Hank's jaw tightened. "In the meantime, the rest of my team can work on finding the bastard who raped you thirteen years ago."

Mia looked from Hank to Sadie and back. "I came back to Eagle Rock not just to write a script. It wasn't until I started the script that I realized that, by not telling, the man who'd raped me was free to attack other women. I came back because I needed to make sure he wasn't hurting anyone else." She nodded. "Yes, I'd like to hire your team to investigate."

"And protect you," Sadie added.

Mia chewed on her lip. "I have a gun. I just haven't had a chance to dig it out of my suitcase."

"Do you know how to use it?" Hank asked.

"I do. I've been to the firing range many times, and I have a concealed carry license for the state of California."

"Sweetie, I think that's great," Sadie said. "But you need someone who has your back until we find out who kicked in that door and who was responsible for the rape all those years ago."

For a long moment, Mia stared into Sadie's eyes. "All these years, I swore I wouldn't let my fear run my life."

"You're not hiding anymore, Mia," Hank said.

"You're taking matters into your own hands," Sadie said, running a soothing hand down Mia's arm. "Hiring a bodyguard is just one way of doing that."

Mia nodded. "Okay. I'll do it."

"Good." Hank faced Bear. "I'll talk to Swede when he gets back. I know he'll be on board. How about you, Bear?"

"I'm all for finding the lowlife." Bear's fists ached for the opportunity to pound the son of a bitch into the ground.

Hank shook his head. "Swede and I will take the lead on the investigation. If Mia's okay with it, I'd like you to be her bodyguard."

Bear's gaze shot to Mia. "I'm not so sure she'd want me to be, not after what happened."

Mia gave him a crooked smile. "If Sadie and Hank think you're the man for the job, I'm okay with it. To make it official, will you be my bodyguard?"

Bear's lips twitched at the corners. "I don't know. I'm not sure my shins and ankles can take it."

Mia raised her hand. "I promise not to kick or hit you, as long as you promise not to grab me in the dark." Then she held out her hand. "Deal?"

Bear didn't hesitate. He closed the distance between them and shook. "Deal." The protector in him couldn't let her go back to that house alone. His brows furrowed. "You know, it might be best if we don't advertise that we're looking for the rapist."

Hank nodded. "It might work even better if no one knows Bear is actually Mia's bodyguard."

Bear grunted. "Right. Whoever he is has gotten away with the crime all these years. He might be trying to scare Mia away so that she doesn't out him."

Mia nodded. "I could say that I hired Bear to renovate my family home." She glanced at him. "Have you ever done any carpentry?"

Bear nodded. "A little, when I spent summers at my grandfather's farm."

"Good enough. As soon as I have internet, we can look up whatever needs to be done. That is, if you don't mind doing some handiwork while I'm writing…"

Bear grinned. "Beats standing around, and it keeps me close to the house in case you need me."

"Then, it's settled," Hank said. "You've got yourself a body-guard-handyman, and we have some work to do finding your attacker."

Sadie smiled at Mia. "But tonight, you're staying here. Tomorrow, your handyman can fix the doorjamb and the lock."

Mia hugged Sadie. "I'll sleep on the couch, if that's okay."

Bear shook his head. "Take my room. I can't sleep in a real bed anyway."

"Sorry," Hank smirked. "I don't have a foxhole handy for you."

Bear snorted. "Watch it, frogman."

"Boys," Sadie warned. "Let's call it a night. Tomorrow will be a busy day. Come on, Mia. I'll show you to the room."

"Just shove my stuff to the side."

Mia started to pass Bear and stopped, touching him on the arm.

A jolt of electricity shot through his arm and into his chest.

"Are you sure you don't want the bed?" Mia asked.

"I'm sure. I couldn't sleep, anyway."

"That's right. You were on the porch when I drove up." She frowned. "Why?"

He rubbed his leg. "Guess I needed some air."

Her eyes narrowed, but she didn't push for more answers.

If she knew he was disabled, would she change her mind about him being her bodyguard?

Bear hoped not. For the first time in a long time, he felt like he had a purpose. He hoped like hell he didn't let her down.

3

MIA LAY in the bed Bear had been in earlier that night. The sheets still smelled like him. That faint musk of male and outdoors somehow made her feel safer. Now that she knew he wasn't just a shadowy figure in the night, bent on raping or killing her, she was glad he would be watching over her, making certain no one crossed the line or tried to hurt her.

When she'd come back to Eagle Rock, she'd thought she could handle being in the hometown where she'd been brutalized by a coward wearing a mask. Thirteen years had passed. Mia had taken half a dozen self-defense classes; she owned a gun and knew how to use it. But after her home had been broken into, she wasn't sure she could stay in Eagle Rock, knowing her attacker could still be there, possibly lurking in the shadows, planning his next attack on her or some other unsuspecting female too weak to resist.

She finally drifted off, exhausted from the stress of the trip, her little bit of housecleaning and being scared half out of her mind by a broken back door, and then being grabbed on the porch by a man in the shadows. In a house full of people who had sworn to help and protect her, Mia was able to sleep dreamlessly, something she hadn't done since she'd first contemplated returning home.

Mia woke to sunlight filtering around the curtains drawn over the window. She stretched in the bed and remembered she'd left all of her clothes at her house. All she wore was the T-shirt she'd slept in. At night in the throes of terror, she hadn't cared what she'd worn. Her only concern had been getting to safety as quickly as possible.

With daylight shining through the window, she realized she still had to get back to her house and her suitcase before she could dress presentably.

Her cheeks heated as she thought of the man she'd hired on as a bodyguard. How could she face him that morning in nothing but a T-shirt that barely covered her backside?

A knock on the door made her start and pull the blanket up to her chin. "Who is it?" she asked, her breath catching in her throat. What if it was Bear wanting in to get his things?

"It's me, Sadie. I thought you might like something to wear down to breakfast."

At once relieved, Mia let go of the breath she'd been holding, confused by the pang of disappointment that it wasn't Bear on the other side of the door. Why would she want to see him first thing in the morning when she looked her worst? "Please, come in." Mia flung back the blanket and swung her legs over the side of the bed. "I was just about to get up."

Sadie pushed open the door and stepped in carrying a pair of jeans and a belt. "These will probably be too big for you, but I figured something too big was better than nothing at all."

"Thank you so much." Mia took the jeans and jammed her legs into them. "These will work until I can get back to my place." She slid the belt through the loops and cinched the waist tight enough the jeans wouldn't slip off her hips.

Sadie chuckled as she eyed the material bunched around Mia's ankles. "Sometimes, I forget how much taller I am than you."

Mia bent to roll up the pant legs to keep from walking on them. "My mother always said the world would be a boring place if we all were the same shape and size."

She pulled on her cowboy boots and straightened with a

smile. "I'm grateful for the jeans. I was wondering how I would get from here to my place without being seen in nothing but the T-shirt."

"No one would have been the wiser. That T-shirt covers all the right places." Sadie grinned. "I left a new toothbrush and hairbrush in the bathroom. When you're ready, I'll have breakfast on the table for you."

"Oh, Sadie, you don't have to wait on me. *I* should be waiting on *you*. You're the one who's pregnant."

"Don't be silly. I'm only five months along, and I'm as healthy as a horse. Let me take care of you this morning. Later in my pregnancy, I might need your help."

"And I will be honored to provide it." *If I'm still here.* Mia hugged her friend. "I'll be down in a minute." She glanced around. "Are the guys up?"

"They've been up for a couple of hours. They're outside taking care of the animals."

"Oh. What time is it?"

"After ten."

Mia gasped. "Ten? Why didn't you wake me? I never sleep past eight."

Sadie arched her brows. "Apparently, you needed it after your eventful night. When you go back to your house, Hank and I are going with you—and Bear. We'll want to notify the sheriff of your trespasser."

Mia chewed on her bottom lip. "Oh, I don't know."

Sadie touched Mia's arm. "Sweetie, you can't count a busted doorframe as a product of wind or ghosts. The sheriff needs to know. What if someone else is having the same problems? Or better yet, what if the sheriff catches the one who busted your back door before he does it to someone else? You'd be saving that other person from the fright of his life."

"I suppose you're right." Mia didn't know why she hesitated. Whoever had broken in her back door should be caught and punished. She just didn't want people to think she was scared. Which she was.

Sadie left her to complete her ablutions. After brushing her hair into some semblance of order and running a tooth brush over her teeth, she hurried downstairs in her oversized jeans.

Even before she reached the bottom of the staircase, she could hear the rumble of male voices. Her pulse picked up, and her breathing grew shallow. After her embarrassing display of cowardice the night before, she wasn't looking forward to coming face to face with Bear. He must think she was some twit from the city, scared of her own shadow.

Throwing back her shoulders, she faked a smile she didn't feel and entered the kitchen.

Hank and Bear stood by the back door, their boots dusty, their shirts already showing sweat from hard work, Sadie looking on.

"We loaded some lumber and nails into the back of Bear's truck." Hank said, giving her a glance. "You'll still need to make a trip to the hardware store, for paint and new locks. You'll want to do that before they close this afternoon. Bear can have the locks installed before dark."

Sadie waved at the men. "Sit. Have a cup of coffee. Mia hasn't even had breakfast yet, and you're organizing her day for her."

"If you don't mind, I'd like to head on over to the house and unload," Bear said.

Mia nodded, her cheeks warm. She hadn't been shy with anyone since she'd moved to L.A. Why was she timid with the bodyguard? Perhaps she felt that way because he'd seen her afraid and in her night clothes.

Well, she'd just have to get over it. The man would be all over her house, repairing what needed fixing and being there in case she had another incident.

Hank interjected. "I'll ride over with Mia in her car, and Sadie can follow us. We've got you covered, Mia, so Bear can get started."

Mia smiled. "Sounds like you have a plan."

"Now, don't let the men bully you into decisions you don't like. It's your house, your schedule and your call." Sadie gave Hank a stern look. "Don't be pushy."

With a laugh, Mia touched Sadie's arm. "No, really. I appreciate that the guys are helping me with the repairs. And, yes, the sooner they get the door fixed and the locks changed, the better I'll feel about staying there."

Sadie didn't back down. "I love Hank to death, but I know how he gets when he's in 'go' mode and bulldozes everyone around him."

Hank slipped an arm around her waist. "But you love me for it."

"I do." Sadie wrapped her arms around his neck and kissed him.

Mia looked away from the couple. The only other place her gaze could go was to the man standing in the doorway.

Bear stared back, his gaze unreadable but not disturbing. "I'll just be going to the house."

"Do you have the address?" Mia asked.

He nodded. "I'll unload the lumber and be ready to start as soon as the sheriff's had a chance to look over the place."

"Right." Mia's stomach knotted. She knew how small towns worked. As soon as the sheriff's department was notified, everyone in the community would know someone had broken into Mia's house. That could work in her favor. The trespasser might not attempt it again, knowing she'd alerted the law, and that they might be patrolling her stretch of the road in response.

"We won't be long," Hank called out to Bear.

Sadie laid a plate full of bacon, eggs, toast and hash brown potatoes on the table. "Sit."

Her stomach growling at the wonderful smell of fried bacon, Mia obeyed. "I won't be long," she assured Bear.

"Take your time. I'll be at the house." Bear left, closing the door softly behind him.

Hank spun on his boot heels. "I'll call the sheriff. That'll give him time to head on over to the Chastain place while Mia finishes her breakfast."

When both men had left the room, Mia tucked into the

food Sadie had provided, surprised at just how hungry she was.

"Coffee or tea?"

"Tea," Mia said, not looking up from her plate.

Sadie poured hot water into a teapot, set two cups and the pot on a tray and carried it to the table. She sank into the seat opposite Mia. "I think you'll like Bear."

"I don't know anything about him. I'm going on Hank's recommendation."

"Actually, Swede, one of Hank's SEAL teammates, met Bear when he was going through physical therapy in Bethesda, Maryland. Bear was a member of the Delta Force. He's a highly decorated war hero."

"And he's going to be a bodyguard and handyman?" Mia shook her head. "How will he feel about that? Seems like he's overqualified for the job."

"Folks who haven't been in the military don't always understand what our guys have gone through." Sadie stared down into her cup as if looking into a crystal ball and seeing the man, not the tea. "Reintegrating into the civilian world is really tough after what they've been through. Especially if they've suffered injuries. All they knew was fighting and war. Some of those battles are still raging inside their heads."

Mia stared at the doorway Bear had passed through. "And Bear?"

"He was one of three men in his unit to survive an ambush." Sadie smiled sadly. "Swede said he was pretty banged up. Bear nearly lost his leg in that attack."

Mia had noticed a decided limp in his gate. "Will he be able to protect me any better than I can with a gun?"

Hank reentered the kitchen. "Bear might have a limp, but he's got the experience and the grit needed to be a top-notch security specialist." He tipped his head toward the hallway. "The sheriff's on his way to your house now."

Mia pushed away from her half-eaten breakfast and stood. "I'm ready as soon as I brush my teeth." She ran up to the bathroom and was back in two minutes.

Hank and Sadie led the way out to the vehicles.

When Hank rounded the side of Mia's car, she frowned. "Hank, you need to ride with your wife. I can drive by myself. Nothing's going to happen in broad daylight."

"I don't mind going with you. And I trust Sadie to drive right with our child in the car." He winked at Sadie.

"I drive better than you do," she said.

"Really, I can do this." Mia got into the car and started the engine. "See you there."

Hank and Sadie followed her in Hank's truck.

They all arrived at Mia's house, turning into the drive behind two sheriff's vehicles.

Mia cringed. She hadn't wanted to come back to town and stir up a lot of trouble. But she wasn't backing down. This was her house. No one was going to scare her away.

Bear came around the side of the house, his gaze going to Mia, his brows rising slightly as if asking if she was all right.

Mia felt warmth spread through her at his look of concern. She gave a slight nod and then turned her attention to Sheriff Bob Wilson, a man who'd been sheriff in Eagle Rock for as long as Mia could remember. He'd been the one she'd called a year ago when her parents hadn't answered their phone. He was also the one who'd called her with the bad news.

Sheriff Wilson and her parents had been friends. Their deaths had hurt him almost as much as it had hurt her to learn they'd passed. "Mia." He met her halfway and engulfed her in a typical Bob Wilson bone-crunching hug.

When he released her to breathe again, Mia stepped back and smiled. "Sheriff, it's good to see you."

"And you, little girl." His glance shifted to the house. "Although I would rather have had coffee with you than investigate a break-in." He turned to the deputy standing nearby. "You remember Larry Maynard? Weren't you two in high school at the same time?"

Mia's eyes narrowed as she studied the tall, sandy-blond-haired man in the deputy's uniform. He looked familiar, maybe a little fuller around the jowls. "Did you play football?"

Maynard grinned. "Every guy in our high school played ball or we wouldn't have had a team. I think I was two years ahead of you in school."

"Were you the quarterback?"

He nodded. "I was during my senior year."

Mia nodded. "I remember. You always dated pretty cheerleaders."

"I married a cheerleader," Maynard said. "What about you? What brought you back to Eagle Rock? I thought when people escaped they didn't come back."

Sadie stepped up beside her. "She's here to find the—"

"Inspiration." Mia grabbed Sadie's hand and squeezed hard.

"Ow." Sadie pulled her hand free and stared at Mia as if she'd lost her mind.

"I'm here for the peace and quiet. I'm on deadline to produce a screenplay," Mia continued.

"That's right," Larry said. "You're a big-time movie writer. I read about you in the Eagle Rock News."

Mia almost laughed. The local news was nothing more than Margie Rodman's blog announcing births, deaths and who'd been hauled into the tiny county jail for public intoxication. When one of their own did good, and Margie got wind of it, it became front-page news on her internet blog site.

"I don't know about big-time, but that's what I do. I write screenplays."

"Mia, we're all so very proud of our local celebrities." Sheriff Wilson smiled from Hank to Mia and Sadie. "Between the two of you, Eagle Rock is back on the map." His smile faded. "Now, Mia, show me the damage."

Mia drew in a deep breath and nodded. She led the way around the side of the house, stepping around a stack of lumber.

Bear had unloaded the truck, laying the boards neatly to the side of the porch.

The back door stood open just as Mia had left it. She'd been too afraid of being caught and raped to worry about closing it before she ran out of the house.

The sheriff climbed the back porch steps, pulled his cell phone out of his shirt pocket and snapped shots of the splintered doorjamb and lock. "About what time did this occur?"

Mia climbed the steps, a shiver rippling down her spine. "I don't know. Maybe around two AM. I don't remember exactly. I woke when I heard the door crash open. I was a little disoriented at the time." From an intense and frightening dream, she didn't add.

"Was anything taken?" Sheriff Wilson asked, stepping into the kitchen.

"That, I wouldn't know. I ran out the other side of the house and haven't been back since." Mia followed him, the hairs on the back of her neck rising. She could almost sense the presence of the intruder, which was ridiculous considering the sheriff was there, and so were five other people.

"Let's check through the house," the sheriff said. "Let me know if you notice anything gone. You can always make a list and send it to me later if we miss something."

Mia walked with the sheriff room by room.

Deputy Maynard followed, holding a pen and notebook as if prepared to take notes.

It was hard to tell if anything was missing since she hadn't removed dustcovers in the living room and spare bedrooms. Everything in the kitchen seemed to be where it was supposed to be—except the doorjamb and a butcher knife left on the floor.

When the sheriff completed his rounds, he stepped out on the porch where the rest of the group waited.

Sadie slipped an arm around Mia's waist. "Well, Sheriff, what do you think?"

"My initial inclination is to think some kids were playing a prank on Miss Chastain. They've got some fool notion this house is haunted. Maybe they're trying to make others think the same. I can't imagine any other motive, seein' as they didn't take anything that we know of."

Mia could think of one other motive.

Sadie cut a sideways glance at Mia.

Mia shook her head slightly.

"What about the rest of town?" Hank asked. "Has anyone else had similar problems? Anyone report attacks?"

The sheriff shook his head. "Not since you and your boys cleared up the trouble with your sister Alyssa's former fiancé. That was some nasty business. How is your sister?"

"She and Swede should be back from Vegas in a day or two."

"I'm glad they were able to get away for a few days," Sheriff Wilson said. "I keep meaning to take the missus back to Vegas. She likes the shows. I like the craps table." The sheriff glanced around. "I'll have a deputy do drive-bys at night as a warning to whoever did this."

"Thanks, Sheriff," Mia said.

The sheriff descended the stairs. "Welcome back, Mia. I'm glad to see you back in town." He climbed into his SUV and drove away.

Deputy Maynard crossed to his SUV, tipped his hat and said, "Good to see you again, Mia." Then he drove away, leaving Mia standing on the top step feeling no better about her house than before the sheriff had arrived.

"Don't worry." Sadie hugged her. "Now that they've left, Bear can fix the doorframe."

A loud crack behind her made Mia jump.

Bear, armed with a hammer and a pry bar, had gone to work removing the splintered wood.

"Do you need help?" Hank asked.

Bear shook his head. "I've got this. Thanks."

"I can stay, if you want," Sadie offered.

Mia smiled. "No. I think we can handle it from here. You should go put your feet up or something."

"No, I shouldn't," Sadie said. "But I get it. You need to write." She let go of Mia and took Hank's hand. "Come on. I want to go look at paint colors for the baby's room."

"Bartlett's Hardware doesn't carry a lot of choices."

Sadie smiled. "I know."

"The closest paint store is in Bozeman."

Her smile widened. "I know."

Hank sighed. "I guess we're going to Bozeman."

"And they say you can't train men." Sadie winked at Mia. "Let us know if you need anything from Bozeman."

"If they don't have door lock hardware at Bartlett's, we might be calling," Bear said.

Hank waved. "Gotcha. We'll be back early enough to give you time to switch them out."

Hank opened the SUV door for Sadie. She climbed in, smiling.

Mia hoped to be as free and easy with a man as Sadie. She and Hank were so good together, and the love between them was so strong Mia could feel it.

A loud bang shook her from her thoughts, and Mia turned toward Bear, her pulse kicking up a notch.

He had the pry bar between two boards in the door frame and he leaned back as hard as he could, holding onto the pry bar, his muscles straining.

The wood creaked, and then split again. He grabbed the splinter and ripped it off the doorframe.

"Is there something I can do to help?" Mia asked.

BEAR STRAIGHTENED, his gaze skimming Mia, his pulse kicking up a notch. She was beautiful, even in baggy jeans and a T-shirt. "As a matter of fact, there is."

"I've never done any carpentry, but I'm willing to learn."

"No specific skills necessary." He pulled a screwdriver from his belt. "All I need is for you to hold the door while I remove the pins from the hinges. Just hang onto the doorknobs and keep it steady until I've knocked out the pins."

"I think I can manage that." Mia held the doorknobs while Bear whacked the pins out of the hinges and slid them into his pocket. When he had all three loose, the door wobbled.

Bear reached around Mia and grabbed the door as the

hinges parted and the door fell away from the jamb. His body pressed against hers as he absorbed most of the weight of the heavy door. Pain shot down his leg, and he grunted, fighting the urge to let go of the door and fall to the ground himself. He closed his eyes and held on until the worst of it subsided. In a tight voice, he said, "I've got this. You can let go."

Mia didn't move away as he expected.

"You can let go," he repeated.

"Um. No," she said. "I can't."

Bear took stock of the situation, his gaze shifting to her hands, trapped beneath his. So intent on keeping the heavy door from crashing down on their feet, he hadn't realized he'd pinned Mia's hands beneath his. "Damn. I'm sorry." Balancing the door with one hand, he shifted the other, moving it off hers. Then he removed the hand on the other side.

Still, she didn't move. "I seem to be pinned."

"If I move too much, I'll lose my grip," he said. "You're going to have to wiggle your way out from between me and the door."

Mia ducked her head beneath his arm and dragged her body against his in an attempt to slide out from under him.

The more she wiggled against him, the more aware of her he became, until his jeans grew so tight, he thought they might cut off the circulation to—

Mia broke loose and flung herself free of his arms.

The heavy door leaned precariously toward her. Bear shifted to balance the weight, putting so much pressure on his bad leg, the pain throbbing there made him break out in a cold sweat. He gritted his teeth and held on. Once he had control, he bent, settling the door on the floor of the kitchen and leaning it against the wall. Then he dropped to the tile and stretched his bum leg out in front of him, pulled his toes upward, to work out the charley horse, and cursed softly beneath his breath.

He hated showing weakness in front of anyone, especially in front of his client. But what disturbed him more was the raw lust that had ripped through him when Mia had wiggled her pert little butt against his groin.

Somewhere in the Brotherhood Protectors rule book—if there was such a thing—there had to be something about not lusting after the client. If there was, he was doomed to fail his first solo assignment before it barely had a chance to get started.

4

———

MIA'S HEART pounded hard against her ribs. For a moment she thought it might actually burst from her chest. Being trapped between Bear and the door had caused so many mixed emotions she wasn't sure if she had been frightened by Bear or by her own reaction to his body pressed so tightly to hers.

Her core throbbed with an aching need she'd never felt before. The desire was so profound, she could barely breathe.

When she was finally free, she bent over and sucked in deep breaths to refill her starving lungs. Not until she heard a soft thump did she look up to see Bear set the door on the kitchen floor, and then drop down beside it.

He thrust his leg out in front of him and rubbed his knee and thigh, his face pale, sweat beading on his brow.

Pushing her own desires to the back of her mind, Mia knelt beside Bear. "Are you okay?"

"I'm fine," he said through tight lips.

"No, you're not." She glanced at the leg he rubbed.

"I tell you, I'm fine. Just leave me alone for a minute."

"Does it help to massage the muscle?"

"I can manage. I'll be up in a minute." When she didn't move, he glared at her. "Don't you have some writing to do?"

He rolled to his side and tried to get his leg under him. When he put weight on it, he collapsed, cursing.

Mia winced, empathy making her want to ease his pain. She reached out to touch his leg.

He pushed her hands away. "I don't need help."

Anger stiffened her backbone. "Look, mister. You're in pain. What does it hurt to let someone help you?"

"You're the client. I'm supposed to be helping *you*. Not the other way around."

"Don't be ridiculous. You *are* helping me. Let me help you." She reached out again.

When he started to push her hands away again, she gave him a hard stare. "Don't be a big baby. Let me massage it until the pain lessens. Then you can go back to being your big, grumpy macho self." She ran her hands over his thigh and knee, gently at first, adding a little pressure with each pass until she was leaning into the massage. "Better?" she asked and glanced up.

Bear leaned back on his hands. "Yes."

Mia continued until Bear grabbed her hand and held it still. "You can stop now."

"But if you're still hurting…" She looked into his eyes.

"If you don't stop now, I won't be able to move for an entirely different reason."

She frowned. "Why?"

He shook his head, his lips quirking upward at the corners. "Just trust me and stop. The charley horse is gone. I think I can stand."

As his meaning dawned on her, heat rushed up her neck into her cheeks. Mia pulled her hands back to her sides and rose to her feet. "Well, if you think you'll be okay."

"I will." Bear pushed to his feet and eased his weight onto his bad leg. "See? Better." He touched her arm. "Thanks."

She willed the heat in her cheeks to subside. "You're welcome. Now, I'd better clear a space in the study to write. Let me know if you need my help again."

He adjusted the angle of the door leaning against the wall to keep it from falling. "I will."

Mia scurried from the kitchen, ducked into the study and closed the door. Pressing a hand to her chest, she felt her heartbeat thundering against her ribs. What was it about Bear that had her in a constant state of agitation?

For one, he wasn't even that handsome. Unless a woman was into the ruggedly attractive guys with permanent five-o'clock shadows on their jaws and shoulders so broad they filled entire doorways.

No, he wasn't the type of man she was normally interested in. Hell, she didn't know any men like Bear. He was so big, raw, muscular and utterly male. Not the usual artist types she ran into when she corroborated with other screenwriters.

For the most part, she'd avoided men. Sure she'd dated, preferring to meet the man on her own terms. She never let him pick her up at her place, preferring to meet at a public restaurant. And she never went home with one.

Since her rape, she'd never actually had sex with another man. Yes, she'd been in some intensely heavy petting sessions, but she'd always frozen up at the last minute. Okay, frozen wasn't the right description. Her reactions were more like full-on panic attacks. Needless to say, those had been final dates with those particular men. They'd never called back, and she'd been glad.

Mia might not be a virgin, but she had never experienced the big O.

So, why was she thinking about it now?

It was him. Bear. Shoot, she didn't even know his full name. In the rush to get inside Sadie's place, full introductions hadn't been made. Now she'd feel silly asking the man whom she'd hired to be her bodyguard what his name was.

Straightening away from the door, Mia tried to pull herself together. She might as well do what she'd told him she was going to do and clean the study. Maybe if she had a spotless, quiet place to write, she'd get some words down.

Mia hitched up the borrowed jeans and thought better of starting to clean. First, she needed to change into her own clothes, and maybe freshen her face and hair. Just because she wasn't interested in a relationship with her bodyguard didn't mean she had to run around the house in baggy clothes with her hair unkempt.

Peeking out the door, Mia glanced toward the kitchen. She didn't hear any hammering or banging. Nor did she see Bear

Quick, while the coast was clear, she hurried up the stairs and into her bedroom. After she changed into her own jeans and a tank top, she hurried across to the bathroom, brushed her hair, applied a little concealer to the dark circles beneath her eyes and a little blush to her pale face. Feeling a little more presentable, she walked out of the bathroom and into the wall of muscle that was her bodyguard.

Bear gripped her arms to steady her.

As soon as Mia had her feet firmly beneath her, Bear released her and backed away, holding up his hands. "Sorry. I didn't mean to grab you and violate rule number one."

"No, it was my fault. I didn't look before I charged out the door. And I wouldn't think of it as a rule so much as a guideline."

His lips twitched, almost a smile. "I wouldn't be up here, but I need some supplies. Do you have time to go to the hardware store?"

She snorted. "Since I haven't started cleaning or writing, I'd say yes."

"We can wait if you need to do something else first," Bear offered.

"No, I don't want to hold you up on fixing that door." She chuckled. "Let's just go and quit dancing around the issue. Hopefully, we'll get used to each other and stop being so awkward."

He grinned. "You're my first personal security client. I don't want to screw it up."

"And you're my first bodyguard. So we'll both bumble

around until we get it right." She grabbed her purse from the top of the dresser. "My car or your truck?"

"My truck. In case you want to load up on other supplies to continue the repairs to this place. I've made a cursory inspection. I have a list in my head."

Mia followed him out to his truck. "What did you find?"

"The back porch is sagging, the steps are rotting, and I think you have a hornet's nest in the eaves at the front of the house."

"Oh, really?" Mia winced. "We definitely want to take care of those things right away. I can't have guests falling through the boards and being stung by angry hornets."

Bear walked with her to the passenger side of the truck and opened her door.

Mia climbed in, entirely too aware of Bear's burly body as she slipped past him.

He walked around the truck and slid in next to her. After starting the engine, he shifted into reverse.

Being inside the cab of the truck brought her close to Bear in a confined space. Her pulse quickened, but not like it did in a panic attack. This feeling was new, a raw excitement she couldn't deny.

As they continued down the drive, her gaze returned to Bear again and again, no matter how hard she tried to focus her attention on the road ahead.

Bear pulled the truck to a stop at the juncture of her driveway and the highway. Without glancing her way, he asked, "How did it happen?"

His question pulled Mia back to reality with a jerk. "Sorry?"

He softened his tone. "Thirteen years ago, how did it happen?"

Mia stared at the highway, her pulse rampaging through her veins, sweat beading on her upper lip.

"If you don't want to talk about it, I understand. But to find out who did it, we'll need details. You'll have to talk to someone."

Mia stared at the corner where she'd gotten off the bus and waved at her friends as the bus pulled away all those years ago.

"Forget it. I don't want to make you uncomfortable." Bear shifted his foot from the brake to the accelerator.

"It was a school day like any other," Mia blurted out. "I got off the bus here, like I had every day for the previous seven years."

She glanced at the trees and vegetation near the corner. "He must have been waiting in the brush. I didn't see him at all, just walked toward my house, like I did every day."

Her fingers curled around the armrests. "Then something came down over my head. A bag or burlap sack. I couldn't see. Whatever it was covered my head, shoulders and arms. Then strong arms wrapped around me. I couldn't fight with my arms and hands. They were trapped against my sides. He must have wrapped rope around the sack to keep me from getting loose. I kicked and screamed, but it didn't do any good. He threw me over his shoulder, carried me a short distance, and then dumped me in the backseat of his truck. He drove across some very bumpy roads and stopped."

A shiver rocked her body. For a long moment, Mia didn't say anything, as she relived the terror and pain of that day so long ago.

Bear took her hand in his and squeezed gently. "You don't have to go on."

Mia found his big, callused hand comforting. "No, it's okay. Sometimes, I pretend it was someone else, not me, who was attacked. But I wouldn't wish it on anyone else. I can truly say it was the worst day of my life." She stared down at the scars on the back of his hand. "You must think I'm foolish." She traced one of his scars with her fingertip.

"I don't think anything of the sort." He glanced her way. "Why do you say that?"

She shrugged. "I was raped and lived. I didn't lose a limb or suffer a spinal injury. Basically, I came out of it intact."

Bear shook his head. "Nobody comes out of anything as traumatic as what you went through intact. I suspect you had posttraumatic stress issues, just like soldiers who survive wartime attacks."

She shrugged. "I don't know about posttraumatic stress. A lot braver men have suffered more than I have and are managing to live normal lives."

"And a lot of them commit suicide because they can't manage day-to-day life as a civilian." Bear shook his head. "How did you manage to get away from your attacker?"

"He left me tied to a tree. I think he expected me to die of exposure that night. It got really cold, but I didn't give up. I rubbed the ropes against the tree bark until they frayed and finally broke. When I pulled the bag off my head, it was already getting dark. I didn't know which way to go.

"I remember being worried about my parents. I wondered if they'd found my backpack, or called the school to see if I'd taken the bus home."

Bear slowed his truck, letting her finish her story before they entered Eagle Rock, for which she was grateful.

"I found my clothes, but not my shoes. After dressing, I walked for a long time, until I came to a paved road. Then I walked some more, barefoot, bleeding, and probably in shock." She drew in a deep breath. That feeling, as though all that awful day had happened to someone else, blanketed her, insulating her from the horror.

"I finally saw a light in the distance. It was a vehicle coming my way. I was afraid it was him, coming back to finish me off. I dove into the bushes and hid until it went by. Then I continued until I came across a mailbox. Then another, the one with our address on it. Somehow, I'd found my way back to where it had all begun. I ran all the way down our driveway, ran through the door and collapsed in my mother's arms."

"If you didn't tell your parents what happened, how did you explain your disappearance and battered condition?"

"I told them I'd chased a rabbit into the woods, got disoriented, lost my way and fell down a ravine. They'd called the sheriff and had half of the county out looking for me when I showed up."

"Why didn't you tell your parents what really happened?"

She laughed, though the sound was hollow, even to her own ears. "I was sixteen, scared, deeply ashamed and horribly embarrassed."

"Jesus, Mia. You had no reason to be ashamed or embarrassed. You were brutally attacked."

"I know that now. As a sixteen-year-old, all I could think of was what my friends would think. They would never look at me the same. Hell, *I* didn't look at me the same. Most of my friends had already had sex with their boyfriends. I didn't want to be the victim, someone to be pitied."

"Why didn't you tell the sheriff when he came out to your house to investigate the break-in?"

Mia shrugged. "It's been thirteen years. I'm sure some statute of limitations would protect him from being prosecuted."

"Do you know that for certain?"

She sighed. "No. To tell the truth, I kind of want to wait and see if I can figure it out without making a big deal of it."

"Mia, it *was* a big deal."

"I know. But I don't want to turn the town upside down looking for someone who might not even live here anymore. What if the attacker was someone from somewhere else?"

"He hid in the bushes, waiting for you," Bear said. "The guy had to have known you, and watched you enough to know when you would get off that bus, and that your folks wouldn't be waiting for you."

Mia had thought of that. "Still, I don't want to disrupt lives of those who weren't directly involved, or cast doubts on innocent people."

"If you want to find the guy, you have to ask questions," Bear insisted.

"So, maybe I'm not sure I want to find this guy," she snapped.

Bear released the hand he'd been holding. "Sorry. I thought that was the reason you came back to Eagle Rock."

"I came back to write a script and deal with my parents' house." Mia closed her eyes and focused on remaining calm.

For several minutes she remained silent, knowing what she had to do, but not liking it any more now than when she was sixteen. She drew in a deep breath, released it and opened her eyes. "You're right. I came back because I wondered if anyone else had suffered an attack like mine. I couldn't live with the guilt. If I had reported the attack when it happened, my attacker could have been identified and put in jail. Instead, he's been free to commit more attacks. Because I was a coward, others could have been hurt."

"Others could have been hurt because of *him*, not you. He's the bad guy in this situation."

As they entered town, Mia stared at passing vehicles and people on the sidewalks. "I really have no idea who it could have been."

"Was there any guy who'd made a pass at you? Someone you might have rebuffed?"

Mia shook her head. "I barely knew what a pass was. Yeah, I watched guys and girls flirt, but I guess I wasn't ready for it. We were in a small school. Everyone knew everyone else."

"Meaning, he knew you, and you knew him," Bear said quietly.

A chill slipped across her skin. "As far as I knew, I didn't have any enemies. I was an introvert, more into my books than boys. My friend Kylie was the social butterfly, the cheerleader and popular girl. Why would someone target me?"

"Maybe he saw you as a challenge?" Bear suggested.

Mia shot a glance his way. "A challenge?"

Bear nodded. "Some sick bastards like the challenge of getting away with things. Especially with women who would be too shy to call the police and report an attack, if she lived to tell."

That had been exactly what Mia had done. Or not done.

She pointed to the right. "This is the hardware store."

Bartlett's Hardware was a small building, probably as old as the town of Eagle Rock. The windows were gray with dirt and age. The sign listed to the right, in need of a more secure mooring, and the paint on the side of the building curled from the harsh Montana winters and age.

For bigger projects, most people drove into Bozeman to the shiny, newer warehouse stores with huge selections. At Bartlett's, a rancher could get the basics. Nails, boards and fencing materials.

Mia used to accompany her father to Bartlett's when she was little. She'd found the aisles full of interesting items. Her father had patiently answered her questions about everything from electrical fuses to gardening shears.

Her chest tightened as she entered the store, half-expecting to see her father pouring nails into a paper bag.

"Mia?" a voice said from across the floor.

Mia glanced up at a familiar face. Thirteen years was a long time, but she recognized Phillip Townsend instantly. Still tall, he'd filled out in the shoulders and arms. Mia remembered him as long and lanky, like a young colt. The bulkier football jocks had picked on him, relentlessly.

Mia waved. "Hi, Phillip."

"Let me know if I can help you," he said, from behind the counter.

Mia nodded. Turning to Bear, she noted the narrow-eyed stare he gave Phillip. She touched his arm. "What do we need?"

"Nails, woodscrews, white exterior paint and lumber," Bear said. "I'll get the nails and screws and then meet you at the counter." Her bodyguard veered off to the left, down an aisle with metal bins filled with nuts, bolts, screws and nails of many shapes and sizes.

Mia wandered along the other side of the same aisle, staring at the hinges and cabinet doorknobs without seeing them, memories of her father filling her with sadness.

Phillip appeared beside her. "The hinges are on sale. Two for one."

Mia smiled. "Thanks. I'm not sure we need them, yet. We're here for boards, screws, nails and a can of white exterior paint. My bod—handyman is making repairs to my house."

Bear rounded the end of the aisle, carrying two paper bags bulging with nails and screws. "I could use six eight-foot-long two-by-fours, treated pine, and eight ten-foot one-by-six decking boards."

Phillip nodded. "Just got a load in yesterday. I'll notify the guys out back to set them aside." He hurried back to the counter and lifted an old rotary dial telephone.

When Mia started to follow Phillip, Bear touched her arm, holding her back. "You know him?"

"We went to high school together," Mia said. She glanced at Bear's face and frowned. "You don't think he could have been the one, do you?"

"He's a guy." Bear's lips pressed into a tight line. "As far as I'm concerned, all males in Eagle Rock are suspects until proven innocent."

She frowned. "And that's why I don't want to file a report. Phillip is one of the nicest guys I know. I doubt he had the strength to toss me around back then. He was nothing but a twig, tall and painfully thin."

"You'd be surprised what a thin, wiry man can do when he sets his mind to it."

"Yeah, well, Phillip isn't the one," Mia said and stalked to the counter.

Phillip glanced up from the phone and smiled. "The guys are bringing the boards around. Where do you want them to load them?"

"Into the black pickup," Bear said.

"So you're Mia's handyman?" Phillip asked.

Bear nodded and stuck out his hand. "Tate Parker."

Phillip reached across the counter and shook Bear's hand. "Phillip Townsend."

So now, Mia knew her bodyguard's full name. *Tate Parker.* She studied him from beneath her lashes. Yeah, she could see him as a Tate. But Bear suited him more.

"I'm glad to see Mia back in town," Phillip said. "We haven't seen her in Eagle Rock since…" His smile faded, and his gaze met Mia's. "Sorry."

That pang of loss still hit Mia hard, but she pushed it aside and focused on the man in front of her. "Don't be. I haven't been back in the year since my parents' funeral." She took both of his hands and smiled. "How are you? I didn't get much of a chance to talk to anyone last time I was home. Weren't you engaged? I seem to remember my mother saying something about that."

Phillip's hands tightened in hers, briefly, and then he pulled them away. "I was. Not anymore."

"I'm sorry things didn't work out," Mia said.

"Allyson and I were supposed to have gotten married last August. She had it all planned, the venue chosen, bridesmaids lined up and a dress purchased.

The pain in the man's face was more than Mia could take. She touched his arm and asked, "What happened?"

His lips twisted. "I don't know. One day she was happy and excited about the wedding." Phillip's head dipped. "The next moment, she was dead."

Mia gasped and pressed her fingers to her mouth. She didn't know what she expected him to say, but dead wasn't it. "What happened?"

Phillip looked up and away. "I wish I knew. Maybe the stress of wedding planning got to her. I thought we had it together. We had a plan. Then she was gone."

"I'm so sorry," Mia said.

"I just wish I'd known she wasn't happy. I'd have done anything to change that, even give her up, if that's what she'd wanted. I just wish I'd seen the signs."

"Signs?" Mia frowned. "Was she ill?"

Phillip nodded. "Allyson committed suicide."

Mia's heart seemed to hit the bottom of her belly like a solid lead weight. Pretty Allyson Severs, with her dark hair and bright blue eyes, had always had a smile on her face. How could anyone so happy hide such darkness inside?

Mia paid for the boards, nails, screws and paint and left the hardware store, her heart heavy. As Bear pulled out on the road, Mia pointed. "Go right at the first road."

"Where are we going?" Bear asked.

"To the cemetery," Mia said. "I haven't been there since the funeral last year." She turned away from Bear and stared out the window as tears slipped down her cheeks.

It wasn't as if she'd expected coming home would be easy. She'd come, knowing it would be hard.

5

———

BEAR PARKED the truck in a gravel parking lot across the street from a small wooden church. A wrought-iron fence surrounded a cemetery filled with grave markers and head-stones with the names of people who'd been a part of the Eagle Rock community as far back as the eighteen-hundreds.

Mia sat staring at the view out the window of the pickup, her cheeks streaked with tears.

Bear's chest squeezed. He knew the pain of losing loved ones. He and his army brothers had been through so much together. When one died, the others grieved. Bear never forgot the faces of his fallen brothers.

Staring at the cemetery reminded him of those men who'd died and the families who'd been there to receive the caskets draped in U.S flags.

Forcing back the raw emotion threatening to overwhelm him, Bear eased out of the truck. His leg ached, but he didn't let it slow him down as he rounded the front of the vehicle and opened Mia's door.

When she didn't move, he waited patiently.

Then she turned and slid down, her foot missing the running board. She would have fallen if Bear hadn't held out his arms and caught her, pulling her against his chest as he

319

staggered backward, unsteadily. When he had his balance, he loosened his hold and stared down into her face.

"Thanks." Mia swept her hair back from her face, and then laid her hands on his arms. "I've got this."

Bear released her and let her lead the way through the headstones. He followed ten feet behind, giving her the space she seemed to need.

Mia wandered through the rows, pausing briefly at a large headstone with the names Harvey and Lois Chastain inscribed. Based on the dates the couple had lived, they would have been Mia's paternal grandparents. She ran her hand over the smooth granite and moved on, coming to a halt near the back of the graveyard. This row didn't stretch all of the way to the end like the others had.

Stopping at a pink and gray granite headstone, the second on the row, Mia dropped to her knees and stared at the names.

Bear leaned against a tree and let Mia have the time to visit the graves of her beloved parents. She murmured something to their ghosts, more tears trickling down her cheeks. Then she stretched out, lying face-down across the grass.

Bear started toward her, but stopped when another woman he hadn't seen before straightened from a grave at the end of the short row.

Blond hair streaked with gray framed a sad face. The woman laid a single pink rose on the grave, kissed her palm and blew the kiss to the headstone. Then she turned toward Mia and frowned. "Mia? Mia Chastain? Is that you?"

Mia pushed to her feet and looked at the woman. "Oh, Mrs. Severs. I just heard about Allyson. I'm so sorry. Allyson was a sweetheart. Everyone loved her."

As Mrs. Severs closed the distance between herself and Mia, Bear straightened away from the tree and took two steps toward the pair.

Mrs. Severs pulled Mia into her arms and held her, rocking slightly back and forth, like a mother rocking her child. For a long moment, the two women hugged.

Bear stood back, reluctant to interrupt the touching moment.

Finally, Mrs. Severs leaned back and held Mia at arm's length, "I'm sorry about what happened to your parents."

Mia brushed tears from her cheeks. "Thank you. I didn't know about Allyson until today."

Bear moved closer to Mia as Mrs. Severs let go of her arms, her shoulders sagging. The woman glanced over Mia's shoulder at Bear.

"This is my handyman, Tate Parker," Mia said, waving her hand toward him. "We just saw Phillip at the hardware store. He still can't believe it. He said she seemed so excited about getting married. Everything seemed to be going so well."

Mrs. Severs gave a half-smile that didn't reach her blue eyes. "I'd never seen her so happy, what with all the wedding planning. Allyson and Phillip were perfect for each other. Then one day, it was as though the light went out of her. Her father and I had spent the weekend at our cabin in the mountains. When we got back, Allyson didn't seem the same. She refused to come out of her room, and she'd quit eating. Whenever we tried to talk to her, she just cried and locked the door." The older woman seemed to choke on her words.

Mia slipped an arm around Mrs. Severs, her own eyes filling with tears.

"We talked to Phillip," Mrs. Severs continued. "He said he hadn't spoken to Allyson since they'd been out the night we left. He'd said they were fine. They'd talked about the honeymoon, and Allyson had seemed happy. The next morning, he called. She didn't answer. He came to the house to speak to her, but she didn't come to the door. He went around the house to her bedroom window and knocked on the glass. She came to the window, but said she wasn't feeling well and didn't want to make him sick, too.

"When we got home, we could tell she'd been crying, but she didn't want to talk about it. It went on like that for two days. The third morning after our return..." Mrs. Severs sucked in a shaky breath. "We found her hanging from the ceiling fan in her bedroom."

Bear's heart broke for the mother. No parent should outlive a child. He couldn't begin to imagine finding his child the way Mrs. Severs had found hers.

For a long moment, Mia held Mrs. Severs. The woman's shoulders shook with her silent sobs.

"Why?" Mia whispered. "She was a beautiful, happy person."

Mrs. Severs dug a tissue out of her pocket and blew her nose. "We didn't know. I looked for a note, anything that would explain what she had been going through. She left her engagement ring on the nightstand. That's it."

"No fight with Phillip?" Bear asked.

"Phillip was just as torn up about it as we were. He swears they didn't fight the night of their date. Everything was normal when he left her." Mrs. Severs drew in a ragged breath. "I even read through her daily journal, hoping to understand." The woman paused, her brows wrinkling.

"What did you find?"

"It was odd. She'd written an entry the night she'd gone out with Phillip. It was all about the honeymoon plans. Every word seemed upbeat and happy. But she didn't finish the page like she usually did. It was as if she'd stopped in midsentence and never went back to finish the entry. I found the journal underneath her bed. Not tucked in, but upside down, as if it had been thrown or fallen from her desk and kicked across the floor."

A cold sensation washed over Bear. He touched Mia's back.

She glanced over her shoulder at Bear, nodded, and then turned to the older woman. "Mrs. Severs, would you mind if I looked at that journal?"

She shook her head. "No. I suppose you could. Although I don't see why. Nothing's going to bring her back."

Mia squeezed the woman's hands. "I'm so sorry. Allyson was my friend. I'd just like to read through those last couple of days, as a kind of closure."

"Certainly," Mrs. Severs said. "Phillip has been so good to us. The poor man seems so lost without her. I don't have the heart to tell him that it hurts when he comes over. Just his being there reminds us of what we're missing. They would have been married. She might have been pregnant with our first grandchild. Now, we'll never have grandchildren."

Mrs. Severs stood with her eyes closed, tears dripping down her face. After a moment, she wiped her cheeks. "If you want to see the journal, please come during the workday. I'd rather my husband didn't know. He gets upset every time Allyson's name comes up. You know how close they were."

Mia nodded. "I remember." She hooked her arm through Mrs. Severs's arm. "Let me walk you back to your car."

"Thank you, dear," Mrs. Severs said.

Bear fell in step on the other side of the frail woman in case she collapsed from her misery. When they arrived at her car, he helped her into the driver's seat.

Mia leaned into the open car door. "Do you mind very much if I follow you back to your house to have a look at that journal, now?"

Mrs. Severs glanced at the clock on her dash. "I suppose that would be okay. I didn't have any more plans for the day. I'm never much good after I visit Allyson."

"Do you want me to drive you home?" Mia asked.

Bear's fingers curled into fists. He didn't want her to drive with someone else. How could he protect her if she wasn't with him at all times?

"No, thank you, dear. I can get myself home." She gave Mia a wan smile. "I'm sad, not helpless."

"We'll be right behind you," Mia said and closed the car door.

Mrs. Severs backed out of the parking lot and pulled onto the road heading back into town.

Mia and Bear hurried to follow.

Once inside the truck, Mia turned to Bear. "I didn't want to see or talk to anyone after I'd been attacked."

"We don't know why Allyson shut down," Bear said. "It could have been something else."

"But if it was him…" Mia pounded her fist on the armrest. "If only I'd—"

Bear reached out and touched her arm. "Stop it. You are not responsible for that bastard's actions."

"You didn't know Allyson," Mia cried. "She was so beautiful, loving and full of life. I can't think of anything else that would make her want to take her life. I wanted to take my own life when it happened to me. But I was too much of a coward to do even that."

"Sweetheart, you were anything but a coward. You did the bravest thing of all…you lived and made something of yourself, despite your fears and insecurities." Bear shook his head. "You're an amazing woman. Sadie said you write scripts for movies. The scripts you write make people laugh, cry and feel."

"But Allyson might be alive today if I had reported my rape thirteen years ago."

"You don't know that."

"Why else would a woman on the verge of the happiest day of her life take her own life?"

Bear couldn't explain why Allyson Severs had committed suicide. Only Allyson could answer that. Unfortunately, the woman had been successful in her attempt to end her torment.

Bear's fingers tightened on the steering wheel. If he ever found the guy who'd raped Mia, and could potentially have raped Allyson and caused her to commit suicide, he'd kill the bastard, inflicting on him a slow, very painful death.

AT MRS. SEVERS'S HOME, the older woman invited them to visit Allyson's room. "The journal is on her desk. I'm going to make a cup of tea and take something for a headache. Can I get anything for you two?"

"No, thank you," Mia said, anxious to read Allyson's last words. She hoped to find a clue as to why the young woman had taken her life.

"I haven't changed anything in Allyson's room since she passed. I can't bring myself to do it. I keep hoping I'll wake up from this horrible nightmare and she'll come dancing into the room, laughing." Mrs. Severs snorted and turned toward the kitchen. "If you don't mind, I'll let you go look. I can't go into her room."

Mia watched as Mrs. Severs walked away. She supposed a mother never got over losing her daughter. Mia wondered if she'd get over losing her parents. Like Mrs. Severs, it was difficult to enter those places that reminded her of them. Coming back to her parents' home had been one of the hardest things Mia had ever done. She kept expecting her mother to be in the kitchen when she walked through the door. But her mother wasn't and never would be again.

As Mia entered Allyson's room, her heart constricted, and her throat all but closed. A wedding dress, wrapped in clear plastic, hung on the closet door. *Bride* magazines littered the desk, and what appeared to be the couple's official engagement picture had been framed and placed on the nightstand, facing Ally's pillow.

She found the journal on the desk, lying open across the array of magazines. The page on the left had writing halfway down the lines. The right page was completely empty.

Mia sat in the chair and turned back to the beginning of the entry for the last day of Allyson's happiness, if not the last day of her life. What had happened to make her so depressed she'd taken her own life?

Mia bent to the journal and read from the beginning of that day's post to the abrupt ending.

Bear stood behind her, leaning over her shoulder, reading along.

Just as her mother had said, Allyson posted about her day at work as a kindergarten teacher, how the children had made her laugh. She'd written that she'd barely been able to focus, because she'd been so excited to see her fiancé that night to talk about where they would spend their honeymoon. And the evening had been magical. Phillip had taken her to a nice restaurant in Bozeman where they'd talked about the different places they could go.

We finally settled on the beach vacation in—

"It's as though something interrupted her," Bear said.

"I agree." She turned back several pages and read through a week's worth of entries. Nothing jumped out. The entries were similar to her last one, all about her days at work and her wedding plans.

Mia flipped back even farther to two weeks before Allyson's last entry. She happened to land on a weekend page. Allyson had gone to Bozeman with her bridesmaids for them to try on their dresses. She'd left it up to them to choose the style they preferred as long as the dresses were in the same material and color. They'd made a party of it.

Though it was a great day, one thing disturbed me. We were supposed to stay the entire day and return late this evening, but one of my bridesmaids had to get back early. She said it was because she needed to bake cookies for her Sunday school class, but I think she didn't want her husband to get mad if she came back really late. I'm not sure what's going on with her, but the others were disappointed to leave early.

The passage didn't name the bridesmaid, and Mia wasn't convinced it meant anything, so she moved on, reading the rest of the entries for that week.

"See anything that stands out?" she asked Bear.

With Bear hovering over her shoulder, Mia became hyper-aware of his body so close to hers. Several times she lost focus on the words, breathing in his outdoorsy scent. She could feel his heat, and it made her pulse quicken. What would it feel like to lie next to him, to be held in his arms and feel his hands sliding across her body?

Her naked body?

Mia closed the journal and stood, putting as much distance between her and Bear as possible in the small room.

He walked around the room, looked out the window and checked under the bed.

"What are you looking for?" Mia asked.

"I don't know. I feel like there's a missing piece to this puzzle."

Mia rubbed her arms, a chill raising gooseflesh across her skin, now that Bear wasn't standing over her. "Why did she stop writing in the middle of a sentence, and why did she then get so depressed she'd take her own life?"

"Do you think maybe she got a call from someone?"

"We thought of that." Mrs. Severs stood in the doorway, a cup of tea in her hand. "We checked her cell phone records. The calls she'd made that night after she got home were to her bridesmaids. We asked them what the calls were about, and they all said Allyson had called to tell them about her and Phillip's choice for a honeymoon location. They said she sounded happy. They couldn't understand what could have made her so sad."

Mia hugged Mrs. Severs once more, careful not to spill her tea. "Thank you for indulging me. I can't begin to tell you how sorry I am that Allyson is gone."

"Thank you for caring," Mrs. Severs said. She glanced at her watch, and her eyes widened. "My husband will be home in ten minutes."

"We're leaving." Mia hooked Bear's arm and followed Mrs. Severs out of Allyson's room and through the front door.

Once they'd reached the porch, Mrs. Severs seemed to relax. "It was nice seeing you, Mia. How long will you be in town?"

"I'm not certain. At least until I complete a project I'm working on."

"Congratulations on your success in the movie industry. Everyone in Eagle Rock is excited by our local celebrities."

"Thank you," she said with a small smile. "I do my best."

"I find it ironic that Allyson never wanted to leave Eagle Rock. If she'd left when you and Sadie did after high school, she might be alive today. I sometimes wonder if I made the right choice, encouraging her to live here. Or if my husband and I had stayed home that weekend we went to the cabin, maybe we could have prevented whatever happened to make Allyson so sad."

Mia touched the woman's hand. "Don't blame yourself."

She gave a sad smile. "I know. Nothing I wish I could have done will bring her back. But still..." She shrugged.

As soon as Bear drove out of the Severs's driveway, he turned to Mia. "I know you don't want to hear this, but I think you need to talk to the sheriff about what happened to you, Mia. He might have other unsolved cases that could be related. He also will have access to the state's crime database. If other women in neighboring counties have been assaulted, we might have a serial rapist on our hands."

Mia had been thinking along the same lines. Everything about Allyson's abrupt change in personality and outlook screamed trauma. And what trauma would make her pull back from everyone she loved? The situation felt eerily familiar. "You're right. I need to talk to the sheriff. But I only want to talk to Sheriff Wilson. Not any of his deputies. The sheriff is an old friend of the family; he'll be discreet."

"When?" Bear persisted.

"I'll set up an appointment with him for the morning."

"Why not now?"

Irritated, she shot a narrow-eyed glance in Bear's direction. "Anyone ever tell you that you're pushy?"

He grinned, the expression transforming his face. "All the time."

Mia sat frozen in time, the smile on Bear's face lighting up the interior of the truck cab. "You really should smile more often."

His grin broadened. "The same goes for you."

Mia couldn't help the infectious grin catching her and making her lips twitch at the corners. The man had her charmed, and he was smart. But that didn't make him right for her.

She had too much baggage. No man wanted to navigate the minefield of her sexuality. He'd step on one of her booby-traps and boom! That would be the end before it really began.

With a sigh, she focused on the road ahead.

Bear's smile faded and he too trained his attention on the highway. "Where to?"

"Home. We only have a couple hours left of daylight to get that door back in place and install the knobs Hank will be bringing. I won't sleep comfortably until I know the doors will hold up next time someone decides to kick them in."

6

___

BEAR USED the new lumber to replace the broken and splintered portions of the doorframe, drilled the holes for the deadbolt and covered all of the doorframe with a fresh coat of white paint. By the time he was finished, his stomach rumbled, and he remembered he hadn't eaten lunch.

He'd bet Mia hadn't eaten either. With the intention of finding her and insisting they get some food, he started to go into the house, but stopped when he heard the sound of a vehicle's engine and the crunch of gravel on the drive.

Hank's truck pulled up to the house. He and Sadie climbed down. Sadie carried a bag.

"Did you think we'd never get back with the hardware?" Hank asked.

"Blame it on me," Sadie grinned. "I never knew there would be so many doorknobs and locks to choose from. I had a hard time deciding which ones to purchase."

"I finally had to make the choice." Hank took the bag from Sadie and handed it to Bear.

Footsteps behind him alerted Bear to Mia's presence. Warmth spread through him. He'd steered clear of her all afternoon, afraid the closer he got, the more he'd want to reach out and touch her.

She smiled and took the bag from Bear, riffling through the contents. "Thank you so much for going all the way to Bozeman to get these. We probably would have been fine with what Bartlett's Hardware had in stock. I didn't need fancy, just strong. These look like they'll fit the bill."

"We got enough to replace the front and back doors, and had them keyed to match the new locks," Sadie said.

Hank climbed the porch steps and held out his hand. "Let me have one of those. I can switch out the front doorknob while Bear installs the back."

Within fifteen minutes, the new knobs and deadbolt locks had been installed.

Sadie and Mia sat on the steps of the back porch talking about renovations while the men worked.

Bear found the sound of their soft voices to be oddly soothing as he worked fitting the knobs and lock mechanisms into place. It made him wonder what it would be like to live in one place and have a home to go to.

His mother had moved him from place to place, always living in cheap apartments, unable to afford a house with a yard. Bear had played in the streets or at whatever basketball court he could find. He'd never known his father, so he'd never missed him.

Looking around at the old house, he knew it needed a lot of work, but at one time, it had been a home Mia had loved. And it could be again, if she chose to stay in Montana instead of going back to live in L.A.

Hank came back through the house, holding up a key. "Mine works. Are you about done here?"

Bear tightened the last screw and straightened. "Done."

Hank handed the key to Mia and descended the stairs to join his wife on the steps. "You should sleep a little easier tonight."

"I hope so. Last night wasn't much fun." Mia's stomach gurgled. She pressed a hand to her belly. "I can't believe we missed lunch." She frowned and stared across at Bear. "You should have said something. I imagine you're starving."

"I'm okay, but getting a little hungry."

"We were about to head into town for a bite of dinner at the diner," Sadie said.

"We were?" Hank asked.

Sadie elbowed him in the gut. "We *are*. You two want to join us?"

Mia glanced at Bear. "I don't have much in the refrigerator. I'm game, if you are."

"Give me a minute to wash up. I'm covered in sawdust."

"Go on," Hank said. "But hurry it up. These women are starving."

Bear grabbed his duffel bag from his truck and hurried into the house. Ten minutes later, he emerged with a clean body, wet hair and clean clothes.

They piled into Hank's extended-cab truck and headed for the diner in Eagle Rock.

"The diner is the only restaurant in town," Hank said. "At this time of day, it's usually pretty full."

"The food's good, and it beats cooking dinner," Sadie added.

Fortunately, they were able to find an empty booth. A waitress hurried by, slapped menus on the table, and continued walking, calling over her shoulder, "I'll be back in just a minute to take your orders."

The waitress, looking frazzled, stopped at a table with only one guest, the deputy who'd been at Mia's house earlier that day, Larry Maynard, still in uniform.

"It smells good in here," Bear said, his stomach knotting, he was so hungry. He lifted the menu and stared down.

A loud crash made him glance up.

The waitress bent to collect broken shards of a water glass from the floor. "I'll get you another," she said and hurried away from the deputy.

"Don't bother. I'm heading home. I'll see you there."

Maynard rose from his chair, stretched and glanced around the room. When he spotted Bear and Mia, he frowned and headed their way. "I hear you've been asking around about the Severs girl."

Bear frowned. How had Maynard heard about their visit?

"Not really." Mia glanced up at the deputy. "We ran into Phillip at the hardware store. I had no idea about Allyson."

Maynard shook his head. "That was a sad situation. I was the first deputy on scene. I couldn't believe she'd done it until I saw her there."

Bear felt Mia stiffen beside him. He reached beneath the table, found her hand and squeezed it.

"Did you conduct the investigation?" Mia asked. "Any idea what happened to her that she would want to take her own life?"

"She didn't leave a note. I can only guess," Maynard said. "Such a shame, losing her so young. Well, like I said, I conducted the investigation. If you have questions, ask me. I may or may not be able to answer. In the meantime, I'm off duty and headed home. It's been a long day." Maynard left the diner.

"He knew Allyson," Mia whispered. "How could he be so casual about her death?"

"Maybe it's his way of dealing with the loss," Bear reasoned, though he felt the same. If Maynard knew the woman, he should feel something. But the man had responded like it was just another day at the office.

"Sorry I took so long. What can I get you?" The waitress pushed a lank strand of dirty-blond hair out of her gaunt face and finally made eye-contact with them. Her gaze snagged on the woman sitting beside Bear. "Mia?"

Mia's eyes narrowed as she stared up at the woman. "Yes?"

The waitress's mouth twisted, and she touched her hair again. "It's me. Kylie."

Mia's brows dipped, and she leaned closer, studying the waitress. Then her eyes widened, and she smiled. "Oh, my God, Kylie."

Bear slid out of his seat to let Mia stand.

Mia hugged the woman, stood back and held her hands. "I haven't seen you in a decade."

"Wow, that makes it sound like forever," Kylie tugged at the food-stained apron around her waist. "You look amazing," she said, a wistful tone in her voice. "You did it, didn't you? You got out of Eagle Rock and made something of yourself."

"I did." Mia smiled kindly at the woman. "What about you? Married? Children?"

Kylie nodded and held up her hand, displaying a small diamond ring and a thin gold band. "Married. No children."

Bear noted bruises on the woman's arm, and frowned.

"Who did you marry?" Mia asked. "Tom Gruehot? You two were a thing for a while."

Kylie shook her head. "That was back in tenth grade. Besides, Tom joined the army right out of high school. I believe he's somewhere in Texas now. No, I married Larry Maynard. He was just here." She turned toward the exit, as if she expected him to be there.

"Larry did mentioned he married a cheerleader."

Kylie smiled. "But enough about me. What would you like to drink?"

Mia took her seat, they placed their orders and Kylie hurried to the kitchen.

"I barely recognized her," Sadie said, her gaze following Kylie. "She looks worse than the last time I saw her. And that's only been a couple of weeks."

Mia nodded. "She used to be the best dressed, most put-together girl in our school. She let me follow her around. I was the ugly friend." Mia's brows dipped. "Did you see the bruises on her arm?"

"I did. Do you suppose she got them from carrying those big trays?" Bear asked.

"Maybe," Mia said, not sounding convinced.

When Kylie returned with their drinks, Bear studied the woman's arms. The bruises were oval shaped and on the inside and the outside of her arms, almost as if someone had grabbed her hard, leaving fingerprints.

The meal passed with discussion of people Hank, Mia and Sadie knew from their school days.

"Sorry, Bear, this must all be boring," Hank said. "Not having grown up in Eagle Rock, you wouldn't know any of these people."

"No worries. I always wished I'd lived in one place all my life. I don't remember anyone from my childhood."

"If the Delta Force is anything like the SEALs," Hank said, "your teammates became your family."

"They were." And he missed them. What he'd done in the army was so far removed from that diner in Eagle Rock, Montana, he could have been on another planet.

"Let me know if any of your teammates are getting out of the army anytime soon. I could use more good men like you."

Bear raised his brows. "Will you have enough work to hire more agents?"

Hank nodded. "Word is getting out. Sadie knows a lot of folks in the movie industry who've purchased ranches or ski chalets in and around Montana. I have inquiries coming in every day. I could use more men today."

"Good to hear," Bear said. "I'll put out some feelers. I know a couple guys who are qualified and looking for work."

"Send them my way. I'll interview them for the jobs."

Bear hesitated. "What about women?"

Hank smiled. "If they can shoot straight and can throw me in hand-to-hand combat, I'm willing to consider them."

With a nod, Bear thought about the men and women he'd met in his career. Some were already out of the military and others were up for re-enlistment soon and had made noises about getting out.

Mia tapped his arm. "Excuse me. I need to go to the ladies' room."

Bear scooted out of the booth and stood back as Mia passed. When he started to fall in step behind her, she pressed a hand to his chest and smiled. "I can do this on my own."

For a moment, Bear frowned. "I don't mind walking with you."

"I mind having a shadow when I'm only going to the restroom." She squeezed his hand. "I'll be all right."

Bear wasn't so sure. He settled in his seat, his gaze following her all the way across the diner floor to the short, dark hallway leading to the restrooms. He counted the minutes.

"Worried?" Sadie asked. "Do you want me to go check on her?"

Bear let go of the breath he'd been holding. "Would you?"

About the time Sadie stood, Kylie, the waitress emerged from the hallway, her eyes red and puffy. A moment later, Mia stepped out of the darkness, her lips thin, her gaze following Kylie.

Bear guessed they'd had a discussion about the bruises on the waitress's arm.

"Thank goodness. Here comes Mia." Sadie sank back into the seat beside Hank.

Bear scooted over on the bench seat and let Mia take the outside. Bear leaned close. "Are you all right?"

"Just dandy," she replied.

"Ready to go?"

"After I finish my drink." Mia tossed back the soda she'd ordered to go with her dinner and set the glass on the table. She obviously didn't want to talk about her encounter in the bathroom, and the strained expression on her face didn't encourage Bear to press.

When they'd finished and paid for their meals, the foursome rose from their booth and headed for the door.

The trip back to Mia's house didn't take long. When they arrived, Bear said, "I'd rather you two ladies stayed in the truck until we have a look around."

Mia nodded. She and Sadie remained in their seats.

Hank and Bear made a cursory pass around the exterior of the house, checked the doors and entered from opposite sides. When confident there weren't any bad guys hiding behind the bushes or under a bed, Bear returned to Hank's truck to collect Mia.

As he and Mia entered the house, Hank and Sadie drove away.

"ALL OF THIS checking and double-checking seems like a lot of trouble for one person." Mia laid her purse on the counter in the kitchen.

Bear's lips pressed together. "I prefer to be thorough. No surprises."

She turned to watch him as he twisted the lock in the door handle and turned the deadbolt. "I'm sure you had more than your share of surprises in the Army. How long were you in?"

"Fourteen years." Bear faced her.

"I take it that you would have stayed longer, if they'd let you."

He nodded, his jaw tightening.

His blue eyes darkened, the intensity making her long to reach out and touch his cheek. Apparently the Army had been more to him than just a job. Her chest tightening, Mia turned and walked a few steps away.

Alone with Bear in the confines of her house, Mia had the sensation of the walls closing in, making the kitchen seem more intimate. The silence lengthened, stretching her nerves with each passing second.

What was she afraid of? Bear was a man of honor. He wouldn't attack her in her own home or outside of it.

What Mia didn't want to admit to herself was that the closer she was to the man, the more heat built inside her body. His broad shoulders and thickly muscled frame made her want to reach out and touch, to feel, to run her hands over the hard planes of his chest and torso. And that would be completely inappropriate between a boss and her bodyguard.

Afraid to face him in case he saw her growing desire, she kept her back to Bear. "Would you like a cup of coffee or tea?"

"No, thank you."

At a loss for something to say, she said the only thing she could think of. "Is there anything I can do to make your stay here more comfortable?"

"Where do you want me to put my things? I left my duffel

in the upstairs bathroom earlier."

"You can have the first bedroom on the right. I'm in the one on the left, across the hallway." She didn't have the heart to move into the master bedroom, where her parents had slept up until the day they'd died. Then she remembered. "Oh, wait, I haven't cleaned that room, yet."

"No need. I can do that. I'm not a guest. I'm the hired hand."

"Still, you shouldn't have to clean your own room." Mia moved toward the staircase.

Bear caught her wrist and pulled her back. "I'm quite capable of taking care of myself. Aren't you supposed to be writing or something?"

Mia stared at his hand on her wrist as electrical impulses ran up her arm and spread throughout her body. Her core tingled and heated in response to the signals zinging from nerve to nerve. The longer he held her wrist, the faster her heart hammered against her ribcage. "Um, I..." Hell, she couldn't think when he held any part of her. His touch had the effect of scrambling her wits. "I can't think... I mean, I can't concentrate when you...when I—" She shut her mouth to keep from saying even more inane comments. "I'm tired. I think I'll go to bed."

Bear glanced down at his hand, and then dropped her wrist and stepped back. "Sorry. I'll have another look around the house, then call it a night as well."

"Okay." Mia dragged her gaze away from his, spun toward the stairs, and ran. Her heart raced with each step taking her father away from the man who made her insides tremble with a need she'd never felt, until him.

Once in her room, she shut the door and leaned against it, dragging in breath after ragged breath until her pulse returned to normal. She gathered fresh underwear from a drawer, put them back and selected the lace thong she'd bought on impulse one day in the lingerie section of her favorite store. Feeling a little foolish, she selected her usual oversized, faded T-shirt to counter the frilly panties.

Armed with her nightclothes, she opened the door, peeked

out and ran for the bathroom door farther down the hallway. Safely inside, she locked the door and turned toward the shower. On impulse, she turned back and untwisted the button on the doorknob.

The lust-driven woman inside hoped Bear would find the door unlocked and enter before he realized she was there. The idea was senseless. Bear wasn't the kind of man who would barge into a room with a closed door. He'd knock before entering. Mia would feel obligated to answer, and nothing would come of her insane attempt to have an "accidental" naked encounter with the hired help. Still, the thought tantalized.

She stripped out of her jeans and shirt, unhooked her bra and glanced toward the door as she shrugged out of it. Breasts hanging free, she had only to slip out of her panties, and she'd be naked. Who was she trying to kid? The man wasn't interested, nor was he coming through the door any time soon.

With a sigh, Mia shed her panties and stepped into the tub. A long cold shower would clear her thoughts, chill her desire and pull her together.

And it did, no matter how disappointing.

The shower also gave her time to think about the discussion she'd had with Kylie in the bathroom. Her old friend swore her bruises were from working at the diner. Mia suspected her husband was the one who'd inflicted them on her skin.

Mia had told her she had choices. She didn't have to stay in an abusive relationship. "When you're ready to get out of it, call me," she'd offered.

Kylie had stared straight at her and said, "I don't know what you're talking about." Then she'd run out of the bathroom, her eyes filled with tears.

The woman needed help.

With her wet hair brushed straight, and dressed in her thong and the T-shirt that hung down past mid-thigh, Mia abandoned the bathroom. Any fantasies about showering with her bodyguard remained unrealized as she padded barefoot down the hall to her bedroom.

Inside, with the door closed behind her, Mia took stock of the room she'd grown up in. It appeared to have been arrested in time, bearing the same decorations and paint from when she'd been a teen.

If she kept the house, she'd update the furniture and bedding to something that would appeal to her guests, if she ever had any. The entire house needed a facelift.

Slipping her feet between the clean sheets, she pulled the blanket up to her chin and closed her eyes. In an attempt to keep her mind off the handsome bodyguard, Mia tried to picture the room and how it would look updated.

No matter how hard she focused, an image of Bear kept popping into her mind. He stood in her room, his broad shoulders filling the small space with an overabundance of male pheromones eating away at the walls Mia had constructed around her heart.

She glanced away from the door, but her mind couldn't erase the image. Mia punched her pillow and visualized sheep, counting them one at a time.

The phone Bear had moved from the living room and installed earlier on her nightstand jangled, abruptly.

Mia's eyes flew open, and she clapped a hand over her mouth to keep from crying out in the darkness. Having lived with cell phones in L.A., the harsh, tinny jangle of the vintage phone made her start and sit up. Next on her list of things to buy was a more updated version with caller ID.

She grabbed the receiver and lifted it to her ear, wondering who would be calling at that hour. More importantly, who knew she was home? "Hello."

Nothing. No static. No voice. Nothing.

Then a hint of a sound, like someone releasing a breath, made her strain to listen.

Mia swallowed hard, her pulse racing. "Who is this?"

Light clicking sounded above her head. Mia screamed, dropped the phone and rolled out of bed onto her knees.

Footsteps pounded down the hallway and Mia's door crashed open.

Bear, wearing jeans and nothing else, rushed in. "Mia? What's wrong?"

Mia leaped to her feet and threw herself into his arms. "I answered the phone. No one spoke, but I heard someone breathing. Then there was a clicking sound."

With Mia tucked against his side, Bear scooped up the phone, listened and shook his head. "Whoever it was hung up. We'll see if the phone company can trace the call. Maybe the sheriff can help us with that."

Mia burrowed her face against Bear's naked chest. "I'm not normally spooked, but the breathing and the clicking…"

Both of Bear's arms circled her and held her close. He smoothed her hair with one hand as he spoke soft, soothing words. "It's okay. It was only a phone call."

"I just had the phone company turn it on yesterday. How could anyone know the number already?"

"Probably a wrong number," he murmured.

"What about the clicking? What does that mean?"

"Nothing." He tucked a strand of her hair behind her ear and tipped her face up to his. "I'm here to protect you. I won't let anything hurt you."

Mia's heart skipped several beats as she stared up into his incredibly blue eyes. She believed he wouldn't let anyone harm her. But she had the feeling she would be hurt anyway.

This was the kind of man she could fall for, and what would that get her? Even if he wasn't her bodyguard, and they were just a man and a woman, he wouldn't want her. When he learned she was hesitant when it came to intimacy, he'd grow frustrated when she shied away from his touch.

Well, she wasn't shying away yet, and his arms were firmly around her. At this point with anyone else, she'd fight to be free, panic taking over and ruining her chances of making love.

Mia stared up into Bear's eyes and waited for the familiar anxiety to take control. But it didn't.

Clicking sounded again. This time, Mia realized it wasn't on the telephone. She looked up at the same time as Bear.

More like a scratchy tapping sound, it moved from one end of her room to the other and faded away. Then it started again.

For a moment, Mia considered the idea that the house was truly haunted.

"Have you been in the attic since you've been home?" Bear whispered.

"No," Mia said, perfectly happy to remain in Bear's arms until the horrible scratchy sound went away.

"Do you know what's up there?"

"Christmas decorations, old keepsakes, boxes of my grand-mother's things that my parents couldn't bring themselves to throw away. I don't know." She'd only been up in the attic on a few occasions when her mother had her help get the Christmas decorations down for the holiday.

Bear loosened his hold on her. "I'm going up to check."

Mia curled her fingers around his biceps. She didn't want him to leave her and opened her mouth to tell him so. Before she could, the clicking sounded again. A shiver shook her body, and she released him. She couldn't sleep knowing some-thing was up there.

"Show me to the attic door," Bear said.

Mia led him out of her room and into her parents' bedroom at the end of the hall. The trap door to the attic was in her parents' closet. She pulled the cord hanging from the ceiling and the door came down. "There's a light at the top of the stairs. Just pull the string."

Bear unfolded the stairs and climbed into the attic. A light blinked on up above, shining down into the closet. Bear disappeared.

Alone at the closet door, Mia wrapped her arms around her body. She stared up at the gaping hole in the closet ceiling, counting the seconds that passed. The sound of footsteps crossing the plywood flooring of the attic only slightly reas-sured Mia.

She strained to hear.

Something hissed, Bear cursed, and the clicking, tapping sounded, coming fast toward Mia.

"Look out!" Bear called out.

Something gray and furry skittered past the open trap door.

Mia jumped back and pressed a hand to her mouth to keep from screaming again. "What was that?" she cried out.

"You have a squatter up here."

"What do you mean?"

"Just a minute, and I'll show you." Bear's footsteps sounded again as if he were moving quickly around the space above. Then he appeared at the top of the stairs with a sheet bundled in his arms. He backed down the steps until his feet touched the floor.

Mia's eyes narrowed as the sheet in his arms moved. "What is it?"

"Not it. Them."

"Them?"

"Come with me. I don't want to open the sheet until we're outside."

Mia followed Bear out of the bedroom and down the stairs. Once outside, he dropped to his haunches and unfolded the sheet. Tucked inside were four tiny little balls of gray and black fluff.

When he laid them on the ground, the four babies scurried toward the brush.

"Raccoons in the attic?" Mia laughed. "So much for ghosts."

His mouth quirked upward at one corner. "Thought you'd get a kick out of them."

She frowned. "Will they be all right?"

"Their mama will find them pretty quickly. She hustled out of the attic through a hole in the siding. I'll get up there and patch it temporarily until we can get new siding to do a better job."

"You don't have to do that. I'm almost certain all this carpentry is not part of your job description."

"It is if we want it to look like I'm your handyman, not your bodyguard."

A cool breeze swept across her skin, making Mia shiver.

"It's too cold to be standing around outside. Let's get you inside." He hooked his arm around her waist and walked her back into the house.

"You go get some sleep. I can handle plugging the hole."

"I won't rest until I know the hole is covered." She didn't add that she wouldn't be happy until Bear was down from the attic, away from the raccoon that could attack him. "I have a hammer and nails in the drawer in the kitchen." Mia hurried into the kitchen and found the hammer and nails her mother had kept for hanging pictures on the walls. "The nails aren't very big, but they should work for a temporary fix."

Bear smiled. "Looks like we'll be making another trip to the hardware store."

"My father might have left some plywood in his shed," Mia offered.

"I saw a small sheet upstairs in the corner. I'll use it." Bear waved toward the hallway. "Ladies first."

Not until they stood at the base of the staircase did Mia remember she only wore the thong panties beneath the T-shirt.

With Bear following close behind her, Mia was even more aware of her bare bottom beneath her shirt. She climbed the stairs, tugging at the hem, in an attempt to cover her backside, while her insides heated and her core throbbed with desire.

At the top of the stairs, Bear cleared his throat.

When Mia glanced back at him, he averted his gaze, his cheeks turning a ruddy red.

He'd seen her thong. Or rather, he'd seen her bottom beneath the T-shirt. And he wasn't going to say anything to embarrass her.

Not only was the man kind to animals, as evidenced by his rescue of the baby raccoons, he was concerned about her, enough not to cause her discomfort. Those two qualities only made her want him more.

Damn.

Too bad she would only freeze. They might get as far as a kiss and a touch, but then she'd push away and run. He'd be left frustrated, and then their situation would be even more awkward.

Her cheeks burning, Mia ducked into her room, letting Bear pass her and go on to the closet in her parents' bedroom. When he'd disappeared, she followed more slowly, ending up at the bottom of the attic stairs, wishing she had the courage to follow her desires.

She climbed the steps as the sound of a hammer hitting nails echoed through the attic. At the top, she looked around, spotting Bear holding a hammer and placing a nail against a small sheet of plywood. He slammed it home and set another. With each nail, the muscles in his back flexed.

God, he was gorgeous, strong and sensitive. Everything a woman would want in a man.

Soon, he had the board secured, and he turned toward the stairs.

Caught staring, Mia backed down the steps too fast, missed the bottom rung and fell backward, landing hard on her bottom.

Bear was down the stairs and lifting her into his arms before she could figure out where she'd gone wrong on her descent.

"Are you all right?" he asked.

"Yes," she said, her words strangled in her throat as her body pressed against his. "The only casualty is my pride."

"Can't help you there, but I can help get you to bed." Holding her close to his chest, he carried her into her bedroom where he laid her gently on the mattress.

"You didn't have to carry me," she said.

"Consider it one of the perks of my job." He winked.

Before he could straighten, she touched his arm. "Bear?"

"Yes?"

"I hate to impose, but could you stay for a little longer?"

He froze in position, his body still bent over hers. "Why?"

She stared at her hand on his arm and realized how needy

she sounded. Drawing in a deep breath, she shook her head. "Never mind."

"I don't mind staying. I just need to know what expectations you have."

"I don't have any," she said too quickly. "I'm just feeling a little unsettled with the phone call and intruders in the attic. What if the mama comes back to find the attic shut? Could she get in through another way?"

"I didn't see any other holes in the siding. You should be all right. And if the phone rings, let me answer."

"How? You'd be in your room. If I'm not mistaken, there isn't a landline in there."

"I could sleep downstairs in the living room," Bear suggested.

"No." Mia bit her bottom lip. "Don't worry about me. I'll be okay."

He nodded. "Okay." Bear turned and walked to the door.

With every step that carried him across the floor, she fought to keep from calling out for him to stay. When he reached the door, he looked back once and then disappeared.

Mia pulled the sheet over her bare legs and lay staring at the door, wishing she'd had the courage to tell him to stay.

Forcing her eyes closed, she lay still, trying to focus on those dratted sheep she was supposed to count. No number of sheep made her any sleepier. When she thought she might never go to sleep, the bed beside her dipped.

Mia's eyes popped open.

On the bed beside her lay Bear, propped against the headboard with a pillow he'd brought from his own room. "Hey," he said softly. "I'll stay until you go to sleep."

She nodded and closed her eyes.

If she'd thought sleep was elusive without Bear in the bed, it was doubly so with Bear beside her. It was all she could do to resist reaching out to touch him. Sweet heaven. She wished he would initiate a hug...a kiss...a touch...

Mia snorted softly. With her record of stiffening at the last minute, what could possibly go wrong with that scenario?

$$7$$

BEAR LAY beside Mia afraid to move lest he reach out and pull her into his arms. She'd asked him to stay, not to make love to her. For the love of God, the woman was his client not his lover!

Then why the hell was he even having thoughts of holding her? He should have told her flat out he wasn't interested in staying in her room for any amount of time. Being this close to Mia only made him want to drag her up against his body and bury himself deep inside her.

If he wasn't mistaken, the look in her eyes when he'd walked away had been anything but telling him to get lost. She'd appeared vulnerable and maybe a little afraid of sleeping in the house by herself.

A proper bodyguard would sit in a chair outside her door, or inside the room, but far enough away the client wouldn't have to worry that she would be accosted by the very man sworn to protect her.

And with Mia's background of having been raped as a teen, she was bound to have residual trauma involved when a man touched her.

Holy hell. He'd set himself up for a long night of frustration.

"Would you rather I sat in a chair outside your door?" he asked, his whisper sounding like a shout in the silent room.

She touched his arm, her fingers digging into his skin. "No. Please stay." Mia rolled onto her side, facing him. "I'll try not to snore."

Bear chuckled and turned to face her. "It wouldn't bother me if you did. Several of my Delta Force brothers snored like freight trains." He smiled. "I kind of miss it."

She stared at him for a while. "You were close to your teammates?"

"Very." His smile faded. Many of them were dead. Some were still at Bethesda recovering from wounds that had ended their careers.

"What about your family?"

"My mother died a couple years ago. I never knew my father."

"I'm sorry."

"Don't be. My mother did the best she could. I think I turned out okay."

"I think you did, too." Her lips curled softly.

Bear fought the urge to bend closer and taste them.

"It's hard coming home to an empty house," she whispered.

"Tell me about it." He brushed a strand of her hair back behind her ear. "In my case, it was coming home to an empty apartment."

Mia cupped his face, her eyes darkening in the pale light from the nightstand. "It doesn't have to be that way."

"In my line of work, it was easier than dragging someone else through the many deployments, not knowing if I would return in a body bag."

Mia shivered. "I'm glad you didn't."

"It doesn't matter anymore. The Army won't have me back. I've been medically discharged."

"I'm sorry." She brushed her thumb across his cheek. "And yet, I'm not sorry. Their loss is my gain." She leaned forward and touched her lips to his. "I'm glad you're here."

Electricity shot through him, sizzling a path through his

veins then dropping south to his groin. His cock stiffened, swelling at the feather-soft touch of her lips against his.

He started to reach for her, but caught himself before he did. Though her kiss had sparked an inferno inside him, to her it could have meant nothing more than an empathetic display of sorrow for all he'd lost.

Bear had no right to touch her.

Think with your head, not your dick, he told himself.

Hell, but it was hard. And getting harder.

Mia scooted closer and kissed him again.

A groan rose up Bear's throat and nearly escaped before he swallowed it back. "Mia."

"Mmm." She rested a hand against his chest. Her mouth hovered close to his, her eyelids resting at half-mast.

"Do you know what you're doing to me?" His hands curled into fists to keep him from reaching out.

Her eyes widened. "I'm sorry. I shouldn't have done that. I'm taking advantage of you."

"Believe me, I don't mind. But if you continue to do what you're doing, I don't know how long I can hold back."

"Really?" Her fingernails scraped across his chest. "I'm afraid I don't have a lot of experience with men."

"And I don't want to damage our business relationship."

She inched away from him. "You're right. Please, accept my apologies. I shouldn't have kissed you."

"It's okay. I liked it."

"You did?" She chewed on her lip. "You're not just saying that because I'm your boss?"

"Oh, hell no." He lifted his fist. "If we were in any other situation, I'd be all over you."

"In what way?" she asked, her voice catching, her breathing becoming more ragged.

He couldn't believe he was lying next to a beautiful woman without touching her, about to describe how he would. "I'd start by sweeping my hand along the side of your face."

Mia closed her eyes, a smile tilting her lips. "And then?"

"I'd trail my finger down the long column of your neck to your shoulder and brush across your collarbone."

She lifted her hand to her cheek and traced the path his words described, pausing at her collarbone. "And now?"

He drew in a shaky breath and let it out slowly, willing his pulse to calm. "You really want me to go on?"

She opened her eyes. "Please."

Holy hell. Mia was so damned sexy in her T-shirt. And he'd caught a glimpse of the thong string between her butt cheeks. God, he wanted to trace that line with his tongue, to run his hands over the smooth mounds of her ass.

Instead, he took it slower, talking his way across her body, one excruciating inch at a time. "I'd cup one of your breasts in the palm of my hand." His skin burned with the need to touch her. "With the tips of my fingers, I'd roll the nipple until it tightened into a hard little bead. Then I'd lift your shirt and suck that breast into my mouth, pulling gently, tonguing you until you cried out, begging me to suck the other."

Mia swept her hand down to her breast and pinched the nipple between her fingers through the fabric. Then she slipped her hand down to the hem of the T-shirt and dragged it up her torso, exposing the nipple.

Bear couldn't stop the moan. Her rosy nipple had tightened into a smooth, round button.

He drew in a ragged breath, swept his tongue across his dry lips and forced his glance upward to connect with her gaze. "I can't do this. If I continue, I'll want to do all the things I'm describing."

She stared into his eyes, her forehead wrinkling. "I don't want you to stop. But you should know that I've never been good at this. I don't want to disappoint you."

"Oh, sweetheart, how could you disappoint me?"

Her lips twisted. "Trust me. I've disappointed a number of men when they tried to make love to me."

Bear wanted to smooth away the worry wrinkle on her forehead. What man could this woman disappoint? "Did you take the lead in any of those situations?"

She shook her head.

"Then here's your chance." He held up his hands. "I won't touch you unless you tell me when and where."

Mia clasped his hand and guided it to her breast. "Now. Here." She pressed his hand to her.

"Say the word, and I'll stop." He closed his eyes, the warmth of her breast against his palm wreaking havoc inside him. Bear opened his eyes and stared into hers. "It won't be easy, but I will."

"Thank you." Her eyelids lowered, and she rested her hand against his chest, her fingers finding and tweaking his little brown nipples. "Tell me what you would do next."

His body tense, his fingers curling around her nipple, he spoke, talking her through what he wanted to do to her body. "I'd roll you onto your back and move to the other breast."

Mia rolled to her back, grabbed the hem of her shirt and pulled it up over her head. A shiver rippled across her body, raising gooseflesh on her skin.

She captured his head between her hands and guided him to her breast

Careful not to alarm her, he flicked the tip of her nipple with his tongue.

She arched off the bed, a soft moan escaping through her parted lips. Mia threaded her fingers through his hair and pulled him closer.

Bear sucked the nipple and half the breast into his mouth and pulled gently.

"Oh, yes." Mia squirmed beneath him, her legs thrashing, her fingers digging into his scalp.

When he pulled away, she captured his head and guided him to the other breast, where he teased and rolled the nipple with his tongue.

"Now, what would you do?" she asked, her voice wispy, as though she couldn't get enough air to her lungs.

"I'd brand you with kisses down the length of your torso, passing your bellybutton and going lower still."

"Show me," she whispered, her stomach taut, her fingers digging into the bedding on either side of her hips.

Bear dragged his lips down her ribs, counting them one at a time, moving so slowly he thought he might explode before he reached heaven.

One...two...three... He skipped past the rest, dove his tongue into her bellybutton and swirled.

Mia bucked, her back rising off the bed. Her eyes were shut tight, her fingers gripping the blanket. "Lower. Please, go lower."

"Open your eyes," he insisted. If he was going there, he wanted her to see and know he wasn't there to hurt her.

Her eyelids lifted.

Hooking his thumb into the elastic of her panties, he dragged them down to her ankles and dropped them to the floor.

"Now, spread your legs," he urged, lightly sweeping a finger down the inside of her thigh and back up to the juncture of her legs.

She hesitated on briefly. Then she drew her knees up and let them fall to the sides. Her eyes widened as he slipped between her legs, still wearing his jeans that had become uncomfortably tight.

"What next?" she whimpered, her muscles tense, her bottom lip caught between her teeth.

"I'd touch you here." He pressed his finger to the mound of curls over her sex.

"Oh, sweet Jesus," she moaned. "Do it."

Bear chuckled softly and carefully parted her folds with his thumbs, exposing the strip of flesh between. He blew a warm stream of air over her heated flesh.

"Is that it?" she cried. "Surely not."

"Sweetheart, this is only the beginning."

"Tell me," she pleaded.

"I'd tap you with my tongue. Like this." He flicked her clit. Once.

And he lifted his head.

Mia dug her heels into the mattress and raised her hips, bringing her sex closer to his lips. "Do it again."

He complied, this time sweeping the length of the little nubbin in a warm, wet laving motion.

Mia gasped, and her head fell back. "I never knew…"

"Never knew what?" he asked. Then he tapped her lightly with the tip of his tongue…once…twice…swirl.

"That it could feel this amazing."

He frowned. "You've never had an orgasm?"

She shook her head, her cheeks turning pink. "Is this what it's like? My vibrator never brought me this far."

"Baby, you're not there yet."

"There's more?" She let out her breath. "I don't know if I can take it. I feel like I'm coming apart."

He grinned. "Then I must be doing it right. Do you want me to continue talking, or would you rather that I show you?"

"Show me. I don't think I can last much longer."

Bear hooked his arms around the underside of her thighs, parted her folds again and bent to the task of giving his client her first ever orgasm. He'd never been one to judge his own prowess in bed, but he had to make sure whatever technique he used, he didn't scare Mia.

She'd never had an orgasm. Nothing like a little pressure to make a guy tense.

Bear licked her clit, flicking and teasing until she squirmed beneath his mouth. He dipped his thumb into her entrance, circling with her juices. She might not know what to do, but her body knew exactly what she needed, and provided the lubricant necessary to ease a man's entrance.

His jeans were so tight now, he dreamed of unzipping the fly and releasing his cock to the warm night air. But he didn't. This time was about Mia. He needed her to know that making love wasn't all about a man fucking her. To do it right, the woman had to be as satisfied as the man.

He pressed his thumbs into her pussy, widening her entrance, then tongued her there, flicking and twisting. Alternating between her clit and her channel, he swirled, laved and teased her.

He knew she was there when she gripped his head in her hands, her fingers pulling at his hair. "Please. Oh. My. Please."

"Stop?"

"Sweet heaven, no! Yes!" Then her body stiffened, her hips raised. Her fingernails dug into his scalp.

He sucked her nubbin into his mouth, burying his nose against her and held steady until she finally dropped down to the mattress.

Bear climbed up her body and leaned over without pressing his weight against her. "Like that?"

She opened her eyes and stared up at him. "Can we do that again?"

Bear chuckled. "If you like."

"What comes next?"

"Sleep."

Her brows wrinkled. "Sleep? You can sleep after that? We're not stopping now, are we?"

As much as Bear wanted to take it all the way, he couldn't.

Mia's confession about never having had an orgasm probably meant she hadn't had much in the way of good sex. For a female, half the enjoyment was the foreplay, the anticipation of what came next. Before Bear slaked his own desires, he wanted to be absolutely certain Mia was ready.

With his pants still zipped, Bear rolled to one side of Mia, pulled her back to his front and spooned her naked body against his. Though he couldn't finish what he'd started, he could at least hold her in his arms and feel the warmth of her skin on his.

Holy hell. He was in for a long night.

MIA LAY in the curve of Bear's body, wishing he hadn't stopped. Her core ached with an intensity she'd never imagined. Yes, she'd found release in Bear's expert foreplay, but something was missing. Her body pulsed with need, her channel contracted, thirsty with desire that could only be quenched by Bear.

She should be happy she hadn't frozen when he'd gone down on her, his mouth taking her to a place she'd thought only existed in romance novels.

For a long time, she lay nestled in the warmth and safety of Bear's arms, counting the breaths he took, her pulse slowing to match the beat of his heart. All the years she'd shied away from men and their lusty intentions, she hadn't known making love could be so good. Now that she knew, she wanted to take it to the next level.

With a yawn, she closed her eyes and listened to Bear's steady breathing. The telephone didn't ring, and the raccoons didn't return to the attic.

She must have fallen to sleep soon after. The next coherent thought was irritation at the light streaming through the window straight into her eyes.

Mia lifted her arm to block the sun shining through her bedroom window. She couldn't remember ever sleeping so soundly. Yawning, she stretched, feeling her body slide across the sheet. Her eyes popped open and she jackknifed to a sitting position when she realized she was naked. The pillow beside her was empty, with a deep indentation in the center, proving the night before had really happened. It wasn't just a figment of her imagination. The beard burn across her breasts tingled, and her nipples tightened.

Deep inside, her core pulsed, reminding her of the need left unsatisfied.

She cocked her head to the side, listening for the sound of Bear's footsteps in the hallway outside her door. When no sounds came to her, she swung out of the bed, dressed quickly and ran barefoot for the bathroom. There she combed her tangled hair, washed her face and brushed her teeth. For a moment, she hesitated over her makeup, wondering if she should apply a little foundation and blush. One glance at herself in the mirror, and she nixed the idea. Bright pink spots of color filled her cheeks, and her eyes glowed brightly. No makeup necessary.

She wore the afterglow of great sex on her face, and she couldn't be happier. For the first time since she'd been raped, she'd enjoyed having a man's hands on her body. And not just his hands.

Heat rose up her neck, brightening the rosy hue of her cheeks. Mia splashed cool water on her face, hoping to douse the fire. How could she face Bear if she couldn't stop blushing?

At the top of the stairs, she inhaled the scent of fresh coffee brewing and toast.

With her stomach rumbling, Mia hurried down the steps and into the kitchen, determined to face the day and Bear. No regrets.

Bear turned with two mugs of coffee. "Have a seat. I made eggs and toast. I hope you like your eggs scrambled."

His face impassive, Bear set the mugs on the table and turned back to the counter.

Mia didn't know whether to be relieved or annoyed that he hadn't mentioned anything about what had happened the night before.

For her, it had been a life-changing event. Probably to him, it was just another night in the sack with a woman. Unfortunately, he'd had to lead her through everything like a virgin on her wedding night. How tedious.

Her heart sinking to her shoes, Mia ducked her head and took a seat at the table, her appetite vanishing in the wake of her humiliation.

A plate slid in front of her, and Bear said, "Hey." With the tip of his finger, he tilted her chin up, forcing her to stare into his eyes. "Last night was amazing."

Tears welled. "How could it have been? You didn't get anything out of it?"

"Are you kidding?" He drew her out of her chair and into his arms. "Nothing is sexier than a woman crying out your name in the heat of her passion."

"Unless it's a man going all the way with the woman." She leaned her forehead against his chest. "Why did you stop?"

"I want you to be absolutely sure."

"I was."

"You had a bad experience when you were little more than a child. I won't be the man to compound the terror by rushing you into something you're not quite ready to handle."

"How will I know I'm ready?"

"You'll know."

She wanted to argue with him, to tell him that she'd known the night before that she wanted him inside her.

Then she wondered how she would have reacted with him on top of her, forcing his way into her. No one had penetrated her since the rape all those years ago. Then, it had hurt terribly. She'd been unable to fight off her attacker. He'd forced himself on her, thrusting into her, ripping through her hymen, tearing the narrow channel of her sex. She remembered bleeding afterward. She'd worn pads to catch the blood. If her mother had asked, she'd been prepared to tell her she was on her period.

Her mother hadn't suspected a thing.

Perhaps Bear had been right to wait. She would have hated freaking out when he entered her.

Pushing thoughts of making love to Bear into the back of her mind, Mia focused on what she hoped to accomplish that day. She moved out of his arms. "I want to talk to the sheriff today."

Bear's downward glance sharpened. "Are you prepared to tell him everything?"

She nodded. "I'd like to see him alone."

"I'm sure we can make that happen."

They both took their seats and ate in silence. When they were finished, Mia rose and collected Bear's plate. "Since you cooked, I'll clean."

"I don't mind pulling KP duty."

"KP?"

"Kitchen patrol." He grabbed a dishtowel. "I'll dry."

Working side by side, Mia washed while Bear dried. More times than she could count, she bumped into him. With each contact, electric impulses raced through her body, making her wish they could go back to her bed and pick up where they'd left off the night before. By the time the last dish had been stowed in the cabinet, Mia's nerves were stretched thin.

"I just need to brush my teeth, put on some boots, and I'll be ready." She hurried from the kitchen and ran up the stairs to the bathroom. After brushing her teeth and hair, she ducked into her room, pulled on socks and cowboy boots. A minute later, she stood outside Bear's truck.

"You really should wait until I'm ready to come out of the house." Bear locked the door behind him and hurried down the steps. "You don't know who might be out here."

"Sorry. I didn't think." *Hell,* when had she stopped thinking of Bear as her bodyguard, and started thinking of him as her lover?

Probably about the time she'd kissed him last night in bed. She prayed she didn't get too involved with the man. When she found the rapist, she wouldn't have a need for a bodyguard anymore. Then he'd be gone from her life.

A deep sadness spread through her. God, she was already getting too deeply involved with a man who would be moving on to his next assignment all too soon.

The drive into Eagle Rock passed in silence. Mia couldn't think of anything to say, afraid if she opened her mouth, she'd ask him to stay on forever. That would be silly and unrealistic of her. The man had better things to do than play bodyguard to a woman who wouldn't need one after she found the man who'd attacked her when she was a young teen.

Bear parked outside the sheriff's office and rounded the front of his truck to help her down.

Mia slipped from her seat and dropped to the ground before Bear could get to her. The less he had his hands on her body, the less she would erupt into full-blown lust.

He rested his hand at the small of her back and guided her into the sheriff's office.

Just inside the door, they ran into Deputy Maynard.

Larry glanced up from the counter. "Mia, what brings you here?"

"I'd like to speak with the sheriff," she said.

"Is there something I can help you with?" he asked.

Mia shook her head. "No, thank you. I'd like to speak with the sheriff. Alone."

Larry's eyes narrowed ever so slightly, then he spun away, heading for the back of the building.

A moment later, Sheriff Wilson stepped out of an office. "Mia, my dear. Please come on back, and bring Mr. Parker with you. We'll meet in the conference room."

"Thank you." Mia smiled, slipped her hand into Bear's and followed the sheriff. She felt like she could handle anything with Bear beside her.

The sheriff closed the door to the conference room and pulled out a chair for Mia. "Please, have a seat."

Mia drew in a deep breath and let it out. "What I'm about to tell you, I'd rather not advertise to the rest of Eagle Rock."

The sheriff grinned. "Sounds clandestine." He held up his hand as if he were swearing on a stack of bibles. "I promise; I can keep your secret.

Mia stared hard at her parents' old friend. Then she dove in, telling him of the day she'd been kidnapped, tortured and left to die. When she reached the end, she straightened. Strangely, sharing the burden made her feel more in control.

"Mia." Sheriff Wilson touched her hand. "I'm so sorry this happened to you. I'll do everything in my power to find and prosecute the slime ball for everything he put you through."

"What happened to me was a long time ago. I've learned to deal with it," Mia said. "I came back because it occurred to me he might be doing this to other women."

Sheriff Wilson's brows puckered. "I'll do a search on the database for rape cases in and around Eagle Rock over the last dozen or so years."

"Thank you."

"There is one I know of that occurred around six years ago."

Mia leaned forward. "Could I have her name? I want to compare notes. If her attacker is the same man as the one who attacked me, we need to stop him."

"I understand. If it were anyone else, I'd hesitate to give out a name, but this woman made a name for herself as a victim's rights counselor. She lives in Bozeman and has regular office hours."

Mia could hardly believe she'd already found one victim. "Who is she?"

"Valerie Sanders. You can find her in the phone book under Dr. Sanders. Tell her I sent you. Better yet, don't, and see what she has to say about her experience." Sheriff Wilson laid a hand over Mia's. "And let me know what you find out. Any information could help lead us to the attacker. Anything, no matter how insignificant it might seem."

"Will do," Mia promised.

"And I'll do a search on the state-wide database of similar attacks to see if we get any more hits in the surrounding areas."

"Thank you, Sheriff." She stood. "Do you mind if I borrow a computer to look up the phone number and address of Dr. Sanders?"

"Not at all. You can use mine." He led her into his office and offered his chair.

Mia sat in the man's chair and brought up the browser on his computer, keyed in "Dr. Sanders" and "Bozeman". Within seconds she had the address and phone number.

Sheriff Wilson handed her the telephone. "You might as well call her and set up a time to meet."

"Thank you." Mia dialed the number.

A woman answered. "Dr. Sanders's office. How may I help you?"

"I'd like to schedule an appointment with Dr. Sanders."

"When would you like to see her?"

"As soon as possible."

"Can you be here in an hour? We just had a cancellation."

"Yes." Mia couldn't believe her luck.

"Your name, please."

"Mia Chastain."

"Dr. Sanders will see you in one hour."

Mia replaced the phone in its cradle and glanced up at Bear. "We have an hour to get to Bozeman."

8

———

BEAR OPENED the door to the sheriff's office and held it for Mia. "An hour gives us more than enough time to get to Bozeman."

Mia stepped past him. "I want to stop by the hardware store. I thought of another question I wanted to ask Phillip."

"Mia?" Sheriff Wilson's voice pulled her to a halt.

She turned. "Sir?"

The older man rounded his desk and rested a hand on her shoulder. "I wish you had come forward sooner. But it's never too late to nail the bastard for what he did." He shook his head. "I'm sorry this happened to you."

"I survived. I just wish I'd come forward sooner. Allyson might still be alive."

His gaze widened. "Allyson Severs? You don't know that she was attacked."

"You don't know that she *wasn't* attacked," Mia argued. "What else could have made her withdraw like that?"

"She could have had a fight with her boyfriend. One he didn't want to own up to."

Mia stared at the sheriff. "You don't believe that, do you?"

The sheriff sighed. "No. But it doesn't mean the same man who attacked you attacked Allyson."

"But if it did happen… I should have said something back then."

"You were a scared kid." The sheriff hugged her. "Let's end this."

Bear's fists clenched. "That's the plan." When he found Mia's rapist, he'd rip the man apart with his bare hands. No man had the right to force himself on a woman. Hell, Mia had barely been a woman. She'd been little more than a child. His chest tightened.

The bastard deserved to die.

"Come on." Mia grabbed his hand and dragged him toward the door. "I'm anxious to see what Dr. Sanders has to say."

Bear passed Deputy Maynard standing at a coffee machine in a break room just past the sheriff's office.

The man lifted his coffee mug as Mia passed. "Hey, Mia."

Mia nodded, but continued on, her focus seeming to be on the conversation she planned to have with Dr. Sanders.

Bear hoped she'd let him sit in on that conversation, but he wouldn't push the issue if Mia chose to go in alone. The two women had something in common Bear could never experience.

The trip to the hardware store took less than five minutes. Mia insisted she could run in and back out without his assistance, but Bear wouldn't hear of it. He accompanied her inside.

Much to Mia's disappointment, Phillip had called in, needing the day off to take his mother to a doctor's appointment in Bozeman.

"What did you want to ask Phillip?" Bear asked as he slid into the driver's seat.

"I wanted to know exactly what he and Allyson had been talking about on the date the last night he saw her. I want to be absolutely certain about what caused Allyson's sudden depression."

"Allyson's diary said they'd been talking about their honeymoon."

"Those were Allyson's last written words, but she didn't get to finish her entry. What if there was more after the discussion about their honeymoon? I can't rule out Phillip until I know for sure."

"Do you really think the guy has it in himself to make a woman so unhappy she'd commit suicide?"

Mia shook her head. "The Phillip I knew in high school was always a people pleaser. He would never do anything to hurt another person. But as crazy as it might seem, I can't—"

"—rule him out," Bear finished. "I get it. Given that he's not working today, you'll have to hold that thought until we have a chance to talk to him again."

"True. In the meantime, we're heading for Bozeman, aren't we?" Mia leaned forward, her gaze riveted to the road in front of the vehicle. "I'm interested to hear what Valerie Sanders has to say about her encounter."

"Are you sure you're up to it?"

Mia nodded. "I was sixteen. What happened to me was a long time ago. I can handle it."

Once again, Bear couldn't imagine what sixteen-year-old Mia had gone through. How horrific to be kidnapped, trauma-tized, sexually abused and left to die of exposure. She was one tough lady to have lived through it and gone on to live a fairly normal life. He could take a lesson from her book and look at the positives in his own life.

So, he'd lost the only job he'd known since getting out of high school. The men he'd adopted as his family were either dead or scattered to the winds in the military or back home in the States. As sad as that was, he had a meaningful job, protecting an amazing woman. The sun shone down on him, and the scenery didn't get much better.

To the west, the Crazy Mountains rose high against the sky, their jagged peaks still frosted with a cap of snow. Montana's big skies and rugged mountaintops inspired Bear like no other place he'd been on earth.

He needed to remember to thank Hank for giving him the opportunity to work in Montana. With this woman who'd proven to be passionate and resilient in the face of danger.

He rounded a curve in the road and passed through a straight stretch of highway through a narrow valley. A stream paralleled the road, the water bubbling so clear and bright, it shined in his eyes.

Something hit the windshield of his truck on the passenger side. Mia grunted softly and slapped her left hand over her right arm.

It took less than a second for Bear to realize the small round hole in the glass couldn't have been made by anything other than a bullet.

He swerved sharply and straightened the steering wheel. "Fuck!" He slammed his foot to the accelerator. "Get down, Mia!"

She bent over, ducking her head below the dash.

"Are you okay?" He asked, zigzagging along the straight road to make it harder for the shooter to aim.

"I'm okay," Mia said.

A quick glance in her direction, and Bear could tell she wasn't okay. Her lips pressed tightly together, and her face had paled.

Another bullet pierced the windshield, cutting through the middle, missing them altogether.

Bear wanted to stop and tend to Mia's injury, but to do so put them in more danger. Instead, he increased his speed. He had to get out of the valley.

When he passed another curve in the highway, and he was certain the shooter couldn't have followed as quickly, he slowed.

"Don't stop," Mia said. Her lips were pinched and her cheeks had paled. "Get us to Bozeman."

"I don't want you to bleed out on me," Bear argued.

"It's just a flesh wound, and I'm applying pressure. I'm barely bleeding now."

Bear studied her for a long moment. "Okay, but first stop is the ER."

Mia chewed on her lip. "I don't want to miss my appointment with Dr. Sanders."

"First stop is the ER. Bullets aren't necessarily the cleanest objects that can pass through your body. Even if it is only a flesh wound, I don't want you getting an infection and dying of gangrene." He held up his hand when Mia opened her mouth to dispute him. "Sorry. I'm driving, and you're going to the hospital."

Her lips quirked. "Yes, sir," she said, like a new recruit to her drill sergeant.

"That's more like it." Bear tried to keep a straight face, but he couldn't help the grin. The woman was injured, but she had spunk. Though he grinned, he worried she wasn't giving it to him straight. Entering Bozeman, he didn't slow much. With Mia giving him directions, he broke every speed limit getting to the hospital, thankful he wasn't tagged on the way by a police officer. He'd take the ticket later, but he wasn't stopping until he got Mia to medical care.

As he pulled into the emergency room drop off area, a siren sounded nearby.

When Bear started to get out of the truck, Mia touched his arm.

"There's an ambulance coming, and there's another car behind us," she said. "Let me out. I can walk in while you park."

An ambulance pulled into the hospital driveway.

Bear glanced in the rearview mirror.

A car had pulled up behind them.

"Are you sure?" he asked. He didn't want her out of his sight for even a moment.

"Positive." She pushed her door open and dropped down from the truck. "Go."

Bear drove around to park in the emergency room parking lot, got out and hurried inside.

Mia sat in a chair with a wad of gauze pressed to her arm. "Victims of a multi-car accident are being brought in. It could be a while before they see me."

"Is there another hospital?"

"I'm fine here. We can wait. In the meantime, could you call Dr. Sanders and ask if she has time to see me later today?"

Bear dialed the number Mia gave him and waited.

The receptionist answered and listened while Bear explained the situation.

"I'm so sorry to hear Miss Chastain has been injured. I'd reschedule her, but Dr. Sanders has a group session this evening, and it usually goes late. The soonest I can get Miss Chastain in is tomorrow morning. Will that be okay?"

"It'll have to be," Bear answered. "Thanks."

Mia glanced at Bear as he ended the call. "What did she say?"

"Tomorrow morning is the soonest she could get you in."

Mia started to get up. "Then let's make today's appointment. By the time I get back to the hospital, they should be ready for me."

Bear shook his head. "I like your determination, but I'm certain Dr. Sanders wouldn't want you bleeding all over her waiting room. It might upset her other patients."

"Mia Chastain?" a voice called out.

Bear and Mia glanced toward the door to the examination rooms. A nurse carrying a clipboard smiled. Beside her stood a police officer.

Bear helped Mia to her feet and walked with her toward the nurse.

"Miss Chastain, this is Officer Petty," the nurse said. "After we get you taken care of, he has some questions to ask you concerning your injury."

"I'm sorry to bother you," the officer said, "but it's routine when an injury is thought to be caused by firearms."

"That's fine," Mia said. "I'd like my friend to accompany me."

"Then please follow me." The nurse led the way to the examination room.

Two hours later, after a thorough cleaning, a butterfly bandage applied by the doctor, and a barrage of questions from the police officer, a nurse brought Mia her discharge papers with instructions on how to take care of her wound.

As Bear led her out of the examination room, doors burst open down the hall and two EMTs pushed a gurney through with a third one kneeling on top, applying CPR compressions to the woman beneath him.

"Need a crash cart, stat!" one of them shouted.

Nurses and a doctor rushed in from all directions.

Bear pulled Mia out of the way as the gurney was wheeled into one of the rooms.

"What do we have?" the doctor called out.

"Thirty-four-year-old female, involved in a hit-and-run in the parking lot of her business. Multiple contusions, head trauma and a possible collapsed lung. Her heart stopped twice on the way over."

"Name?"

"Valerie Sanders."

Mia gasped, and her knees buckled. If not for the strength of Bear's arm around her, she might have collapsed on the floor of the emergency room.

A nurse rolled a cart into the room with the unconscious woman, and the professionals went to work, attaching the necessary equipment to the woman's chest to jumpstart her heart.

Mia stared, unable to move.

"Come on." Bear's arm tightened around her as he urged her toward the exit. "We need to get out of the way so the doctors and nurses can do their job."

"Dear God. That was Valerie Sanders." She glanced up at Bear. What were the chances of there being more than one Valerie Sanders in Bozeman, Montana?

"I'll call Dr. Sanders's office and verify it's her. But right now, we need to get you out of here." He led her to the exit and out to the parking lot. Once they were inside his truck, he pulled out his cell phone, hit redial for Dr. Sanders's office, pressed the speaker button and held the phone where Mia could hear.

After two rings, a message played, *You have reached the number for Dr. Valerie Sanders. We're sorry to inform you that Dr. Sanders has been involved in an accident. All of her appointments are cancelled until further notice.*

Bear ended the call and shifted the truck into drive. "Is there another route back to Eagle Rock?"

Mia shook her head. "Not really."

"I don't like the idea of going through that valley again."

"The only alternative takes hours to get home."

"It might be worth it," he said.

"I'll take my chances," Mia said, and then frowned. "But I don't want you hurt."

He shook his head. "I'm not worried about me. Whoever is doing this is after you."

"I could lie down in the back seat all the way back, if that makes you feel any better."

His brows furrowed. "If you promise to stay down the entire way home, that might work." He stopped in the hospital parking lot, jumped out, opened the passenger door and helped Mia out of the front seat. When her feet were firmly on the ground, he paused and stared down into her eyes. "So far, I'm not doing such a good job of keeping you safe, am I?"

She smiled up at him. "How could you know someone would be waiting to ambush us on the road to Bozeman? This isn't your fault." Her smile faded. "Do you think whoever shot at me got to Dr. Sanders?"

"I don't know. It's too much of a coincidence to discount."

"Maybe I shouldn't have come back to Eagle Rock, after all." Mia plucked at Bear's shirtsleeve, staring at her fingers, thinking about all that had happened since she'd come back. "If I hadn't stirred up this hornet's nest, Dr. Sanders wouldn't be in the hospital fighting for her life."

"If we don't stop this guy, he could go on to attack more women. Could you live with yourself if another Allyson took her life because she was attacked?"

Mia chewed on her bottom lip. She'd barely been able to live with herself, knowing that sadistic son of a bitch was still free to terrorize other women. Knowing he might have been the cause of Allyson's depression and subsequent suicide, and possibly the hit that had put Dr. Sanders's life in danger, made anger burn in Mia's gut. "I can't let him get away with this." She gazed up into Bear's eyes, her resolve strengthening. "He can't continue to hurt other women."

"Then we don't stop now. At the same time, we don't have to paint a target on your back." Bear bent and kissed her lips. "Please get in the back seat and stay down until we get to your place."

Mia's lips tingled at the brief brush of his lips. "This situation is getting too dangerous. I know you signed on to protect me, but you can back out any time you want. I would completely understand."

Bear's lips thinned into a straight line. "I'd hoped you'd figured out what kind of man I am by now. I don't run from a fight, and I don't leave a defenseless woman to take care of herself. Even if you weren't my client and I wasn't your body-guard, I'm in this for the long haul. Mia Chastain, you're stuck with me until this is over." He yanked open the back door and pointed. "Get in. I'm taking you home."

Mia's heart fluttered at the harshness of Bear's tone. The fierceness of his expression set butterflies loose in her belly and made her body tingle in anticipation of being alone with him in her house.

This man was a warrior, fearless and undaunted by a man with a gun, firing at them like an enemy sniper. Mia was thankful the deadly gleam in his eyes was aimed at the bastard who'd tried on more than one occasion to scare her away from Eagle Rock.

If anyone should be afraid, it should be the man who had attacked Mia, Dr. Sanders and possibly Allyson. His days of hurting others were numbered. Mia wasn't running anymore.

9

ON THE WAY BACK to Eagle Rock, Bear drove as fast as he could through the narrow valley where Mia had been shot. He held his breath across the straight stretch and kept a close watch around each curve in the road for movement or anything out of the ordinary.

They made it all the way to Mia's house without incident. By the time he pulled into the yard, his nerves were stretched tight. "Stay here while I check the house. And stay out of sight."

He waited until she bent over, out of line of sight, before he dropped down from the truck. With his weapon drawn, Bear made a complete circle around the house. He quickly entered the structure and went from room to room. When he was satisfied the house was clear, he hurried out to the locked truck and opened the back door.

Mia lay across the back seat, her eyes closed, her uninjured arm tucked beneath her head.

"Mia, sweetheart?" he whispered. "The house is all clear."

When she didn't respond, he looked closer, his breath lodging in his throat until he saw the reassuring sight of her chest rising and falling. Bear gathered her in his arms and carried her into the house and up the stairs. The added weight caused his sore leg a twinge of protest, but he ignored the pain and continued to her room. He laid her across her bed, pulled off her boots and covered her with a blanket.

For a long moment, he watched her sleep, wanting to crawl onto the bed and hold her in his arms.

The gunfire that day had scared him more than he cared to admit. He'd been trained to operate under live fire. His experience in combat had prepared him for battle and casualties among the people he cared about. But nothing had prepared him to lose his heart to a stranger he'd only met a couple of days before.

Maybe he wasn't cut out for this line of work. It couldn't be normal to be so incredibly attracted to a client. It inhibited his ability to think straight. Complete focus was what he needed more than anything right now.

Someone was willing to kill Mia and Dr. Sanders to keep his victims from comparing notes. Perhaps they were getting too close to unveiling his secret, and he was running scared.

Reluctantly, Bear left Mia's room, descended the stairs and found a telephone in the hallway. His cell phone had spotty reception this far out of town, if any at all. He dialed Hank and waited for him to pick up.

"Patterson speaking," Hank answered.

"Did you hear about Dr. Sanders?" Bear asked.

"What about her?"

Bear filled him in on the information Sheriff Wilson had given them regarding the Sanders woman's rape, what had happened on their way to Bozeman and Mia's short stay in the hospital.

"Where is Mia now?" Hank asked.

"She fell asleep on our mad dash home."

"You should have called me. I would have covered for you on your way through that valley."

Bear had thought of calling Hank, but Mia had been in a hurry to get home, and he figured it would be okay, as long as she stayed low and out of sight. He now realized how wrong he could have been, and how much he had risked her getting hurt all over again. He had to start thinking through all the possibilities if he was going to be any good at being a body-guard. Thus, the reason for his call to Hank.

"I'm concerned about Sanders," Bear said. "If someone thought she might have information that would implicate him in the rape cases, he might go after her again."

"I could go to Bozeman and provide her protection, or I could come to Mia's house and be your backup."

"I'll take care of Mia. I don't think she'll sleep the rest of the day away. When she's up, we'll contact the sheriff and let him know about what else happened."

"Okay, then. I've got Sanders. Let me know if anything changes."

"Same to you. If the doctor comes to, get a description of her attacker and the vehicle he was driving."

"Will do."

Bear returned the phone to the base.

"Who was that?"

He spun to find Mia standing behind him in her socks, her hair rumpled and her face soft from sleep. Without thinking, he opened his arms.

Mia walked into them and rested her face against his chest.

"That was Hank," he murmured against her hair. "He's going to keep an eye on Dr. Sanders in case whoever hit her comes back."

Mia's gaze shot up to his. "You think her attacker will try to finish the job?"

Bear didn't want to worry Mia, but he couldn't sugarcoat what was going through his thoughts. "If the hit-and-run was deliberate, the man who did it might come back to pull the plug on her."

Mia gasped and buried her face in his shirt. "I should have come forward back when I was a teen."

"You can't blame yourself for someone else's brand of crazy."

"But none of this would have happened if I'd done it then. Allyson would still be alive, Dr. Sanders wouldn't have been raped and now run over. That sick bastard would have been in jail."

Bear gripped her arms and leaned back to stare hard into her eyes. "You did not do these horrible things. You were a victim, just like the others. A child victim. The bastard who is terrorizing the woman of Eagle Rock needs to be caught and put out of everyone's misery." He pulled her back into his embrace and held her for a long time.

Eventually, she relaxed against him, her hand splaying across his chest. "What next?" she whispered.

"We contact the sheriff and tell him about the gunfire in the valley and the attack on Sanders in Bozeman."

Mia nodded. "I'll get my boots."

"No. I'll have him come here." He smoothed the hair back from her face and pressed his lips to hers in a brief kiss. "You've been through enough."

Mia touched her fingers to her lips and gazed into his eyes. "I haven't been through what Dr. Sanders has."

"Thank goodness." Bear kissed her again. He knew it was wrong, but he couldn't resist, and she didn't push him away. Reason warred with desire, finally winning. Bear started to raise his head. The next step was to put distance between him and his client.

Mia raised her arms, entwined her hands behind Bear's neck and dragged him down to her mouth.

He couldn't hold back any longer. He wrapped his arms around her waist and pressed her body to his, the hard ridge of his cock nudging her belly.

In the middle of the day, with sunlight streaming through the glass of the front door, Bear held his client in his arms and claimed her lips as if there wouldn't be future kisses for them.

He traced the seam of her lips with his tongue.

Mia opened to him and met him halfway, her tongue twisting around his, thrusting and tempting him to tighten his hold on her.

He slipped his hands lower, cupping the backs of her thighs

and lifted. "Tell me to stop, and I will," he whispered into her mouth.

"Don't stop," she replied and wrapped her legs around his waist, her sex riding the ridge of his jeans.

Bear moaned and turned, pushing her back to the wall. "I'm on fire."

"Me too." She pulled her head back. "What are we going to do about it?" She kissed his chin, his neck and nibbled on his earlobe, before returning her gaze to his.

Bear glanced toward the staircase. "The bedroom's too far."

Mia tipped her head toward the living room. "There's a nice soft rug in the living room." Her lips curled upward in a sexy smile.

Holding her tightly against him, he carried her into the living room and let her body slide down his.

She didn't stop when her feet touched the floor. Instead, she sank to her knees and tugged his hand, urging him to do the same.

Bear pulled his gun out of his shoulder holster, set it on the coffee table, and then unbuckled and shrugged out of the holster straps.

He knelt on the floor in front of Mia, knowing this wasn't what Hank had had in mind when he'd asked him to protect Mia. "This is wrong in so many ways. We shouldn't be doing this."

She raised his hand and slid it beneath her shirt to cup her breast. He could feel the rapid beat of her heart. "Yes. We. Should."

Mia pressed her hand to the back of his, and then slid it down her torso to the waistband of her jeans. "I'm ready. Please don't make we wait."

"Are you sure?" he asked. "I don't know if I can be as gentle as you need me to be."

"I won't break." She cupped his face, her gaze capturing his. "Show me that this can be…good. Teach me."

His pulse racing, Bear laid his hand over hers. "I don't want to scare you."

She flicked the button loose on her jeans and ran the zipper downward. "I've never felt this way before, and I'm not afraid, anymore. Now I want this more than I've wanted anything else in my life. I trust you."

Her words sealed the deal for him. Once he unleashed his desire, he knew there was no going back.

MIA HAD SHIED AWAY from making love with a man since she'd been raped. Not one of her dates had ever broken through the barrier of her fear to awaken desire strong enough to push her past the memories.

Here, on the floor of her parents' living room, she couldn't think of anything else but wanting to lie naked with Bear. Her core ached with the need to have him inside her, filling that empty space she had thought would be forever untouchable. He was the only one she could imagine herself with...this broken warrior, sent to protect her from a frightening adversary she couldn't name.

Mia reached out to flick open the buttons of his shirt, making quick work of them.

Bear shrugged out of the garment, letting it fall to the floor. Then he curled his hands around the hem of her shirt and dragged it over her head, tossing it to the coffee table beside him.

A shiver rippled through her that had nothing to do with the cool air caressing her heated skin. Every nerve stood at attention, anticipating his touch.

Mia reached behind her back and unhooked her bra.

Bear slipped the straps off her shoulders and palmed her breasts, as if weighing them, before he bent to take one into his mouth.

Her breath catching in her throat, Mia arched her back, urging him to take more.

He feathered his tongue across her nipple, moistening the tip, and then rolled the bud between his teeth, gently biting down.

Mia threaded her hands through his thick hair and pressed him closer, eager to speed this along. Every fiber of her being ached to feel his thick shaft inside her channel. This would be the day she pushed the memory of her rapist out of her mind. She'd have a better memory to fill the dark nights. Memories of Bear, his gentle hands, his thick muscles and his rugged body sliding across hers.

She slipped out of Bear's embrace and lay on the rug. "Don't take it too slowly. I don't know if I can wait much longer."

Bear drew in a shaky breath. "*You* can't wait?" He chuckled. "I thought that was my line."

She guided his hand to the open fly of her jeans.

He helped her push them over her hips and down the length of her legs. When she was free of them, she slipped her fingers into the elastic of her panties and tugged them downward.

Bear took over, easing them over her hips, bending to press kisses along her bared skin, following the panties down to her ankles.

Blood surged through Mia's veins, spreading the heat to all of her extremities and inward to the aching center of her being. This was going to be it. Her virginity taken by force, Mia was now eager to give herself to a man for the first time. She might as well be a virgin, and suddenly she was very conscious of her lack of experience.

Was she being too forward?

Bear touched the inside of her thigh with a kiss.

Mia arched her back off the floor, the rush of sensations washing over her like a tidal wave. "You aren't doing this because I'm the client, are you?"

His breath warmed a path to the apex of her thighs where he parted her folds with his fingers. "I'm doing this *in spite* of the fact you're my client." He flicked the nubbin of tightly packed nerves, setting off an explosion of tingles, shooting from her center outward.

"Oh, thank God!" she cried. "There. Oh, sweet Jesus. There!"

He flicked, teased and sucked her clit until all logical thought scattered to the wind. He pressed his two fingers into her entrance, swirled his tongue along that highly sensitized strip of flesh until her body tensed, pushing her to the very edge. Then she rocketed into the stratosphere, her hips undulating to his strokes, her breath catching in her lungs.

She laced her hands in his hair and tugged him upward. "Now. I have to have you inside me. Now!"

He climbed up her body and settled between her legs. With a quick flick of his fingers, he loosened the button and zipper, and released his cock from the confines of his jeans.

Mia pushed the denim downward, too caught up in the rush of desire to care if he stripped all the way. She had to have him. Wanted him inside her. Couldn't breathe until he consummated their lovemaking.

With the tip of his shaft pressed to her slick opening, Bear paused, his face tense, his muscles straining. "Say the word, and it stops here."

"Oh, sweet Jesus. Don't stop now." Mia wrapped her legs around his buttocks and tightened, urging him to enter her.

"Not yet." He leaned onto one hand, fished in his back pocket and tossed his wallet onto the rug beside her. "Protection."

"Oh." Too lost in the moment, Mia hadn't even thought of protection. Thank God, one of them was thinking. Her hands shaking, Mia grabbed his wallet and flipped it open.

"In the center pocket," he bit out between clenched teeth.

She found the square foil packet, tore it open and rolled the condom over Bear's pulsing shaft. "Does that feel all right?"

He let go of the breath he'd been holding. "You can't even imagine how right that feels."

"Show me," she said.

"Don't you want to be on top?" he asked.

She shook her head. "No. This feels natural. The way it should be."

He eased his thickness into her channel, moving ever so slowly, his gaze locking with hers.

Her juices lubricated the path, making it easier for her tight channel to accept his girth.

Bear kept going until he filled her completely, and then stopped. He bent to kiss her forehead, her eyes, her nose and finally her mouth. "Are you okay?"

Mia dragged in a ragged breath and nodded. "I've never felt so…" She shook her head, too lost in the moment to come up with the right word.

"Complete?"

"Yes," she said on a gasp. "You feel amazing."

"I was about to say the same. You're so tight. So wet." He kissed her again, his tongue seeking hers, thrusting and twisting in a long, breath-stealing caress.

Then he pulled out of her, all the way to the tip.

Mia cried out, reached for his buttocks and dragged him back inside.

Bear moved in and out of her, again and again, the speed of his thrusts increasing with every stroke.

Soon, Mia's fingers dug into the hard muscles of his ass as she rode the wave to her second climax of the day.

Bear thrust one last time, burying himself deep inside her, where he held still, his body tense, his eyes closed as his cock pulsed inside Mia's channel.

Mia eventually drifted back to earth, her heartbeat slowing to normal, a warm flush spreading over her.

Bear rolled over to lie on his side, taking Mia with him, still retaining the connection. "Are you all right?"

She smiled, a hazy euphoria making her feel slightly drunk. "I don't think I've ever been better."

He chuckled and tucked a strand of her hair behind her ear. "You were amazing."

Her smile slipped. "I never knew it could be like that."

Bear's brow wrinkled. "Good or bad?"

Mia cupped his cheek. "Neither. It was incredibly…" She shook her head, struggling to describe what had just taken place. "Like you said...amazing." She kissed him and wound her arm behind his neck. "When can we do that again?"

Bear opened his mouth to reply.

Before he could, something hit the picture window. Glass shattered, the curtain flew upward and a projectile landed on the floor a few feet away from where they lay, splattering liquid all around. Flames spread everywhere the liquid landed.

Bear leaped to his feet, yanked Mia off the floor and pushed her behind him. He gripped the end of the rug they'd been lying on and tossed it over the fire, smothering the flames.

Mia snatched up her shirt and jeans and jammed her arms and legs into her clothes as fast as she could.

Within seconds, Bear had the fire out. The scent of gasoline and smoke lingered in the air.

"Stay inside, and make sure the fire doesn't reignite." Bear slipped into his jeans, grabbed his gun and ran for the door.

Mia hurried after him. "Where are you going?"

"To find the bastard who threw that Molotov cocktail through your window."

10

BEAR RAN out the door and leaped off the front porch. The sound of an engine caught his attention. He raced toward it, but it was speeding away too fast to catch on foot. He stopped at the edge of the woods and searched for tire tracks in the dirt. He found a single set, probably belonging to a motorcycle.

Afraid to leave Mia for too long, Bear returned to the house.

Mia met him at the door, dressed but tousled. God, she was beautiful with her lips swollen from his kisses. But he didn't have time to dwell on how much he wanted to kiss those lips. Once again, someone had attacked her home, and he was no closer to discovering who it was.

Pulling her into the circle of his arm, he led her toward the hall phone and dialed the number Sheriff Wilson had given him.

"Sheriff Wilson speaking."

"This is Tate Parker at Mia Chastain's house. How soon can you get here?"

"Ten minutes, tops. What's going on?"

"Two, maybe three attacks today. We'll explain when you get here."

"Ambulance?"

"No. We're okay." Barely. If the fire bomb had been a few feet closer, an ambulance would have been in order.

Bear's heart squeezed hard in his chest. They'd had too many close calls in the past couple of days. He wanted to go out and find the bastard, but he couldn't leave Mia. Wouldn't leave her. Not when she was the target of the madman.

The sheriff arrived in less than five minutes, lights flashing on his service vehicle. Another deputy pulled in shortly afterward.

Together, they processed the scene, gathered evidence and took notes.

"I'll get my latent print expert working on whatever fingerprints we can lift from the glass shards. We'll also look through the licenses of all motorcycle owners in the area and see if we can narrow down the owner to a list of reasonable suspects. But that won't account for those who have motorcycles they only use on their ranches. Those might not be licensed."

"Any clue, no matter how big or small, is better than nothing, at this point," Mia said. "This guy can't keep getting away with what he's done."

"Dr. Sanders might be our best bet at this point," the sheriff said. "She's possibly the only person who has seen her attacker's face."

"Hank's pulling guard duty. He'll make sure she stays safe."

"Good." Sheriff Wilson nodded. "I'll put in a call to the Bozeman Police Department and see if they can provide a uniform as well."

Sheriff Wilson touched Mia's shoulder. "I'm sorry this is happening to you. I had ordered my men to circle past your house at night. It appears they need to be watching it on a 24-hour basis."

"We were shot at on the road to Bozeman." Mia's lips thinned. "You can't be everywhere."

"I'm short-handed as it is. The county doesn't have the money for a larger staff."

Mia slipped her arm around Bear's waist. "That's why I have a bodyguard."

"Lot of good that's doing you." He didn't like that whoever was targeting her was getting past him to hurt her. Some bodyguard he was.

Her arm tightened around him. "If I hadn't hired you, I might not be here at all."

The sheriff left shortly after.

Bear helped Mia clean up the gasoline and the damaged carpet. He found a piece of plywood in the shed and nailed it over the window until they could order replacement glass.

Dusk settled in early around Mia's house, with a bank of clouds blocking the setting sunlight.

"What do you want to do for dinner?" Mia asked. "My refrigerator is pretty empty. I could stir up some scrambled eggs."

"I'm almost afraid to let you out of the house after all that happened today, but dinner at the diner might be the ticket."

"At least we won't be smelling gasoline and smoke while we eat," Mia pointed out.

"The diner it is."

"I need to shower and change before we go." Mia stepped up to him and laid her hand on his chest. "You could use a shower, too. Care to join me?"

He caught her hand in his, tempted to take her up on the offer. Very tempted. "I'd better not. I need to stay vigilant. That last attack was close."

Mia's lips pressed into a thin line. "That jerk has to be stopped. He's cutting into my pathetic attempt to seduce my bodyguard."

"Babe, any other time and I wouldn't hesitate. But your life is more important to me than incredibly satisfying sex against the shower wall." He bent to claim her lips in a long, soul-defining kiss. "Can I get a rain check on that shower?"

"Count on it." She turned and pulled her shirt over her head, dropping it on the floor behind her. A sassy glance over her shoulder made his blood hum and pool in his groin. "That's just a little of what you'll be missing."

He picked up her shirt and popped her ass with it. "Go, before I forget why you hired me in the first place."

Mia laughed and ran for the stairs.

A moment later, Bear heard the shower running, and he sighed. He'd much rather be upstairs with Mia than watching for an attacker. But he'd already let himself be distracted far too much.

Mia hurried through the shower, eager to rejoin Bear downstairs. She couldn't believe she'd been brave enough to try to seduce her bodyguard. That was another first for her. She was glad it was Bear who'd been the first man she'd really flirted with, the first man to give her a full-blown, unforgettable orgasm, and the first man to make love to her since that horrible day when she'd been so brutally attacked.

Bear was kind, gentle, tough, strong and everything a woman would want in a man. And Mia couldn't wait to get back down the stairs to be with him.

She wondered if he felt nearly as strongly about her as she did about him. Hell, she'd only known him for a couple of days. Was she having her first case of puppy love? Sure, she wasn't a teenager, but she'd been robbed of her childhood infatuations because of the attack. She'd felt dirty, soiled, unworthy and just plain icky about the usual sexual explorations of a teen and young woman.

Perhaps she was reading too much into what she was feeling for Bear. Her footsteps slowed on the stairs leading down to the first floor.

Then Bear appeared at the bottom, with that quirky smile aimed in her direction.

Mia's heart filled with an unequaled joy, and she practically flew the rest of the way down the staircase and into his arms.

He chuckled and held her close. "Hey, what's this all about?"

"I don't know." Mia felt silly, giddy and shy. "I just felt like being in your arms."

"Good. I kind of like it when you're here." He kissed the top of her damp hair and tipped her face upward, forcing her to look into his eyes. "Everything okay? No regrets?"

"None." She smiled, her lips trembling. "What about you?"

"My only regret is that I couldn't be in that shower with you." He set her away from him. "I did a spit bath in the sink down here, but I still smell like smoke and gasoline. Can you put up with me for now?"

She leaned her face into his shirt and sniffed. Wrinkling her nose, she gave him an assessing glance. "I suppose I can put up with it. As long as I get that shower with you later."

"As soon as we resolve this case." He kissed her soundly. "You're on."

Mia liked the big, burly soldier when he was playful and teasing. She liked him even better when he had her completely naked on the floor. But that was for another time, not when they were headed out the door to visit the diner in Eagle Rock.

She'd have to keep it together a little longer. At this point, Mia was almost willing to set herself up as bait to lure her nemesis out of hiding. Ready to be done with this investigation, she'd do just about anything. Then maybe, she could get on with her life. Hopefully, Bear would be around a little longer to be a part of it.

It didn't matter if she lived in L.A. or in Eagle Rock. She could write scripts from anywhere. Speaking of which, she needed to get a good start on the one due in less than a month.

The drive into Eagle Rock didn't take long. Soon, they pulled up to the diner. At six-thirty in the evening, a line of cars clustered around the only restaurant in town. Men in cowboy hats and dusty jeans sat at the tables, eating a hearty dinner. Families gathered in the booths, with little ones popping up to stare at the occupants of the other booths.

As Mia walked through the door, she inhaled the scents of meatloaf, hamburgers, chicken pot pie and steak, and her stomach rumbled. "We didn't eat lunch, did we?"

His hand pressed to the small of her back, Bear nodded. "We were otherwise occupied."

Either being shot at or making love, they hadn't gotten around to lunch. Mia didn't mind missing a meal. Having experienced the best sex she could have imagined, she'd give up lunch any day to make love all over again.

"Find a seat." Kylie rushed past them, carrying a tub full of dirty dishes. "I'll be with you as soon as possible."

Mia led the way to the booth Kylie had just cleared and slid across the seat.

Bear sat opposite, his gaze scanning the room, as if searching for anyone who looked even remotely suspicious.

Mia did the same, seeing only the people she'd known since she was a child. They were a little older, some had children of their own, but no one appeared to be ready to take a shot at her. She smiled and waved at an old rancher who'd been one of her father's fishing buddies. "Until I came back to Eagle Rock, I didn't realize how much I missed it here."

"Seriously?" Bear stared at her as if she'd lost her marbles.

Mia laughed. "Seriously."

Bear reached across the table to take her hands. "You've been threatened, shot at, almost had your house burned down, and you have nostalgic feelings for this town?"

She shrugged, trying to play it cool when electric tingles spread from where his hands held hers to the farthest reaches of her body. "It's my home. I know most of the people who live here." *And now, you're here.* She didn't say it out loud, but part of the reason she was glad she was back was that she wouldn't have met him unless she'd come home when she did. God, she hoped she would have the opportunity to get to know him better. He was the kind of guy she could fall for. She just hoped she was the kind of girl he could get to like, given the chance to really know her.

Kylie hurried up to the table, breathing hard. "Sorry, I had to take the dirty dishes to the back, then they had me running the trash out." She raised her hands. "Don't worry. I washed my hands afterward." She waited, pen poised over her pad. "What can I get you?"

Once again, Mia noticed the bruises on Kylie's arms. There were three new ones next to the ones she'd seen before. Mia reached out to catch Kylie's hand. She gently pulled her arm out straight, her lips pressing into a thin line. She glanced up at Kylie. "You don't have to put up with this," she said, her voice low enough others wouldn't hear her.

Kylie snatched her hand out of Mia's grip. "You don't know anything about my life. Either order your food, or better yet, let me find someone else to take your order."

Before Mia could say anything else, Kylie spun on her heel and hurried away.

"More bruises?" Bear shook his head. "No man should hurt a woman like that."

Mia's heart constricted. She wanted to take Kylie and hide her away from her husband. "How can anyone who has promised to love, honor and cherish someone, until death do they part, end up hurting that very person?"

"Does the sheriff know his deputy is an abusive ass?"

"I don't know, but I mean to find out." Her gaze followed Kylie to the hallway leading to the bathrooms and the back office area.

A moment later, a confused older waitress arrived at their table. "Hi, I'm Linda. I'm taking over this table for the evening. What can I get you?"

"I'll take the chicken pot pie," Mia said.

Bear ordered the homemade meatloaf the waitress recommended. When Linda left with their requests, Mia pushed to her feet. "I'm going to the restroom."

"I'll walk you there."

Mia smiled. "We've been through this before. I made it to the bathroom and back without incident then. I can do it, again."

Bear frowned. "I don't like letting you out of my sight."

"I'll take that as a compliment." She rested a hand on his shoulder. "But for now, stay."

She waited a moment to make sure he wouldn't get up and follow her. When she was sure he would stay put, she headed for the bathroom, hoping to catch Kylie alone.

The hallway was dark, the overhead light burned out. Mia pushed her way through the bathroom door.

"Kylie," she called out softly.

A toilet flushed, and a woman stepped out. "Sorry. I'm the only one in here." She washed her hands, dried them on a paper towel and left the room.

Just to satisfy herself, Mia checked all three stalls, washed her hands and left the bathroom. She'd seen Kylie head down the hallway, assuming she'd gone to the ladies' room. Perhaps she'd gone farther down the hallway to one of the other doors.

Mia turned away from the dining room, and walked along the hallway to the next door, determined to find her friend. Upon opening it, she discovered a closet with cleaning supplies and mops. The door across the hall led into an office with an old desk and a filing cabinet. It was empty.

When Mia backed out of the office, she heard another door open behind her. She turned to find Kylie standing at the rear exit, her face flushed, her eyes wide.

"Mia? Oh, thank God." Kylie ran toward her and wrapped her arms around her. "You have to help me."

Adrenaline rushed through Mia's veins as she held Kylie close to her. "What's wrong?"

"You have to get me out of here. Larry's mad. Really mad. If he catches me, he'll beat me all over again."

"Why is he mad at you?"

"Does it matter? He gets mad at the stupidest things and, when he does, he hits me. The bruises on my arms are nothing compared to these." Kylie lifted her shirt, exposing her torso and belly. Huge bruises colored her body in an ugly array of blue, purple and yellow.

"Oh, Kylie. You can't go back to that monster." Mia hugged her tightly. "Come home with me. Bear and I will make sure Larry never touches you again."

"I can't go out in the diner. Larry's out there. He's looking for me. I can't go out there. Please. Let's go out the back. We can slip away, and he won't know. He won't find me." Tears slipped from her eyes. "I can't let him find me."

"I need to tell Bear where we're going."

"No! Don't leave me." She clung to Mia, refusing to let her go back into the diner. "I have to get away. Now. You told me you'd help me. I'm asking for your help. Please."

Mia rubbed her friend's back, glancing over her shoulder to the lighted diner beyond. Now would be a good time for Bear to come looking for her. He didn't appear in the hallway and Kylie was edging for the rear exit, pulling Mia with her.

"Please help me," she pleaded.

Mia's heart banged against her ribs. She couldn't leave Kylie in the hallway. If Larry came along, he'd take her home, and the Lord only knew how he'd punish her for trying to run away.

Stiffening her back, Mia gripped Kylie's arms. "Okay. I'll get you out of here. But we're going straight to the sheriff's station and filing charges on your husband."

"I don't care where we go. Just get me out of here." She flung the door open and ran out.

Mia raced after her. "Kylie, wait for me." As the door closed behind her, she searched the encroaching darkness for Kylie.

She spotted her racing around the corner of the diner and out of sight.

"Kylie!" she called out.

Then a burlap bag descended over her head, and strong arms wrapped around her, locking her own arms to her side. The nightmare she'd endured when she was sixteen started all over.

Mia screamed as loud as she could, the bag muffling the sound. This time, Mia knew a little more about self-defense. But without her arms, she could do little more than stomp on her attacker's instep and kick his shins with her heels. She dug her heels into the dirt and tried to flip him over her head, but he was bigger, stronger than last time, and he had her completely trapped.

She kicked him again, wiggling and ducking, trying to work her arms loose. Mia fought desperately and pounded her heel into the man's foot.

He cursed and hit her hard in the temple.

Mia's thoughts turned to haze. She blacked out.

11

———

THREE AND A HALF minutes passed before Bear finally got out of his chair and marched toward the hallway through which Mia had disappeared. Something wasn't right. He could feel it in his gut. In all his years in the Army, his gut had never lied.

He stormed into the ladies' room only to find it empty. By now, his mind and body were at full alert. "Mia!" he called out. He raced down the hallway opening doors along the way. All he found was a broom closet and an empty office. At the end of the corridor was an unmarked door. He pushed through to the outside, and his blood ran cold.

No one was there. Bear ran to the corner of the building and around the side and back to check the other side. He couldn't find any sign that Mia had been there, or which way she might have gone.

He'd watched the hallway from the moment Mia entered. She hadn't come back into the diner, meaning she had to have gone out the back. Whether she'd gone out on her own, or was forced, Bear didn't know.

He had to find her.

Weaving through the cars in the parking lot, staring into the windows of each parked vehicle, Bear pulled his cell phone out of his pocket. With limited reception, he prayed he'd have enough to get through to Hank. Before he could press the call button, the phone buzzed in his hand and Sadie's caller ID came up.

"Sadie, where's Hank?" Bear demanded before she could say a word.

"This *is* Hank. When I walked out of the house, I grabbed Sadie's phone instead of mine. I have some news for you. Dr. Sanders woke up. She can identify her attacker."

"Mia's gone," Bear said, his voice flat, his heart sinking to the pit of his belly.

"When? Where?" Hank demanded.

Bear told him. "She's only been gone for less than three minutes. She can't be too far."

"Call the sheriff. Have him check all roads in and out of town."

"They don't have enough people available to look everywhere."

"I'm leaving the hospital now. The Bozeman PD will keep an eye on Dr. Sanders. Oh, and the man who ran her over was driving a sheriff's deputy's car. He had sandy blond, curly hair and sat fairly tall in his seat. She said she thought he might be Larry Maynard."

Bear's heartbeat stuttered, and then raced ahead. "I'm going to talk to Larry's wife, if I can find her."

"Do that. I'll be back in Eagle Rock in thirty minutes. Keep me informed."

"Will do." Bear clicked the end button and ran through the front door of the diner, nearly running over Linda as she carried the tray of food he and Mia had ordered.

"Your food is ready," she said.

Bear took the tray from her and set it on the table behind him. Then he gripped the woman's arms. "Where's Kylie?"

"I don't know. She was in the kitchen just a minute ago. I think she got something in her eye."

Bear set Linda aside and raced for the kitchen. A big burly man with tattoos lacing his arms looked up from the stove.

"Employees only back here," he said, his voice like rough gravel.

Bear didn't flinch. "Kylie Maynard."

The cook jerked his head to the far corner on the other side of the industrial, stainless steel sink. "She's been back there blubbering like a baby. Get her out of my kitchen."

Bear hurried past the cook and found Kylie curled in the corner, her knees pulled up to her chin, tears streaming down her face.

"I didn't want to do it. She was my friend."

Bear's gut clenched. Kylie had just confirmed that her husband, Larry Maynard, had Mia. "Where'd he take her?"

Kylie sobbed louder and buried her face in her hands. "I don't know. He said he couldn't let her talk. She would ruin his life if she found out."

"Found out what?"

"He'll kill me. You don't know what he's capable of..." Her words ended on more sobs.

Bear lifted her out of the corner and stood her on her feet. "Think, damn you! Where would he take Mia?"

"I don't know." Tears streamed down her face and her body shook.

Bear took a deep breath and tried to talk calmly. The woman was hysterical. Shouting at her wouldn't bring him any closer to finding Mia.

"Kylie, look at me." He tipped her chin up and stared into her red-rimmed eyes. "Does your husband have a place he likes to go to get away?"

She sniffed and wiped the tears from her cheek. "He likes to take his dirt bike up into the mountains outside of town."

"Does he stop anywhere? Is there a cabin or hut or campsite he likes to visit? Does he go hunting?"

Kylie's brows furrowed and she stopped sobbing long enough to think. "I think he has a campsite up there. He goes up there to hunt in the fall." Her eyes widened. "He took me there once." Her bottom lip trembled, and the tears ran down her cheeks again. "He was terrible to me. He…he…" She buried her face in her hands again.

"Tell me, Kylie. I won't let him hurt you again."

"It was shortly after we were married. He took me up there and made me… He tied me to a post and he…he hurt me. God, he raped me. I didn't say anything to anyone. We were married. I thought he had a right to use my body any way he wanted, but he hurt me. I think that's why I haven't gotten pregnant."

Anger burned in Bear. If he got his hands around Maynard's neck, he wouldn't stop squeezing until the man stopped kicking.

"Think, Kylie. Where was the campsite?"

"There's an old road a mile or so out of town. You can barely see it. It's past the turn-off to Mia's house. The road winds up into the hills. I rode with him on the back of his motorcycle. The trees hung over the road so much we had to duck several times. It might be completely grown over by now." She glanced up at Bear. "Do you think he took her there?"

"You have to show me where the road is."

Kylie shook her head. "I can't."

"You have to. If Mia truly is your friend, you can help her by getting me to that road. You can leave after we find it. I don't care, but you have to show me where that road is."

Kylie's bottom lip trembled. "I'm not sure I can find it."

"I need you to help me. You're all I have. Mia needs us."

Kylie nodded, her shoulders stiffening. "You won't let Larry hurt me?"

"I promise."

For an excruciatingly long moment, she stared up into Bear's face. "Okay."

Bear hooked her arm and led her out the back door and around the side of the building to his truck. There, he helped her up into the passenger seat.

He pulled out his phone and called Sheriff Wilson. "It's Maynard. He's the rapist, and he has Mia." He told the sheriff what Kylie said about the campsite. "It's a long shot, but it could be the place he originally raped Mia."

"I'll have someone check his house. I'm on my way from north of town. You might get there before I do."

"I'm taking Kylie Maynard with me. I'll leave her at the entrance to the road. Make sure she's safe."

"Will do."

Bear drove his truck out onto Main Street and sped through town, headed south toward Mia's house. As he passed her driveway, he slowed to a crawl.

Kylie leaned forward until her nose practically pressed to the front windshield. "I don't know. It wasn't dark outside when he brought me here; and it's been several years." She watched the tree line to the right as Bear drove slowly past.

"There," she pointed to the right. "I remember seeing an old fence post with a NO TRESPASSING sign on it."

An old post, weathered by the sun and snow, listed to the side with an equally old sign hanging at an angle. When Bear turned toward the post, his headlights shined off the sign. He could barely make out the faded lettering. NO TRESPASSING.

His pulse raced as he noted fresh tire tracks in the dust. He might be on a wild goose chase, but if there was even half a chance of finding Mia out there, he had to check it out.

"I'm getting out here." Kylie opened the truck door. "He'll kill me if he knows it was me who led you to find him."

"Stay low in the bushes. The sheriff is on his way."

She nodded and slipped out of the truck and into the darkness.

Bear drove along the rutted track, branches scraping the sides of his vehicle. He had to progress with his lights on to keep from running into trees. He prayed Maynard wouldn't spot him until he was close enough to help Mia.

The going was slow and finally, Bear stopped altogether, preferring to continue on foot.

He pulled his gun out of his shoulder holster. Following the road using only the light from the stars above, he jogged up the hillside, pushing back the pain in his bum leg, afraid he was headed the wrong direction. Even more afraid he wouldn't be there in time to save Mia.

Mia surfaced to consciousness as she bounced against a hard, lumpy floor. The burlap bag, now loose, kept her from seeing around her, but by the dust filtering through it and the shape of the objects in front of and behind her, she reasoned she was wedged into the back floorboard of a truck or SUV.

Dust filtered through the doors and windows, tickling her nose and making her want to sneeze. She fought against the urge, preferring to keep the fact she was awake from her captor, whom she had yet to see.

Instead, she shifted her head, trying to work the burlap bag off so that she could take stock of her situation and come up with a plan to liberate herself.

Her head ached, and when she tried to move, hard plastic zip-ties constrained her wrists behind her back.

Using her teeth to pull and lifting her shoulders, she inched the bag over her head until she could see again. As she'd suspected, her attacker had dumped her into the back floorboard of a pickup, and, based on the bumps and ruts, he was taking her out in the wilderness.

Her heart beating hard in her chest, she wiggled her wrists, straining to loosen the zip ties. When that didn't work, she rubbed the plastic against the metal fixtures holding the front seats in place. After several attempts, the plastic broke, and her wrists were bleeding, but free.

Just when she got the courage to sit up and take matters into her own hands, the truck jerked to a stop.

Mia might only have one chance to escape. She had to make it good. No one would find her in the Crazy Mountains. Not until it was too late to help her. She wanted to live to see another day. To make love to Bear. To have children and be happy.

She waited for the man to open the back door. When he

reached for her ankles to drag her out, she let him pull her halfway through the door.

The bag fell away from her head, and she saw that he wore a sheriff's deputy uniform. When she could finally see his face, Mia swallowed her gasp, fighting to keep her eyes as closed as possible.

Larry Maynard leered at her. "Mia, Mia. You should have stayed away from Eagle Rock. Now, I have to kill you, like I should have all those years ago."

Inwardly, she railed, *You bastard!*

But she kept her arms behind her, pretending they were still tied. When he leaned forward to lift her onto his shoulder, she grabbed his hair, yanked his head down, and slammed her knee into his face.

Larry staggered backward, his eyes watering, blood gushing from his nose. "You bitch!"

He reached for her, but Mia ducked out of his reach and ran as fast as she could, heading for the brush. If she could make it that far, she had a chance. She could hide in the shadows until he gave up looking for her. Then she'd find her way back to a road, back to civilization, and bring the sheriff back to arrest his ass and hit him up with attempted murder.

She ran across an open clearing, the stars in the big Montana sky lighting her way and making her all too visible to her pursuer.

When she'd almost reached the edge of the encampment, something caught her ankle and she pitched forward, landing hard on her chest, the wind knocked from her lungs.

"Bitch! You're going to die, but now I'm going to make it slow and very painful." The hand gripping her ankle tightened.

Fear and adrenaline running high in her veins, Mia kicked hard, aiming for Larry's wrist, trying to dislodge his hold. His other hand slapped at her flailing foot, and finally caught her other ankle.

"No," she cried. He couldn't take her again. This couldn't happen. She hadn't taken all those self-defense classes to end up a victim yet again. To the same man who'd attacked her before.

"I'm going to make you cry and scream for mercy, just like you did when you were sixteen. And it's going to feel so good when I drive my dick deep inside you. Again. And. Again." He dragged his body up her legs, his weight heavy against her.

When his chest crushed her body into the ground, Mia worked her knee free. Grabbing his face with both hands, she dug her thumbs into his eye sockets and jammed them hard at the same time as she jerked her knee into his groin.

Larry screamed and fell onto his side.

Mia shoved him hard, rolled out of his reach and scrambled to her feet. She ran for the brush and dove into the shadows. She landed near a pile of rubbish and splintered boards that might once have been parts of a hunter's deer stand. Her hand curled around a three-foot long two-by-four.

"I'm going to kill you!" he called out, blinking hard and rubbing his eyes. "I'm going to fuck you like I fucked the good Dr. Sanders. Like I fucked that stupid Severs twit, and the woman from Bozeman. You're going to squeal like the redhead I strangled and left for the vultures to pick her bones clean. Mia, you're going to wish you were dead when I finish with you. You're going to wish I'd killed you when you were sixteen."

Anger roiled inside Mia. This bastard had raped and murdered his last victim. If he came one step closer...

Larry Maynard pulled a gun from his pocket and straightened. He pulled a flashlight form his other pocket and shined it toward the bush behind which Mia hid.

"Come out, little Mia. It's time to face the music. You've caused enough drama."

Mia waited, shrinking lower to the ground as the flashlight's beam swept past her, swung wide and started back toward her position.

Two steps closer, and he'd see her. He'd also be within her range.

Mia took a steadying breath and tensed her muscles, ready to spring.

Larry stepped closer. One...two...the light edged toward her.

Mia waited until it was almost to her.

"Maynard!" a voice called out. "Drop the gun."

A thrill raced through Mia. She recognized the command in that voice. She should have known Bear would find her.

Larry spun toward the voice and stared into the darkness. He pointed his gun toward Mia. "No, you put your weapon down, or I'll shoot your girlfriend."

"You don't know where she is."

"You don't know that for sure, do you?" He edged toward the bush, getting closer to where Mia huddled in the shadows.

"My finger's on the trigger. One step closer, and I'll pull it."

"You're bluffing."

"Are you willing to risk her life, calling my bluff?"

Bear didn't respond.

Larry inched closer.

Mia bunched her muscles, tightened her grip around the board and shouted. "Don't shoot!" Then she launched herself at Larry, swinging as hard as she could. She caught him in the side of his head. His gun went off, the bullet missing, skimming past her head without touching her.

Larry dropped to his knees and toppled onto his side. His pistol slipped from his fingers and fell into the dirt.

Mia stood over the man, tempted to hit him again. And again. Until the man was nothing more than bloody pulp. He deserved it. But if she did that, it would make her no better than him.

She tossed the board to the side and stepped past him. Then she was running toward the emerging shadow that was Bear.

Almost to him, she noticed he had lifted his weapon.

"Get down!" he shouted.

Mia dove for the dirt.

Bear fired his gun at the same time as another shot rang out.

Bear jerked backward and clutched his arm, dropping the gun to the dirt.

Mia rolled to her haunches and spun.

Larry fell backward in the dirt, the gun he'd held went with him, and he lay still.

"Is he dead?" she asked.

"I hit him in the chest," Bear scooped up his gun, walked over to the man, nudged him with his foot and kicked the gun away from his hand. "He's not going to hurt any more women."

"Thank God." Mia rose to her feet and met Bear in the middle of the clearing. A dark stain spread across his shirtsleeve. "You've been hit."

"It's just a flesh wound." He shoved his weapon into his holster, circled his arm around her waist and pulled her against him. "Are you okay?"

She nodded. "He didn't have time to hurt me. I wouldn't let him."

"You're one tough little lady, you know that?"

"Damn right, I am. I refuse to let any man do what he did to me, ever again."

"I'm sorry I didn't stop him before he got you this far."

"It's not your fault. If I wasn't so hard-headed, you would have followed me to the restroom."

"That's what I get for listening to you. From now on, I'm going to listen to my gut."

She leaned into him, her hand on his chest, her eyes gazing up into his. "And what is your gut telling you now?"

"That I need to redeem my rain check on a shower."

She laughed. "After you have that arm checked out by a doctor."

"Why, when I could have you play nurse?" He nuzzled her neck and flinched when he tried to wrap his wounded arm around her.

"Uh-huh. Not happening. First, the doctor. Then I'll play nurse and we can get that shower." She wrapped her arm around his waist and led him toward the trail leading into the campsite.

"How about we just stay here and neck a little?"

"Not here." She nodded toward the headlights pushing through the woods toward them. "Besides, we have company."

"Damn. And I was hoping to make good use of the Montana starlight."

"We will, sweetheart. We will." She leaned up on her toes and pressed her lips to his. "I promise. In the meantime, I bet we'll be answering a lot of questions. But one thing is for certain. There are a lot of women who will sleep easier tonight with one monster less in this world."

Bear nodded. "I know I'll sleep better."

Mia frowned. "I guess this means I don't need a bodyguard anymore."

Bear's arm tightened around her. "I guess you won't. I hope it's not too late to ask you out on a date."

Mia smiled, her heart lightening. "I thought you'd never ask. The answer is a million times yes!" She wrapped her arms around his neck and kissed him, happy and free of the shadow that had haunted her for so many years. She dared to open her heart for the first time and hope for a beautiful, loving future. And maybe, just maybe, Bear would be a part of it.

Brotherhood Protector Series
Montana SEAL (#1)
Bride Protector SEAL (#2)
Montana D-Force (#3)
Cowboy D-Force (#4)
Montana Ranger (#5)
Montana Dog Soldier (#6)
Montana SEAL Daddy (#7) Summer 2017
Montana Rescue (#8) Fall 2017

Take No Prisoners Series

SEAL's Honor (#1)

MONTANA RANGER

BROTHERHOOD PROTECTORS SERIES
BOOK #5

New York Times & USA Today
Bestselling Author

ELLE JAMES

1

———

"Are you sure you don't want me to stay?" Gavin Blackstock straightened, after hooking up the mower to the oldest tractor on the Brighter Days Rehabilitation Ranch. He shook his shaggy black hair out of his gray eyes and wiped the grease from his hands.

Hannah Kendricks sighed. Yeah, she wished Gavin could stay and cut the hayfield instead of her, but...

"No, we need the supplies and tomorrow is Sunday. The feed stores are closed." She stared at the aging farm machinery, wondering if it would conk out in the middle of the field and leave her to walk all the way back to the barn. "I'll keep the tractor going long enough to cut the hay." She held up her hand as if being sworn into office. "Don't worry, I promise to baby it."

"Why don't you let Percy do the cutting?" Gavin suggested.

"I would, but he's better at manning the baler. The hay I cut three days ago is dry and ready to bale. If we want to get all of it baled by Wednesday, we need to cut today."

Gavin opened his mouth to protest.

Hannah held up her hand. "We've got it covered. I hired three hands to help."

"Troy Nash got here early this morning." Gavin frowned. "Why did you hire that boy?"

"I heard he'd been fired from his job at the feed store. I figured he could use the money since his daddy had his heart attack."

"You've got a soft spot for those down and out."

She shrugged. "We take care of our neighbors in these parts."

"Yeah, but Troy's a known troublemaker."

"Maybe he just needs someone to believe in him." Hannah ran her hand across the smooth seat of one of the saddles stacked on a saddletree. "Besides, I hired Abe and Mark. They're good, hard-working teenagers. Don't worry about us."

"Why the hurry? If it doesn't get cut today, we can do it tomorrow when I'm here to help."

Glancing up at the bright Montana sky, Hannah shook her head. "A storm's headed our way from off the Washington coast. You know as well as I do that we can't bale it if it's wet. And if we don't cut the field now, the hay won't have time to dry and be baled before the storm hits."

"So?"

Hannah's lips tightened. "You know we need two cuttings from those fields to keep us from having to buy hay to get us through the winter."

Gavin glanced at the old tractor. "This hunk of junk gets crankier every time we use it. I brought it up to Holloway when he was here last month, but I'll mention it again. He's supposed to be here tomorrow."

Hannah bit down on her bottom lip. Holloway was the young financial manager of the Brighter Days Rehabilitation Ranch. He showed up once a month to do the accounting and make any big buying decisions. Otherwise, he left the ranch for Hannah to run as she saw fit, making the day-to-day hiring, firing and maintenance decisions. "He can be pretty tight with the purse strings."

"Maybe you can turn on some of the charm you reserve for our clients." Gavin cocked his brows.

Hannah glanced down at her faded shirt and jeans and gave her best friend a very unladylike snort. "I'm not very convincing as a girl."

Gavin laughed out loud. "Don't knock yourself, Hannah. From where I stand, you're all female. And you do it better than most women I know."

"Yeah, but where Holloway comes from, I'm nowhere near the kind of woman he's used to dealing with. I don't even know how to bat my lashes." To prove it, she fluttered her eyelashes. The action felt as clumsy as it probably looked based on Gavin's grimace.

"Yeah, don't do that. It just looks weird." He limped to the truck. "Just try to be nice."

Hannah followed. "I'll see what I can do. We really need at least one newer tractor before next season." She hugged Gavin. "Thanks for giving it your best shot. At least, it's running."

"Hopefully, it will remain running until you get through the cutting." Gavin glanced toward the barn. "Looks like Percy has his team of helpers ready. I'd better get to Eagle Rock and back so that I can be of some assistance before the day's over." He gave Hannah a stern glance. "Be careful out there. We don't want any more 'accidents'. We can't lose our best therapist."

"Your *only* therapist," Hannah muttered. "I'll be all right. Quit worrying. What happened recently was just a couple of accidents. They could have happened to anyone." She gripped Gavin's arm and stared directly into his eyes. "There's no conspiracy going on here at Brighter Days."

Frowning, he touched her cheek. "I'm not so sure. You're the only one the accidents have affected." He drew in a deep breath, released it and nodded. "I should stay and do the cutting."

"Go." Hannah gave Gavin a gentle shove. "I can handle this. And nobody is going to mess with me. I want to be here for the guys. Once I finish the field, I'll help load hay on the truck and trailer. I need to be there to watch and make sure none of them does anything that will set them back on their roads to recovery."

"Yes, you do need to be there. They wouldn't be nearly as far along as they are without your help." He glanced down at his leg. "I never thought I'd walk again, and look where I am, because of you."

Hannah's chest expanded. Nothing was more rewarding than helping wounded veterans regain mobility and some semblance of a life worth living.

Working at the Brighter Days Rehab Ranch, she got the best of both worlds. She got to help people, like her best friend from childhood, and give former soldiers, sailors, marines and airmen a reason to keep fighting, for a great cause—rehabilitating horses rescued from horrible situations.

And she wouldn't have had this opportunity if not for the benevolence of the investment group who'd purchased the ranch and allowed her to make it into the thriving therapy center it was.

Gavin paused before climbing into the truck. "Oh, and Hannah, you might want to think about being the girl you are and date or find someone to love. You need a life outside of this ranch."

"Says the man who hasn't had a date in over a year?" She shook her head. "I'll date when you date." Narrowing her eyes, Hannah tilted her head. "Maybe I'll date you."

Gavin gave her a twisted smile. "Thanks, but it would be like dating my little sister. No can do."

Hannah nodded. They'd tried kissing, once, but the sparks weren't there and the connection didn't feel right. Like Gavin said, it was like kissing a sibling. Bleh! "You're right. We weren't made for each other in that way. Why spoil a perfect friendship? But that doesn't mean you can't find a woman to love you and all of your faults."

Gavin crossed his arms over his chest. "Same to you, Han. Same to you. I'll date if you date."

"Watch what you dare. I've been known to rise to a challenge."

"I'm counting on it." He stood for a moment longer and

then dropped his arms. "Go cut they hay, but don't forget…I dared you."

As Gavin climbed into the farm truck and spun around on the gravel, heading for town, Hannah watched, something tugging at her heart, telling her that Gavin had a point. Since she'd left college, she hadn't been on a date. Perhaps it was time.

Ranch foreman, Percy Pearson, appeared from around the side of the barn on the ranch's other tractor, towing the hay baler. He waved as he passed Hannah. "Ready?"

She nodded, climbed onto the old tractor's seat and waited for the farm truck, driven by medically retired Staff Sergeant Lori Mize, to pass. A motley crew of wounded warriors and hired hands filled the bed of the pickup, laughing and joking about the work ahead. She hoped between the group of able-bodied hired hands—Troy, Abe and Mark— and the three veterans—Franklin, Vasquez and Young, with their varying degrees of disabilities— they'd get the work done quickly.

Hannah started the engine and shifted the tractor into first gear. Resigning herself to a long day in the field, she adjusted her cowboy hat over her forehead and drove the tractor through the gate into the pasture. The clear sky promised to turn the cool Montana morning into a warm, early summer day. Hopefully, free of strange accidents.

Cookie, the ranch cook, waved and closed the gate behind her. He always stuck around for the warriors who weren't ready, or weren't capable of the heavy lifting needed to throw fifty to eighty-pound bales onto the trailer. Not that they had any other veterans staying behind. All men, and women, were on deck that day. Cookie would have a huge meal waiting when they returned, tired and starving, having burned a ton of calories.

Hannah followed Percy until she came to the field she was to cut that day.

He pressed on to the one farther out, taking with him the truck with the crew that would load what he baled.

Hannah would spend the day alone, driving the tractor

with the mower on the back. This particular field had its share of hills. She hoped and prayed the old tractor wouldn't bog down and give up while climbing the hills, and that the brakes would hold on the way down.

Starting at the far end with the steepest slopes, Hannah worked her way up and down the hill. She kept a steady pace, careful not to push the tractor's engine too hard. On the way down the hill, she moved as slowly as she could, shifting into low gear to let the engine help, rather than relying totally on the worn brakes.

After the first pass, she felt more confident the tractor would handle the job. She settled back in her seat and let her mind wander away from the hayfield.

Hannah thought about how far she'd come and how satisfied she was with where she'd landed in her life. Growing up on this ranch as the daughter of the owner's housekeeper, she'd learned to ride a horse almost before she'd learned to walk.

She'd never known her father. Her mother had instilled in her a love for the outdoors and ranch life. And she had all the male role models she needed to teach her what was expected of a man and how he should behave toward a woman. Preferring the outdoors to housework, Hannah had grown up working alongside the cowboys and ranch hands, doing everything they did to care for the animals, buildings and land.

Her mother had insisted she go to college, scrounging and saving so that her daughter wouldn't have to take out loans to pay for her tuition.

Hannah would rather have stayed at the ranch and worked with the horses, but she knew a college education meant a lot to her mother, so she'd gone.

Gavin, her best friend from high school, had joined the marines and gone to fight in the Middle East. Two years into his enlistment, Gavin had been injured in battle, taking a hit to his leg. He'd come back to the States where he'd undergone multiple surgeries in an attempt to remove all the shrapnel, repair the damage and save the leg. Finally, they'd had to amputate below his knee. Once he'd lost his leg, he'd been fitted with a prosthetic and sent to rehabilitation therapy to learn how to deal with his loss. After several months, Gavin was medically retired and sent home where he struggled with depression and trying to fit into a place where he felt he no longer belonged.

Hannah had been on the fence about what to study. When she'd gone to visit her best friend in the hospital, and later in physical therapy, she'd made her decision. She wanted to help people like Gavin regain use of their limbs, or learn how to get along without them, and in the process, regain their independence, confidence and self-respect.

She'd studied hard so that she would be accepted into the physical therapy program and graduated at the top of her class. Her mother had been so proud.

She'd taken a position at a rehab center in Bozeman, working with people who'd had knee and hip replacements, rotator cuff surgeries and more. But she wanted to work with veterans.

Gavin had stayed in DC, looking for a job. He couldn't find anything that suited him. He liked being around horses more than people, but he still felt drawn to his comrades in the marines, wishing he could be back in battle, helping to fight for his country.

Hannah had applied to work at Walter Reed in Bethesda, Maryland. The same day she'd received an invitation to interview, her mother had suffered a fatal stroke.

Though three years had passed, the pain of her loss still pinched Hannah's chest.

She pulled her mind out of her memories as she reached the end of the row. Turning the tractor, she started mowing the next row, heading down a hill toward a ravine lined with trees. The rhythmic chug of the engine lured her back into her memories.

Her mother died the day after her stroke, never having regained consciousness. Hannah had delayed her interview in Bethesda for two weeks to give herself time to arrange for her mother's funeral and to settle her affairs. She'd buried her mother, her only living relative, in the cemetery outside Eagle Rock, the nearest town to the ranch her mother had called home.

Percy and Gavin had stood by her side, along with the handful of ranch workers and the ranch owner, Mr. Lansing. They'd buried her mother on an ironically bright, sunny Montana day. She would have loved the sunshine.

In a domino effect, Mr. Lansing had a heart attack that night and ended up in a long-term care facility. Percy and Hannah knew the event was the beginning of the end of their little hodge-podge family of ranch workers.

Her heart heavy, Hannah had said her goodbyes to Gavin and the ranch hands. Then she'd entered the ranch house, packed up what she would keep of her mother's and arranged for the rest to be donated. Heartsick and so sad she could barely breathe, she'd set her suitcases by the front door, with the intention of leaving the ranch in the morning.

That's when Percy had come to her. Someone had asked to speak with her on the telephone.

She hadn't wanted to, but Percy insisted it was important— something to do with the sale of the ranch.

With a knife twisting in her heart, she'd taken the call. An attorney requested a meeting with her the following day. He had information about her mother's will and news about the sale of the ranch.

Reluctantly, she'd agreed to meet him at his office in Eagle Rock the next morning before she left town.

Hannah's lips lifted. Even from the grave, her mother had been looking out for her. She must have known the day would come soon when Mr. Lansing couldn't manage the ranch. He didn't have any heirs, and he'd need to sell. She'd left Hannah her life savings, a modest amount of money stashed away in the bank for her own retirement she'd never see. And she'd left a letter for Hannah.

Dear Hannah,

If you're reading this letter, I've managed to die before I had a chance to tell you about your father. I didn't talk to you about him as you grew up, but I wanted you to know he was a good man. I never told him about you, so don't blame him for not being a part of your life. Blame me. Maybe I didn't make the right decision by not telling you about him, but I felt it was the right one for you and for him. Just don't hate your father. And no matter what, I have always and will always love you with all of my heart. Love, Mom

Hannah barely heard the rest of what the lawyer had to say, so deep was she in her own misery.

He paused, expecting an answer to a question she hadn't absorbed.

Clutching the letter to her chest, she looked up and asked him to repeat it.

"Will you stay and help manage the transition from cattle ranch to a rehabilitation ranch for wounded warriors and sick or injured horses?"

Hannah blinked. "Who? Me?"

The lawyer nodded, repeating the proposition presented by the new owners of the ranch. "He—they want you to think about it." The lawyer leaned forward and touched her arm, his brows furrowed with obvious concern. "If you stay, the other employees will keep their jobs and you could do a whole lot of good for veterans and animals."

Stunned, she left his office in a daze and returned to the ranch where Percy met her with his duffel bag in hand.

He set down the bag and gripped her arms. "Hannah, are you okay?"

She nodded and then said, "Percy, I've been so wrapped up in my own grief, I didn't stop to think about you. What are you going to do when this ranch sells?"

He shrugged. "I don't know. I thought I'd head out to my sister's place in North Dakota."

"But you hate going to your sister's for more than a day...two tops."

"It's the only place I know to go." He forced a smile. "But don't worry about me. I always land on my feet."

She tilted her head and given him a stern stare. "You've

worked here as long as I can remember. When was the last time you had to look for a job?"

He glanced away. "It's been about thirty years or so."

For the first time, Hannah noticed the gray in his brown hair and the deeply grooved lines around his eyes. The man had leathery skin from years in the sun and weather and he had to be closing in on sixty years old. Who would hire him?

Staring at her old friend, the man who'd been the closest thing to a father she'd had, Hannah had made her decision. "We're staying."

Her lips curled at the memory of Percy's expression when he realized he wouldn't have to go to his sister in North Dakota. She'd called Gavin the next day and begged him to come work for the Brighter Days Rehabilitation Ranch where he could help veterans and horses. He'd be doing his part for his brothers-in-arms.

Hannah pressed her foot on the tractor's brakes as the hill dipped sharply toward the ravine. She'd made the turn on the previous pass with no problem.

But something snapped, making a clanking sound of metal hitting metal, and the brakes failed.

Hannah's heart jumped to her throat. Instead of slowing, the tractor picked up speed, the weight of the tractor plus the mower, pushed it even faster down the hill.

Hannah's fingers tightened on the steering wheel and her pulse raced. She debated turning to slow the vehicle in its headlong rush toward the ravine. But turning at that pace was a surefire way to flip the tractor.

She tried to shift to a lower speed to let the tractor engine slow her descent, but no matter how hard she shoved the lever, it wouldn't shift to low. Her gut clenched as she ran out of options.

With trees and rocks waiting for her to crash into them, Hannah had no other choice but to get off. Her only problem being, if she jumped, she stood a strong chance of landing in the mower. At which point she'd be cut to pieces.

She stared at the trees and rocks ahead, her mind working

through the scenarios at lightning speed, survival instincts kicking in.

That's when she spotted her only chance. The option was risky, but slightly less risky than crashing into the ravine. She turned the tractor's steering wheel ever so slightly, careful not to cause it to flip, and angled it toward a large tree with a long branch hanging just low enough for her to reach out and snag it with her arms.

Hannah held on to the steering wheel, fighting to keep it headed toward the tree, wondering if she could pull off what she planned.

With no time left to change her mind, she released the steering wheel, pushed to her feet and threw both arms over the branch.

Her chest crashed into the solid limb, knocking the air from her lungs. But she held on.

The tractor and mower continued on their course straight toward a large boulder, smashing into it with enough force the front end of the tractor crumpled. Momentum carried the mower forward, flipping it up and over the top of the tractor, crushing the seat where Hannah had sat moments before.

All of these actions happened in a matter of seconds. Hannah's arms slipped on the rough tree bark and she fell from her perch, landing on her back. Pain shot through her head and darkness enveloped her.

Brotherhood Protector Series
Montana SEAL (#1)
Bride Protector SEAL (#2)
Montana D-Force (#3)
Cowboy D-Force (#4)
Montana Ranger (#5)
Montana Dog Soldier (#6)
Montana SEAL Daddy (#7) Summer 2017
Montana Rescue (#8) Fall 2017

ABOUT THE AUTHOR

ELLE JAMES also writing as MYLA JACKSON is a *New York Times* and *USA Today* Bestselling author of books including cowboys, intrigues and paranormal adventures that keep her readers on the edges of their seats. With over eighty works in a variety of sub-genres and lengths she has published with Harlequin, Samhain, Ellora's Cave, Kensington, Cleis Press, and Avon. When she's not at her computer, she's traveling, snow skiing, boating, or riding her ATV, dreaming up new stories. Learn more about Elle James at www.ellejames.com

Website | Facebook | Twitter | GoodReads | Newsletter | BookBub | Amazon

Or visit her alter ego Myla Jackson at mylajackson.com
Website | Facebook | Twitter | Newsletter

Follow Me!
www.ellejames.com
ellejames@ellejames.com

ALSO BY ELLE JAMES

Hearts & Heroes Series

Wyatt's War (#1)

Mack's Witness (#2)

Ronin's Return (#3)

Sam's Surrender (#4)

Brotherhood Protector Series

Montana SEAL (#1)

Bride Protector SEAL (#2)

Montana D-Force (#3)

Cowboy D-Force (#4)

Montana Ranger (#5)

Montana Dog Soldier (#6)

Montana SEAL Daddy (#7)

Montana Ranger's Wedding Vow (#8)

Montana Rescue

Take No Prisoners Series

SEAL's Honor (#1)

SEAL's Ultimate Challenge (#1.5)

SEAL'S Desire (#2)

SEAL's Embrace (#3)

SEAL's Obsession (#4)

SEAL's Proposal (#5)

SEAL's Seduction (#6)

SEAL'S Defiance (#7)

SEAL's Deception (#8)

SEAL's Deliverance (#9)

Ballistic Cowboy

Hot Combat (#1)

Hot Target (#2)

Hot Zone (#3)

Hot Velocity (#4)

Texas Billionaire Club

Tarzan & Janine (#1)

Something To Talk About (#2)

Who's Your Daddy (#3)

Love & War (#4)

Hellfire Series

Hellfire, Texas (#1)

Justice Burning (#2)

Smoldering Desire (#3) TBD

Up in Flames (#4) TBD

Plays with Fire (#5) TBD

Hellfire in High Heels (#6) TBD

Cajun Magic Mystery Series

Voodoo on the Bayou (#1)

Voodoo for Two (#2)

Deja Voodoo (#3)

Cajun Magic Mysteries Books 1-3

Billionaire Online Dating Service

The Billionaire Husband Test (#1)

The Billionaire Cinderella Test (#2)

The Billionaire Bride Test (#3) TBD

The Billionaire Matchmaker Test (#4) TBD

SEAL Of My Own

Navy SEAL Survival

Navy SEAL Captive

Navy SEAL To Die For

Navy SEAL Six Pack

Devil's Shroud Series

Deadly Reckoning (#1)

Deadly Engagement (#2)

Deadly Liaisons (#3)

Deadly Allure (#4)

Deadly Obsession (#5)

Deadly Fall (#6)

Covert Cowboys Inc Series

Triggered (#1)

Taking Aim (#2)

Bodyguard Under Fire (#3)

Cowboy Resurrected (#4)

Navy SEAL Justice (#5)

Navy SEAL Newlywed (#6)

High Country Hideout (#7)

Clandestine Christmas (#8)

Thunder Horse Series

Hostage to Thunder Horse (#1)

Thunder Horse Heritage (#2)

Thunder Horse Redemption (#3)

Christmas at Thunder Horse Ranch (#4)

Demon Series

Hot Demon Nights (#1)

Demon's Embrace (#2)

Tempting the Demon (#3)

Lords of the Underworld

Witch's Initiation (#1)

Witch's Seduction (#2)

The Witch's Desire (#3)

Possessing the Witch (#4)

Stealth Operations Specialists (SOS)

Nick of Time

Alaskan Fantasy

Blown Away

Warrior's Conquest

Rogues

Enslaved by the Viking Short Story

Conquests

Smokin' Hot Firemen

Love on the Rocks

Protecting the Colton Bride

Heir to Murder

Secret Service Rescue

High Octane Heroes

Haunted

Engaged with the Boss

Cowboy Brigade

Time Raiders: The Whisper

Bundle of Trouble

Killer Body

Operation XOXO

An Unexpected Clue

Baby Bling

Under Suspicion, With Child

Texas-Size Secrets

Cowboy Sanctuary

Lakota Baby

Dakota Meltdown

Beneath the Texas Moon